"I Want you dead!"

Another piece clicked in. "You can astral project. I wasn't hallucinating." Eric laughed in relief. "So you were going to seduce me, drug me, and stab me?"

The word "Yes" came out on a whisper. "I wanted to bash your head in right there in your room. I couldn't." The weight of those last words sounded as though they crushed her as much as his weight on top of her.

"So your plan to kill me was out of revenge? For Jerryl. Not anything someone ordered you to do?"

"For everything you destroyed. The program. Jerryl. Me."

"It was a war, don't you understand that? People die in war."

Fonda took a breath. "Then you'll understand why I have to kill you."

Their bodies were hot against each other. Was he crazy that her venom and emotions were actually a turn on? They sparked something primal in him. It wasn't helping that they were sealed together from leg to chest.

"The war is over." He leaned closer to her, the heat enveloping his face. "Let it go."

Her mouth tighte_____ _____ _____ line. "There's where you're wrong_____ _____ until you're dead."

By Jaime Rush

BURNING DARKNESS
TOUCHING DARKNESS
OUT OF THE DARKNESS
A PERFECT DARKNESS

BURNING DARKNESS

JAIME RUSH

AVON

An Imprint of HarperCollins*Publishers*

This is a work of fiction. Names, characters, places, and incidents are products of the author's imagination or are used fictitiously and are not to be construed as real. Any resemblance to actual events, locales, organizations, or persons, living or dead, is entirely coincidental.

AVON BOOKS
An Imprint of H arperCollins*Publishers*
10 East 53rd Street
New York, New York 10022-5299

Copyright © 2011 by Tina Wainscott
Teaser excerpt copyright © 2011 by Tina Wainscott
ISBN 978-0-06-201885-4
www.avonromance.com

First Avon Books paperback printing: February 2011

Avon Trademark Reg. U.S. Pat. Off. and in Other Countries, Marca Registrada, Hecho en U.S.A.
HarperCollins® is a registered trademark of HarperCollins Publishers.

Printed in the U.S.A.

10 9 8 7 6 5 4 3 2 1

To my wonderful fans, who make it all possible.
To Kyle Kollarek, just 'cuz.

To My Readers:

If you've read my previous books, welcome back to the Offspring series! If you're picking up one of my books for the first time, this is the fourth book in the pulse-pounding series that started with *A Perfect Darkness* and continued with *Out of the Darkness* and *Touching Darkness*. Fear not! You'll get caught right up with what's going on, like jumping on a moving train. This book isn't directly tied into the story arc of the first three books. And I predict that you'll want to go back and read the rest of the books so you can experience all the excitement you've missed.

Cheers,
Jaime Rush

BURNING
DARKNESS

CHAPTER 1

Fonda Raine stepped out of the back end of a month in hell a hardened warrior, ready to undertake the most important task of her life: kill Eric Aruda. She knew she wasn't worthy of taking another breath if she didn't wipe that son of a bitch off the surface of the earth.

Everything in her D.C. suburb looked so much fresher and cleaner since the last time she'd been there. Or maybe it was her mind that was clearer, now that she'd buried her grief and anger beneath a huge mound of determination. She paused on the sidewalk and breathed in air teased with the scent of baking pizza crusts. She soaked in the clarity of the streetlights, the crispness of the music drifting from a jazz bar. Even the homeless seemed less bedraggled. She sought out one homeless man in his usual spot at the entrance of the alley past Sal's Pizza Joint.

"Hey, George."

A big smile broke out on his face, his teeth white against his dark skin. He'd obviously been using the toothpaste she'd given him.

"It's the Cinnamon girl. Wondered where you've been."

They'd met six months ago. She'd eaten only half her Italian sub and had searched for someone to give the other half to. The guilt of throwing away a perfectly good sandwich when there were people starving on the streets . . . unthinkable. There had been George with his warm eyes and surprised smile that someone was looking at him. He'd confided that the hardest thing for him was feeling invisible.

She crouched down to his level. He'd never explained why he called her the Cinnamon girl, but she guessed it was a good thing. "Had some business to take care of. You got the stuff I sent?"

"Yeah. Been a long time since I got a care package. You're a sweet girl."

"Not really, George." She took a quick breath. "Maybe I'm a killer."

He looked into her eyes and shook his head. "You're no killer. Don't have the eyes of a killer."

She stood, not wanting to believe that. She *had* to be a killer. "You warm enough?" The odd cool snap in July made it feel like a fall evening.

He nodded toward the old army jacket he wore. "I'm jus' fine. You look tired. You takin' care of yourself?"

She handed him some folded bills. "I'm okay. Here, buy yourself some dinner. I'll see you around." Maybe.

One habit she'd never shaken from her years growing up was checking her surroundings. Her gaze scanned automatically and connected with a man in a long beige coat. Her heart thudded heavily in her chest. Hadn't she seen him, like, blocks away? Three turns ago, at least, which meant he'd kept pace with her . . .

Fear prickled across her skin. Heat flamed her cheeks, adrenaline shot through her body like arcs of electricity. How long since she'd felt like this? Scared. Geared to fight. Alive.

Yeah, alive, but maybe not for long.

She reached beneath her oversized sweater and slid her fingers across her switchblade. Her brief glance shouldn't have given away that she'd noticed him. Wouldn't it figure? Spend a month in a low-income area with a crack house a block away and no problems. Come back to her relatively safe neighborhood and get stalked.

It had been three months since she lived in her apartment, but she remembered the shortcuts. She maintained her casual pace, pretending to look in the shop windows at an angle where she could see the man. He remained a certain distance from her, pausing to look at a darkened window. Yeah, he was definitely watching her.

Come on, you sleaze bag. You think you can, what, jack me up? That because I'm five-foot-two I'm weak and helpless? Don't mess with me. I bite.

Her internal diatribe bolstered her confidence, but she wasn't going to stand him down if she didn't need to. Best course of action: give him the slip. She had a knife, but if he had a gun, gun trumped knife every time. She'd seen firsthand what a gun could do.

She continued on, forcing herself to keep her pace when she wanted to sprint. Dammit, if her heart would stop racing, she could breathe so much better. If her knees weren't wobbly, she could walk in her vintage clogs.

She turned the corner, kicked off her shoes and ran. The alley on the right led between two brick buildings and took another sharp left. Her feet pounded on the concrete and God knew what else. She scooped up a bottle as she ran, tossing it to the left, and slid between the brick wall and a Dumpster. She mouth-breathed, so she wouldn't gag on the smell of rotten food.

He entered the alley in a fast walk, still trying to maintain the look of someone not hunting down someone else. He headed around the corner where he'd heard the bottle fall, and she raced back the way she'd come, staying close to the wall. Emerging on the street, she scooped up her clogs and ran to her apartment building.

Her fingers fumbled with the key to the entrance door. She closed it behind her, making sure it clicked, and ran to the stairs. Elevators gave her the creeps: a small box where someone could corner you. Or press a button to a vacant floor and pull you out. It didn't matter that there weren't any vacant floors in her building. Old habits, old fears . . .

But I gave him the slip.

She blasted into her apartment and slammed the door shut behind her. Snapped the two dead bolts. The air was musty. She went right to the bathroom and started the shower, not brave enough yet to look at her feet. Her clothes piled on the floor, clogs next to them. The switchblade fell with a thud on the tile. She stepped into the flow of water even though it wasn't warm.

"Nobody scares me. Nobody can touch me."

Her words echoed in the small room, sounding loud and hollow.

She tried again, deepening her voice. "I'm not afraid of anyone. I am not afraid. I'm not . . ."

Her body shook, and she slid down the wall to crouch in the tub. The words wouldn't come, but the fear did. She fought it, denied it, but it roared through her and devoured her courage.

Fine, let it come, she thought. Let it come now, because when I go after Eric, there won't be any room for it.

Fonda lifted her head and looked at the clock on her nightstand: two in the morning. *It's time.* She sat up, her heart thrumming. Eric Aruda had taken everything from her: her job, her sense of importance, and her lover. He had destroyed her life, and she'd never even met him. Hopefully she could kill him without coming face-to-face with him. For revenge, yes. For her self-worth. Reason enough, but she had another, higher reason: for her country.

But could she do it?

You're no killer.

"Yes, I am."

Death was no big deal. She'd always told herself she could kill if another creep tried to force himself on her. She'd seen two people gunned down and one person die from an overdose right in front of her. Death was a by-product of life. She was tough, more than tough. She could kill Eric.

She would have bought She Wants Revenge's CD for the band's name alone, but the song, "Tear You Apart" fit her mood perfectly. She put that track on repeat, grabbed the shears from the kitchen drawer and returned to the bathroom. She mouthed the lyrics she'd memorized as she stared at the mirror, a ragged breath coming out of her mouth. "It's war-time."

Her blond hair curled up just past her shoulders, giving her a soft look. Time to become a warrior, like she had when she was thirteen and her father's drug buddies began to see that the sulky girl was becoming a woman. She'd chopped off her long hair and camouflaged her body in oversized clothing.

She'd been entranced by Helen Slater in the movie, *The Legend of Billie Jean*. Billie Jean had cut her hair super short as she prepared for war in a beachside town.

Hanks of white-blond hair rained down in the sink. She searched the cabinet beneath the sink and pulled out a box of hair dye. An hour later she had her "war paint," a dark pink streak on her right side. Her fingers sifted through her locks, still longish in front and short in back. She gave her reflection a hard smile.

"Time to kick Aruda ass."

She reclined on her bed and got into the meditative state she'd taught herself to sink into at fifteen, when escaping her surroundings became necessary for her sanity.

The memory of the picture of Eric that used to be on the "Targets" bulletin board filled her mind. Her soul lifted out of her body. She loved the weightlessness of this state, the freedom. The humming sound started here, pleasant but pervasive.

All around her, clouds swirled like a gentle tornado, sweeping her through the ethers. She had learned to go along for the ride, keeping her mind clear. The humming turned into a loud buzzing that hurt her ears and vibrated right through her. When she couldn't stand it anymore, the sound faded, the clouds cleared, and she stood in a bedroom.

A light on the nightstand lit the small room. She scanned her surroundings. Eric was stretched out on the bed, his head propped up slightly on the pillow. Her heart sprang to her throat. His eyes were open and staring right at her! She retained her overall appearance when she projected, though it was diaphanous in nature. If he saw her, he'd probably know who she was and that she was targeting him. She was about to return to her physical body but stopped. He hadn't reacted. His stare was . . . blank. Was he dead?

She shifted her gaze down to a chest dusted in golden hairs; it rose and fell evenly. Breathing. Her gaze continued down, following the line of smooth hairs that pointed lower. She swallowed. He was lying on top of the rumpled sheets naked. She forced her gaze farther down to his legs, then back up to his chest. If she had a twin sister, they could both recline on top of him without falling off. His body was absolutely magnificent.

Who cares? Who freaking cares! That body is going to be lifeless. Dead!

But *her* body wasn't lifeless. She felt her astral body stir. Self-hatred cut into her like jagged bits of glass.

You worthless bitch. This man killed Jerryl, and here you stand feeling . . . aroused. Slut! Whore!

She shoved her gaze back to Eric's face. Even slack, his expression retained a hardness. His icy blue eyes were glazed. Bloodshot. He was in some kind of catatonic state. Maybe drunk.

His questionable state made it tricky. What if he was aware of her and pretending to be out of it until she made a move? Not that he could hurt her, but if he saw her, she would lose the element of surprise. Getting to him would be a lot harder.

She studied him. His breathing didn't change. His hand was splayed across his ridged stomach, long fingers flexing involuntarily.

With a groan, he shifted to his side, the white skin on his hip translucent in the light. A large tattoo adorned his biceps, a blue eye with slashes in the iris. Okay, he definitely wasn't cognizant. He wouldn't put himself in a vulnerable position where he couldn't see her. She advanced on him and stopped beside his bed, tensed for any sudden movement. After several minutes, she relaxed.

Once, she and Jerryl had a lot of fun practicing her ability to touch objects at the target location. She would astral project into his bedroom and wake him in intimate ways.

Her heart ached, but she pushed the thought away. *Focus. Grief will weaken you.*

Though she was good at projecting, she was like an astronaut in a space suit when it came to manipulating physical objects. Even with practice, her movements were clumsy and unwieldy, but she'd learned to lift larger objects. She searched the small room for something she could use as a weapon. The walls were covered in oil paintings, and every piece depicted either a couple in a provocative position or a naked woman in a sensual pose, all by the same artist. The one of a female angel, a man kneeling before her, grabbed her heart. Was he begging for redemption? She tore away and kept searching.

The lamp on the nightstand had sharp edges at the base. If she could smash it down on his temple, she might render him unconscious. Then she could keep bashing until he was dead.

She concentrated and grabbed the lamp. She might as well be wearing boxing gloves. It tipped. *No, don't fall!* She swung her ghostlike hand to keep it from toppling. She couldn't feel the cold brass, only a dense energy. She pushed it back, and it settled on the surface. Eric didn't move.

Damn. Now what?

Frustration swamped her.

Don't give up. I could try to strangle him.

The light gilded the coarse hairs on legs thick as pilings. His chest was deep, and she could see the faint indent of ribs beneath the pale skin on his side. Big, strong . . . cruel murderer. She leaned toward him, flexing her astral fingers.

Eric rolled onto his back and looked right at her. His eyes focused. She held her breath, so frozen she couldn't leave.

He propped himself up on his elbows. "Great. Now I'm friggin' hallucinating." His voice was slurred.

He closed his eyes and opened them again. "Still there." He closed them for another few seconds and reopened them. His smile surprised her. "Maybe something good'll come of sleep deprivation." He reached out to her. "Come here, beautiful, and gimme some love."

Sleep deprivation. That was why he seemed out of it. So he wasn't totally awake, but he wasn't asleep either. Her gaze slid down to his penis, which was now fully engorged. He wanted her.

Again, her body stirred. *Stop that!* It was Jerryl's fault, in a way. For years she had associated sex with lewdness, fear, force, and just plain depravity. Jerryl had awakened the sexuality she'd stuffed deep down inside her. For a month she and Jerryl had crazy, hard, wild sex at least once a day, and her body now craved it.

The last person on earth she wanted to have sex with was Eric Aruda. Unfortunately her body wasn't on board with that idea.

His eyes drifted shut, his hand lying on the bed stretched out toward her. She had to get out of there, think of another way to get to him.

Wait. She could use this. She might not be able to kill him psychically. So she would have to do it physically. The plan clicked into place. Eric was obviously hungry for sex. Could she seduce him, maybe plant an idea in his mind to meet her somewhere? When he showed up, she would have to play dumb. She couldn't admit she was the one he was seeing in his sort-of dreams, after all. No, she'd pretend she was just at the same place, wanting the same thing he did. Lure him to a cheap hotel room, drug him and tie him to the bed so he couldn't use his strength or his deadly ability. She knew he was deadly. He'd torched two CIA agents and shot another one.

But she wanted him to know why she was killing him. Needed him to know. So she'd wait until he started coming out of it. The hard part would be pushing back her hatred enough to seduce him.

Spies had to do shit like this. Mata Hari or whatever her name was, I think she slept with the enemy. For those moments forget who he is, what he's done. Use your hunger. Focus on the physical aspect of his body. The hate can come when you're driving a knife into him.

She reached out and touched his arm, and he

opened his eyes again. Her fingers slid down his fore-arm. Like when she'd touched Jerryl, Eric's energy was so thick and hot, it was almost like touching his skin. She forced a smile, sly and coy. "Hi, sexy." She leaned closer and pressed her lips against his neck.

"This isn't real." His words were a half groan.

Her hand slid over his chest and across his stom-ach. "But doesn't it feel good?"

His answer was another groan, and he tilted his head back and closed his eyes in pleasure. She knew he could feel her, her touch as soft as cashmere, with the same heat she felt from him.

She closed her eyes for a moment, reliving how it felt with Jerryl, wishing it were him. She hadn't thought she would ever feel this again. The heat, the intensity, only came with touching another person like her. During training, she had touched someone without psychic abilities and felt no heat.

Eric was . . . well, he was big. *Everywhere.* She teased all around his erection, running her fingers over his inner thighs and then up to the pale skin of his pelvis. He was tensed, making every muscle stand out, sculpting his body like one of those statues she'd seen in pictures.

He reached out again, and his hand went through her ethereal body. "My . . . imagination," he whis-pered, a shadow of agony on his expression.

"Maybe," she said, giving him her coy smile again.

"Who . . . are . . . you?"

She liked that he couldn't catch his breath as she moved her hands over his body. "Call me whatever you'd like."

He laughed, soft and husky. "This has got to be a dream, which means I'm finally asleep. Thank God."

He looked up at her. "I'll call you Tawny. Come here, Tawny. I want you to sit on me. I'm going to grind into you and suck you raw."

The words stirred her. Yes, raw. She leaned down, as though to do much more than just place a kiss on his stomach. She bet his skin was soft and that those fine golden hairs would tickle her lips, and if she impaled herself on his massive erection and drove her fingernails into his shoulders when she came . . .

Shock and disgust threw her out of her mission. She blinked to find herself back in her own bed, covered in a fine sheen of perspiration. Her breath came in shallow pants. The worst, the absolutely worst part was the throbbing between her legs.

She got to her knees and smacked her forehead against the wall. "Whore! Slut!" Her body had responded to her enemy's. She was weak, a traitor. "Piece of trash."

Those were her stepmother's words, echoing in her brain as they often did. She deserved every one of them. Back then, no. Now . . . yes.

With her forehead pressed against the wall, she banged her fists on either side of her head. Big, gulping breaths kept away her fury and tears. She sagged back onto the bed. Fatigue came from the tension that it took to keep that fine, tenuous thread between body and soul. When her soul thrust back into her body, the rush of energy was the final, exhausting straw.

"I will do this. I'll kill him even if I have to die trying."

Eric blinked as the sexy nymph disappeared. He propped himself up on his elbows and looked around. Was he dreaming? He felt as awake as he'd been for the last many days. He even pinched himself and felt the pain of it. Damn. Awake. Bleary-eyed, rubber-brained, but awake, and with a junior-high boner. He dropped back on the bed.

"Hell. I *am* hallucinating."

This wasn't good. How many steps away from insanity? First, visions of naked women because it had been way too long since he'd had sex. Then what? Would he see the enemy sneaking in with guns and kill them, only to discover he'd killed his friends?

Psychosis.

The warning Eric had gotten echoed in his head. Another one of their kind had suffered from sleeplessness right before he went whacked and killed his mother. Eric hadn't slept since he'd burned Jerryl. Overuse of their abilities could push them over the edge.

He had rushed headlong into dangerous situations. He'd faced death. Never had he felt afraid. What the sleeplessness and hallucinations meant . . . the prospect scared the hell out of him.

CHAPTER 2

An urgent knock on her door shot Fonda out of bed. She had the trippy mental picture of Eric standing there.

Who the hell is it?

It was seven-thirty in the morning. Even during decent hours, she rarely had visitors. She let no one into her life, so there wasn't a chance that it was some friend in need. Maybe a neighbor, like that elderly lady who had given her a wary smile when she offered to carry up the woman's groceries once.

She grabbed her switchblade and peered through the door's peephole to see a man she didn't recognize. Wait a minute. She did recognize him! The man who'd been following her last night. Holy crap, how had he found her?

"What do you want?" she called out, hoping he couldn't hear the tremble in her voice.

"Fonda Raine?" He knew her name. Stalker? Crazed rapist?

"Who wants to know?"

"Agent Westerfield with the FBI. I'm here to ask you about your work with Gerard Darkwell."

That threw her. She tried to get a better look at him. His long coat was draped over his arm. He wore a simple suit, hair brushed back in a neat style, posture straight and businesslike, sort of Fox Mulderish, she supposed. She'd had a ginormous crush on David Duchovny in the *X-Files* days. He believed in monsters and psychic abilities, in oddities like her. The man at her door was handsome, but he was no Fox.

"Hold on a minute."

She ran to the bathroom, grabbed the switchblade from the floor, and pressed it behind her back as she opened the door a crack. "Your ID?"

He showed her a badge that *looked* authentic, but how could you really know? He was probably in his late forties, his brown hair streaked with silver. He glanced in both directions before saying, "The FBI is studying the unusual project in which you were involved. With the fire, some of the data is lost. I need you to fill in the gaps."

She didn't want to go back there. Only look ahead, not back. But the words came out: "Will the FBI continue the project?"

"Possibly."

Darkwell, a muckety-muck at the CIA, had tapped her for a top-secret government program. She, a nobody from the projects, doing important work. For the first time in her life, *she* had felt important. And the money had been great, enough to give her a cushion of security she'd never had.

"Come in." She opened the door and gestured for him to sit in the bright yellow vinyl chair, a relic from the sixties. "It's a rocker," she warned as he eyed it dubiously. "Or you can have the bubble chair."

He cleared his throat. "This is fine."

She loved things from the past. Life seemed safer then, more innocent. She tucked the switchblade beneath her leg as she sat on the arm of the couch.

He settled into the chair, steadying it, and then looked at her. "We've been trying to track you down since the fire at Darkwell's estate."

The fire Eric Aruda had no doubt set, which destroyed the mansion where she'd been living and working, and that killed Darkwell. "I spent some time with my father." Sounded so nice and heartwarming, going home for support. "What do you want to know?"

He held up a digital recorder. "May I? I want to get the details right." He flipped it on and held it in his hand. "Tell me about your work with Darkwell. I know it was of a supernatural nature."

"We considered it paranormal. How much do you know?"

His mouth twitched, but he kept his expression passive. "To be honest, not much." He paused, maybe giving her a chance to start rattling away, which she didn't. "Let's start with you. You obviously have a super-paranormal ability that Darkwell considered valuable."

"I can astral project." It had been so odd to hear Darkwell casually put into words what she had hidden for so long.

Westerfield gave no indication of what he thought. "You and the two other contractors were using your abilities to do what, exactly?"

"Find and kill terrorists. It was supposed to be

ones in the Middle East, but a local group called the Rogues were trying to sabotage the program, so we were mostly targeting them. They also have abilities."

Finally something made him react. His light gray eyes glittered with interest. "Tell me everything you know about them."

She did, ending with, "They're dangerous. Will you kill them? That's what Darkwell was trying to do."

Instead of answering, he verified the spelling of the names he'd written down. "Just before the fire that destroyed the house there was another fire that killed one of Darkwell's contractors."

A gasp escaped her throat. "Jerryl Evrard," she whispered. *Say it without emotion.* The horror had spliced her open and let her deepest fears and feelings bleed out. "Eric Aruda psychically set Jerryl on fire."

While we were making love.

Those horrible moments came roaring back: Jerryl's scream, the eruption of flames, the ungodly smell of burning flesh. She had been right there, dammit, and couldn't help him. She tried to smother the flames with a blanket, but it had done nothing. She still had nightmares, still heard his screams of agony, and worse, the silence of death. She had lived, and he had died.

Even that didn't shock Westerfield. He took it in as though she'd told him about a summer storm, impassively jotting something down. "There was a prisoner at the estate named Sayre Andrus. What do you know about him?"

"I knew there was some guy locked in the attic, under guard, but that's about all. He might have died in the fire. I heard they found two bodies in the rubble."

He gauged her every word, her expression, or at

least it seemed that way. She felt that power of being important again.

The chair wobbled as he shifted, and he planted his foot to steady it. "You were not at the estate when the fire broke out?"

"Darkwell told me to go home, that he suspected there might be trouble from the Rogues." She'd been angry that he didn't think she could handle it or help. Maybe she could have taken out one of them. Maybe she could have killed Eric.

"What did Darkwell tell you about your abilities? About how you came to have them?"

"He said I inherited my ability from my mother."

"That's all he told you?"

"What else is there to know?"

He stood. "Thank you, Ms. Raine. I don't have to tell you that this subject remains highly classified and should not be discussed with anyone. I trust you haven't."

She shook her head, coming to her feet, too, gripping the switchblade behind her back. "Who would believe me?"

His mouth betrayed a trace of a smile. "True."

"Do you believe me?"

"We'll be in touch."

She watched him walk to a black sedan parked out at the curb and get in, though the car remained in its spot for several minutes. Did she want to work for the government again? She couldn't think about that right now. She couldn't think of anything but her mission. Revenge kept her going, a gnawing hunger that filled her being. She was afraid that after Eric was dead, she would have a big, gaping hole inside her. Maybe a new top-secret mission would fill that hole.

Her phone rang. She walked over to the red acrylic telephone stand but let the machine pick up.

"Hey . . . hon. It's your dad. I see your stuff is gone, so I'm figuring you went home. That's okay," he hurried on to say. "Could you give me a call and let me know you're all right?" A pause, then a nervous laugh. "I guess I got a taste of how it was living with me all those years . . . like living with a zombie. One day I'd like to . . . well, I can't make it up to you. But I'd like to try. Funny how it's easier to say this to a machine than it would have been when you were here." Another pause. "Okay, I'll talk to you soon."

Her fingers gripped the phone but she couldn't pick it up. She had never said a thing about why she'd shown up at his house with a duffel bag and a request to stay for a few days, which ended up being a few weeks. He'd never asked.

"As long as Connie's in the picture, you'll never make it up to me," she said to the phone. "She'll be out of jail soon, and you'll go back to using. I can't lose my dad again. I've lost too much already."

The man posing as John Westerfield closed the car door and dialed his brother. He knew Malcolm would be in a private place awaiting his call.

"It's Neil. Darkwell was doing exactly what we suspected. He recreated the program with the offspring of the original program."

He could feel Malcolm's fury pulsing in the silence but knew restraint would overcome it. After all, restraint had been bred into them from birth.

"Why didn't he come to me?" he said at last, a rhetorical question, but Neil answered anyway.

"He knew you would shut him down. You have

a lot more to lose now if this gets out. The seven off-spring Darkwell called Rogues are a big problem. She gave me a rundown of their abilities. Eric Aruda is the most dangerous. I'll fill you in on the details later."

"Seven. Seven people who know about Darkwell. Possibly about their origins. It's messy. I don't like it."

Neil stroked the vehicle's shifter. "Messy but manageable. Remember what I did last time. I was brilliant, if I don't say so myself."

Malcolm released a breath, possibly of relief. "Yes, it did work out well. But they weren't expecting it. These people are. They all have to go. Start with Fonda, as she'll be the easiest to dispatch. Target Eric next."

"Now? She's still in her apartment, so small, my fingers could go around her neck twice."

"You're salivating, aren't you?"

Neil swallowed. "It's been a long time since I've killed someone. I'm so ready."

"Not now. Someone might have seen you or there could be cameras. We have to be careful. Everything we've worked for is at stake. She's bound to go someplace where you can take her out neatly and quickly. Make it look like a simple mugging, nothing weird that will pique a medical examiner's interest or show up as an oddity in the news." He let those words settle for a moment like dust. "Then you can work on finding the rest of them. You'll get to kill plenty. That should keep you happy for a while."

As though he could be placated like a demanding child. Neil disconnected.

They had been raised to eschew emotions and follow rigid rules, but the world had infected them with its emotions. They were everywhere, filling the air with their intoxicating scents. He breathed them in, made them his own: jealousy, rage, bitterness. How unfair that his brother should still impose rules on him. To preserve Malcolm's career, he had curtailed himself. Now he was being given *permission* to kill, but with limitations. There was another emotion he had assimilated: anger.

Maybe he wouldn't take Fonda out quickly. He could take her to the lab. Like Darkwell had experimented with people with enhanced psychic abilities long ago, though he himself would work with Fonda for fun.

Neil pulled away from the curb and into the flow of traffic. People hurried about their business, unaware of the magnificence in their midst. Hunger and lust filled him, sharpened by anger. He stopped at a red light and watched a man crossing the street with a group of pedestrians. Another drone. A drone that reminded him of his own role here . . . a drone in his brother's hive.

Neil reached toward the man, feeling the power surge inside him. He imagined his hand thrusting into the man's chest, the soft squishiness of his heart pumping in his palm. He squeezed. The man grasped his chest and dropped to the ground, his face a mask of agony. A shame to use his powers in such a hidden way. Much more exciting would be to make his heart explode right out of his chest, splattering blood all over the people around him. So spectacular. Too weird.

Someone knelt by the man and checked his pulse. Neil kept squeezing. A horn blasted behind him. Impatience. Annoyance. Traffic did not stop just because a man was dying. The driver behind him gestured for him to go.

Neil looked at the drone, sprawled out on the asphalt, no longer moving. Fonda Raine would soon be the same.

* * *

Eric flopped down in bed, but his eyes were open, his brain wired awake. Why couldn't he sleep?

Too much on your mind, that's all.

But there wasn't that much going on. After a month and a half of hell, no one was trying to kill him and the people he cared about. The damned thing of it was, he couldn't even enjoy it.

Eric opened his nightstand drawer and took out a Ho Ho. As his teeth sank into the chocolate cake, his mind went to his current task: find Sayre Andrus. Without Darkwell's directive to kill the Rogues, Sayre had been happy to menace them for personal pleasure. So far Sayre had thwarted their efforts to find him.

He would find Sayre, torch him, and then stop using his pyrokinesis unless absolutely necessary. He no longer had the taste for watching the flames. Yes, he'd felt victory when he sent Jerryl to his fiery hell, but something had changed, erasing that sensuous pull of destruction. He had inadvertently caused two sort-of innocent people to die. He wasn't even pissed that he hadn't been the one to kill Darkwell.

At least he'd had a sweet hallucination. More like a succubus, seducing him and then torturing him with an unresolved hard-on. He looked at the Thomas Rut paintings that adorned his walls, his one luxury. He half expected one of those women to step out of the painting and start talking to him.

Eric closed his eyes, willing sleep to come. He managed to grab snatches here and there, but never deep enough for dreams. He drifted into that jagged sleep, also a tease. He didn't know how much time passed until he opened his eyes again. His chest tightened. The hallucination was back. Tawny.

Ghostly, shimmering, beautiful in a flowing dress with a long scarf flowing from her hair.

"Go away."

She walked toward him like a cat, her hips swaying, movements fluid. Her smile reminded him of the Cheshire cat, conspiratorial, mischievous. "I don't want to. And I don't think you really want me to either."

Oh, he liked the seduction. It was what her presence meant that bothered him.

He turned his head. "You're not real."

She touched him in that not-real way, running her finger down the center of his chest, following the line of his hair just past the blazing erection he had despite the fact that he didn't want her there.

Just to further prove how nuts he was.

"Mm, I see you do like me here. You can feel me, can't you?"

He could, a soft, hot energy that left a burning trail across his skin. "My imagination," he managed on a whisper. Damn, he had to get laid. He couldn't handle this craving, this hunger. Maybe the hallucination would go away if he wasn't so horny.

"What if I was real? What if I'm a soul fragment of a lonely girl? A dream connection, two souls meeting . . ."

"Like Lucas and Amy."

She paused. "Who?"

He waved his hand. "Never mind."

She continued running her hands over his chest. He grabbed for them, but his hands went right through hers.

"How come I can feel you touching me, but I can't touch you?"

She shrugged, though her fingers trailed first

around one nipple, then another, causing them to tighten painfully. "I don't know how this works."

His body involuntarily rose to her touch, seeking the heat of her. "If you're going to touch me, do it where it counts."

She smiled. "I'm saving that for later."

"What, you going to keep coming back night after night, driving me crazy with your teasing?"

She liked the idea of that, apparently, giving him a look of interest. "Or we could meet." She leaned closer, her expression becoming more urgent. "Find my lonely soul."

He snorted. "Your lonely soul is hanging out with my lonely soul in Crazyland."

Her fingers touched his cock this time, sending his body into a spasm. "Are you sure about that?" She trailed her fingers down the length of him. "Aren't you up for a little adventure?"

"That's an adventure in"—damn, she was taking his breath away—"insanity."

"You're not afraid, are you? Big guy like you . . ." Her gaze went to his cock on those last words, but her eyes and voice held a definite challenge.

"Where?"

"There's a place where my lonely soul likes to hang out. It's a bar called the Dew Drop Inn." She gave him a location northwest of Annapolis.

"Oh yeah, that sounds real."

"Well, I didn't name it." She planted her hands on either side of his waist and leaned down over his stomach. Her gaze, though, was on him. "Don't you want to find out? What if I'm there?"

"Then this is plain weird. Or you're an Offspring."

"An Offspring? What's that?" She didn't seem to know.

He wasn't about to get into it right now, not with a hallucination. "Never mind."

She leaned lower, kissing down the center of his chest, following the line she'd drawn with her finger minutes earlier. "I'll be waiting for you." She stopped just short of the tip of his cock. "Then we can continue this in person." Her dress slipped off her shoulder as she sat up. Her shoulder looked so soft and smooth, the skin above her still-concealed breast pale. "As soon as you can get there."

And she was gone.

He shoved out of bed. "Friggin' crazy hallucinations. Now she wants me to head out into the night and make an ass out of myself . . . to myself."

So why was he shoving on a pair of jeans and flinging on a black cotton shirt?

He looked at his reflection over the dresser mirror as he pushed the shirt buttons through the holes. "Because you're friggin' crazy, that's why."

He had to admit, though, that a diversion was what he needed. An adventure, as she'd said. He'd elected to stay in the Tomb, their name for the bomb shelter that had been their safe haven, because of the warrant out for his arrest. Darkwell's doing, and just because he'd gone away didn't mean the warrant had.

He went into the bathroom and pulled a brush through his hair. He looked like hell. Eyes red and listless, skin pale from lack of sun. He looked like a vampire. He palmed some gel and spiked his hair. Not that he expected to meet Tawny at the Dew Drop Inn, but maybe he'd meet someone else in need of a romp. Chicks were hot for vampires right now; he could get lucky.

He walked toward his door, hoping Amy and Lucas, the only other Rogues still at the tomb, were asleep. For one thing, he still had a boner. For another, being around them was painful. As much as he'd once felt jealous of their all-consuming passion, the tension between them lately weighed heavy on him.

A chest of drawers was lodged in front of their bedroom door. Amy was sleeping on the floor in the hall. She looked so small and so pained, even in sleep. Lucas insisted that he be locked in his bedroom—alone—every night so Sayre couldn't possess him and cause them harm. He kept Amy out for her own protection, but they had other issues, too.

Eric clamped his bottom lip with his teeth as he pulled his door closed. The tiny click didn't wake Amy. The groan of pain in the bedroom did, though. She shot to her feet, eyes wide in fear. "Push it away, push it away," she said, shoving at the dresser.

Eric gave it a hard shove, and she wedged herself through the crack between the dresser and the door frame before he'd even finished. Lucas was contorted on the bed, his face in a grimace. She crouched next to him, shaking his shoulders. "Wake up! Wake up!"

"It's not Sayre," Eric said after a few seconds. "It's another storm of images."

When Sayre possessed, he had Lucas do things, like get a gun. The storms dropped him, and as he described it, images of something terrible that was either happening or about to happen tore across his brain like an electrical current.

"No." Amy shook her head, still patting Lucas's cheek. "We're not in danger anymore. No more storms."

Eric's chest tightened at the thought of more danger. "Maybe it's an accident. I'll check with the others."

A few phone calls later and he returned. "Everyone's fine. We won't know what he saw until he wakes up. That should be in about five minutes."

"Eric! He's bleeding!" She started crying, pulling Lucas against her chest. Blood trickled from his nose. "Get me a tissue!"

He brought a box, and she dabbed at the blood.

A stab of panic hit him. "Amy . . . he's bleeding from his ear, too."

Her yelp of fear shot right through him. "This is killing him. I can't . . . I have to . . ."

"Wait it out. Let's see what he says when he comes out."

They waited, but he didn't come out. Her frantic gaze went from the clock to Lucas, like a mad tennis match. Twenty minutes. Thirty minutes. Forty. He watched, his chest frozen.

"He's not coming out." She felt for his pulse. "It's so shallow. I can't go through this again." She looked at Eric, pleading with her eyes.

"I won't do it."

"I'm not asking you to." She kept looking at him.

"You want my blessing?"

"Your agreement that it has to be done."

He looked at Lucas, willing him to wake so he wouldn't have to make a choice. This was the worst storm ever. If it killed him . . . "Do it."

She ran out of the room. He watched Lucas while she was gone, and his body tightened as though electrical currents were going through him, too. He wiped at the blood continuing to drip down Lucas's face.

Amy returned with a small box and pulled out one

of two syringes. She stared at Lucas, torn but resolute, then looked at the bluish liquid in the syringe: the antidote. She had gotten it from the botanist who found the substance given to their parents to boost their abilities . . . what the Offspring had inherited. Even the botanist admitted it was unstable. One of his sons had lost his abilities after taking it—the one who went psycho. The other son hadn't. Lucas had refused to take it, fearful of losing his ability to foresee the future, which helped him protect Amy.

"He probably won't ever forgive you." He met her tear-filled gaze. "You know that, don't you?"

"It's not fair. We've been through so much. I've almost lost him twice."

He took her hand. It should be him breaking down, not Lucas. "No matter what happens, your love changed him, made him stronger, better. What you two have . . . it's incredible."

"I know." Her voice was a raw whisper. "I'm going to lose him either way. I'd rather he be alive and mad at me than . . ."

It killed him to watch the man who was like a brother to him and the woman who, as it turned out, was his half sister, in agony. She had risked her life for Lucas, and he'd done the same. Eric didn't understand that kind of love, but it stunned him anyway. Watching the little ways they touched each other, the looks they traded that smacked of such intimacy, it made him feel he should leave the room. Sometimes it made him ache, though it could have just been heartburn.

"I'm sorry, Lucas," she said on a whisper, pulling his arm into position. "I love you." She pushed the plunger, and the liquid disappeared from the syringe.

She removed the needle and threw it into the box as though it had burned her fingers.

Eric pulled her to her feet and held her, and she cried in his arms.

Some time passed. He didn't know how much. She disengaged and lay down next to Lucas. "He'll sleep for twenty-four hours. That's what they told me would happen. He'll wake . . . and he'll be okay."

Lucas did seem relaxed now, and the bleeding had stopped. Eric could only nod, but he wasn't so sure. Taking the antidote was as scary as going psycho.

She held onto Lucas but looked at him. "Why are you dressed? You still can't sleep, can you?" Her gaze flicked to the box. "Eric—"

"I'm not taking that stuff. Unless I'm bleeding like Lucas. Dying." He wasn't going to chance losing his abilities until Sayre was dead. "I'm heading out to get some fresh air. I'll have my phone if you need me." He put it in his pocket. "Amy . . . I won't take sides. It's going to be rough. But . . ." He wasn't good at this kind of thing. "I'll be there for both of you."

She nodded, a faint smile on her face. "Thank you. I won't tell him you agreed. That was for me."

There was nothing he could do now. He left, feeling the pressure in his chest ease as he emerged aboveground and walked to the garage where Lucas's Barracuda waited. Maybe all he needed was to drive. Fast. Find a remote road and hit the gas. The car kicked ass. If he ended up near the Dew Drop Inn, he could always check it out. What could it hurt?

CHAPTER 3

The Dew Drop Inn way passed Eric's expectations, which were of a small, quaint building with a piano player doing the standards. No, this place was a two-story, shit-kickin' country dive, complete with a neon boot sign.

Country music wasn't his thing, but he was craving something, and maybe he'd find it here. If a hot chick was wearing boots, well, she wouldn't be for long.

Who are you kidding? You're going to see if you're crazy. Because she won't be here and then you're going to have to take that antidote, too.

He shoved that thought away. The parking lot was still full even at this late hour, but that wasn't surprising on a Friday night. A couple was making it in a nearby car, and the woman's groans were so loud they rivaled the music coming from the building.

He hated when women faked it, and that chick was definitely putting on a show. Still, the sounds of her dramatic gasps kicked his libido into overdrive, and that didn't take much on a good day. When he was undersatisfied, overtired, and ramped up from being teased two nights in a row, it rolled over him like a wave of hot water. He adjusted his jeans and started walking toward the entrance. Music and cigarette smoke billowed out when he held the door open for a couple who were leaving. He stepped inside and paid the cover charge.

Okay, he was looking for his succubus. Several women were dressed in tight jeans and plaid shirts, as were the men. Most folks were too involved in their drinking, talking, and dancing to pay him much notice. A couple of women did, however, their smiles predatory as they took him in. Getting laid should not be a problem.

Eric walked up to the long bar covered with peanut shells to order a beer, and that's when he saw her. More like felt her watching him. She shifted her gaze away, a shy smile on her face. She sat at the end of the bar, a full shot glass and lime wedge in front of her, an empty shot glass next to it. Not exactly his succubus, but damned close. Long blond hair, eyelashes so thick they had to be those stick-on type. Bright pink lipstick on lush lips. Her black miniskirt, paired with textured tights and red, high-heeled boots, made her legs look long. She didn't fit in either. She turned her stool around to watch the dance floor, her gaze sliding across him as she did.

He ordered a Heineken and wandered over, his body buzzing. She wasn't looking at him directly, but she was aware of him. Her body straightened, her fingers messed with her hair.

"You don't want to go there, buddy," a man at the bar said. He nodded toward the woman. "She's cold. Cut you right down."

He could have told the guy to mind his own business, but hey, he was only trying to save his dignity. "Thanks, man. But I'll take my chances."

The woman glanced at him as he came to a stop beside her, but looked back at the dance floor. He looked at it, too, taking a sip of his beer and remaining just outside her boundaries. Damn, it had been friggin' forever since he'd been out on the scene. He suddenly felt old and out of touch, as though he'd just come back from war. In a way, he had. He'd been to the dark side of the physical world, human nature, and himself.

"Do you dance?"

The soft, sweet voice, nearly obliterated by the music, pulled him back to present. She was talking to him. Had she asked him to dance? No, just if he did.

"Not to this stuff."

They weren't line dancing, but most were kicking up their boots to the twangy song.

He gestured to the dance floor with his bottle. "You?"

"Only the slow songs."

He wasn't going to get in her face and drop a lame line or offer to buy her a drink. Or check her out. Well, not in an obvious way. He pretended to scope out the place while taking her in with his peripheral vision. The Cheap Trick song "She's Tight" came to mind, though it was quickly buried under the song, something slower now.

She threw back her shot, licking her hand and squeezing the lime into her mouth. Damn, he wanted to lick off the drop of juice that dripped down her jaw. Now he felt right about offering to buy her a drink.

Before he could, she turned to him. "Dance with me."

Not quite an order, and not a request either. He hated slow dancing with a woman he'd just met. Where to put his hands, how close to hold her, and for God's sake don't stomp on her feet.

He set his bottle on the bar. "How can I refuse?"

She stood, and he took her hand and led her to a dance floor that was rapidly crowding in with couples. She moved into his arms, not a damned thing about her cold. Her movements were a bit awkward, telling him she didn't like slow dancing as much as she'd said. Small, brightly colored rings circled her right upper ear but not her left. The big red hoops that hung from her lobes brushed against her neck as they moved. He was way too tall for her, his hands coming down on her shoulders, leaving her hands to wrap around his waist.

Which felt good. He willed his cock not to jump to attention, but it didn't listen, as usual. She had to feel it, but she didn't move back. He looked down at her, but she stared straight ahead at his chest. She was worrying her lips. Probably feeling his erection. She met his gaze and smiled, but he saw nervousness in her big brown eyes.

She said, "I have a bottle of tequila back at my hotel room."

Whoa. He actually stopped moving. Had he heard her right?

"Tequila works for me."

"I don't want you to think I'm cheap. It's just . . . I could use some company. Know what I mean?"

He had to keep the words *Hell, yes* from roaring out of him.

She'd stopped moving, too. "I swear I've never done this before."

He saw something in her eyes, maybe that need, pain, but not desperation. Without another word he took her hand and led her from the dance floor. The guy who'd warned him about her now gaped as they wound their way through the crowd toward the door.

This seemed too easy. They'd hardly traded smoldering looks, casual conversation, or even names. They exited the building into the cool night.

"I'm Eric," he said.

She covered her mouth. "God, we haven't even told each other our names. You must think I'm a—"

He kissed her word away. She tasted like tequila, musky and rich, with a hint of lime and salt. Beneath the smoke he smelled a clean scent, like soap. She looked fragile, despite her bold request.

"I don't think you're an anything."

She looked away at that, swallowing hard. "Follow me. I'm staying at a little motel down the road. I was going to head back to D.C.—I went to Annapolis on business—but I wasn't ready to go home."

"You wouldn't happen to be married, would you?" he asked as he followed her to a deep yellow 1976 Mustang.

A shadow crossed her eyes, which was why he was surprised when she said, "Widowed."

Damn. "Sorry. I shouldn't have—"

"No, it's okay."

It was only then that he thought of his succubus. Hadn't she insinuated that she belonged to the soul of a lonely woman?

She paused beside her door. "Would you have backed off if I was married?"

"Depends on the situation, but definitely if you had kids."

She started to get in, but he held her door open and leaned down to meet her gaze.

"You never told me your name."

"Oh. Sorry. I'm Edie." She reached out and shook his hand, which struck him as so odd he almost laughed.

Thank God he caught himself and didn't. "Nice to meet you, Edie. I'm driving a 'Cuda. I'll pull up to your car and we'll head out."

The motel, twenty minutes down the road, was as old as the car he was driving. It had about twenty units, and one car sat in the parking lot. It reminded him of the kind of place his dad, or the man he had thought was his father, chose when they went on a trip.

Edie's long blond hair swung against her back as she walked to the door with the number 19 on it. Her unit was almost at the end of the strip of building. She didn't turn on the light, and when he reached for the switch, she said, "Don't."

Ah, one of those women who only had sex in the dark. To mask their shame, maybe.

She turned on the bathroom light and closed it within an inch, letting a stream of light into the room. "More romantic this way."

She'd invited him to have sex with her without even knowing his name and now she wanted romantic? Naw, it was shame. Was she married after all?

She walked over to the dresser. "I've got orange juice on ice. I was going to have a couple of drinks in the room and then drinking alone seemed pretty pathetic, so I went out instead."

She went to work unwrapping a couple of cups, scooping ice into them, and then opening the bottle of tequila.

He moved up behind her, covering her shoulders with his hands and kneading them. They were rock hard. "We don't have to drink."

She met his gaze in the mirror. "Yes. I do. We do."

Okay, she had issues. She wasn't drunk, despite the tequila on her tongue. So something was haunting her, and she needed a drink to loosen up so she could exorcise it by having sex with a stranger. He checked her ring finger. She wore lots of rings but nothing that looked like a wedding ring, nor a telltale white band.

He pushed her long hair away from her neck and leaned down to kiss her soft skin, but she shifted away.

"Can you turn the air conditioner down?"

She was acting strange, but if she was telling the truth about this being her first one-night stand, that might explain it. Oddly enough, he felt a bit weird, too. Probably picking up her energy. He walked over and futzed with the controls, one of which was missing a knob.

She walked over with the drinks when he was done, handed him one, and raised hers. "Cheers."

"Cheers." They tapped cups, and he took a drink. He wasn't a tequila drinker, or really much of a liquor drinker in general. When you had a tendency to set fires with your mind, losing control was a bad idea.

She sat down on the bed, tucking one foot under her thigh. "When we finish these, we can . . ." She gave him that shy smile again. "Well, you know."

He quelled the urge to say *Bottoms up!* But he did drink.

She cat-walked across the bed to her small purse and pulled out a condom. Her ass swayed with her movements and her skirt rode up the backs of her thighs. She moved with a feline grace, but she also had a nervousness that kept her moving.

The liquor was relaxing him, that was for sure. It stole over him like a mist. She twisted around and smiled. Beautiful smile. He smiled back, though his lips felt rubbery.

She crawled toward him and looked in his cup. "Finish up."

"I don't want—"

She pushed the cup toward his mouth. "I want you to feel nice and loose."

"I already do."

"More loose." She reached down where she'd set her cup and finished hers in one gulp.

Okay, finish it up, get laid. She tossed her cup on the floor and came up behind him. Her fingers kneaded his shoulders as he'd tried to do to her a few minutes ago. He melted beneath her touch. The room even shifted, as though he were on a ship in rolling waves. His head lolled but he caught it. He was way too relaxed.

"How are you feeling?" she asked, her mouth near his ear, her breath warm against his neck.

Only garbled sounds came out. His mouth wouldn't work. What the hell?

She pulled him down and leaned over him. "Are you all right?"

He tried to lift his hand. To speak. To think. *I've . . . Too . . .* His thoughts kept scrambling. *No, not right . . . not all right.*

"Can you scoot up on the bed?" she asked.

She tugged on his arms, and he sloppily moved with her. His arms were like overripe celery. He felt as though he were sinking into the mattress. She leaned closer, her face warped. She looked strange in the near-darkness. Her eyes were as sharp as blades, her mouth in a tight line. And her hair . . . it wasn't long anymore. It had a streak of a darker color. No, none of this made sense. Except now she looked like his succubus.

"Eric?"

He couldn't focus anymore. Her mouth floated away from her face, her eyes wobbled. His eyes wanted to roll back but he fought to keep them facing forward. "Can't . . ." More garbled nonsense.

She moved away, and then he felt something tighten around his wrist. His arm finally moved, but not his intent. Then his other wrist. Arms over his head.

The girl . . . what was her name again? She leaned close again. "Eric Aruda . . . welcome to the last day of your life."

Then he lost the battle and his eyes crashed shut.

Fonda leaned down into Eric's face. He was definitely out. She closed his eyelids as one does with the dead.

Not yet.

She'd gotten a couple of pills from her old neighborhood. She didn't even know what kind of drug it was, didn't want to, only how much to give him to knock him out.

She took the ropes she'd brought and anchored his wrists to the cheap headboard. She wasn't going to wait long. As soon as he started coming around, she would tell him why she was killing him. Maybe it didn't matter once his soul left his body and went to hell. It mattered to her. She'd ditched the wig and changed clothes, black pants and a moss green shirt, black boots that looked more industrial than glamorous. She pulled a knife out of her bag. Long and sharp. She had planned and daydreamed about this, but now that she was here . . . killing someone was harder than she thought. Even for good reason. The blood would leave a terrible mess for that nice man at the check-in desk to deal with. It probably wouldn't be as easy as it looked on television. She'd cut a man once, in self-defense, but that was all reaction and instinct.

She put herself back in the moment when the fire had broken out. Jerryl's screams. Her agony and the guilt she carried that she couldn't help him. Her anger shored up her determination. *You can do this.*

She unbuttoned Eric's shirt and traced the space between the ribs on his left side. Stabbing his chest wouldn't be as gory as cutting his throat. Either way, the flashbacks would haunt her just as the fire did.

She straddled him, feeling his hip bones beneath her thighs. He was as beautiful in person as he'd been during her astral visit. That didn't change anything. He was still a killer. And soon she would be, too.

CHAPTER 4

What the friggin' hell?

Eric's muddled mind put those words together first, and it took everything in him to do that. He could hardly open his eyes. His instincts, though, were on alert. Danger vibrated through his being, but this was a different danger than he'd ever felt.

Stay calm. Don't move. Think. He fumbled with putting together his most recent memories. Bar. Hot chick. Went back to her motel room. About to have sex. How did he go from there to flat out on his back with his thoughts tumbling as though they were in a dryer?

Listen.

No sound.

His arms ached, and he realized they were above his head. He gave them a tug. Panic sliced through him, springing his eyes open. He looked up, finding his hands tied to the bedposts. Still in the motel room. Where was the hot chick? Light crept around the edge of the bathroom door. Someone turned on the water in the sink.

The heaviness in his brain and body . . . Hell, she'd drugged him. Hadn't he seen her pour the drinks? No, she'd had him adjust the air conditioner, distracted him.

Damn, hadn't he known the pickup was too easy? Crap. He'd picked up some homicidal bitch. Or at best, a thief. But he could feel his wallet in his back pocket, so back to the homicidal option. He pulled on the ties, his eyes on the door.

The water stopped.

His metabolism was always fast for running alcohol through him. Thank God that seemed to be the case for drugs, too. The right rope snapped. Then the left.

The toilet flushed.

He bounded off the bed and toward the door just as it opened. She walked through, her long blond hair now short. Different clothing. Same girl.

She stiffened at the sight of the empty bed, and he grabbed her. He saw the flash of a blade as she tried to bring her hand up. He twisted her arm. She gasped in pain, and the knife fell with a thud to the floor. He pushed her toward the bed, falling so he landed on top of her with all of his weight. Her breath left in a gasp. He smashed his hand over her mouth, crushing her into the bed. Her eyes, huge in her face, were already tear-streaked, the thick black liner smudged.

His teeth were gritted, jaw tight. "Who the hell are you, what the hell did you give me, and why the hell are you trying to kill me?"

He lifted his hand enough for her to answer, ready to slam it down if she screamed.

"You killed him!"

Those words threw him. "Killed who?"

Hatred permeated her hoarse voice and darkened

her brown eyes. "You burned him, you son of a bitch. You *burned* him!"

The pieces clicked into place. "You're Fonda." He tried to remember what he knew of her. She was one of the enemy Offspring, Jerryl's lover. Small but fierce was how someone had described her. As she struggled beneath him, he agreed. But not fierce enough to budge him.

She gave up the struggle, aiming her anger at him instead. "I want you dead!"

Then another piece clicked in. "You can astral project. I wasn't hallucinating." He laughed in relief, but his humor was short-lived. "So you were going to seduce me, drug me, and stab me?"

The word "Yes" came out on a whisper, no shred of remorse. "I wanted to bash your head in right there in your room. I couldn't." The weight of those last words sounded as though they crushed her as much as his weight on top of her.

"So your plan to kill me was out of revenge? For Jerryl. Not anything someone ordered you to do."

"For everything you destroyed. The program. Jerryl. Me."

"It was a war, don't you understand that? People die in war."

She took a breath. "Then you'll understand why I have to kill you."

Their bodies were hot against each other. Was he crazy that her venom and emotions were actually a turn on? They sparked something primal in him. It wasn't helping that they were sealed together from leg to chest.

"The war is over." He leaned closer to her, the heat enveloping his face. "Let it go."

Her mouth tightened to a hard line. "There's where you're wrong, Eric Aruda. It's not over until you're dead. I couldn't live with myself knowing you were still out there alive, knowing I didn't do what I needed to do. You're a cold-blooded killer. It's what you deserve."

She meant that, too. Maybe she was right.

"So you're still going to try to kill me?"

Pain burned in her eyes. "Hell, yes. You'll think I'm a dream, but someday I'm going to perfect my skills." He saw the hunger in her eyes that he'd felt when he talked about killing Jerryl.

Just what he needed, a homicidal female after him this time. Did she know what skill she might have inherited from her mother? No, she'd be using it now. If she learned, she'd be deadlier.

He sighed. "You're going to make me kill you, aren't you?"

"Do it," she dared. "Why stop now? You probably enjoy it."

She was taunting him. Those words stung, though, because he had enjoyed torching his enemy. The allure of the flames, the power . . . He was pissed enough to kill her, just on principle. What he couldn't figure out was why she didn't pretend she would accept a truce. Was she crazy? Suicidal?

He looked down at her face, in a mask of hatred, her small wrists pinned to the bed beside her head. Shame now flickered inside him at those lustful feelings.

"I didn't enjoy killing Jerryl. It was kill or be killed."

"Stop. You don't get to talk about him. And you sure as hell aren't going to convince me that you were doing the right thing by killing him."

No, he wasn't. "Look, little girl, I don't want to kill you."

If he killed her, then Sayre would be the only threat. Part of him craved the adrenaline rush of being hunted, but a bigger part just wanted peace and quiet for a while. He wasn't going to get that as long as Fonda lived. He could swear she wanted him to kill her. There was a reckless part of her that plugged right into that same part of him.

No way was he going there again. He flattened his palms over hers. "I could let you go. *We* could let this go, get on with our lives. It sucked, what happened to all of us. But Darkwell's dead—"

"Because you killed him."

"I wish I had. That man was evil."

"You're evil."

He closed his eyes on that word for a second. "I'm not evil. Aren't I proving that by offering to let you go? But you have to promise you'll forget this revenge plan."

"I won't promise you anything."

He wasn't going to change her mind. Damn. He wasn't evil. The flashbacks pulsed through his mind, not paranormal like Lucas's storm of images, but nearly as painful. The things he'd done . . .

Now he was going to have to kill this beautiful girl to stay alive. Even with a good reason, it still didn't feel good.

He unconsciously lifted his weight off her, and she took advantage and kneed him in the balls. *Bitch!* Pain shot through him, twisting his stomach into nauseous knots. He reflexively curled up. She dodged to the left and dropped down to grab the knife that was on the threadbare carpeting. She came at him, sharp point slashing down. He grabbed her wrist and slammed her against the wall, sending a picture to the floor. She kicked at him again, and he had to slam his body against hers to stop her. He wrestled the knife out of her hand and held it to her throat. His breaths sawed in and out, blood pulsing so hard it pounded in his ears.

Just do it! Kill her.

He pressed harder, and a drop of blood dripped down her throat. He didn't see fear in her eyes. Only a resoluteness, with her chin tipped up, eyes narrowed at him. If looks could kill, he'd be writhing on the floor.

His hand started shaking with the effort . . . the effort *not* to do it. His body was in full survival mode. *Kill, kill, kill.* So why couldn't he finish her?

He remained there for several seconds, their gazes locked. "I'm not going to kill you." Because he couldn't. It stunned him. Scared him. He couldn't do what needed to be done.

She sneered. "*Now* you become a coward?"

He shook his head. "That shit doesn't work. Ask my best friend who tried to get me to kill him."

"What?"

"Never mind. Think about whether you really want a war with me. Because I don't want one with you. I'm done with war." Fatigue seeped through him at the thought of it.

A scrape of shoe on concrete made them both swivel their heads toward the front window. He remote-viewed, and what he saw made him eat his last words: a man approaching the window, his hand on a gun tucked into his waistband.

He whispered, "You have company? There's a guy with a gun outside our room."

"Maybe someone heard us and called the police."

"Not likely."

He remote-viewed again, seeing the man sticking a long pin into the door lock.

Her eyes had closed, but they snapped open. "I know him! He's an FBI agent. He asked me about Darkwell's program. Why is he here?"

Frustration and fear gripped him in a cold tight hold. *Hell.* Someone else wants me dead." He turned to her. "And if he's not your buddy, he wants you dead, too."

"Why?" Her voice was strained, eyes wide. "Why would he want to kill me?"

"Because you're an Offspring." *No time for more of an explanation. Have to get out of here. Save yourself. She's on her own.*

But even as he thought it, he grabbed her hand and pulled her next to the door as they heard a click. He gripped the knife in his other hand. The door opened, and he lunged. The man, taken off-guard, fell backward. The blade slashed down his chest. That's all Eric had time to notice. They took off toward his car, he patting his pocket for the keys. His other hand was clamped over hers, though with her shorter legs, she couldn't run as fast as he. The two working lights made puddles of piss-yellow glows in the narrow parking lot. They reached the car, swinging around to see if the agent was on their trail.

Eric saw him press his hand over the cut in his chest and look to see if anyone was around. One of the rooms was occupied, and even at this late hour a glow emanated from behind the curtains.

Fonda whispered, "Should we call for help?"

"Not if this guy has government ID on him. Get in

the car," Eric said, shoving her in through the driver's door and following her in.

The agent reached out and pointed, and a small explosion tilted the car. They both flung themselves down in reaction. No glass had shattered.

"He blew the tire out," Eric told her, peering above the edge of the window. "But . . . he wasn't pointing with the gun. Come on."

They scrambled out on the opposite side of the car. Eric saw him standing several yards away, an odd smile on his face. This was one person he didn't mind torching. He narrowed his eyes and concentrated.

Nothing. He tried harder. Fear pulsed through him. *Have I lost my abilities? No, not now! Blowtorch that son of a bitch!*

Anger heated his face but didn't produce one tiny flame.

The man's smile grew. Then he held out his hand like he was gesturing for Eric to stop. One second Eric was facing him, wanting to smash his face. The next, his body was flying backward as though an invisible wrecking ball had slammed into him. He landed on the asphalt, banging his head with a jarring thud. For a moment the night sky spun, stars dancing, his stomach churning.

No time for lying down. He sprang to his feet, holding onto a car's front fender for balance and facing an enemy who was quickly gaining the upper hand. *Hell, who is this guy? What is he?*

"Are we having fun yet?" Westerfield taunted. "Well, I am, anyway." He turned to Fonda, who was standing a few yards from Eric. He curled his hand into a fist and thrust it toward her.

With a gasp, she clutched the sides of her head and

crumpled to her knees. "My head . . . it feels like his hand is inside, cr-crushing my brain."

Eric ran over and pulled her up by the arm, but never took his eyes off the agent. "What the hell?"

Westerfield took a step closer.

Fonda stumbled, grimacing in pain. Her eyes were squeezed shut, her body contorted in on itself. "He's . . . doing it, isn't . . . he?"

"Yeah, I think he is." *Unknown enemy. Unknown power. Unknown motive. Not good.* He knelt beside her. "Listen to me. You have to get him out of your head . . . your body. Someone gave me good advice once. Don't fight it. Imagine steel doors slamming shut, and this son of a bitch getting thrown back."

"Have . . . to . . . fight."

The man was walking closer.

Eric turned back to her, grabbing her shoulders. "Look at me."

She opened her eyes halfway, an obvious struggle.

"Put your energy into those doors, not fighting."

"Fighting . . . is all I know."

"Yeah, I can see that. But it's not working, is it? So focus on the doors."

She gripped his arm, her face a mask of concentration. Blood vessels stood out at her temples. With a breath, her eyes widened. "He's out."

"Let's go." He pulled her to her feet and they ran around the corner of the building. The motel backed up to woods. He pulled her close as they ran. Yeah, she'd been an enemy minutes ago. He'd deal with her later. Right now, though, he wasn't going to let the homicidal maniac get her. No time to figure out why.

They reached the line of dense trees and ran into the shadows. Beyond that, who knew? But woods was better than homicidal maniac with skills. Except that maniac was probably going to follow them in.

Amy brushed Lucas's hair, way overdue for a trim, back from his forehead. His eyes fluttered open, making her jerk in surprise.

He struggled to sit up, his gaze going to the clock: five in the morning. "How long have I been out? It might be too late."

"Six hours." Her stomach clenched. "Too late for what? What did you see? Eric called everyone, and they were fine."

His blue-gray eyes were stark with a fear that was contagious. "They're not going to be. None of us are."

"What are you talking about?"

"I saw all of us . . . dead. The ones who are out there"—he nodded toward the ceiling—"die out there. Run off the road. Shot." His face was paler than she'd ever seen it. "Eric and some woman lying on the ground. I don't know how, but they're . . . they're dead."

Her throat tightened so much, she could hardly push out the words: "We'll call them."

They decided who would call whom, and reached everyone but Eric, urging them back to the tomb.

Lucas paced the large living area, shoving his hand through his hair. "Where did Eric say he was going?"

"He didn't. Just that he needed to get out. We'll keep trying him. Maybe he hooked up with someone and that's why he's not answering."

Lucas nodded but didn't look mollified by that possibility. After what they'd been through, no one was likely to ignore their phone. But there wasn't supposed to be any danger now.

Amy had to tell him what she'd done before the others arrived. She watched him rub at the spot on his arm where she'd injected him, but he'd been too preoccupied to take conscious notice of it. Now he looked down at the quarter-sized bruise.

She walked closer, and his questioning gaze turned to her. "Lucas, you had the worst storm ever. You were bleeding from the nose and ears." She showed him the bloody tissues in the garbage can, her hands shaking. "And you were out a lot longer than normal. I—"

His eyes hardened as she talked. "You gave me the antidote."

"I had to. You were going to die."

He looked at the bruise again, as though he couldn't bear to look at her. She saw the fear in his eyes, the pain of betrayal. He would view it that way, because being able to see the future was worth dying for if it meant saving his people.

"I thought the danger was over," she tried again, hating his silence.

"I had a storm." His words were ice-covered. "You know what that means."

"You were bleeding. I couldn't let you die."

When he looked at her at last, his eyes were shuttered. Worse than the way he'd looked at her after she sneaked away to get the antidote without telling him.

He walked toward the opening that led downstairs.

"Lucas." She followed but remained in the doorway. "Yell at me. Tell me how angry you are."

He paused midway down the stairs but didn't even turn to face her. "I don't feel anything right now, Amy."

He kept going and eventually disappeared. She knew this is what would happen; she'd told herself losing his love was worth saving him. She slid down to the floor, realizing she hadn't taken a breath in so long her chest was hurting. The harsh intake of air was followed by a sob. Hopefully, he wouldn't lose his abilities. Maybe he would forgive her then. Love her again, no. If he could just forgive her, she could somehow go on without him. If she'd let him die, she would never have forgiven herself.

She let herself cry now. Soon, there would be no time for crying.

CHAPTER 5

Fonda's chest hurt like hell. Racing through the woods in near pitch-dark, her sworn enemy helping her, an unknown enemy somewhere behind them . . . she could hardly wrap her head around it.

Eric slowed, thank God, and tugged her closer.

She felt his finger press against her mouth, and in the watery moonlight saw him looking behind them. Her pounding heartbeat and harsh breathing obliterated any other sounds. She hadn't felt that insane crushing feeling in her head after they'd run from the agent. Just before her head would have probably exploded, Eric ordered her to do that visual thing. It worked.

Their breathing quieted. There, in the far distance, the sound of footsteps. Walking, not running.

A vibrating noise came from the vicinity of Eric's jeans. His cell phone. He jabbed the button to stop it. She started to say something, but he pressed his finger over her mouth again. Then they were off again, his fingers still clamped over hers, drawing her through the trees as though he had night vision.

Maybe he did.

Eventually he let go of her hand and slowed to a walk. The pursuing footsteps were farther away each time they stopped to listen.

Eric leaned close and whispered, "Maybe his injury is dragging him down. I cut him pretty good back at the motel."

The air was chilled, and her face felt numb. The sun was only thinking about coming up, lightening the sky to a dull gray. They couldn't hear anything that sounded like footsteps, only the sound of birds waking and road noise in the distance. He nodded toward that but said nothing. Every time she started to say something, he either put his finger over her mouth or made the cut sign across his throat.

They broke out of the woods as the sun started filling the sky with streaked pink light. It wasn't the highway they saw, though, but what looked like a shantytown: rows of little buildings, if you could call them that, cobbled together, some two stories, some painted and some gray, weathered wood. Some of the booths had signs tacked onto the front of their open spaces, the letters too faded to read. Grass grew tall between the buildings, caressed by the breeze, and the huge parking area was all dirt and weeds. Once, the place must have been filled with sounds and activity, but now nobody cared about it.

Not liking the direction of her thoughts, she turned to something she liked even less. It was the first time she'd gotten a good look at Eric since they left the motel room. His shirt was still unbuttoned, showing a damp slice of his chest. His blond hair at his neckline was also damp, though if not for the twigs, it would have been as perfectly mussed as it was at the bar. Like flames, she'd thought then. She was sure her hair looked much worse. He walked into the jumble of buildings, his expression tense, as though he expected someone to jump out at him.

Standing in the opening between the buildings and the woods felt too vulnerable, so she walked toward shelter. The place smelled of moldering wood. Eric moved among the shadows and shafts of light that poured down between the slats, but glanced up occasionally, obviously checking for her. No, she hadn't run off. Yet. Or maybe he was worried that she would sneak up on him, a shard of wood clutched in her hand. She glanced at herself, no real weapon, a third his size. Probably not. Even when he had been drugged, she couldn't overpower him. Their glances held for a moment, giving her a tight feeling in her chest, and then he kept looking.

One grouping looked like it held concession stands, and an old sign, hanging crooked from only one hook, said, SHANTY FLEA MARKET and below that, PRETZELS. One stall had a pile of old trophies in the corner, another had a rusty BBQ grill that still smelled like smoked meat, but most were empty. Her stomach twisted when she saw a roach run across the grate.

She paused, listening and watching the woods. Cardinals sang their loping call and a breeze stirred the pines, but nothing sounded like a human—or whatever he was—coming after them. She made her way toward Eric, who was circling back.

He pulled out his cell phone and made a call. "Hey, it's Eric. I saw that you tried to call me a few times . . ."

He listened, his eyebrows knitting together at what

he was hearing. She caught the sound of a female voice that sounded frantic.

He leaned against one of the sturdier beams, pressing his fingers to his forehead as he listened. "I think I know why. Someone's been after us."

Fonda heard the "Us?" on the other end.

He looked at her, his mouth twisting into a smile. "Yeah, guess who I happened to run into? Fonda Raine . . . Yeah, that Fonda. Long story, but there's some dude after us. And he's got powers. I think that whatever he does with his hands, he can do with a psychic ability. He's too old to be an Offspring, probably late forties. We ditched him for the time being, but we need to get out of here. We're at some . . ."

"Shantytown flea market," Fonda supplied, stepping closer so she could hear the other side of the conversation. He hadn't told the woman that she'd tried to kill him. Interesting.

He repeated what she'd said, and added, "It's just off a highway." He gave them a general idea of where they'd started from. "Can you come out and get me? Once everyone's together we can figure out our next move."

Fonda heard the woman ask, "Lucas saw you and a woman dead. It must be Fonda. Is she joining up with us?"

Eric looked right at her, and she felt an odd twist in her chest. "I don't know what I'm going to do with her. I'll figure it out by the time you get here." He disconnected, sliding down to the wooden floor, arms draped over his bent knees. He tilted his head, his gaze still on her. "What *am* I going to do with you?"

"*You* are not doing anything about me. I'll be gone

before they get here. What did she mean, Lucas saw me dead?"

"He gets storms of images, glimpses of the future. He probably saw us being attacked back at the motel."

She stepped closer. "Why didn't you just leave me behind? You could have—should have—left me to fend for myself."

"Is that what you wanted me to do?"

"Yes." She didn't want to think about him saving her. "That's what ruthless people do."

He rubbed his eyes. "Yeah."

While they were on the run through the woods, they were united against an even deadlier enemy.

"Besides the fact that you had every reason to kill me."

He laughed softly, shaking his head. "You know, I might have felt that way once." The humor in his eyes, thin as it was, faded. "But as I said, I don't want a war with you. You're free to go."

For some reason, that left an empty feeling inside her. She knelt down in front of him. "Why? You're a cold-blooded killer."

"Not when I needed to be."

"With me?" Because she'd seen the rage in his eyes, when he had the knife at her throat, before it was replaced by resolve. She touched the cut and felt the sting, but it wasn't bleeding. Resolve that he couldn't do it. Fear at his failure to kill when it was necessary and justified.

She knew exactly how he'd felt. In those minutes before she returned to the room, she'd been battling that same thing. While straddling Eric's limp body, she had lifted her hand, ready to bring the knife down . . . and she couldn't do it. Nausea had risen in her throat, sweat popped out on her forehead and neck, and her hand froze in mid-motion.

He'd been watching her thrash herself. "I couldn't use my pyrokinesis on that guy," he said. "Now I know why. He's got powers like us."

"You told whoever you were talking to that he wasn't an Offspring. You said something about that when I projected to you, too. What's an Offspring?"

"You. Me. Do you know anything about your history? About why either your mom or your dad died when you were a baby?"

"I only know I inherited my paranormal ability from my mother." Hadn't Westerfield asked if she knew anything else? Insinuating that there *was* something else.

"Did Darkwell tell you how he knew your mother?"

She sat down, facing Eric. It felt intimate somehow, but she pushed that thought away. He knew things, things she needed to know. "Just that he'd read about her ability in some report. I wanted to see it, but he pretty much blew me off, promising he'd try to find it but never doing it."

He held up his finger. "Lie number one. He recruited your mother and several others, including my mother, to join a program called BLUE EYES back in the eighties. He gave our parents something that boosted their abilities, and he used them to kill people. Only that substance made them go crazy. And that made the project one big fat liability, so it was shut down and covered up. How did your mother die?"

It was none of his business, that's what she wanted to say. "She killed herself."

"Lie two." He held up a second finger, and his certainty shifted something inside her. "They killed her.

Darkwell couldn't afford to have anyone start questioning why the people in his program had become unstable."

She could barely push out the words, "Darkwell killed her?" She hadn't committed suicide? Hadn't abandoned her?

"He denied it, and in that I think he was telling the truth. There were two men behind the program. We thought the other one was Sam Robbins, but he wasn't"—he raised his eyebrow at her—"ruthless enough. So maybe someone behind Darkwell, a silent partner. Maybe the guy who's after us now."

She'd unconsciously moved closer to him, wanting to soak in his words about her mother. "That guy killed my mom?"

He shrugged. "It's possible. We're the offspring of the people in the program. We inherited the supercharged ability. And we inherited the possibility of going crazy, too, if we use our abilities too much." He leaned back. "How did it feel, having someone gunning for you without even knowing why?"

"Awful."

He nodded. "That's how I felt, before I knew what I know now. Someone hunting me down because I'm a liability. How did it feel that he could get *inside* you? That it was so hard to fight, you thought you were going to die?"

She frowned. "The worst—one of the worst things I've ever felt."

"Now you know how I felt when your boyfriend was screwing around in my friggin' head, trying to make me do things I didn't want to do." His words were like a slap in the face.

She pushed to her feet and turned away. Eric was

the enemy, not the victim. "What about this substance you mentioned?"

He stood, though she saw how tired he was. He reached up and held onto a loop of rope hanging from the ceiling beam, flexing his biceps in the process. "We just found out it was some kind of alien DNA. We inherited that, too."

He liked the shock and revulsion on her expression; she could tell by his smug smile. "That's plain freaky."

He shrugged. "Yeah, but it opens up possibilities. Who are our ancestors? What else can we do? Look at what that guy can do. He must be infected with the same stuff."

She shot him a look. Was he making this up? No, he was excited about the alien DNA.

She looked at her hand. What she expected to see that she hadn't already noticed, she didn't know. As though just knowing would now reveal itself with webbing between her fingers or a green glow.

"Can we get it out of us?" she asked, feeling her skin itch.

"I doubt it. It's pretty cool when you think about it."

"No it's not. It's icky." And scary.

He walked up some rickety stairs that led to a small deck with picnic benches. It had a corrugated tin roof but was open at the sides. She followed, seeing that he was using it as a lookout. He scanned the surrounding area, his eyes narrowed. She looked, too, as though she'd come up for the same reason.

"I don't see him," he said.

She sank down on a bench.

He stretched out on another bench. "I'm going

to close my eyes for a few minutes, though I'll keep checking the perimeter." He slid a narrow-eyed gaze at her. "Being drugged doesn't constitute a good night's rest. What was that stuff you slipped me, anyway?"

"I don't know. I asked a dealer for something to knock a person out. He gave me some pills, which I ground up and put in your drink."

"Great." He tucked his hands beneath his head and closed his eyes.

"I'm sure it was heavy-duty sleeping pills. That's what I asked for. Nothing addictive like heroine."

He wriggled on the bench, as though to make himself more comfortable. "That makes me feel a whole lot better."

She couldn't tell if he was being sarcastic. The thought of it being something like heroine yawned in the pit of her stomach. He could be tweaking right now, or craving more. Shaking. That stuff was wicked. Thankfully she only knew secondhand, seeing her dad and his friends suffer through it. The one thing her dad *had* done to protect her was threaten anyone who offered her dope in his rare sober moments. Not that she would have touched the stuff. "How are you checking the perimeter?"

"I can remote-view. Kind of like your astral projecting, only I can't be seen. And I can't touch objects . . . or people at the location."

Heat flashed into her cheeks and she looked away. Was he viewing her now? Seeing her reaction? She stuffed it, hunkering down, burying her face against her knees. She hadn't slept all night. On top of that, the adrenaline surge and exertion had drained her.

Still, she peeked at Eric, barely fitting on the bench. "Was there a third lie?"

He opened his eyes only as much as necessary to see her. "Hm?"

"You said lie one and lie two. I just wondered if there was a third one."

"Yeah." He settled back into his resting mode. "That we were the bad guys."

As tired as she was, that propelled her to her feet, and she walked the edge of the deck to check the woods again. It was chilly, though getting warmer now that the sun had risen. She needed food, a soft bed, and most of all, she needed to be gone by the time the Rogues arrived to pick him up.

Where was she supposed to go? The psychic creep knew where she lived. But he hadn't found her when she was living with her dad. Going back there filled her chest with a dark cloud. Connie would be out of jail soon. As for herself, she was done spending time in hell.

Fonda wrapped her arms around a square column, her gaze going to Eric. His shirt had slid open, revealing that muscled stomach and deep chest. *Stop looking at him! He's infected you like that horrible alien stuff he was talking about.*

She banged her forehead against the column, trying to drive the thoughts out of her head.

"You'll give yourself a headache doing that."

His voice stopped her.

"Why *are* you doing that?" he asked, his eye cracked open.

I hate myself, because I can't totally hate you.

"Trying to drive the headache I already have away," she said at last, when nothing clever came to mind.

A vibrating sound made her stiffen. The Rogues

were probably there. She would be on her own, and somehow that was scarier than being with Eric.

"Yeah," he said after listening on the cell phone, his expression screwed up into fear and anger. "Crap. Everyone's there? . . . Damn . . . You don't think they know about the shelter, do you? . . . The guy who's after us posed as an FBI agent, so he's probably connected to the government. I'll bet he ran the tags on the 'Cuda and tracked it back to Lucas. I can be there—" He pinched the bridge of his nose. "All right. Hang tight, then. Keep in touch."

"What's wrong?" she asked when he put the phone away.

He paced, scanning their surroundings. "The police raided my friend's art gallery. Our hiding place is nearby. They're all stuck until it's clear."

She didn't want to feel anything for the Rogues. They were terrorists. To see big bad Eric worried, though, touched a spot inside her. She shut it down. "And we won't be able to get back to our cars."

He shook his head. "But Olivia said I could get her car in D.C. I doubt these people—and now that the police are involved, I'm sure there are more than one—know she defected. I can take you to wherever you need to go."

Her hand went to her mouth.

"What?" He walked closer.

"I told Westerfield—the supposed FBI agent—everything. He said he knew a little about the program but he wanted me to fill in the holes. So I did."

She cringed, ready for him to slap her or worse. His jaw tightened and his hands balled into fists, and then he slammed one into the post she'd just been holding onto. But he didn't hit her or even look as though he would.

She said, "I did contract work for the CIA. I wasn't looking at an FBI agent as someone to distrust."

"Well, here's the game plan now: don't trust anyone. Not the police, not anyone at any government agency. Darkwell had ties that reached far and wide. I'll bet whoever this guy's affiliated with does, too."

"I'm sorry I outed your friends. I knew you as the enemy."

"So you didn't mind if we were all killed."

She turned away. Her voice went soft. "Like you said, it was war."

He reached out and turned her face to him. *"Was?"*

She moved away from his touch. "Maybe the Rogues aren't the bad guys."

"But?" he asked, hearing her unsaid exclusion.

"You still killed the man I loved. And you almost killed me." She looked at him then. "You meant to, didn't you?"

His expression shadowed, but he shook his head. "No. But if you were in my way, I would have. You were just as much an enemy as he was, at least in black and white. The others—particularly Nicholas—made me promise not to hurt you. I kept that promise."

She could see he was telling the truth. "So I owe him for you not torching me." She gave a quick nod, bringing back that terrible day again to remind her that she should not let herself fall into a sense of false security where Eric was concerned, even if they were on the same side right now. "I hope you weren't expecting me to slobber all over your shoes in gratitude."

He laughed, the jerk, not the reaction she'd wanted to provoke.

He rubbed his hand over his mouth as though to erase the smile. "That was an interesting mental picture."

"I'm getting out of here." She started walking toward the stairs but halted at his words.

"You might have inherited a skill from your mother."

He'd worded it oddly. Had he forgotten she'd inherited astral projection from her? "You mean *another* skill?"

He paused for a moment. "Yeah. You might need it out there by yourself."

She walked closer, her arms still wrapped tight around her. It was an old gesture, but a hard one to break. "What is it?"

He leaned against the beam, tilting his head as though he now wasn't sure he should tell her. "You have to promise not to use it against me or my people. Remember, I kept my promise."

"Fine."

He held out his hand. "Shake on it." He was serious. "Not all that long ago, you were trying to kill me. Humor me."

She reached out, and her hand was enveloped in his. When she tried to pull free, he held tighter. "Say the words."

She let out a huff of breath. "I promise not to use this new skill to hurt your friends."

"Or me."

Her mouth twisted. "Or you."

He let go, leaving her hand feeling cold because his had been so warm. He leaned back again. "Your mother could freeze time. I got this secondhand, so I don't have all the details, but she could change the perception of time. In the example my friend was given, your mother froze time so that someone else could come in and shoot the target and leave without anyone seeing the assassin."

She absorbed that for a few moments. "How did she do it?"

"That's the part we don't know."

"And who told you this?"

"Ever heard of Richard Wallace?"

She shook her head, still wrapping her brain around it. Stopping time. That would have come in handy when she was younger. "Why did you take the chance of telling me this? You don't know how good I am at keeping promises."

"No, I don't. And I know you think you have every reason to want me dead. But you need all the help you can get out there. So consider it ammunition that I'm hoping you won't use against me."

The sound of a broken twig in the distance halted all conversation. His eyes closed, then snapped open. He held his finger to his mouth and gestured for her to follow him. Oh, God, not again.

They walked quietly and swiftly through the maze of buildings, careful not to kick any debris. Once again he took her hand and pulled her behind him up stairs that hardly looked safe. They were sturdy enough and didn't creak, and looked a hell of a lot safer than where he was gesturing next: a ledge that went around a fake water tank. The tank would block them from sight from below and almost every angle. He gestured for her to go first. Sure, so she could be the one to fall if the plank gave out. She took one step, then another. The plank bounced but held. Luckily she had great balance. She used to walk along the edge of the roofs in her neighborhood just to feel the thrill.

When she was tucked into the corner, he backed in front of her, effectively blocking her from sight.

There wasn't much room, and the front of her body was pressed against his back. He leaned close to her ear and whispered, "If he gives me the chance, I'm going to jump down and nail him with this." He held up a piece of metal she hadn't even noticed him picking up. "If he finds us first, jump to the ground and haul ass. I'll keep him busy."

She just stared at him, though with his back to her, he couldn't see her stunned expression. Was he really trying to protect her? No, he was up to something. What he didn't know about her was that she wasn't a scared rabbit. She *was* very uncomfortable being so close to him. She smelled the musk of his sweat, an earthy scent she caught herself breathing in. She stepped onto an even thinner plank that went around the tank to get a better look below. Eric turned and furrowed his eyes in a gesture she took to mean *Get back here!*

She saw a shadow cross the floor and move out of her sight. The board bent down beneath her weight, unanchored at the other end. She walked back to the wall that was Eric's back.

The scrape of shoes froze her, and her hands involuntarily flattened against his back. Westerfield's voice sent creepy crawlies over her skin:

"I know you're here. I can smell your emotions." He made loud sniffing noises, as if taking in the scent of baking cookies. "Are you afraid now? Yes, I can smell fear. Yours, Fonda Raine. There's nothing to be afraid of. Come down, and bring your boyfriend with you. Let's get acquainted."

They remained where they were, of course. She tamped down her fear. Could he actually smell their emotions? Eric's body tensed rock hard.

"I have to say, I'm surprised you were holed up with him after you told me he'd killed someone you obviously cared about. I could smell your anger and grief, like the salt of the ocean. Was having sex with him some kind of punishment?"

Her mouth tightened, wanting to set him straight. Just what he wanted.

"Tsk tsk, Aruda. Your skills won't work on me."

It didn't seem like the injury Eric had inflicted was slowing Westerfield down. He walked around, humming a song, moving things across the floor, perhaps, as he looked for them. Finally he stopped, and she sensed him below. She dared to look down, and between the board and the tank saw him looking up. He had that creepy smile on his face, as though he knew he would win but was enjoying the game.

He raised a gun and aimed it at them.

She shoved Eric forward, throwing herself against him. A bullet splintered the wood where she'd been standing.

Eric lost his balance and jumped to the ground. When Westerfield aimed at her, Eric rushed him. The bullet went wild, hitting the tank.

"Run!" Eric yelled at her.

The two men wrestled, Eric with a grip on the gun, too. He shoved Westerfield against one of the columns. It didn't seem to faze him. Fonda prepared to jump down, but not to run away.

Eric rammed his knee into Westerfield's stomach with the same result. Except the column buckled, tilting the platform she was on. She fell, grabbing onto the edge and swinging her body down. Using the momentum, she aimed her legs at Westerfield, sending him flying several feet to a pile of boards. She landed hard on her back, banging her head and seeing stars, then Eric's face as he leaned over her and helped her up.

The tank and platform it was on crashed to the ground behind them. Fonda and Eric moved to the side as boards skittered across the concrete floor. They spun to face Westerfield, who was still sitting. Though his shirt was cut and had dried blood on it, she saw no sign of the wound he'd recently sustained. He held out his hand, looking at Fonda. Her body lifted and she flew backward. She hit the ground with a thud and rolled, her insides tumbling.

Don't throw up. Get up.

She lifted her head, which was aching without supernatural help. Eric had his hands around the man's neck. With a gasp of pain, Eric dropped to his knees. Westerfield was clenching his hand into a fist aimed at Eric's stomach. She started running toward them, but he threw out his other hand and sent her flying again.

Eric's face was red and he was writhing on the ground, his hands clutching his abdomen. "Stop!" she screamed, trying to get to her feet again.

Stop time.

But how?

Eric's groans grew more raw. The veins in his neck stood out, and his face deepened to a sick shade of purple.

Focus. Time stops. Time stops. Freeze!

She put all of her energy into freezing time, so much that she was gasping for breath and squeezing her eyes shut. Suddenly everything went quiet. No more groans. She opened her eyes. Both men were frozen. They broke out of the spell a second later, though now Westerfield was staring in surprise.

Again, she told herself, and focused, her whole body tightening with the effort. The groans stopped, and she opened her eyes. Even the trees weren't moving in the breeze. A bird was suspended in the sky. She got up and hobbled over to Eric, frozen in his contorted position.

"Come on! Get out of here!"

He was as frozen as Westerfield. Damn. No way could she haul him out of there. She didn't have much time.

Now's your chance. Forget about Eric. Save yourself.

Instead she pushed Westerfield over. He landed on the concrete with a hard thud, but she was already grabbing the planks of boards in the pile and throwing them onto him. She grabbed his gun and stuffed it into the waistband of her pants. She dragged the tank over by the board it was still attached to and dropped it on him.

The sounds of birds started again. Eric looked around in bewilderment, gasping for breath.

"Help me!" she said. "Throw boards on the pile."

"What—" But he didn't stop to question. He'd already taken in the situation and knew acting was better than figuring things out.

Westerfield was trying to push the boards away.

She pulled out the gun and aimed it at him. *Remember how to do this.* She'd practiced a few times with a friend's gun when she was a teenager but never aimed at anyone. She squeezed off three shots, punching holes through the boards and getting thrown backward with the kick. Eric took the gun and squeezed off three more. Blood splattered on the aged wood. Westerfield groaned, his fingers sticking out between the boards.

Eric grabbed her hand again and started running toward the woods. As they ran, boards flew into the air, one next to her head. She spared a glance back, seeing Westerfield struggling to get up. He was flinging the boards with flicks of his arms.

What the hell was he?

Eric flung his hand back and shot at him. Westerfield ducked out of sight. As they ran alongside the buildings, boards exploded from them. Westerfield was making the motions of smashing everything and sending it toward them.

One board hit her in the back, sending her flying forward. Her hands skidded across the hard ground and dried grass. The air was filled with debris, as though a minitornado had hit. Eric shielded his head as another board flew past, ducking down and pulling her to her feet. They both looked back. Westerfield was walking toward them. Walking, not running, in no hurry, which was the scariest of all. No, the scariest was the smile on his face.

Her back ached, but she pushed forward. Eric, still gripping her hand, led her to a sharp left. Her hand ached, too, but she wasn't about to complain. Once again it felt as though she wore a boxing glove, but this one was two sizes too tight.

Her brain screamed. Pressure. Crushing pain. She looked back as they entered the edge of trees. Her legs went weak, but Eric jerked her to the right. Her vision began to blur, and then Westerfield was out of sight. The pressure eased. She shuddered at the thought of him getting into her.

Eric kept looking behind them. "I don't see him, but that doesn't mean anything. I'm going to check on him real quick." He came to a stop, and so did she, nearly stumbling into him.

He closed his eyes and his face tensed for a few seconds. His eyebrows furrowed. She knew better than to interrupt him. When he opened his eyes, he said, "He's still there. No sign of any wounds, though there's blood on him. I wonder if he can heal himself like my sister Petra can."

"She can heal herself?"

"I don't think she's ever tried to heal herself."

So *that* was why Eric wouldn't die.

He said, "I saw him on the phone reporting to someone that we'd gotten away. He's definitely not working alone."

"Does he look like he's going to come after us?"

"No, but I'm not taking any chances."

She trailed her hand against the trunk of a tree as they passed. The canopy allowed the early sun to stream through in places, warming her as she walked through the sunbeams. "I don't think he can use his skills unless we're in visual range. That squeezing in my head . . . as soon as we were out of his sight, it stopped."

"Good. We need to know his limitations." He slid her a glance. "Especially since he knows about our abilities."

"Sorry," was all she could say. "I grew up in a neighborhood where the cops weren't always to be trusted. But FBI, CIA . . . I figured they could be."

He huffed, a hard expression on his face. "Mostly

they can, but there's corruption everywhere. The government has been doing people wrong for a long time. BLUE EYES was only a small chapter in the book of Heinous Crimes Against U.S. Citizens. There have been all kinds of secret programs that infected people with biological chemicals, smallpox, you name it." His mouth tightened. "Darkwell was probably the worst. He used our parents, and then he tried to use us again to do the same thing."

Darkwell had used her. Maybe. She'd trusted him once. She wasn't so sure she could trust Eric.

He turned to her. "You froze time. You really friggin' froze time."

She nodded, feeling a smile spread on her face. Her mother's legacy. "But I didn't think about you freezing, too."

"I'm surprised you didn't haul ass while you could." And leave him there, he didn't say.

Me, too. She shrugged. "It was only fair to help you; you told me about it." At his surprised expression she added, "Don't make more out of it than that." That's all it was.

"I won't." He looked at her. "Let's get to someplace safe and figure out what to do next."

Let's. Meaning *let us.* She didn't like the sound of that. Getting someplace safe sounded good, but no way was she staying with Eric Aruda, even if she didn't have any good options.

Neil stood in the wreckage of the building. He didn't want to chase them into the woods. They had the advantage there, and they were skilled enough to push him out, unlike the average human. He looked down at one of the bullet wounds, running his finger inside the hole in his shirt and touching the weal of healed skin. He hated getting shot. Worse, was getting badly cut. He slid his finger down the cut Eric had made. Even though it was healed now, it hurt like hell and drained him.

He pulled out his phone and called his brother. "They escaped, but I'll find them again. Any luck on your end?"

"You're not exposing yourself, are you?"

He smiled at the wreckage strewn all around. It felt good to wreck things. To create chaos. To breathe in the emotions of fear. He inhaled now, at the memory of the sweetest scent, fear flavored with anger.

"No worries. I'm in a remote location." It would look like vandals had torn up the place.

"And you couldn't take them down?"

Oh, but he loved the chase so. They would die, he had no doubt of that. They could not go to the authorities, nor could they hide forever. He had waited so long for this, obeying, curbing his desires so his pretty brother could have all the power and glory.

"Remember, they're not ordinary humans," he said. "They're strong—stronger than I thought they'd be. I can get into them, but they can push me out. Don't worry; I'll wear them down."

The silence was filled with doubt. Malcolm had no choice but to trust in him. Who else could handle this?

"Have you taken care of the others?" he asked.

"No. There's a block on them, and I suspect they're all together somewhere. I have a feeling it's near Lucas Vanderwyck's gallery. Darkwell noted that they saw activity in the house above his art gallery, though when they went in, no one was there. I don't want to pull in any more of my people than necessary. It's a delicate situation, one I expect you to remedy immediately. Take care of Aruda and Raine now, so they're not loose ends. Then we'll be ready for the rest of them."

Neil heard someone address Malcolm in the background. "Sir . . ." The rest was too low to hear.

"I have to go," Malcolm said to him. "Be effective. I'll do a locate as soon as I can. Maybe Aruda will lead you to the rest of them."

He disconnected. Neil shoved the phone back in his pocket. He wished he could locate. Even Malcolm had to look into something, akin to a crystal ball, to see a distant location. They had always been competitive, but Malcolm was the golden, older brother. He was all right with that . . . as long as he could kill.

CHAPTER 6

Someplace safe, after hitching a ride on the back of a farmer's flatbed for an hour, turned out to be Quiet Waters Park in Annapolis. Not that he cared, at that moment, about getting back to nature, fresh air, all that crap.

Eric knew he needed time to think. Sitting on the flatbed, the air rushing around, whipping Fonda's white-blond hair into a frenzy, was not the time he'd needed. She had a dark pink streak on the right side. He knew she had a white-hot streak inside her, but didn't want to think about that.

They walked into the park. The day was warming up, and people were arriving to take advantage of it. He watched one family lay out their blanket, mom telling the kids to stay close, dad unpacking coolers. He watched them so intently as they walked that the woman called her kids even closer, staring him down.

No, I'm not stalking your rugrats. Just wondering what it would be like to have that life. To not have demons tearing up your insides and devils hunting you down on the outside. He looked at Fonda. *And let's not forget the succubus.*

As though she'd been reading this thoughts, she turned to him. "We're having a picnic?"

"Yes."

The two bags he carried contained food and drink. She carried another bag with a change of clothes for both of them, courtesy of Wal-Mart. Her hair was still windblown, though she'd finger-combed it once they got off the truck. He'd wondered at that. Was she vain or neatening up for him? Yeah, right. He must be tired.

Dead dog tired.

Once they passed the building and main area, they took one of the paths and found a spot nestled in the trees that overlooked the water. He set the bags on a picnic table, took out his phone and called Amy.

"Just checking in," he said when she answered.

"They're still out there, several cops posted." He could hear the fear in her voice. "It makes me wonder what these people know. This is too close for comfort."

"Give me their positions. I'm in Annapolis. I'll take them out." The gun was hidden in the clothes bag, and they'd bought ammo.

"No, don't do that. We're trapped, but for now we're okay. If they come down here, we'll be ready for them. If you come, they'll know for sure we're here, and you might get killed."

"I'll hold for now." He filled her in on what they knew about Westerfield. "I'll try to find this guy. Or probably he'll find us. I've got to figure out a way to take him out."

"Is Fonda still with you?"

He glanced at her, opening the bags and setting out the food on the picnic table, not unlike the woman he'd seen earlier. Fonda had obviously been looking at him, because she quickly shifted her gaze away. Damn, she was small. Small but fierce. Some part of him only saw vulnerable with a shell of toughness, a shell that would crack without too much pressure.

"Yeah," he told Amy.

"I'd love to hear how you two connected."

"Yeah, well, we'll save that for another day."

"Is she on our side now?"

Their eyes connected, and he felt something tighten in his chest. "I wouldn't say that exactly. How's Lucas?"

"He won't even talk to me. But it helps having everyone else around. It doesn't help being stuck down here."

"Let me to talk to him."

"He's not going to listen to anyone. I've got to let him be angry about it. He hasn't had any storms, but that's no comfort. He hates not knowing the future."

He could hear the pain in her voice. "Put him on for a minute."

After a pause she said, "All right."

A few seconds later Lucas said, "I heard you and Amy talking about me. You of all people should understand why I'm so pissed."

"I do, but you weren't there, bro. I mean, you were but you weren't. There was blood, and you were out a long time and—I told her to give it to you."

Silence for several seconds. "You *what*?"

"Yeah, it was my idea." Okay, he'd screw up his relationship with Lucas, but they'd been family for a long time. Maybe theirs could withstand this. Lucas and Amy's, he wasn't sure.

"Your idea." Except he didn't sound convinced.

"Totally."

"Eric, you are full of shit. You're the last person who would put that stuff in me. Why are you trying to cover for her?"

Eric pinched the bridge of his nose. "Because I don't want you to mess up what you have. She loves you, man. That's the only reason she did it."

"Don't get involved in our business. I've had enough deception." He let those words sink in before changing the subject. "Were you able to get one of the cars?"

"No." He didn't want to get into how Fonda had outed them. "That's not an option. They know about everyone."

"Call Magnus. I'll bet they don't know about them."

"Good idea." He memorized the number Lucas gave him. "I'll keep in touch. Let me know if you need me."

Eric disconnected and then programmed the number into his phone. He sat down across from Fonda and started eating his sub. She was purposely not looking at him, instead focused on the greenery and water beyond. They were alone, since there was only one table in the area.

A thought occurred to him. "Have you ever heard of Magnus or Lachlan MacLeod?"

She shook her head. "Are they Rogues?"

"No. But they're like us. Offspring."

Good. They were safe. He continued eating. He'd hoped food would give him energy, but it seemed to make him sleepier. Had she drugged him again? No, he'd either carried the food or had it in view. Did she still want to kill him? Sure, she'd saved his ass back there, but that could be instinctual. Obligatory. Wasn't that why he'd done the same for her?

He crinkled up his sandwich wrapper and set it aside, then ripped open the box of Ho Hos. Tearing into the package, he actually let out a sigh. Damn, did he need this.

She watched with an amused and curious expression. "Like it, do you?"

"It's my one vice."

"Why don't I believe that?"

"You're right. My other vice is having sex. Lots of hot, sweaty, monkey sex. Except it doesn't look like that's going to be happening anytime soon, so I'll have to settle for these."

She shifted uncomfortably, exactly what he'd intended. That would teach her for judging. As a peace offering, he held out the box to her, but she shook her head.

He tossed the last piece of cake into his mouth, savoring the chocolate and icing. "I always use a condom. Don't want you to think I'm a slut or anything."

She narrowed her eyes at him, then planted her elbow on the table, hand up. "Arm-wrestle me. At least give me the satisfaction of kicking your ass one way."

"You don't want to arm-wrestle me, little girl."

"Don't call me that, and yes, I do. Afraid I'll beat you?"

"No, I'm afraid I'll hurt you. I used to hit the bars and wrestle for money. This body builder challenged me, thought he was some big shit. His bone snapped and poked right through his skin here." He pointed to his biceps. "Wasn't pretty."

She kept her arm in position, challenging him with her eyes. Her arms were pretty toned, just short of being muscular. With a sigh, he engaged her, their hands locking. She took him by surprise, gripping him hard and slamming his hand down almost all the way. Recovering in time, he fought her within a half inch of the tabletop. He didn't want to hurt her but couldn't let her win. She gritted her teeth, her arm shaking, but she held. That surprised him, too. He could see the anger she was dredging up. She needed to punish him. If she couldn't kill him, she'd humiliate him.

He eased up and let her bang his knuckles on the table. "You're strong."

She pushed to her feet, crossing her arms over her chest. "Did you usually give in when you wrestled a woman?"

"After that guy's bone poked through his skin, yeah, pretty much. Mostly I didn't wrestle women, unless it was some butchy chick who I thought could handle it. But you put up a good fight."

"Did you win a lot?"

"Yeah. Made some good money for a while. Then it lost its allure. People take it too seriously, especially when money's involved. Especially when money is going from their pocket to mine. Makes 'em grumpy."

"I bet."

The sugar he'd eaten backfired, making him feel even more drained than before. He pressed his forehead to the table, bracketing his head with his arms and closing his eyes. "Let's rest up. Then we'll figure out our game plan." He lifted his head to look at her. "Don't leave."

Fonda walked away, just to be stubborn, he was

sure, because she only went to the edge that dropped down to the water. She sank to the ground and leaned against the tree, bending her knees and pulling them against her chest. Damn, she looked like a little girl. Even with her new skill, she was no match for Westerfield, not in the long run. While he knew he shouldn't care what happened to her, the hell of it was, he did. Must be that chivalry crap he'd seen from the other guys. But they were in love, and he was not. The thought was so ludicrous, he had to stifle a laugh.

How'd you two meet?

Ah, my little sweetie here tried to kill me. It was love at first sight.

He watched her, seeing only the side of her face, the curve of her jaw. It amazed him now to think she had the balls to try to kill him. No doubt Jerryl had been feeding her with his hatred of him, and then he himself had gone and given her a reason to hate him. He'd remote-viewed them and seen them making love, a perfect opportunity to take out a dangerous enemy while he was distracted.

At the time, he hadn't cared that Fonda was there, that she was witness to the immolation of her lover. Now, he allowed himself to see it as she had, how horrific it must have been for her. She wasn't a robot enemy; she was human, real . . . like him. As mad and vengeful as he'd been when Jerryl nearly killed Petra, he understood her reasons for trying to kill him.

He could keep her safe for a while. Wasn't that the least he could do? She was the last thing he saw as his eyes drifted shut and he floated in a dreamless abyss.

Fonda woke, surprised she'd actually fallen asleep. She had curled up in a fetal position. A glance at her watch showed she'd been asleep for two hours. Damn, her body was a train wreck, bruised, scratched, and aching all over. She pushed painfully to her feet, and wouldn't you know, her gaze went right to where Eric had been at the table. He wasn't there now. Had he left? Why did that prospect shoot up her heartbeat in panic?

Hullo, don't want him to be here. In fact, that would be perfectly groovy if he just disappeared.

Except he hadn't. She found him lying on a patch of grass on the other side of the table. She walked over, very quietly. He was lying on his back with his hand on his stomach, a position that reminded her of when she'd astral projected to him. *He'd been naked then and he isn't now, so push that thought right out of there.*

He had buttoned up his shirt when they reached the highway, for whatever good it did with the big rip down the side. They'd picked the twigs out of each other's hair before they faced the world, a trippy scenario in itself. All she could think about was how monkeys did that to their mates.

In a flash an arm grabbed her legs, swiping them out from under her and dropping her to the ground. *What the . . . ?*

Eric was on top of her, his arm across her throat, his lower body pinning her hips to the ground. He blinked, breathing hard, and sat up. "What the hell are you doing? Trying to get killed?"

"I wasn't doing anything. I walked over to see if you were awake. You didn't look like you were."

He still hovered over her, looking dazed. "I sensed someone there. After what I've been through, I'm paranoid. And ready to strike."

"I see that. Can you let me up?"

He blinked again, as if realizing he was straddling her in a provocative way. Bracing his hands on the ground on either side of her, he leaned down, and when she had the bizarre suspicion that he would kiss her, he pushed up and jumped to his feet.

Then he totally surprised her by reaching out a hand. She wanted to refuse, to get up on her own out of principle, but was too tired for that bullshit. He pulled her to her feet with so much power she stumbled toward him. He braced her shoulders until she recovered her balance and took a quick step back.

Eric glanced at his watch. "We got a couple of hours of rest. But one thing we've learned with these people"—he looked at her meaningfully, but without malice—"is that we can't stay in one place for long. This guy can locate, and we're sitting ducks here."

He walked over to the bag and pulled out the jeans and shirt he'd bought. He tore off his shirt, sending buttons flying and reminding her of an erotic male dance show. Then, just like that, he dropped his pants. She had a side angle view, ass to hip, and a glimpse of a semierection.

"What do you think you're doing?" she shrieked.

The naughty son of a bitch turned to face her with a *duh* expression. "Uh, getting dressed." He gestured toward the rest of the park. "No one can see me."

"*I* can see you! Couldn't you have gone into the trees for a little modesty?"

"Do *not* tell me that seeing me naked makes you uncomfortable. You, who sneaked into my room and put her astral hands all over my body."

Dammit, she hated when her flaming cheeks gave her away. "That was different." She was trying not to look; really, the man had no shame. Was he actually getting more erect?

Even worse, he walked closer! He anchored his hands on his hips and looked down at her. "And how is that? Oh, I get it. It's okay to see me naked if you're planning to *kill* me, but not if we're working together."

She turned around. "We're not working together. Okay, back there we were, but not now." She waved her arm at him. "Get dressed. I'm going over there." She snatched her clothes from the bag and stomped off toward the edge of the land. A glance back revealed Eric shaking his head while he bent over to slide on jeans—no briefs!

And you're looking because . . .

I had to make sure he couldn't see me. I didn't want to look.

She kept on going, another glance back, and no, she couldn't see him anymore.

She stripped out of her filthy clothing and was about to slip on new, boring clothes—totally yuck— when a chorus of catcalls sounded from the water. A canoe packed with young men were all waving, whistling, and hollering out God-knew-what while her bare ass was in plain view. Letting out a roar of frustration and embarrassment, she tromped back inland, only to come into Eric's view.

"I'm guessing all of that noise was for you," he said in that snarky way that told her he was enjoying her discomfort. Oh, definitely he was. His eyes sparkled when he took her in, tank top, thong panties, and pants clutched in hand. "You know, it's only fair that I see you, since you saw me."

She yanked on her pants. God, the man was infuriating. "How can you joke about that? Aren't you mad at me for trying to kill you?" Couldn't he just pout about that for a bit and not look at her as though he wanted to eat her?

"Furious." Except that he didn't look or sound furious.

She wadded up her clothes in a ball as she walked back to their table, then shoved them into the plastic bag.

At least he had clothes on now. She grabbed her bottle of Jovan musk from the duffel bag he'd bought to store the gun and their toiletries and dabbed some on. It was a popular fragrance back in the eighties, and she was glad they still sold it.

He waited for her to put the bottle back in the duffel bag and walk closer to him. "Oh, and we *are* working together."

"Excuse me?"

"You heard me. First we have to get a vehicle. I've got a lead on that, though I'll have to do a little groveling. I was sort of responsible for their father dying when I set the estate on fire—which, by the way, I only did because Darkwell was about to shoot us. It's splitting hairs, I know, and I don't blame them for being pissed. But I hope they'll help. They need to know what's going on, anyway." He gave her an odd look, as though something of great interest had just occurred to him.

"Give me the gun," she said, and held out her hand. "Sounds like you can get more, and I don't know how easily I'll be able to get money."

"What do you need the gun for?"

"Uh, psychic creeps who like to squeeze my head. Duh." *So there, a duh for you.*

"The gun will be in here." He tapped the bag. "If

we need it, whoever can get to it first grabs it. Not that it seems to do a lot of good with this guy, but it'll buy a few minutes while he heals. Come on, let's go."

She crossed her arms over her chest. "You're not listening. I am not going with you."

"Don't make more out of it than what it is. We should stick together until we know what we're up against."

She raised one eyebrow. "What, you afraid to be alone?"

His mouth quirked in a smile. "Terrified."

Ooh, when he did that . . . If he wasn't so cute, it would really annoy her. And the thought of Eric being cute was annoying enough.

"So what's the benefit of us staying together, exactly?"

"For right now, what binds us—people out to kill us—is bigger than what tears us apart. Twice now we worked together and did not get killed."

"Out of pure necessity," she added quickly, remembering she'd had that thought, too. "We only forgot that we're enemies because of the bigger enemy on our asses."

"Exactly. You go out there, and you'll die. Is that what you want?"

"Maybe I don't care."

He tilted his head at her. "You acted like you wanted me to kill you at the motel. You dared me to."

Pain tightened her chest and she looked away. "What good am I if I can't avenge Jerryl's death? If I can't kill the man responsible for destroying everything?"

"I'm more than twice your size. Don't be so hard on yourself."

She looked up, her eyes moist. Was he actually trying to make her feel better about not killing him? She swiped at her eyes. "That wasn't why I couldn't do it." Crap, she'd said too much. She walked over to throw the bag of clothes away, but he was standing beside her, his hand on her arm.

"What do you mean?"

"Nothing. Not a damned thing."

She tried to move away, but he held her in his grip. "You'd been crying when you came out of the bathroom. I didn't pay much attention then; I had other things on my mind. But I remember, your eyes were all smeared and you looked defeated."

She tried to shake him loose. "So what?"

He turned her to face him. "You couldn't do it, could you? You couldn't kill me."

That seemed to fascinate, no, cheer him. She didn't want him either fascinated or cheered. "Sure I could. I was crying for Jerryl."

He shook his head. "That's what you meant about not being able to kill me." He actually laughed!

She shoved him away and walked off. "I'm glad it amuses you that I'm so worthless that I can't even accomplish the most important task of my life."

Worthless! Slut! Connie's words echoed.

He grabbed her and spun her around to face him, his hands gripping hers. "If you'd killed me, you'd be dead now. So you would have felt worth living, vindicated, whatever. Then that guy would have come in and killed you. You lived because of me."

Too damned true. She gritted her teeth. "At least I would have died with honor."

He looked into her eyes, and she thought he was probing her soul. Could he do that? "Do you still want to kill me? Would that make you feel better? More worthy?"

She shook her head so slightly she wasn't actually sure he saw. "I've already failed."

"Then let it go. Right now we need to find out who's hunting us and why. Come on."

He hefted the bag and walked toward the road. Paused. Looked back at her.

Being reckless, taking chances . . . that's what made her feel alive. But maybe she wasn't ready to have her head crushed just yet. Maybe she'd find out what was going on instead. Having a big strong guy around, even if it was Eric Aruda, well, that was just practical. She stiffened her shoulders and walked forward.

CHAPTER 7

Eric breathed an internal sigh of relief when Fonda walked toward him. He didn't want to have to throw her over his shoulder, but he wasn't going to let her go off on her own. She did stay a few feet away from him—in protest, he was sure—arms tight around her body. He hid his smile at that. Even at that distance he could smell the light, crispy scent of her perfume.

He pulled out his phone and called Magnus. He hoped Lachlan didn't answer.

A man said, "Magnus."

"It's Eric Aruda. We have another problem."

"What is it?"

That's what he liked about dealing with men. They didn't get emotional, freak out, crack their knuckles. They just wanted the facts.

"It's not over yet. I don't think they know about you, and we're going to keep it that way. But you need to know what's going on, and I need a vehicle. You don't owe me a damned thing, especially after what happened. On foot, we're seriously hampered, and I don't have any other options."

"Hold on." He heard another man, probably Lachlan, in the background. Not surprisingly, his objections were clear, even though Magnus had covered the mouthpiece. He returned a few moments later. "I'll pick you up. I've got an old truck that's registered in my name, but it's going to need some work. I'll have Lachlan get a battery, fill the tires, and get it running. You can stay here until then. Probably a day."

"I don't want to involve you any more than I have to."

"Neither do we. You're trouble, Aruda. But my father inadvertantly created this situation, and we won't turn our back on you. Do you need weapons?"

"We've got one gun. We could use another."

"What about the rest of your people?"

"They're trapped in the shelter, a phony police raid. If we show up, they'll know they're on to something. For now, nonaction is the best course of action. I've got Fonda Raine with me."

Silence for a moment, which meant they likely knew who she was. "Wasn't she working for the enemy?"

He looked at her. "Yeah, but she didn't know any better."

She frowned at him.

He gave Magnus their location and they made plans to meet within the hour. They were nearing the entrance of the park. He remembered this place. It was where he'd torched one of Darkwell's men who was about to take out Amy.

A family was packing up their car, and Eric headed

to the gazebo they'd vacated. He glanced back to see Fonda reluctantly following. He sat at one of the tables, nodding for her to sit next to him. She took a seat across from him instead.

He had a history of being blunt, blurting out his thoughts before thinking. The hell of it was, he should have no problem dumping life-changing information on Fonda. But something about her, despite her tough, angry exterior, softened him.

"Tell me about your father."

Her eyebrows furrowed. "Why?"

"Just tell me, and then I'll tell you why." If her father was some loving guy, he would come up with some reason why he'd asked and leave it at that.

She looked away, her mouth tightening into a stubborn line.

Eric said, "We all have a history that was damaged by Darkwell. We were damaged. Maybe I can give you some missing pieces."

Fonda's body was as closed as it could be, legs crossed, arms tucked around herself. "After my mother died, he married Connie, who got him into meth." Her big brown eyes gave away her pain. "He was pretty much useless after that." She stood, walking to one of the columns, still facing away from him. "But I survived. I didn't need him. Why do you want to know?" A lock of hair fell over her left eye. She didn't brush it away.

He knew there was more to the story, much more, but she wasn't about to share it with him. Which was cool, because he didn't need to know her shadows. He had his own.

He stood, leaning against the edge of the table and stretching out his legs. "My mom died when I was young, too. Accidentally burned herself to death in a lab accident, or that's what they told us. She was out of her mind by then." A stab of fear pierced his chest. Had it been psychosis? Had she gone through a bout of sleeplessness before that? He focused on Fonda, whose eyes were now filled with the horror of what he'd just said.

"My father also married a woman not good for him," he went on, "but in other ways. Lucas was living with us. They'd already killed his mother. And our stepmother wanted us out of the way. She almost had him convinced that sending us to boarding school was a good idea." He swallowed. He hadn't realized how much he would have to tell her, how much he had to reveal about his own pain. "I hated my father for being so weak, letting her manipulate him." It was why he'd sworn to never let a woman get hold of his soul. "I always felt disconnected from him. I don't look anything like him. I was definitely not his favorite child. He doted on Petra. I think he even liked Lucas better than me. Granted, I was a pain in the ass." She nodded in agreement, but he ignored her. "Always getting into trouble, doing things that made him crazy, like jumping off of buildings and stuff."

Her face changed at those words, eyes widening, mouth softening. She didn't say anything, but she was listening at least.

"But it seemed to go deeper than that. When I realized the government was after us, Petra and I went to him for answers about what our mother was doing before she died. He refused to answer. He accused me of being paranoid, which I am, and which is why I even realized someone was following me. Then he threatened to call the police on me. I called his bluff. He wouldn't call the police on his son. That's when he told me the truth: I wasn't his son.

"My mother had an affair with someone in the program. The substance that boosted their abilities boosted their sex drives, too. My mother and Amy's father had an affair. It was a shock to realize the man I thought was my father wasn't, that he knew all along and resented the fact that he'd raised me as his own. But his loyalty vanished at giving us the truth, at helping us. I'm an Ultra, born of two participants who got the substance. Ultras are more powerful. They are also more susceptible to going crazy." Again that spear of panic. He took a breath, letting his words sink in.

Her eyebrows furrowed. "Why are you telling me this? You want sympathy?"

He chuckled at the thought of Fonda pulling him to her and stroking his back. *Poor baby.* Except the image, as unlikely as it was, tugged on something deep inside him. He cleared his throat and the fuzzy emotions. "That's not why I told you."

It didn't take her long. Her expression changed again, tensing as the implication became clear. "No. I don't believe you."

They had so much in common, their pain, the shock of learning the truth about their heritages and why their families were shattered beyond repair so long ago. He nodded. Bizarrely, the image of him holding her now flashed into his mind. Instead he reached over and tucked the lock of hair behind her ear.

"Richard Wallace, the man I asked you about earlier, he's a botanist who was obsessed with slime molds, collecting them and stuff. He also chased meteors and sometimes found something called *powdre ser*, which is some kind of slime found where a meteorite has landed."

"The alien DNA you told me about."

"Yeah. Alien as in foreign, not green men. Wallace accidentally ingested some of the slime mold, and it boosted his psychic abilities. He was working with Darkwell on the program at the time, and he got a hard-on at Wallace's new power. So Darkwell gave it to our parents without telling them what it was. When the shit hit the fan, Wallace became a target, too, and went into hiding for over twenty years. He had two sons, the men we're meeting shortly. They're your half brothers."

She loosened the lock of hair, letting it cover her eye again. "What kind of game are you trying to play?"

"Wallace could astral project. Your mother couldn't. She could only freeze time. So we're pretty sure you inherited that from him, especially since he'd had a onetime thing with your mom. According to Amy, he was happily surprised at the prospect of having a daughter." No need to tell her that at the time, Fonda was his enemy as well.

She paced, working through it if her expression was any indication. She stopped after a few moments. "This man who's supposedly my father . . . he's the one whose death you're responsible for?"

Damn, he hadn't thought about that. "Yeah."

"So you killed my lover and . . . my father."

"I didn't mean to kill Wallace. When I set Darkwell on fire, he tossed his jacket toward the drapes in his office, which set the whole place on fire. He was holding Wallace prisoner in his basement. Magnus and Lachlan couldn't get him out."

"Do Wallace's sons know? About me, I mean?"

"I think so."

She released a long breath. "Why did you tell me this? You could have just taken me there and never said a thing."

"I wanted you to be prepared. And to know the truth. We've all been shut in the dark long enough. Having felt disconnected from family for so long, other than my sister and Lucas, who's like a brother to me, it was nice to discover I had a half sister. And it was nice to know my real father wasn't a wimp who'd served his balls to his wife on a silver platter. I won't ever know my father, but I respect him. That's more than I can say about Rick Aruda."

He grabbed up the duffel bag. "And it explained a lot, like why he never really cared about me. Why we never connected."

Her face went pale and she pulled her lower lip between her teeth. She knew what he was talking about. They had so much in common, and yet, they couldn't be further apart.

He said, "By the way, you're an Ultra, too. Just so you know."

She came up beside him. "Let's go."

With all the new information in Fonda's brain, that psychic creep might as well be squeezing her head, she thought. They walked in silence toward the park entrance. Part of her wanted to scream and cry and scratch Eric's face. The other part wanted to sink into the numbness that had been her cocoon the month she'd stayed at her dad's place.

Her dad. Or not.

That was her life, ping-ponging between drama, feeling alive, and numbness, never feeling what hid in the darkest recesses of her soul.

She slid a glance at Eric beside her. Why had he told her about his childhood, how his father had rejected him? She didn't want to see his pain at that. It triggered hers.

She wasn't about to tell him that she, too, took risks. She'd never jumped off a building, mostly because the ones she'd walked along the edge of were several stories high. Once, someone had called the police because they thought she was going to jump. She'd gotten a big lecture and the next day was back on the ledge.

No, you're nothing like Eric.

Another voice asked, *Weren't you willing to become a murderer? He killed Jerryl in the name of war, and you were going to kill him for the same reason. Wouldn't the people who care about him feel the same about you as you did about him?*

She choked on that realization, looking away from him in case there was anything in her eyes that gave away the horror of that.

He slapped her on the back, sending her stumbling forward. "Sorry. Just trying to help."

She regained her footing. "Well, don't. Don't help me. Ever."

He raised his hands in surrender and kept walking. She maintained the distance between them, determined not to let her anger at him lessen. No, she wouldn't try to kill him again, but she wasn't going to soften toward him. Sure, it made sense to stick together, but that's as far as it would go. She dug her nails into her palms, feeling the bite of the edges. It helped keep the anger close.

They reached the shopping center where Magnus was going to pick them up. Magnus, who might be her half brother.

Within a few minutes a black BMW tore into the parking lot and screeched to a stop in front of them. The passenger window slid down, and the man driving lifted his sunglasses and took them in with his brown eyes. He leaned over and pushed the door open. "Get in, mates." He nodded toward the backseat, sending his wild brown curls dancing. "In the back, Eric. I want to chat Fonda up."

Eric's mouth tightened in annoyance, and she fought a smile watching him squeeze into the backseat of the coupe. Magnus looked as solid and muscular as Eric. She slid into the front seat, her amusement gone. What did chat her up mean, exactly?

He tore out of the lot as soon as she closed her door. With a glance in the rearview mirror, he asked Eric, "You told her?"

"Yeah."

About her possible paternal heritage, no doubt. Good thing he had told her; otherwise she'd have been slammed in the face with it.

Magnus turned to her. "What can you do?"

She blinked in confusion before realizing what he was talking about.

Eric said, "How about I introduce you first? Fonda Raine, this is Magnus McLeod. Magnus, Fonda."

Magnus reached over and shook her hand. "Sorry. You could say I was raised in a barn, but we—my brother and I—were actually raised in the woods, not many new people to meet."

He was still driving fast, even while shaking her hand and looking at her.

She loved going fast, too fast, but right now she was more into finding out everything she could. "I can astral project and touch objects at the target location." She tried not to think about exactly what objects she'd been touching lately. "And I just discovered I can freeze time for a few seconds."

He nodded, finally looking ahead. "Can you project to other time periods?"

Her eyes widened. "I've never even thought about that."

"Our father could do." He had a slight Scottish accent. "My brother inherited that. Give it a try sometime. But be careful." He looked at Eric in the mirror again. "You told her about using her abilities too much?"

"Briefly. But not about Lachlan."

"What happened to Lachlan?" she asked.

"If we overuse our abilities, we can go crazy. Dad called it psychosis. My father worked for years to find an antidote to Blue Moon, using himself as a human guinea pig. It was never stable, which drove him to distraction trying to figure out why. He hadn't felt it was stable enough to give to us yet."

"Blue Moon is what Wallace called the substance," Eric clarified.

Magnus downshifted and took a corner tight and fast. "Lachlan secretly got addicted to astral travel. He'd go down to the basement and hide what he was doing, like doing drugs. He went to the battle of Culloden and slipped over the edge. Killed our mum thinking she was an enemy British soldier. Bad bit of business, that." His eyes darkened, even though he'd sounded casual enough. "After Mum died, Dad gave us the antidote, stable or no. He still hadn't quite got it right when he died. We made up another batch"—again he looked at Eric—"if you need some."

"No way," Eric said. "I can't afford to potentially lose my abilities now."

Magnus glanced at her. "That's a side effect of the antidote. But it's worth it to save your sanity, or your life, if it comes to that. Lachlan lost his powers; I didn't."

"What can you do?"

"Make myself appear to be invisible."

They went over a bridge that spanned a river. Magnus peppered her with questions about the program and Darkwell, then asked, "Where are your loyalties now?"

"To no one."

"You'll have to commit to a side at some point. Best to do it now while you're clear-headed. Waffling will only get you killed."

"I'll remember that."

He looked at Eric in the mirror again. "We did have a problem with the antidote. In the melee before Darkwell's people descended on us, the formula for the latest version was destroyed. My father wrote everything on paper. A typo nearly destroyed one of his experiments, so he never did his important calculations on the computer. He kept everything in a notebook, every version he'd tried in the last five years. The antidote itself spilled onto the notebook and distorted the writing of the last section. The antidote we made up is the version before that. My father tested it on the mice but not on himself or us."

"Well, that makes me want to jump right in," Eric said, his mouth twisted.

Magnus pulled down a gravel road, and Fonda realized he had kept her so busy answering questions, she hadn't taken notice of their route . . . his intention, no doubt. She had lived much of her life in a state of survival, protective and alert, so she couldn't blame him.

They came around a corner on the gravel road and saw an earthen-colored wall with an ornate gate in the center. Beyond it was a lush garden and then the house. Green scrollwork adorned the top of the wall. Magnus pulled up to a building set off to the right, a simple square structure with four garage doors, two of which were open. He slammed into the garage at a stunning speed, hitting the brakes just before they might have smashed into the back wall. When she could pry her fingers off the door handle, she saw that the garage looked like a mechanic's shop.

"We learned to fix our own stuff," Magnus said when she got out and stared at all the equipment and parts hanging on the walls.

Eric pulled himself out of the car with a groan. He also took in the shop, his mouth slightly open. "This is a mechanic's wet dream."

An old white truck was in the bay on the right, and a man who resembled Magnus, only leaner and with long wavy hair, stalked over, a wrench in his hand. It looked like he was going to use it on them. Or, seeing where his angry gaze focused, on Eric. Great. Now what had Eric gotten them into?

CHAPTER 8

Amy had taken to sleeping outside Lucas's bedroom door, by the dresser they had to wedge in there. Later she would get up and go back to the room she shared with Petra. She would not be far away from Lucas, but he wouldn't let her sleep in the same room as him. Before, it was for her safety; now he was angry with her.

She didn't hope for forgiveness or reconciliation. All she wanted was for him to express that anger in ways other than silence. It hurt, in every part of her body, but she deserved it. Now she would pay the price for loving him. Lucas's behavior didn't surprise her; she knew how he felt about getting the antidote. That he tried to take the blame, well, it brought tears to her eyes. Stunned her. What was going on with him?

When she heard Lucas calling for her, she thought it was her dreams. God, if only he would come to her dreams, if only he could. As far as she knew, he hadn't even tried recently.

When he whispered her name again, she sat straight up. "Lucas?"

"I want to talk."

She jumped to her feet and pushed away the dresser enough to slip inside the open door. He closed it, and before saying a word, started kissing her.

She melted into his mouth, craving his touch. Even if he just wanted her body, she would give it without expecting more. Yeah, that's how bad it was.

He stripped off her clothes, kissing her neck, shoulders, and breasts. He nipped at her, and even the pain felt good.

"Lucas . . ."

"Shhh." He moved to the bed, never taking his mouth from her body. He wore only sweatpants bottoms, and he maneuvered those off without breaking his stride. In seconds he also had her long T-shirt and panties off, too. She felt him enter her, felt as though she'd come home after a long cold journey. The room was dark, only the dimmest light coming from the clock on the dresser. She wished she could see his face.

He came, filling her with throbbing heat. He gripped her shoulders as his body arched. Maybe it had just been a while, but usually he lasted much longer. She ached for longer. Would he send her away now or hold her through the night? Could he forgive her that quickly?

His hands slid from her shoulders to her neck, his caress anything but gentle. His fingers went around her throat and started squeezing. Her eyes popped open.

Lucas would never hurt her, not for any reason.

Not Lucas! Sayre!

"Lucas!" Her voice was garbled.

Her heart slammed in her chest, pounding right up into her ears. She tried to bring her knee up into his groin, but he pinned her down. She shoved her head forward, slamming it into his forehead. Taking advantage of his shock, she pushed him aside and then fell on top of him. "Lucas!" She shook him by the shoulders, banging him against the floor.

He blinked and groaned. "Amy?" His voice sounded disoriented. "What—"

"Sayre."

The relief that poured through her! Lucas was back. Then disgust and then grief that he hadn't called her in at all. She got up and turned on the light. He sat up, still naked, rubbing his forehead where she'd banged into him. Her forehead was aching, too. Then his gaze went to her, standing naked by the dresser.

Her voice was shaky. "You called me, and when I came in, you started . . . kissing me. I thought . . . never mind. We made love, but it wasn't you." She shivered. "God, I don't know how to even feel. It was you, your body. But it wasn't you inside."

He came to his feet and pulled her close. "Are you all right?"

She closed her eyes against him. "I don't know."

He leaned back and pushed her hair from her face. "I'll kill him if I can. I don't know if I can get into his dreams, but I'm going to try." He picked up her clothes and handed them to her. "I don't want you here."

"But—"

"Go. It's too dangerous."

She saw his anger at Sayre. She saw that he was

afraid for her. It was what she didn't see that made her the most afraid. She didn't see love.

The man pointed the wrench at Eric, coming to a stop a foot in front of him. "I want you and that girl out of here by tomorrow. Or sooner."

Eric hadn't budged, other than stiffening his shoulders. "I already told Magnus we wouldn't be here long. And 'that girl' is your half sister, Fonda Raine. Fonda, this is Lachlan."

He didn't look as though he was going to shake her hand when he turned his hard gaze to her. "I don't consider you family. Just because my father screwed some tart—"

"Knock it off," Eric said, raising his hand as though he was about to do just that.

Other people's anger always ignited hers, too. "Your father was as much a tart as my mother." She turned to Eric. "And I don't need you to step in for me. I grew up around guys who were as tough as any of you; I know how to take care of myself."

His eyebrow rose, though he looked more interested than annoyed.

Lachlan jabbed his finger at her. "Don't you say a word about my father."

"Well, it appears that he's my father, too, so I'll say what I want."

Magnus stepped in, rolling his eyes. "Lachlan, give it a rest."

Lachlan pointed at Eric, but looked at Fonda. "Be careful with your boyfriend here. He's likely to explode, and he'll take you with him."

"He's not my boyfriend." She could hardly get the words out fast enough. "He killed my boyfriend."

Before they could ask more about that, she asked, "What do you mean, 'he'll explode'?"

"I see the same edge in his eyes that I saw in my own . . . before I exploded." And killed his mother. He looked at Eric. "You won't take the antidote, will you? Have you had any hallucinations?"

Eric flicked his gaze to hers for a second. "No."

"Agitation, impulse control problems, blackouts, or sleeplessness?"

"No."

"Yes," Fonda answered. "He's been suffering sleep deprivation." She turned to him. He looked tired, his eyes bloodshot, but she could also see an edge in them.

Eric glared at Lachlan. "Yeah, and look how happy you are now that you've taken the antidote and lost your abilities."

Lachlan flung the wrench, fortunately not at anyone, and stomped back to the truck. "I don't understand why you insist we help these *people*," he said, presumably to Magnus.

Magnus took a step closer to Eric, his voice lowered. "Be careful, mate. Lachlan didn't know who we were that day. He was locked in another time period, another world. He would have killed us all if we hadn't stopped him. But he'll never forgive himself. And you won't either."

"When I start visiting other time periods, I'll keep that in mind. How long until the truck is ready?"

"Probably tomorrow morning."

"Tonight," Lachlan said in a firm voice.

"Come to the house, get cleaned up. I'll feed you dinner and then we'll get you on your way."

Fonda followed Magnus, trying not to look back to

see if Eric was behind her. Unfortunately, she could feel him back there, that dense hot energy she'd felt when astrally touching him.

The gate was open, and they walked through it into a strange and beautiful garden. Mixed among the flowers were oddly shaped and colored *things* that had little signs with long scientific names. The late afternoon sun that filtered down through the trees lit up copper wires that covered the courtyard like a spiderweb. They followed a curving path to a stained-glass door; the walls on either side were glass.

"It's an enchanting place," she said. *In a strange kind of way.* It made her wonder about the man who'd built it.

"My . . . perhaps *our* father loved fungi and slime molds," Magnus said, as though reading her mind. "Pardon my bluntness, but what is your natural hair color?"

She pointed to her head. "Well, not the pink, of course. People don't believe me, but this is my true color."

Magnus nodded, then opened the door, walked inside and waved for them to follow. Narrow hallways stretched in both directions, and the glass walls looked into another courtyard with even more odd growths and a black pond in the center. She was so entranced, she was surprised when Magnus put a framed picture in front of her face. "Our father," he said, this time a bit more assuredly.

The man in the picture reminded her of Sting, with short, white-blond hair and sea-green eyes. Definitely her hair. She wasn't sure what to feel, but when her eyes tingled the way they did just before she cried, it surprised her. All these years, the man who had failed her, who hadn't loved her enough, wasn't even her real father.

"What kind of father was he?" she asked, embarrassed to hear the hoarseness in her voice.

"We used to kid him that he loved his fungi as much as us, but he was a good man. He did everything he could for us, spent his life keeping us safe. Even to the end."

His words hit her in the chest. Richard Wallace protected his children.

"It's hard to find your father and not be able to know him," Eric said in a soft voice, his gaze on the picture. "I'm sorry I took that away from you."

She looked sharply up at his apology, one she could tell he meant. He met her gaze. She looked back at the picture, unable to deal with the apology. He knew the loss as she did, but she couldn't share that with him.

She handed the picture back to Magnus. "Thank you."

"Maybe another time you can come back, and we'll show you videotapes of him." He waved past a small sitting area intimately lit by small silver lights that dangled from long cords, and beyond that, a kitchen. "Do you need clothes?"

"We bought one change of clothes," Fonda said.

"You'll need more than that. Eric, you could probably fit into mine." He assessed Fonda. "You're a bit smaller than my mum, but I think you could manage." At her surprised look, he said, "My father kept all of her things. And despite the circumstances, she was a generous woman. She won't be haunting me. Or you."

For giving her husband's bastard daughter her clothes. "You're sure?"

He nodded. "Come."

She followed him into a large bedroom that had probably been the master. It seemed preserved, the air stale, a thin layer of dust on the dresser. He opened a door that, amazingly, led into a closet the size of another room.

"Groovy," she said on a reverent breath, taking in the drawers, shelves, and racks of shoes. "I think I'm in love with your mom." She glanced at him. "No disrespect intended."

Magnus chuckled. "None taken. Mum was a clotheshorse, kept her clothes for years. She didn't get out much, but she loved dressing up. I think it filled something inside her, something no one else could."

Fonda walked in, taking in the small chandelier—a chandelier in a closet?—the chair in the center, and then racks and racks of clothing. Being around clothing filled her with a joy she couldn't explain. All those years she'd lived on hand-me-downs, and what she loved most was vintage clothing. Her eyes were wide, and it was the first time she'd smiled, really smiled, in what had to be well over a month. She spun around, taking in all the colors and fabrics, and then came face-to-face with Eric, who was watching her with a bemused expression. She turned away. The swell in her chest was only about the clothing.

She turned back to Magnus, who also seemed amused by her. "Sorry. I love clothing, too. Go ahead and pick whatever you feel is best."

"They're just sitting here, Fonda. It's not as though we'll get any use of them. Take what you want."

Those words soared through her, making her fingers tingle. *Don't get greedy, girl.* She walked slowly, controlling herself, to one rack. *Breathe. Don't act like an idiot.* She started pushing each hanger to the right, taking a look at the items. With a gasp, she took down a mod black twill jacket. "Courrèges, made in France!" She traced her finger along the belt, then looked at the label at the back. "Real sixties era, because it doesn't have the logo on the tag yet." This would fetch well over a thousand bucks at the boutique. She held it up to her and walked to the full-length mirror, then sighed with both awe and regret. No way could she risk ruining something like this. She hung it back up and took down an adorable, blue sixties dress with flowing sleeves. "A boho dress!" She turned to Magnus. "Your mom was cool."

"Yeah, I think she actually wore that in the sixties. I never saw it on her. Take it. It'll look good on you."

"Hobo dress?" Eric asked.

"Boho. Like Bohemian."

Magnus said, "Pick whatever you want to carry with you. I'll get a bag to pack it in and a few things for you, too," he said to Eric, and then added with a saucy lift of his eyebrow, "Unless you want to pick out your own."

Eric gave him a phony laugh, but he was still watching her. She met his gaze in the mirror and shifted back to the dress. "We got one of these in the boutique once, but Marion got first dibs."

"Boutique?"

She hung the dress on a lower rod and kept looking. "I managed a vintage clothing boutique before I worked for Darkwell."

Being here took her back to those days, simple, safe, her only excitement whenever a new lot of clothing came in. Here in this closet she could get lost in that simplicity. She pulled down a dress, held it in front of her and danced around. Again her gaze snagged Eric's in the mirror, and this time a spark of hunger glinted in his eyes. He was leaning against the door frame, easy and relaxed, and yet . . . not.

With a quick breath she hung up the dress and looked for more practical things, clothing she could run in, if necessary. Most of the things here were Jackie O classy, not even close to her own style. She liked sixties and eighties best. Ooh, the tie-dyed yellow jeans and matching jacket with fringe would work perfectly. She hung that next to the dress. A deep pink, linen top and matching pants with a wrap-around style also went onto the keeper rack.

When Magnus returned, he handed Eric a stack of clothing. "This should do. You wear boxers or briefs?"

Fonda waved toward Eric. "He doesn't wear any." Her eyes popped. "I mean—"

"She gives away all my secrets," Eric said with a roll of his eyes.

"No, I didn't . . . at the park, he was . . ."

Magnus held out his hand. "Whatever, mates, no worries. If you want to take showers, or a shower—"

"Showers," she said, a little too forcefully. "Yes, please." She followed him to a door he opened on the other side of the bedroom.

"You can use the one in here. Eric, follow me."

She closed the door behind her and turned on the shower, grateful to wash away the grime and horror of the last few days. If only she could screw off the top of her head and wash it out of her mind. When she turned to the mirror, she let out a startled gasp. Big surprise that the mirror hadn't cracked. Her makeup was gone, and without the thick dark lines around her eyes, she looked odd, washed out. They'd bought basic toiletries at the store, but she hadn't even thought about makeup.

After her shower, she dried off and reached for her clothes. Damn, she hadn't brought them in. She wrapped the towel around her and walked into the bedroom. Eric stepped in, carrying a large overnight bag. He stopped at the sight of her. For that matter, she'd stopped, too. He wore only jeans, and drops of water dotted his broad shoulders. His hair was spiky, as though he'd barely towel-dried it. His jeans were low on his hips and tight on his thighs.

He seemed to push out the words, "The truck's good to go. And Lachlan is ready to see us off."

She nodded, then shook herself out of the moment and walked into the closet.

"Give me whatever you're bringing, and I'll pack it," he said, following her in. She saw her reflection, and here, in the softer lights, her hair playfully mussed, she didn't look so bad. Why anyone put fluorescent lights in a bathroom was beyond her.

He stood close while she took the clothing off the hangers, neatly folded them, and handed them to him. She focused on those clothes, though she could see his bare feet, strong legs encased in blue denim, and then the sprinkling of hair she knew so well just above his waistband. Her eyes drifted up as she handed him the last item. His gaze was on hers as he took it, their fingers brushing.

"I'll let you get dressed." He started to turn and leave.

"Is it true what Lachlan said, that you could go crazy and explode?"

He shook his head. "I've always been on the

edge. Paranoid. No impulse control. The thing that's changed is the sleeplessness, and that's only been since . . ." He let the words trail off.

"Since you killed Jerryl."

His eyes darkened. "Yeah."

She looked for a trace of emotion on his expression, but he'd banked it. "What did you feel when you . . . did that?" She couldn't bear to say the words again.

"Triumphant. But mostly, relief. You don't know what it's like to have some son of a—someone who can get into your head and control you. He tried to make me shoot my friends."

"You shot yourself instead."

He nodded, his mouth tightening at the memory, no doubt.

"You were willing to die for them. To protect them."

"Yeah. But the last straw was when he nearly got my sister to kill herself. No one does that to my family. Not her or any of my people."

She put her hand to her chest, the emptiness, the need, drilling a huge hole there. "It was war. Nothing personal."

His eyes narrowed. "What did he feel when he got me to shoot myself? He must have thought I'd die from the wound. I'll bet he was patting himself on the back, his shoulders all puffed up. It was personal for him, wasn't it? It became personal for both of us, our own war within the war. He hated me, mostly because he couldn't get me. That's why he went after my sister. He tried to get to me through her."

It *had* become personal. She knew part of that was Jerryl's ego. He couldn't stand to lose.

No, don't you dare start to see it Eric's way.

"You'll never get me to understand why you killed Jerryl the way you did. War, a personal vendetta, whatever. You killed the man I loved. The only man I ever loved." She pulled that pain close, needing to feel it again. Needing it to slide that wall between her and Eric.

He walked back to her, his head cocked at an angle. "So what you're trying to tell me is he was the love of your life."

"You say it like you don't believe me."

"How long were you two involved?"

Why exactly had she felt compelled to start this conversation, in a closet, when she was wearing a towel? When he smelled of clean male mixed with the scent of deodorant.

"Six weeks."

He bobbed his head. "He loved you, too?"

"Yes."

"He told you that?"

She adjusted her towel, feeling it slipping low on her breasts. "He wasn't the mushy type."

"He ever say anything like"—he moved closer, his face inches from hers—"'I can't live without you'? Or 'Baby, I need you,' and not mean for sex?"

She pushed him back even as those words dug into her. "Stop it."

He didn't back up far. "You're accusing me of killing the love of your life, so here's your chance to stick it to me. But prove he *was* the love of your life. That doesn't mean having lots of sex."

Her eyes snapped wider at that. "What do you mean by that?"

"Nicholas told us you two were always going at it.

But remember, Blue Moon does that to us. We can go all night, stay hard and hungry, but that's not necessarily love."

She swallowed hard at those words. So okay, she had thought that meant they had something special, because he could control his orgasm, that he wanted her so often.

"Look, I'm no expert at this stuff," he said. "I've never been in love, never said those words to a woman. But I've seen it in my people. I think it's a bad idea to get involved when there are guys out there gunning for you, but nobody listens to me. So Lucas breaks into Amy's apartment to warn her, risks getting caught by Darkwell, and does just that. He'll suffer terrible pain to get glimpses of a future that might include danger, so he can warn us. Rand dove into the water when Jerryl grabbed Zoe and took her for a swim. Nicholas risked getting killed twice to save Olivia. That's what men do when they love a woman. Jerryl ever do anything like that?"

All Jerryl wanted to do was kill. Especially kill Eric. He'd been focused on his job, and she'd been focused on him. The thought of a man doing any of that for her . . . she gripped the edge of her towel. "There was never a reason for him to risk his life to save me." She lifted her chin. "But one of the first few nights we were working together, we went to a bar. Some creep was bugging me, and Jerryl stood up for me. He protected me."

Eric crossed his arms over his chest as though waiting for more. "That's all you got?"

"That's enough."

He snorted. "That's nothing."

"That's everything."

"Why?"

"Because no one ever did that for me." Her voice rose with her words and the emotions behind them. "No one. Not the man who was supposed to be my father, who sat in his drugged haze while his friends said lewd things to his thirteen-year-old daughter. Not when his wife called me names. Not when one of his so-called friends tried to rape me. He didn't even believe me, because, 'No, Willie wouldn't try to hump you. He's my bud.' I had to keep seeing that despicable man in our apartment. Okay, so maybe I built that one act of chivalry into something a lot more, but that was all I had! It was all I had, and you took it away from me."

Damn tears, damn emotions, swallowing her up when she needed to be strong. To make matters worse, Eric put his hands on her bare shoulders. She shoved him away and tried to turn, but he pulled her hard against him. She put her hands to his chest to push him back, but her towel started slipping and she grabbed it with one hand, twisting her fingers into the terry cloth. She kept her face pressed against his chest, fighting to regain control, eyes squeezed shut with the effort.

Dammit, don't let him see you like this.

He lifted her chin, and she felt a tremble in his hands as his thumbs brushed away her tears. "I didn't mean to hurt you. Not then, not now. I did take him away from you, but I didn't take away the only person you ever loved. I didn't take that away from you, little girl. You still have that in your future."

"Why are you trying to make what Jerryl and I had smaller?"

"I want it not to hurt so much."

Didn't he see that he was making it worse? Not because he was making her see that the grand love she thought she had was an illusion. No, because he was being tender, and how was she supposed to hate him when he was being tender?

"No, stop," she said, and the tears fell even harder. The brush of his thumbs on her cheeks was like a knife, scraping away her walls, revealing that place inside that ached to be comforted. That was something no one had done, not her father, not Jerryl.

She'd never let anyone see that part of her, not even herself. She sure as hell didn't want Eric to see it, to expose it, but he wouldn't stop whispering, "It's okay, stop crying." Even worse, he kissed her damp cheek, soft kisses that speared right into her chest. "Please don't cry."

He kissed her other cheek, and she hated that it felt so good. Hated herself for feeling it, for relaxing into his grip, for the heat every kiss left on her skin, because his mouth was moving down, over where her dimple creased when she smiled, the edge of her mouth, and for the way her mouth slackened in invitation. His mouth rubbed across hers, kissing her, the wet sound of their lips connecting, hers moving hungrily to feel more of him, and her chest so tight, so full of something that filled her—

"Fonda." His voice was urgent. "You're bleeding." He touched her mouth and showed her a smear of blood on his finger.

She pressed her finger to her lip and looked at the smear. She'd been biting her inner lip so hard, she'd drawn blood. She ducked her head down to the dark towel wrapped around her, dabbing her mouth with the corner.

The rational part of her brain was objecting, using pain to pull her back to her senses. She wiped her eyes, her gaze on his. She would have been pissed that he'd made her cry, but he looked both sad and baffled.

"Oh—sorry."

Magnus's voice from the doorway jerked them both out of the moment. She stumbled back, grabbing at the towel that started slipping again.

Eric stepped in front of her, giving her privacy. "We're ready. Well, almost." He nodded for the two of them to leave her alone.

When they closed the door, she stared at her reflection, shell-shocked, her whole body trembling. *What the hell was that?*

Madness.

She stepped closer to the mirror. *You failed to kill him. You're teamed up with him. Now you're attracted to him! You were two seconds away from melting into him right after he'd stomped all over your relationship with Jerryl.* It was the glimmer of tenderness he'd shown that had sliced right into her darkness. Ruthless, cold-hearted Eric Aruda begging her to stop crying as though her tears were burning right into him.

She waited for Connie's nasty names to stab at her. They didn't, leaving only an empty humming that reminded her of astral projecting. She let the towel drop, looking down at the tattoo on her right hip: a black kitten with knifelike claws extended. *If you want to keep any scrap of self-respect, of worth, that's how you look at Eric, how you treat him. Then, as soon as you can, you get the hell away from him.*

CHAPTER 9

Eric went through the motions of taking the gun and extra ammunition from Magnus, of stuffing the bag behind the seats of the old truck, but his head was still back in that closet.

That wasn't him, that was a possession, but not by Sayre. No, more like a Lucas possession. That tender, caring shit was something Lucas, not he, would do. Especially with a woman who, not twenty-four hours ago, had tried to kill him.

Tried, but couldn't.

Yeah, and she wasn't real happy with herself that she couldn't. What does it say about you that you want a woman who damned near tried to kill you?

She walked out, wearing the hobo dress with a skirt that came to mid-thigh. In contrast to the dress, she looked mad as hell. Thank God. If he'd seen her come out with a gooey, dewy look on her face or a smidgen of vulnerability, he'd be in big trouble. Damn, he knew women used tears to get their way, but seeing one actually crying—and because of him—sliced and diced him three ways and then some.

She got into the truck, slamming the door closed and slumping back, her arms over her chest, gaze riveted ahead.

Magnus tapped the door. "Good luck, mates. Let me know what's going on." He nodded toward Fonda, his smile barely concealed. "Be on your guard." He walked over to her side, and she rolled down the window. "It was nice to meet you. Could be good to have a sister."

Her expression softened, though Eric could see her surprise, too. Her smile was tentative. "Thank you. I wasn't sure how you felt, being . . . well, the way it happened."

"That my father messed around on my mother? It was Blue Moon. He was devoted to Mum. He would never have hurt her on purpose. We'll see you again?" She nodded. "Be safe," he said, and stepped back.

Eric started the truck. The muffler roared, and the whole truck vibrated with power. "How fast is this thing?" he asked Magnus.

"It's got a turbo 350 with a TH350 tranny, three hundred horses. It'll do."

Eric nodded. "Yes, it will."

Lachlan walked out, his shoulders stiff, his expression in a snarl. Angry. Yeah, he could relate. He waved as they pulled away, but Lachlan stood and glared.

"Don't you ever do that again," Fonda said, her gaze pointedly ahead.

"What, wave at Lachlan? I was just being friendly."

She huffed. "I meant what you did in the closet."

He came to a stop where the gravel drive met the road. "What, exactly?" He'd done a few things he probably shouldn't have. Might as well narrow it down.

"Belittling what Jerryl and I had. Making it seem like he was only using me."

"Maybe he was. Guys are like that sometimes."

Her lips tightened into a hard line. "Maybe you're like that. Maybe you use women and toss them away. But you didn't know Jerryl, so you have no right to insinuate that he was an asshole, too."

"I'm happy to accommodate a willing woman, no doubt. But to repeatedly bang a woman and not be absolutely clear on where the relationship is or isn't going . . ." He shook his head. "Nope, wouldn't do that."

Her upper lip lifted in a sneer that reminded him of Billy Idol. "Because you're so *honorable*."

"Hey, I'm the biggest asshole you've ever met. But I'm an honest one. I call 'em as I see 'em. You can hate me for that, or because I killed him or because I'm a jerk or for any reason you want. You've got a few to choose from. But I didn't take away the love of your life, because he wasn't."

"And that was important to make clear to me because . . ."

That made him stop. Why had it been so important? Because he wanted her free of the illusion that she'd loved Jerryl, and that he'd loved her.

It was more than that, bud.

"I was trying to make you feel better."

She pointed at him, finally looking his way. "You're just doing it to make yourself feel better."

Was he? He did feel better knowing Jerryl wasn't her big love.

"And that other thing you did," she added.

Uh-oh, here it comes. "Kissing you."

"Yeah. That. That was totally . . . totally . . ." Her eyes were wide, searching for the right word.

"Stupid? Wrong? Crazy?" he supplied.

"All of the above." With another huff, she turned to look out the passenger window. She wanted to hold onto her anger at him. It had probably killed her to break down in front of him—especially him—like that.

"Fine," he said. "We'll forget the thing in the closet ever happened."

"Forgotten," she said in a singsong voice, still turned away.

He pulled out onto the road. That was the best thing that could happen. Forget it, bury it deep. Act as though it had never happened.

But he knew that neither one of them was going to forget it, no matter how hard they tried. Something had happened between them. Something had changed, and he had a feeling it was going to mess everything up.

His phone rang: Amy. "Did the cops leave?" he said as a greeting.

"They still have guys posted. They must think one of us will come back here, but so far they haven't made a move to come in or find an entrance. We're all right for the most part, but we have an old problem that's returned: Sayre." She told him about the possession, her voice taut, trembling at times. "So far Lucas can't get into his dreams, but maybe Sayre's not asleep."

Eric felt a swell of anger and resoluteness. "I'm going to get him."

"You have enough going on."

"I don't care. I want this guy out of the picture. Look, I . . ." He glanced at Fonda, who was staring out the window. The hell with it. "I know I've done some reckless things, things that have put you guys in danger. Maybe it's this sleeplessness, but I'm getting flashbacks, and it ain't pretty. Let me do this for you and Lucas."

"I don't know, Eric."

"I'll rephrase. I'm doing this for you and Lucas. For now, we've given this Westerfield dude the slip. So while we're in a safe place, I'll find Sayre. Have Nicholas do a locate on him."

"Thanks, Eric, but please be careful. He's evil." Her emotions were at the surface: gratitude, but also fear.

"I'll talk to you later," he said, not wanting to hear another woman cry. He couldn't take it.

Fonda was now looking at him, her eyebrows furrowed. "Who are you going to take care of?"

"Did you ever meet Sayre Andrus at Darkwell's estate?"

She shook her head.

"Darkwell brought the murdering son of a bitch in from prison, pulled some major strings to arrange his release. Sayre's caused a lot of problems, including trying to rape and kill Olivia Darkwell."

When Fonda winced, he remembered that she'd almost been raped.

"You said someone tried to rape you."

"Remember," she said, "we forgot everything that happened in the closet. So this Sayre was working on the program?"

"Yeah. He can get into a person's dreams and make them do things. But he seems to like attacking women in person. The dude is a first-class psycho. He's been toying with Lucas, making his life miserable. I have no doubt his goal is nothing less than murder. Lucas and Amy, they've been through enough. I'm going to stop him."

"Now? While we've got our own psycho to deal with?"

His mouth tightened. "My friends are hurting, and they're in danger." Not only from above, but from within. "Darkwell had Sayre try to come in through Lucas and kill us all. Since I can't sleep deep, I don't think he'll be able to get into me. But in case he latches onto me, if I have a blank, dark look on my face, get the hell away from me."

She shivered, looking away for a moment. "You do like war."

"I'm not going to let someone kill me." He rubbed his hand across his forehead. *Be honest.* "I did like it. I craved the adrenaline rush, but I'm tired. Tired of hiding and tired of fighting." He had way too much to deal with now. These new people. Sayre. Fonda. All on not enough sleep.

The sun was setting, the most brilliant orange he'd ever seen as it colored a grid of small puffy clouds. They needed to find a safe place to duck into for the night. Westerfield had found them before, which meant they couldn't stay in any one place for long.

The phone rang again, and this time it was Nicholas. "I found Sayre. He's in a small wooded area east of D.C. Looks like he's hanging out with the homeless folks." Nicholas gave him specifics.

"I don't want to be that far away from you guys," he said. "How are things there?"

"Tense, man. A sneeze could shatter everyone. But we're ready for an invasion. Looks like an armed camp. Go, take care of the bastard. You have our blessing."

"All right. If anything changes—"

"We'll call you."

Eric disconnected and looked at Fonda, who had been listening. "Sayre escaped when the estate burned down. Since there hasn't been word one about him on the news, I'm guessing the CIA is trying to keep the fact that he's on the loose secret. They sure as hell don't want to admit that one of their own arranged for his release and now they've lost him. They're putting Lucas's mug on the news, hoping to snag Sayre since they're identical twins. Nicholas found him hanging out with the homeless in the woods."

"So why not let the police know where he is?"

"Because he'll end up back in prison, and that's not good enough."

"I know how you work. Don't you dare hurt those people or burn the woods down."

He raised an eyebrow at her. "Is that an order?" He could see the concern in her face, and oddly enough, it was kind of endearing.

"Yes. Most of those people have some kind of mental thing going. They're—"

"Innocent. Got it. I'm not going to go in and torch everyone, hoping to get Sayre." He headed toward the highway. "Any particular reason you feel so compelled to protect them?"

She looked ahead, something he noticed she did when she was uncomfortable discussing something. "I've known a few homeless people."

She was content to leave it at that, and really, he didn't want to know that much about her.

Except, "How so?" came out of his mouth instead of nothing.

"I grew up in some pretty rough areas. Sometimes I knew their stories. Girls who found it safer to sleep outside than in what you could loosely call their homes. Men who still live in a war, so no one wants to hire them and no family wants to deal with them. Sometimes life sucks."

He looked at her. Her gaze was trained straight ahead, her mouth in a hard line. Her father was drugged out, she'd said. *Forget it. It's none of your business.* "Were you one of those girls?" *Argh.* He could have banged his forehead against the steering wheel.

She flicked a glance at him. "No. I locked myself in my room, cut my hair short and dressed like a boy. And I learned to kick ass."

He could feel her anger. Something about it drew him. Sparked in him. He'd always been angry. Even his father had said he was an angry baby. Here was someone who had a right to be angry. He started to say something else, but she cut him off.

"I don't want to talk about my life anymore. And I really don't want you to have that look on your face—"

"What look?"

"Pity, or whatever it is. I survived. I'm over it. Subject closed. Everything's groovy." She looked out the window. "Yeah, perfectly groovy."

She wasn't over it, though. She'd built a fling into love because of one act of chivalry. Because no one had ever stood up for her, protected her. Damn. He did not want that tight hot feeling in his chest when he thought of it. He turned up the radio and tuned in an alternative rock station.

After a few minutes she looked at him. "I want to go by the motel where . . . well, you know. Even though they've probably cleared out the room, I want to see if I can get my purse and my favorite boots."

Sayre was probably going to be in the woods for the night, so they had time. Westerfield would be long gone by now and most likely wouldn't expect them to return. Not that she'd asked, but he said, "Okey-dokey," drawing an ireful look from her.

They drove in silence, he trying to keep his gaze ahead. He thought about the best way to nail Sayre. Torching him would be the easiest, though if Sayre sensed him, he could push him out. Maybe he'd get lucky and catch Sayre otherwise occupied, like with Jerryl. Except that would put an innocent woman in jeopardy. Seeing it from Fonda's point of view made him think about things like that.

He passed the honky-tonk, glancing over to see if she was looking at the place, too.

Damn. She was curled up against the door asleep. Her palms were tucked beneath her head, eyelashes fanned out above her cheeks. She looked small and vulnerable, hardly capable of trying to kill a guy. Without her anger, she looked sweet, her full mouth sensuous now that it wasn't in that tight line.

Eric realized he was looking at her more than at the road. He pulled up to the motel a few minutes later. Three vehicles sat in the faded asphalt parking lot, none of them his or Fonda's. The bastard had them towed away. Eric didn't know what Westerfield drove. Still, he was on alert. Lights glowed from three rooms, including the one they'd been in. He parked, leaving the engine running, and surveyed the area.

The door to Room 19 was slightly ajar, just as they might have left it when they tore out. Could they get that lucky? He tucked the gun beneath his shirt and stepped out of the truck. Scanned the surroundings. So far, so good. He pushed the motel door open and stepped in, gun now at the ready, and surveyed the room. Ropes still tied to the bed frame. Picture on the floor. Her purse and a duffel bag in the corner.

A sound behind him at the open doorway had him spinning around. A small wiry man with glasses so thick he reminded him of Mr. Magoo stood there. Eric kept the gun at his side but tucked out of sight. Dude didn't look like some maniac, but he'd learned never to judge a book by its cover, scrawny as it was.

"I was about to clean the room," the man said. "I'm running behind, had a stomach bug."

Eric couldn't tell if his eyes were widened in surprise; they were huge in magnification. "We're staying another night."

"Where's the young lady who rented the room?"

"In the truck asleep." He thrust some bills at the man, probably more than the room cost. "That should cover us."

"Who are you?"

"Her boyfriend. We'll be out early in the morning." He stepped toward the open doorway, forcing the little man to back up. He did, indeed, have a cart of cleaning supplies with him. He hesitated, but Eric walked to the truck without any further conversation. When he turned back, Magoo was pushing the cart back toward the office at the far end.

From his angle, Eric couldn't see Fonda's face, but she was still curled up against the seat. He knocked on the glass. "Come on. We're here."

He could see her clearly enough in his mind, mouth soft and tempting, pink even without lipstick. Damn, he did not want to be attracted to the succubus who'd tried to kill him.

"Come on, Fonda!" he barked, his annoyance at

himself bursting out. He yanked open the door, and she fell backward.

He caught her before she hit the ground, scooping her up. Her eyes fluttered open, but they were drunk with sleep. She weighed next to nothing as he carried her like a baby.

"Where . . . ?" she managed.

"I'm taking you to bed."

Her eyes opened at that and she began to wriggle. He replayed the words in his mind, and his body took them the same way she had. "Not that kind of taking you to bed. Get a couple of hours of sleep."

"Put me down."

"We're almost there." He kicked open the door with his foot.

She put up a bigger struggle, the anger taking hold of her face again. He released her, and she dropped to her wobbly legs. She grabbed onto his arm and let go just as fast.

"Sorry, following orders," he said, raising his hands.

She walked in, her gaze going to her purse and the bag. "It's all still here?"

"Apparently the manager spent the day in the bathroom and hadn't gotten to the room yet."

She stumbled to the bed. "So tired. Need sleep." She pulled herself onto the bed, only enough to fit her curled body on it. Her dress slid up mid-thighs, and that display of skin was enough to perk him up even more.

A wave of dizziness swept over him for a moment as he watched her. Lust? Sometimes it did that, washed over him like a wave. No, not lust, not for this one. Sleep. He needed it, too. Neither of them had gotten rest, much less sleep, in the last twenty-four hours. He locked the door, taking one last glance outside. He stripped out of his shirt and lay down on the bed, careful not to touch her. Not that she'd know it; she was out. He watched her sleep, her anger gone again, leaving the sweet innocence. If he didn't know better.

But you do.

He closed his eyes, but they opened again. She filled his vision, her white-blond hair spilling across her cheek, the pink hairs now dispersed rather than being in one streak. She still wore the red hoop earrings, and one draped against her neck. She was one of the most interesting women he'd ever met.

He forced his eyes closed, but he made one detour on the way to trying to sleep. Using the coordinates Nicholas had given him, he zoned in on Sayre, in a sleeping bag on the ground. Damn but he wanted to just torch him and get it over with.

No more jumping in without thinking.

He scanned Sayre's surroundings: trees, several other forms on the ground, a few tents. Homeless people. If he set Sayre on fire, some of those hobos would probably die, too. He envisioned the mansion going up in flames, killing Richard Wallace. The fires he produced psychically were so hot, they got quickly out of control. He would have to approach in person.

Sayre's eyes popped open, and he sat up and searched the area. Eric pulled out. Hopefully Sayre would think the strange feeling was his imagination. Otherwise, getting to him was going to be a lot harder—and more dangerous.

Sayre Andrus searched the woods. Nothing more

than the usual noises and movements: groans, mumbling, and every now and then some guy who'd relive the war, waking up screaming and shit.

The annoyances were worth it. This was the best place to hide out. None of these guys watched the news, and he had shaved his head so he looked nothing like Lucas's picture the police were showing on television. That would die down eventually, and he'd find a way to integrate back into society again. Like taking one of these guys' identity. For now, lying low was working good.

Except for that prickle of sensation he'd just felt. Not his twin brother's energy either. He thought for damned sure Lucas would have dove right into his dreams to teach him a lesson about diddling his girlfriend, but no. Nothing.

He poked into Lucas's head and found him asleep, alone in his bed. *Aw, ain't that a pity? Alone because of little ol' me?* Well, that hadn't stopped him last time. He grinned wide at the memory. He hadn't had a chance to get himself some beaver, not with the bulletins running. No need to take a chance. Getting some through Lucas was only a tease, but one he had enjoyed anyway.

He didn't know whose energy it was he'd felt, but he was going to keep his sixth sense alert. If someone was gunning for him, he'd be ready.

CHAPTER 10

The scream rocked Eric out of half sleep. Fonda's scream. He lurched up and grabbed the gun. Scanned the room. No one. Then looked to Fonda, still screaming and writhing on the bed.

Nightmare.

He hardly had time to register relief. He needed to quiet her down before someone came to investigate.

"No! No, oh, my God," she said in a strangled voice. Her eyes were twitching beneath her closed lids.

He put his hand over her mouth, hovering close. "Fonda. Wake up. It's a dream."

"Jerryl!" she screamed in agony, but it was muffled beneath his hand.

Damn. She was having a nightmare about the fire. Seeing her reliving it yanked out his guts. He shook her, pressing his other hand on her shoulder and pushing her into the bed. "Wake up, Fonda!" She kicked, and he had to press his body down onto hers to keep her from hurting him or herself. "Fonda!" he said into her ear.

He felt moisture on his lip. Tears slid down her temples.

"Put it out! Oh, God, oh, God."

"Fonda, wake up!"

He pulled her to a sitting position, his hands on her shoulders. Her eyes fluttered open.

He didn't dare pull her closer, not after what had happened in the closet. A part of him wanted to, though. "You had a nightmare. It's all right."

Something in her eyes changed as she came fully awake. She looked around her, breathing hard. Not the estate. No fire. She swiped at her eyes with trembling hands. "I tried to put the fire out. I threw blankets on him. But I couldn't . . . couldn't . . ."

"No, you couldn't. There was nothing you could do. What I do, it's too hot to easily put out."

He readied himself for her anger, for her to rail at him for taking Jerryl away again. He saw no anger in her eyes, only guilt. He rubbed his fingers across her cheek, erasing the last of the tears. "No one could have helped him."

"But I lived. He died and I lived."

"Because you weren't my target."

He ran his hand down her arm. She had a fine network of scars crisscrossing her upper arms. His chest tightened.

"Who did this to you?"

She pulled away from his finger, which traced the lines, and scrambled off the bed, her gaze averted. "No one."

He got to his feet, too. "Did your father do that?" he asked, lowering his voice. She shook her head. "Jerryl? No, they're too old for him. Ex-boyfriend?"

"No." After digging in her duffel, Fonda grabbed a small bag and walked into the bathroom. "Why does it matter, anyway?"

"I don't like the idea of someone cutting a woman. It's the kind of brutality that makes me nuts."

"I'm not your concern. Forget about them," she said from the other side of the door.

When she emerged a few minutes later, he was waiting. "Just tell me who did it." His gaze went to her thighs. Above her knees he saw more of the same scars. "You've got a lot of cuts." Most in places people wouldn't see.

"It's none of your business. What's our next step?"

He released a breath. She was right. "I'm going to take care of Sayre Andrus. You're coming with me, but not into the woods. Then we'll find another place to hunker down while we try to find Westerfield."

Fonda pulled some dark clothes from her bag and went back into the bathroom. She moved like a cat, her body fluid in motion. She came out wearing black leggings and a long black top, and slid little feet into the black combat boots. He noticed they had patches, pink cats with X's over their eyes.

She looked up at him. "Let's go. I don't want to be here anymore."

"What's wrong? Don't like the happy memories?" He nodded toward the ropes still hanging from the bedposts.

She looked away, and did he see regret? Probably over not succeeding in killing him. "I just want to go. Put on your shirt."

He only now realized he still didn't have his shirt on. What was the big deal? He slid it on, catching her watching in the mirror over the dresser. He hit the bathroom, splashed water over his face, and put on his shoes. "Ready."

She was about to walk past but paused in front of him. "Don't be nice to me. Holding me, trying to make me feel better . . . don't do that."

He raised an eyebrow. "Why not?"

"I don't want to like you, Eric Aruda. Don't make me."

She walked out to the truck. He remained there for a moment, watching her, a smile tugging at the corner of his mouth. That smile dropped. No one had ever accused him of being nice before. Why was he being nice to her? He was proud of being a butthead. It was his nature. So why wasn't he one around a woman who couldn't stand him? Probably his guilt over what he put her through.

He watched her get into the truck and pull the door closed. She brushed her fingers through her hair, her mouth in that hard line. No, it was more than that. Something about her got to him, reached into his chest and squeezed, not unlike the way Westerfield could, only this felt . . . different. A combination of good and scary. *Don't explore that too closely. Last thing you need is to get involved. Remember, bad idea.*

He closed the door and followed her to the truck.

Fonda tried to keep her gaze from sliding over to Eric as they drove west. She could feel his eyes on her, though. Like he was speculating about her. Wondering about her scars. She had bigger scars inside. She didn't want him wondering about any of them.

Holy crap, to wake up from that horrible nightmare with his hands on her shoulders. He comforted her, smoothed away her tears. She had felt safe and protected, something she hardly ever felt. Only it was in Eric Aruda's arms, and that wasn't a safe place to be at all.

He was dangerous. Evil. Bad. The enemy. Yet, he'd been tender twice, this time absolving her from guilt. Apologizing for her pain and meaning it. She'd heard enough empty words to know the difference.

She found her gaze drifting to him, the line of his jaw, the tendons in his neck, and past his loose shirt to his jeans that encased his thighs. His fingers were tapping on his knee to the Rolling Stones' "Gimme Shelter." Strong hands, long fingers. She'd seen him naked, knew the lines of that big, hard body, the ridges of his flat stomach, the curve of his ass, which was finely dusted in golden blond hairs.

She felt that stirring deep in her stomach. *Stop that!* She was so desperate not to have those stirrings about Eric, she pulled up Jerryl's image in her mind. *Feel how you're betraying his memory. Feel how . . .*

She could only see Jerryl in a hazy way. Bristly hair that was too short to run her fingers through, brown eyes that narrowed in an annoyed way when she'd come to his room and he was concentrating on work. She couldn't picture his mouth at all.

Her eyes widened, and it felt as though someone had thumped her hard in the chest. Jerryl hadn't loved her. What he had loved was killing. And not only killing in general, but killing Eric Aruda. Sometimes when they had sex, she would see a lusty passion in his eyes. As soon as he came, though, the first words out of his mouth were: "I can't wait to kill that son of a bitch." He'd actually been thinking about it while they were having sex! Like a woman who ignores the signs that her man is cheating, she had ignored the signs that he didn't care about her beyond as a sex partner.

When Eric asked if Jerryl loved her, she'd believed her answer. She had told Jerryl she loved him, and what had he said? *That's nice.*

She had heard, *That's so nice that you love me. I love you, too.* That's not what he'd meant at all. It was, *That's nice,* the way someone says those words when you give them an ugly sweater. Her words were an ugly sweater to him . . . because the only reason she'd said them was to hear him say them back to her. She thought sex, and saying the words, meant it was love. Her fingers kneaded her forehead. It wasn't love at all.

It was embarrassing to see now how she had thrown herself at him. The act of chivalry in the bar, that he possessed powers like her, such an allure. All Jerryl had cared about was becoming Darkwell's number one. She wasn't even number three or four on his list. It hurt, but not as much as she thought it might. It also lessened the loss of him, as Eric had intended.

He's done more to protect you than Jerryl ever did.

The thought walloped her upside the head. She hadn't seen it, of course, hadn't wanted to, but there it was. From the beginning, right after she tried to kill him. He'd grabbed her hand when they ran out of the room, helped her get Westerfield out of her head, and stepped in front of her twice, with Westerfield and when Magnus walked into the closet.

Warmth rushed through her body. *No, you're not doing that again. It's probably instinct. He has people. He's used to protecting them.*

She closed her eyes at the thought. *People.* She had no people. Former coworkers that she hadn't let in. Nothing more than that.

"You okay?"

His voice yanked her from her dark thoughts.

"You looked like you were in pain," he said.

She could see by the crease in his forehead—he cared. "Cramps," she said. It was hard to keep from rolling her eyes at that lame excuse.

"Do you need . . . you know, that stuff? Having a sister, I know it's a life and death thing—"

"No, I'm fine."

Double damn him. No, he was probably protecting her because he saw her as weak. That made her feel better.

At a light, he picked up the map. "Almost there. I want you to stay in the truck. I don't want him to know you exist."

There he went again, protecting her. "I have no interest in getting involved in your wars."

"Good."

He pulled down a side street and then to a parking lot. He parked, reached into the back and pulled out a gun from the storage area. "Westerfield's gun has a silencer on it."

"He was going to use that on me."

He tilted it at an angle, looking at it. "Yeah." His mouth tightened. "I don't know why, when he has a far deadlier weapon. Much quieter to squeeze our guts and brains. Or maybe not."

His screams of agony echoed in her memory. She

shook her head. "Not." She glanced at the woods. "What are you going to do to this guy?"

"Can't burn him. Like you said, it'd send the whole place up in flames." He was staring intently at those dark woods. "I'm going to figure out which bundle is him and shoot." The intensity in his eyes burned as bright as any fire. Normally she didn't like men with very light eyes. His were the color of a wintry blue sky reflected in a pond. Icy blue, hard to read. He looked at her. "Be ready for anything. I don't like leaving you by yourself, but I won't be long. Westerfield shouldn't be able to find you that fast. If I'm not back in thirty minutes, drive the truck away and come back in an hour." He pinned her with his gaze. "But come back."

"I will," she said, surprised she hadn't thought of ditching him. No, she couldn't do that to him.

He dug around in the back, twisting his body so his jean-clad ass was right beside her. "I thought I saw a flashlight . . . Ah." He slid back to the front seat. "Do you have a cell phone?"

She nodded, digging in her duffel bag and extracting it from her purse.

"Give me your number." He punched in numbers as she recited it, and her phone rang. "Now you have mine. Put it on vibrate and keep it with you. We've found that's the safest way, so the ring doesn't give you away in case you're in a touchy situation."

He was used to being hunted. Hunted by Jerryl and the man she'd worked for.

He got out of the truck. "Be careful."

After he disappeared into the woods, she sat for a minute, listening to the crickets singing. Most of the time she'd worked for Darkwell, she was left out of the action. What if Eric ran into trouble? Not that she cared about his personal safety, but she had to admit she felt better having a big strong guy around.

Telling herself she could prove she wasn't some scared girl, Fonda slid out of the truck, pocketing the keys, and followed his path into the woods. She listened, tuning into his footsteps in the distance. Her foot hit something lumpy, and a man said, "Ow."

"Sorry." She stopped, looking around as her eyes adjusted. Tents and sleeping bags were everywhere. The homeless. She'd been so focused on Eric, she hadn't looked down.

Ahead, Eric flashed his beam across the ground. Some of the forms on the ground didn't even stir when the beam lit up their faces. Others covered themselves and grumbled. Eric didn't linger for more than a second.

She saw one man standing beside a tree, and something about his posture said *predator*. She picked up her pace. The man stepped closer to Eric. Danger burned her throat with a bitter taste. She lifted her gun but couldn't shoot, not without knowing what was behind the man.

The predator took three quick steps toward Eric, his hand raised in a gesture that screamed *Knife!*

"Eric! Watch out!"

He spun as the man lunged toward him. Both went down, and the flashlight landed nearby, lightening them up. She ran toward them.

A southern-accented voice said, "Who the hell— Eric Aruda, right?"

Eric said nothing as he tried to wrestle something out of the man's hand. Yes, a knife. Fonda stomped on his hand and wrestled the knife from his tight fingers.

"Fonda, get out of here!"

She saw Sayre then, his head shaved closer than Jerryl liked to keep his, blue-gray eyes flat. He was looking right at her, even as he struggled with Eric. And he smiled at her, a smile that sent a cold shiver through her body. The men rolled from one side to the other, both locked in a death grip.

"Nice of you to bring your girlfriend," Sayre said in a strained voice. "I haven't been able to visit Amy lately. Me an' her, we had a good time. Lucas tell you?"

His voice was filled with his taunting as well as strain. Eric got in a punch, which grazed Sayre's cheek. Eric was bigger, but Sayre was quick. That punch would have demolished him if Sayre hadn't moved so fast.

She aimed the knife, hoping to disable Sayre so Eric could get control over the situation, but she was afraid of accidentally stabbing Eric. She jammed the knife into a tree and jumped on Sayre's back when they rolled again.

"Fonda, get out," Eric growled.

Sayre flung his arm back and hit her in the side of the face, knocking her off. She heard Eric's snarl, and by the time she jumped to her feet and faced them, Sayre was also on his feet. Eric rushed him, shoving him against a tree trunk. Sayre's breath rushed out with a groan. He should have collapsed but instead kicked Eric in the stomach. Eric doubled over, only for a second but long enough for Sayre to get another kick in and dodge around him. Eric's hands just missed him. Fonda reached for the knife in the tree but it took several tugs to get it free. By then Sayre was gone, his footsteps retreating into the darkness.

Eric slammed his fist into the tree he was standing beside. "Dammit!"

"Hey, take this somewhere else, man," a man's voice said.

"Are you all right?" she asked, coming up to Eric.

With the light coming from below, his face looked even more intense and angry when he turned to her, his breath coming hard. "What in the hell are you doing here?"

"Saving your ass, as it turned out. He would have ambushed you."

He reached down and swiped up the flashlight with a flick of his wrist. He swept the light around on the ground until it lit up the gun, which had obviously been dropped. "Why didn't you stay in the truck? I thought you didn't want to bother with my wars."

"I'm tired of being left out. I figured I'd be backup."

He straightened up in front of her, his chest still rising and falling, hand flattened over his stomach where he'd been kicked. "You could have gotten killed."

"There's something you don't know about me, Eric. I don't like to play it safe. Feeling fear is better than feeling . . . numb. And you're welcome." She started back, realizing she'd used his name for the first time. Hearing it roll off her tongue felt strange, intimate.

He followed, coming up beside her. "I'm supposed to thank you for what, little girl? Exposing yourself to a psycho bastard?"

She flung a look at him.

"Okay, thank you for saving my ass. That's two I owe you."

"We're not keeping score. I don't want you owing me anything." Or vice versa. Particularly vice versa.

They weaved around the people who weren't quite sleeping anymore. Some were sitting up, grumbling at the intrusion. Within minutes she and Eric walked out of the woods. He smelled of earth and male and had a smear of dirt across his cheek, and somehow those things were arousing in a strange way.

He took hold of her arm, twisting her around to face him. "It was only a figure of speech. You're right. There's no owing anyone anything. Right now we're working together."

The tight feel of his hand around her arm triggered something deep in her body. "Then you shouldn't have your panties in a wad because I went in to make sure the guy didn't whack you. Which he would have. If we're working together, you shouldn't have a problem with that. And I may be little, but I'm not a 'little girl,' and don't call me that again. Just because I made a big deal about Jerryl standing up for me at the bar doesn't mean I'm a frail flower. I've dealt with drug dealers, thugs in the 'hood, I've handled a lot of ugly stuff by myself. So if I want to get in on the action, I will. That is, if we're really working—"

His mouth covered hers, and she was completely thrown off. It amazed her, however, how her mouth jumped right in, kissing him back. Her lips softened and parted beneath his. He took that as invitation and slid his tongue inside, sweeping across her teeth, swirling around her tongue. She couldn't breathe and it didn't even matter. She felt the urge to tear off her shirt and move into his body, and the thought was so jarring, she pushed him back.

She covered her mouth with her fingers. "What'd you do that for?"

"To shut you up. Let's get out of here."

She narrowed her eyes at his back as he walked to the truck. Damn him. Heat was still flushing through her body. She followed, getting into the passenger side.

He started the truck and looked at her. "I know . . . 'Don't ever do that again.' "

"Damn straight." That was the problem. Those weren't the words screaming through her mind. Not *No, no, no!* But *More, more, more!*

She put *No, no, no* on her expression. And what did he do? Laughed! Shook his head and laughed. Honest to God, she didn't know whether to slap him or laugh with him, and the two warring factions twisted her insides like taffy. On top of that, his laugh transformed his face from hard and chiseled to handsome and boyish. His icy blue eyes sparkled, and his mouth, slightly crooked, revealed perfect white teeth.

"You think this is funny?" she asked.

He sobered for a moment. "No, it's very, very serious." Then a laugh erupted again.

"Care to share why you think this . . . this situation is funny?"

He got control of his laughter. "You remind me of someone I know well. Stubborn. Reckless. Lives for drama. Angry. Full of piss and vinegar."

"Who's that?"

He waited a beat, that smile still on his face. "Me."

Her eyes popped. She didn't know what to make of *that.* "So when you kissed me back there, you were . . . kissing yourself?"

He rubbed his fingers across his mouth. "Interesting thought. Maybe I should do it again"—he leaned closer—"and see if I can figure it out."

She leaned back even as her body wanted to meet him in the middle. "Back off, Aruda."

"Just kidding." He was still smiling. Triple damn him. The smear of dirt, the tousled blond hair, the irreverent smile, all made her want to roll around on the ground with him.

Naked.

Hush! Naughty thoughts. Dirty . . . funny. She had the dialogue with herself before realizing that again Connie's vicious words weren't playing in her head anymore.

Change the subject. "You know, I didn't even think about freezing time back there. That was dumb. I could have stabbed him or something. I'm not used to having that skill."

"I didn't think about it either." At least he hadn't agreed on the dumb part.

He pulled out his cell phone and made a call. "Hey, Nicholas, it's Eric." Defeat permeated his voice. "No, I didn't get him. He must have sensed me checking on him earlier, because he was ready . . . No, I'm okay." He glanced at her. "I had some help. I'll try again later. Right now I want to focus on the guy who can squish our guts with his mind. Can you do a locate on someone you've never seen? . . . I figured you'd need a touchstone, and I don't have a picture of him. I can't remote-view unless I have a location. Unfortunately, I think he'll end up finding us; I'd much rather find him first. Everything the same there? . . . Okay. I'm here if you need me."

He disconnected.

She said, "I can locate. I found Nicholas and Olivia for Darkwell a couple of times."

"Do it."

She nodded. It felt good to be useful. "But I need sleep first. I'm exhausted." That last rush of adrenaline had wiped her out. Okay, two rushes: the one she'd gotten when fighting with Sayre and the one that came with Eric's kiss.

"We'll find a motel. But now that Sayre knows about you, be careful because he'll be after you."

"After me?"

"You intrigued him. Plus he'll go after you just to get to me. I'm sure he thinks we're together. *Together* together. Just be aware. He gets into your dreams and makes you do things. You'll feel a prickle at the base of your neck, but you won't notice it if you're asleep. I'll make sure you don't go wandering around."

"Because we'll be in the same room?"

"Makes sense. Money is limited, so might as well keep the costs down. And like I said earlier, you've already seen me naked, and I've almost seen you naked, so we're practically lovers already."

"Don't say that." Boy, those words had come flying right out. *Way to not sound like that bothers you.*

"Unless you don't think you can handle it . . ." He slid her a look that reeked of challenge.

Oh yeah, they were alike all right. He knew exactly how to get to her. *Keep that in mind, little girl. Uh, girl!*

"It won't be a problem."

"Glad to hear it."

"Good." She couldn't leave well enough alone. "Because we're not going there, you and me. Maybe we're working together, but we are not going *there*."

His fingers tightened on the wheel. "Remember those examples I gave you of what Lucas and Nicholas did to prove their love for their women? They put their asses on the line because they were all wrapped up in their feelings. Romantic? Sure. Brave? Yes. Stupid? Definitely. They lost their minds. I have no intention of doing that. So fear not that my hand—or anything else—will go roaming over to your side of the bed during the night. What's going on right now is way too serious for us to get sidetracked, whether we want to or not."

Did he want to?

Forget that.

"What do you mean, 'your side of the bed'? Don't you mean, my bed?"

"Sure, whatever."

"We're not sharing a bed."

"Of course not."

"Good. Glad we got that settled." She glanced at him. " 'Cause we're not." *Okay, you've made your point.* "What will Sayre do if he gets into my head?"

"I can only guess based on his past actions. He'll have you come on to me so he can vicariously have sex. Or he'll have you try to kill me. Maybe both."

"Holy crap."

CHAPTER 11

Fonda and Eric were a half hour closer to Annapolis when they pulled into the gravel parking lot of another cheap motel.

She wrinkled her nose. "Ugh. This place offers the rooms by the *hour*."

He grinned as he read the sign: THE LOVE SHACK. "It's perfect. They won't need a credit card and they won't take notice of us. We're just two more horny people in for a quickie."

Okay, he really hadn't needed to say that. Not on the heels of that kiss. Even now she involuntarily rubbed her fingers over her mouth.

So the first problem was, as they stood at the nicked-up desk in the office, that the fat, greasy man they'd roused from sleep gave them a fat, greasy smile after taking them in, and her in particular.

The second problem: no room had two beds. Of course.

"Don't get a lot of call for twin beds here," he said, now eyeing them with an odder look than he had when they rang the bell at two in the morning, disheveled and dirt-smeared.

"We'll take whatever you've got," Eric said, slapping cash on the counter.

Easy for him to say.

The man gave them a key, sliding a look to her but addressing Eric. "Porn channels are extra. If you want to watch, I'll need your card."

"Pass. But I'll need an extra set of sheets."

The man raised his thick dark eyebrow. He pushed a piece of paper at him and pointed at Rule 5. "No ripping of the sheets to be used as ties. You have to bring your own. Or . . ." He ducked down and produced a pair of fuzzy handcuffs. " . . . you can buy these for fifteen bucks. I've got other toys—"

Eric held out his hand to stop him. "No . . . thanks."

"You have to sign here that you've read the rules and will abide by them. No using chocolate syrup. We lost a room for a whole day because the stuff looks like blood when it dries, and the crime scene unit had to come out."

She got stuck on the chocolate syrup part, dripping it over a hard male body, licking it off.

The man continued, "No—"

"Give me the thing to sign." Impatience saturated Eric's voice.

She peeked at the rules. No lit candles for those who wanted to drip hot wax onto their lover's bodies. No use of oils for lubricants. Oh, boy.

He scribbled his name and took the extra set of sheets from the man.

"Five dollars."

"You're kidding," Eric said in a voice an octave deeper than usual, nailing him with a dark look.

"Uh, yes." The man giggled without a smile. "Have a nice night."

They walked out, grabbed their bags from the truck, and headed to the room. Where one bed awaited them. She hoped the place looked nothing like that first room. The memory of drugging him and trying to kill him struck an ache in the pit of her stomach.

"What are the extra sheets for?" she asked. "You're not sleeping on the floor."

He raised an eyebrow. "You're up for sharing a bed?"

Whoa. She hadn't actually thought that through, only that no way was he going to lay on what she assumed would be the grossest carpet in the whole world. "It's no big deal."

"I'll still use the extra sheets. I don't have anything to sleep in, and I'm not sure I could sleep in clothing anyway." He tugged his thumb on the waistband of his jeans. "Too constricting. So we'll each have our own sheets."

The cat slept in the nude, that's what he was saying. Flippin' great. He seemed to think that because she'd seen him naked, seeing him naked again wouldn't bother her. She couldn't tell him that, yes, it would bother her very much, thank you. As tired as her brain was, her body was awake and prickling like electricity in all the wrong places.

He slid the key into the lock and opened the door. "Nice," he said, drawing out the word.

Oh, boy.

He swept his arm toward the open door. "Ladies first."

She stepped in, her eyes going right to the round bed with the faded leopard-print bedspread. The bed that meant he was going to have to sleep in the middle because his feet would be hanging off the edge otherwise. Even worse, there was a large mirror above it. Metal loops sprung from the ceiling. There were pictures on the wall depicting hearts but on close inspection were actually composed of tiny pictures of erotic parts of the body.

Oh, boy.

Around the television were placards advertising the porn movies available on the pay channel. The pictures weren't exactly modest: a man dipping his tongue into a woman's cleavage in one, another man's face buried in ginormous boobs in another.

Even with the phony, sweet smell coming from an air freshener, the most erotic thing was still the smell of Eric and earth.

She glanced at him, also taking it all in with bemusement. He shook his head and his expression grew serious as he walked around the room, running his hands across the ceiling tiles and the fire sprinkler head. He cut the lights and studied the mirror on the ceiling.

"What are you doing?" she asked.

"Checking for cameras."

"Eww. You think someone might be taping us?"

"Never know with these kinds of places." He went into the bathroom and even looked under the toilet lid.

"And you would know this because . . . ?" She didn't want to think he hung around in sex spots like this.

He came out. "No, I don't frequent these kinds of places." He glanced around. "I'd rather have sex in the dugout of a ball field or a patch of woods in the park than a place like this."

Don't ask. Don't ask. "And I take it you have?"

His mouth curved in a half smile. "I like doing it in places that are just public enough to be risky. Got arrested once doing it on a bench in a ritzy neighborhood. Doing it in a place like this, that's so staged . . ." He shuddered theatrically. "Much better to be spontaneous, out in the open, breathing fresh air, even better to feel summer rain hitting your bare ass . . ."

He wasn't reminiscing about whatever woman he'd done that with. He was looking at her, his gaze sliding down her body. Her eyes filled with the heat of imagining him making love in the rain, his bare ass . . .

"I need a shower," he said, turning abruptly.

And wash off that intoxicating mix of male and earth? "No." He turned at her harsh order. Because she'd actually said it aloud. For all to hear. For him to hear. "Uh, I want to take one first."

"Go ahead."

Even through the jeans, she could see his erection straining against the denim. He walked to the curtains and looked out. She remembered the heady feeling of arousing him when she'd astrally projected to him, but she should not be feeling it now. Shouldn't have felt it then either.

She pulled out the fluffy Marilyn-Monroe-like nightie she'd taken from the wardrobe, all Magnus's mother had for nightwear. She took a shower, and even the flow of the water seemed more sensual, like hands moving over her skin.

Get a grip. You heard him. Getting involved is a bad idea twenty ways around. Yeah, he's nice to have around while that psycho creep is out there, but after that, there's no need to see him again. Then you can go find that cute guy who works at the bookstore who's always hinting about getting together and get the horny out of your system.

Except that guy wasn't big and muscular and gorgeous and dangerous.

She finished, put on the nightgown, made sure the fabric didn't reveal too much, and walked out.

Eric was lying on the bed, wearing only his jeans, eyes closed, hands behind his head. Which made his biceps look even bigger. A sigh escaped her mouth, soft as a whisper. Being able to look at him like this, without him knowing, made the hunger yawn as it came fully awake. She had this illogical urge to run her fingers along the bottom edge of his rib cage and then the waistband of that too-constricting pair of jeans. Why couldn't he have been a scrawny, ugly guy? Would that be too much to ask?

She cleared her throat. "Shower's all yours."

He cracked his eyes open, and then they opened completely. He shot to a sitting position. "Oh, no, you are *not* wearing that."

Heat flushed in her cheeks, and she walked to her duffel bag.

"It's all I have. I wasn't planning to share a room with you. As you say, what's the big deal?"

"Do you have to ask? Oversexed male with blue balls who was recently teased by a sexy nymph. A man can only take so much, and I'm stretched as tight as a rubber band that's been pulled a hundred feet apart." He jabbed his finger at her. "You prance around in that at your own risk."

"I'm not 'prancing' around." She crossed her arms over her chest. "You're sleeping naked. It's hardly fair that I can't wear what I want and you can."

"Look, if you can't help yourself, I'm all for being sexually attacked in the night. Can you say the same?"

The image of his hands sliding over her breasts rocketed through her mind. "Fine, I'll change."

He pushed to his feet and walked to the bathroom. She inhaled softly as he passed. Dreamy . . .

It was lust, a purely physical need for touch, for connection. Maybe it was her reckless streak. Damn. A part of her wanted him. *Well, you're not going to get him*, she told it. *Besides, he's not going there either.*

She listened to the water hitting his body, imagining him running a soapy cloth across his stomach and his chest, the bubbles sliding down his skin. It was only because she'd seen him naked that she could imagine it so damned well.

She put on one of the other dresses and went to work pulling down the comforter and inspecting the sheets. They smelled fresh and clean, no stains. No signs of bed bugs in the creases of the mattress. It was while she was crawling across the bed doing her inspections, with her butt facing the bathroom door, that Eric walked out.

She heard something like a groan as she spun around, and had to swallow hard at the flare of hunger in his eyes. "Checking for . . . bugs. Didn't find any. You know, bed bugs," she finished lamely.

Holy crap. He was wearing a towel wrapped around his waist, and the terry cloth didn't even begin to camouflage what the denim did. She quickly averted her gaze up his chest, water still dripping down from towel-dried blond hair. This sharing a room business suddenly became a really bad idea. Then her gaze hit on the bruise on his stomach.

"Holy crap." She got to her feet and came closer. "Sayre did that when he kicked you."

"No big deal." He turned and tried to look at his back. "What's the scratch look like?"

"Not horrible, won't need stitches, but . . . ouch." She ran her finger alongside the long scratch. "It's clean." He smelled clean. She'd never been aroused by a man's scent before, but the mix of soap and clean skin tickled through her body. Not a bad substitute for earth and male, actually.

"What's the story with the eye tattoo?" she asked, because talking about anything was better than standing there sniffing him and touching his back.

He turned his right arm to look at the tattoo, inadvertently flexing the muscles. "Zoe had a dream about this symbol, and we decided to adopt it as our logo. The program our parents were in was called BLUE EYES. The O is for Offspring. The slashes in the iris look like an R, for Rogues."

"Far out." Now she was touching the lines of the tattoo, and quickly stopped herself and stepped back.

He picked up the stack of sheets. "You have any tattoos? I was a tattoo virgin before this."

She nodded. "Mine aren't for public viewing."

He raised an eyebrow and smiled in that way he did whenever something sensual came up. Slightly crooked, devilish, heat flaring into his eyes. His gaze dropped down to see if he could catch a glimpse, and she felt his eyes slide over her. His smile and the spark disappeared, though, when he looked at her thighs. The scars.

She slipped beneath the comforter completely, not wanting to give him the opportunity to pry. "We should get some rest. It's already late."

He apparently got the hint. "Yeah."

He walked to the window and looked out again, giving her a view of his broad back, tapering down to a narrow waist, and that ass tightly wrapped in a blue towel. He turned back and walked over to his bag. The juxtaposition of the package of Ho Hos and the gun was jarring. He held out the package to her, offering it. She shook her head. He set the gun on the nightstand within easy grasp.

Suddenly she was very glad they were sharing a room. She felt safer with him there, next to her.

Eric tore open the cellophane and sank his teeth into the chocolate cake, checking out the front window again. After a few seconds, he flicked off the light, having left the one in the bathroom on. He laid out his sheets, untied the towel, and got into bed. She saw a flash of pale skin, the curve of his behind, and then he tossed the top sheet over him. She could smell chocolate, and it made her mouth water.

He flopped onto his back with a sigh, looking at the ceiling. "Now that's different."

She looked up, too, startled to see the two of them lying in bed together. Like people about to have sex. Or people who had just had sex. Except they looked too tense to have just had sex. He looked too . . . hard. The sheet was draped across his waist, but she couldn't mistake the rise in the fabric.

Stop looking!

Mm, touch instead.

She blinked at the naughty voice in her head, rolled over and faced the other direction.

"Are you sure you're comfortable sharing a bed?" he asked, damn him, tuning into her discomfort.

She rolled back over. "It's weird, that's all. Being in bed with a man . . ."

"You're not having sex with," he finished.

"That and . . . I've never slept with a guy before. I mean, spent the night."

He raised an eyebrow. "You never spent the night with Jerryl?"

She shook her head. "He had this thing about sleeping alone."

He looked at her, and she couldn't figure out what he was thinking. Finally he said, "What about other guys?"

"I can't believe I'm having this conversation with you." She shook her head, but he was still waiting for an answer, and what did she care if he knew? "I've only been with two guys before Jerryl. They weren't special." Just a way to connect with another human being. "I didn't want to spend the night with them. Didn't seem right somehow."

She saw the slightest smile on his face. Not the sensual one, but an intrigued one. Why the hell should that intrigue him?

"Anyway, it's just weird." She scooted as far to the edge as she could get. The reflection startled her, him laying on his back, their hands only an inch apart.

He had never been in love before. Neither had she. So they were even on that score. She was sure he'd probably spent the night with loads of women, though. Probably held them, curled his body around theirs, the scent of heated sex on their skin. Even though she was imagining it about other women, the image stirred her body.

But he'd never *loved* a woman, and for some reason that made a smile tug at her mouth. She turned to her side, facing him. She watched the rise and fall of his chest, the way his exhalation sank his stomach into a hollow. His Adam's apple bobbed when he swallowed. His eyelashes flicked when he blinked.

The words from her favorite Metric song pounded through her mind, *Help, I'm alive*. Her heart *was* beating like a hammer. And it *was* hard to be soft, tough to be tender.

For so long she wanted him dead. Here he was, alive, breathing, and all she could feel was gratitude that he was.

"I'm glad I didn't kill you."

The words hung in the air, and then he turned his head to her. "What?"

"I'm glad I didn't kill you."

He smiled. "I'll bet you say that to all the guys." The absurdity of that made her smile, and his smile grew even wider. "You know, that's the first time I've seen you smile. You've got dimples."

She was smiling way too much, and oh, yes, heart definitely beating like a hammer. "Good night." She flipped over, squeezing her eyes shut. *Don't, don't, don't get pulled into him. It's got wrong all over it.* There was a more dangerous pull beyond the physical one. The part that responded to his tenderness, his protectiveness. Those two parts mixed together were an explosive, intoxicating brew. Damn him, why couldn't he just be an asshole? That's what she'd expected, even what he'd said he was. But he'd shown her moments of tenderness that had torn down pieces of that wall around her heart.

" 'Night," he said.

She could feel his body heat radiating toward her. She wouldn't be getting to sleep anytime soon. As scary as the fire nightmares were, she was afraid of a whole new dream tonight. Something erotic and sweaty, bodies sliding against each other, breathing heavy, naked . . . sometimes even good dreams were scary.

CHAPTER 12

Neil pulled into the parking lot of the Love Shack. He killed the engine and stepped out, quietly closing the door. He sniffed the air. Mm, lots of emotions here: fear of getting caught, shame, and lust. He breathed them in, letting them shimmer through his body. And somewhere here were Eric Aruda and Fonda Raine. What were their emotions?

His brother had found them. Damned annoying that he had to rely on someone else's skills for that. Especially Malcolm's. He wasn't sure what they drove or exactly which room they were in. Malcolm couldn't get that exact. But Neil would find them. The hunt was as much fun as the kill. There were people around, so he wouldn't be able to use his skills in a spectacular way. Drawing attention to themselves was the ultimate sin. Not that they were following the rules anyway, not completely.

He walked down the concrete strip, pausing in front of the first motel room and listening. Sensing. The woman was shaming the man, calling him names and, if the slapping sound was what he thought, spanking him. People were so odd. They got swamped by their emotions, and that made them weak. Much better to eat them as a delicacy and not be eaten by them.

He sensed the shiver of electricity—the Geo Wave, it was called—of another one of their kind. He scanned the surroundings and his gaze alighted on a man wearing black several yards away. Neil's lips curled into a sneer as he approached the man.

"What are you doing here, Pope?" he asked. "You are not assigned to us anymore."

"And you are not supposed to be here. Leave now."

"You're assigned to them?" Neil nodded toward the motel. "To assassinate?"

"Leave."

He couldn't be sure, not enough to challenge him right there. Pope's powerful abilities were legendary, though Neil had never seen them firsthand. He hated backing down but wasn't about to go head-to-head with him here and now. Besides, an altercation would alert his prey.

He turned and left. Several minutes later he called Malcolm, who asked, "Is it finished?"

"No. Pope was there."

"What the hell is he doing here?"

"Getting in my way. He ordered me to leave. I didn't want to make a scene so I obliged. I was not pleased."

"Pope isn't supposed to use his abilities on you, or interfere with our official tasks, but he can cause problems with our unofficial ones. The question is, why was he there? What does he know about the Offspring?"

"We didn't exactly have a chat," Neil said. "I could take care of him as we did the last one."

"Only if necessary. We don't want to take any risks. We have two factions to consider. I have a lead on the whereabouts of the rest of the Rogues, who must be in hiding together. Darkwell was in the process of obtaining the original blueprints for Lucas's art gallery. I don't know why, but he must have suspected something. I'm pursuing that now. I will continue to monitor all of their abodes for the time being, but I suspect they've been warned."

"And I will take care of these two. It's only a matter of time."

Eric lay there listening to Fonda breathe. She remained awake longer than he thought she would, but finally her breathing settled into a deeper pattern. After those surprising words about being glad she hadn't killed him, he had to lighten the moment. Then he'd gone and made her smile, and those dimples, and the light in her eyes, and the very sad thought that she didn't smile much . . . She'd never spent the night with a man before. That had settled right into his gut, like a warm gift of melted chocolate.

Not a gift to you. Forget that. Last thing you need is to feel anything.

The sleep deprivation was tricking out his mind, weakening him. He didn't want to give in to the illusion of what he felt for her, or thought he felt.

He finally dozed, snatching at sleep, seconds here and there before bobbing back to the surface. A sound snapped him fully awake. Someone beside him, lifting the gun from the nightstand. Fonda . . . pointing the gun at him.

What the . . . ? He lunged for her, twisting her

around and onto the bed, his fingers squeezing hers on the gun. Her eyes were blank. Hell. Sayre.

"Fonda, wake up!" He didn't want to hurt her, but he had to stop her.

She kept struggling to bring the gun barrel back to his face. He pinned her wrist to the bed.

"Fonda!"

She was looking at him, but it wasn't her in there. Her mouth twisted in a faint, evil smile before she blinked. Her eyes widened. "Get your hands off me! What are you doing, coming on to me in my sleep?"

Yep, she was back. He gave her a sardonic look. "Hardly my style." He pulled her hand in front of her, and she could see her fingers holding the gun. "You were about to wipe me."

She released the gun, and he climbed off her and took it. She sat up, looking spooked. "Sayre."

He nodded.

She shuddered. "He was in me. I remember the dream and then I felt him coming in. I couldn't do anything to stop him. He was talking to me, 'Let me in, darlin',' and I couldn't fight him." Her eyes were still wide as she remembered, her arms around herself.

He wanted to put his arms around her, too, but stopped himself. "He's never come into me, but that's what he does."

"If you hadn't woken me up—"

"But I did." He did touch her then, rubbing her shoulder for a second before pulling his hand back. "It's all right now."

"Is this what it felt like with Jerryl, someone twisting their way into your head, the violation of it?" She

looked at him. "No wonder you wanted to kill him."
She looked at him, her eyes intense. "I knew that's
what he was doing, but I never thought about it from
the other side. Your side."

"It's way damned different when you see it that
way, isn't it?"

She put her hands to her temples. "I understand
why you did it." She grimaced slightly, as though she
were in pain. "What I don't understand is why you
didn't kill me. I was the enemy, too."

He could breathe easier for some reason, like
something had opened in his chest. "You weren't *my*
enemy." He gave her a small smile. "I'm glad I didn't
kill you, too."

Her laugh was soft, halting.

He said, "You asked me what I felt when I killed
Jerryl. I said triumphant and relieved. I downplayed
the relief part." He stared past her. "Having him
in my head like that, knowing he could force me to
do something against my will, scared the hell out of
me. Those seconds when he was trying to get me to
shoot my people were the most terrifying in my life.
I've always been strong, tough. But I wasn't strong
enough."

He met her gaze, and he could tell she knew exactly how that had felt. "Killing him was the only
thing I could do. But no, I didn't enjoy it. I thought I
would, but I didn't." He clenched his fist. "I used to
get a rush using my powers. I set buildings on fire to
punish criminal employers, but it was always after
hours when no one was there. Before I knew I could
do it from a distance, I was sending hateful thoughts
toward my stepmother and set the house on fire. She

was too drunk to get herself out and died. That was the first time I killed someone. I didn't mean to kill her." Guilt still gnawed at him over that.

"Your mother set herself on fire by accident, right?"

He nodded. "I learned that before I knew about my ability, but fire had always drawn me. The first time I discovered I could set fires psychically . . ." He shook his head, remembering how it had blown him away. "My father and I had an argument. I was thirteen, I was angry, and afterward I was staring at a patch of ground in the backyard, and suddenly—*poof!*—it went up in flames. I stomped it out, stunned. Then I tried it again, this time on purpose and farther from the house. It happened again. I watched the flames, the way they danced and spat . . . it was sensual. Intoxicating." He looked at her. "But I didn't feel that way when I burned Jerryl. And I won't feel that way when I nail Sayre either."

She tilted her head. "Thank you for telling me that."

He heard a car door close and leapt off the bed. An engine started. He cracked open the drapes and looked out to the parking area. A man stood in the lot as a car tore out, spitting gravel. He was taller than Eric, though not as big. His shaved head reflected the red neon light from the sign. The man turned and looked right at him, as though sensing he was being watched. Eric held his gaze and felt a ripple of electricity go through his chest. The guy wasn't there to catch a quickie. He was there for them.

"We're out of here," he said, snapping the drapes shut. "There's a guy out there who's giving me the creeps."

"Not Westerfield?"

"Totally different dude."

She scrambled off the bed. He pulled on his clothes, which he'd left near the bed on purpose. He checked the window again, but the man wasn't in sight.

She stepped out, wearing dark orange linen pants and a wraparound shirt. Every time he saw her, she looked completely different. "I'm ready," she said, picking up the bag.

He grabbed his bag and the gun and peered outside again. Still no sign of the man he'd seen before. He remote-viewed, scanning the parking lot. "I don't see him at all, but I'm pretty sure it wasn't a hallucination." He looked at her. "So far I'm not that sleep deprived. But we're out of here anyway."

They crept out of the dark room and into the night.

CHAPTER 13

Eric and Fonda drove until the sun began to paint the sky shades of purple and pink. She'd never witnessed a sunrise before, and had now been awake to see two in a row. She picked up a magazine off the floorboard, one she'd bought at a convenience store the day before. Her guilty pleasure had been drinking up celebrities' drama and angst. Cheating sports stars, scandalized politicians, and the latest divorce . . . well, compared to her ordeal, they all seemed boring. She dropped it to the floor and turned to Eric, taking in his profile, square jaw and strong, short chin.

"I'm ready to find Westerfield," she said.

"Okay. I'll find a place to pull over."

Fifteen minutes later he drove through the entrance to a cemetery. "Do graveyards bother you?" he asked, seeing her take in the rows of gravestones.

"Nothing bothers me." Not the remains of the dead, not nightmares about Jerryl's death, and especially and certainly not Eric. She got out of the truck and started walking toward the stones. Some were very old. Those were the ones she liked best, old-fashioned names like Beatrice and Herbert, dual stones for husband and wife. The ones where only the husband or wife was gone always pulled at her heart, like plucking one string of a guitar. One person left behind, waiting to die so he or she could join their love.

She sank to the grass on the other side of a dual headstone, tracing the groove of the heart on the granite. A cold sense of aloneness swept through her, but she erased any mournful expression she might have on her face at the sound of his footsteps coming close.

"Hiding?" he said, leaning on the top of the stone and peering down at her.

"As if I could." Her hand dropped from the groove. "Just getting into the mind-set." She leaned against the stone, and the cold seeped into her back as she closed her eyes. She heard him come around and kneel beside her on the crunchy grass and fought not to look at him.

"He'll be able to see you, right?" he asked.

She nodded. "I'll be quick, in and out. Enough to see where he is."

"If you pinpoint the location, even in a general way, I can remote-view it more carefully. I can do it from a distance, like a few hundred feet above the target, so he won't sense me. We don't want him to know we're looking for him."

They were using their skills in tandem. It felt strange, but she supposed it made sense. "All right."

"Be careful."

She cracked her eye open at that. "What do you mean? About being seen?"

He shrugged. "I don't know what I meant. It just came out."

"He can't do anything to me in my etheric form."

His eyes looked darker than usual, the pupils slightly dilated. "You don't know what he can do."

She tried to hide her shiver at those words.

Her hands flattened on the cool damp ground. She settled into her comfortable spot, sliding through the clouds and the place where the humming started. Just when it got so loud it hurt her ears and shook her body, the clouds parted.

She was sitting in the front seat of a car, Westerfield at the wheel. He was looking out the side window, but, as though sensing her, started to turn her way. She disappeared but kept the connection, reappearing in the backseat behind him. Funny how her heart was pounding as though she were physically there. She took note of the signs they passed.

He turned onto a gravel road overrun with weeds, got out and unlatched a gate. The sign next to the road read CAMDON AIRFIELD. It was faded, the paint cracked, reminding her of the shantytown flea market. He got back in the car and turned down the radio. He sensed her, because his body was alert as he slowly turned.

She pulled out.

Eric was sitting close, too close, watching her intently.

"Back off, Aruda," she said. "You're in my space."

"I'm keeping an eye on you. Whenever one of my people goes off somewhere, we always watch for any signs of trouble."

She pushed to her feet. "I'm not one of your people, and I've been doing this for a long time without anyone watching over me."

He stood, too. "You haven't targeted someone like Westerfield before."

"I can handle it."

She was being bitchy. The bitchiness bounced through her like a pinball, making her restless even as fatigue started to drag on her. She'd let him see her in embarrassing and vulnerable positions twice, and that was enough.

"Darkwell never said there was any danger in leaving our bodies," she said.

"Sure, he's going to tell you that when he wants you to do his bidding? And he probably had no idea if there was danger or not."

The thought of that thread breaking . . .

"Did you find him?" he asked, derailing that startling train of thought.

"Yes." She told him about the sign.

"I'll call my people, have them look it up on the Internet."

My people this, my people that. Did he have to rub it in? He checked on their status and then gave whoever he was talking to the information she'd given him. He spread the map on the ground and traced his long finger along the roadways as he listened. "Got it. That's not far from here. Thanks." He looked at her. "It's in a town named, of course, Camdon. I'm going in for a closer look."

He reclined on the ground outside the line of the graves, she noticed, cradling his head with his hands. He hadn't asked her to watch over him. When he closed his eyes and started breathing heavily, she quietly stepped closer. His eyes twitched beneath his closed lids and the veins in his neck stood out. His body trembled. What would he look like if he ran into trouble? How would she pull him back?

"I see the airfield," he said, surprising her.

She couldn't communicate while under, or at least she'd never thought about trying.

"He's opening the doors to a hangar. There are a few hangars, but they're all empty. Not this one. There's an old plane inside. He's walking to a tool chest in the back . . . taking out keys. I can't get much closer without him sensing me."

He opened his eyes, and she took a step back and looked into the distance, as though she hadn't been watching his every twitch. He pushed to his feet, grunting with the effort.

"Do you get tired after you remote-view?" she asked.

"Yeah. That's why I try not to stay too long. Otherwise I'm out. And we don't have time to wait. He's getting that plane ready, and who knows if he'll come back."

"How far away are we?"

"Probably about forty minutes."

She had that time to rest, but he didn't, not if he was driving.

Once they were in the truck, he turned to her. "Get some rest," he said, as though reading her mind.

"What about you?"

"I'll be fine. My fatigue comes in waves, and for now I'm fine."

"How are we going to get rid of this guy?"

"He blocked me from torching him before, but he might have been expecting it. I need to take him by surprise." He started the engine but looked at her. "Will that be too hard, seeing me do that?"

She shook her head. "Not with Westerfield."

It touched her that he cared. When she met his

eyes, meaning to tell him that she appreciated that, his eyes caught her attention again. "Eric, your pupils are dilated."

He looked in the rearview mirror, blinking as he took in his reflection. "That's weird. Maybe it's the early morning light. Or the aftereffect of remote-viewing."

"They were a little dilated before you remote-viewed. Now they're more so."

He put the truck into gear and pulled out. It wasn't the light. A shiver of unease flowed through her.

She closed her eyes but couldn't drop off to sleep during the drive.

As they entered the small town of Camdon, he said, "There's no need for both of us to go in. I can—"

"This *is* my war. You're not keeping me out of the action."

"I'm just saying—"

"No, don't just say anything about me staying put."

He gave her the look of an impatient parent, which annoyed her all the more. "Remember how he sent those boards flying? If something like that hits you, you're done for. Besides, my plan is to torch the guy, and I'd rather you not be around to see that."

"Oh, please. Just because you saw me get weepy, you think I'm vulnerable. Okay, you caught me at a weak moment. But I'm not weak. I told you I'd be okay if you torched Westerfield."

"Stubborn . . ." He mumbled the rest of the words.

"Bossy . . ." She mumbled stuff, too.

"Look, little girl, this is serious shit here."

"No kidding. And would you stop calling me that!"

His gaze went from her head down to her toes. "You are little. And you are a girl. Unless there's something I should know—"

She smacked his arm. "You are such a—"

"Wonderful—"

"Overbearing—"

"Handsome—"

"Jerk. Sometimes," she added, because he had a playful gleam in his eyes, and she didn't want him to think she was taking this seriously. She raised an eyebrow at him. "Would *you* stay back for any reason?"

"No."

"Remember, I'm like you. Stubborn, yes. So I'm in."

He pulled off just before the entrance to the airfield. Another sign said CLOSED, no surprise there. He shut his eyes and, she guessed, remote-viewed the hangar.

"He's going through what I'm guessing is a preflight check. The plane looks old. I went up high to see the layout of the area." He pointed to the tree line on the right. "If we follow that, and stay inside the trees, we can get to the hangar without being seen."

"Can't you get him psychically, without even going to the hangar?"

"I thought about that, but if I can't, then he'll know we're here. I want to be right on him."

"We can't shoot him, though."

"We can shoot him; he just heals fast. It might still buy some time, sap some of his energy. And speaking of—"

"I won't forget I can freeze time."

"Let's go. We need to keep our conversation to a minimum. We don't know what this guy can do. Petra has extraordinary hearing, so he might, too."

They crept through the sparse pines, barely a cover at all. No sign of Westerfield, but as they got closer, they heard sounds coming from the hangar. They stalked the large metal building from the rear angle, sliding along the wall toward the opening. They peeked through the grimy window. There he was, standing in front of the plane's prop. He turned the prop horizontal, grabbed hold of both sides, and pulled the plane toward the opening.

They ducked down and crept to the side of the opening. The sound of grunting echoed from the cavern of the hangar. The edge of the wing came into view, then the plane, small and old, like Eric had said. Beneath the wings and body was a suspended strip of thin metal. The plane stopped on the tarmac outside the hangar, and Westerfield placed blocks in front of the wheels.

He pulled a cell phone from his pocket and walked back into the hangar. His voice floated from the hangar. "I've got the plane loaded. It would be nice to have some help with this. I've spent the whole morning getting this piece of crap ready . . . Yeah, I know, you've got more important things to do." Bitterness seeped into his words. "I do like the killing part, but this isn't the kind of killing I enjoy. None of these people will die directly by my hand."

My God, he was whining about it. She shivered in disgust. And people were going to die. *People.* More than one.

He came out again and climbed inside the plane. "I don't get to see them gasp their last breath, or groan in their death throes. I don't get to smell their confusion, their shock or fear."

She remembered how he'd smelled her fear. She

looked at Eric, and he seemed to know what she was thinking: *No emotions.*

"It's almost ready. I've still got to check for water in the fuel tanks. I'll let you know when I'm done." Westerfield pocketed the phone and climbed back out again. "Forgot to take the chalks out."

Eric counted on his fingers. *Three. Two. One.* He stepped around the side of the building. She followed, ready for anything, holding the gun to her side.

Westerfield looked up, his eyes wide. They'd taken him by surprise, but their advantage evaporated. She saw the strain on Eric's face, but Westerfield didn't go *poof.* He held out his hand, and Eric flew backward. Then his eyes locked onto her. He pushed her, too, and she hit the asphalt hard, feeling the bite of it on her arm. Her gun skittered several yards away.

He advanced on them like a robot then. Eric looked for her as he jumped to his feet. Westerfield waved his arm like a symphony conductor, and a long metal rod lying inside the hangar flew off the ground right at Eric. She couldn't scream fast enough to warn him.

So she froze time. The metal rod was suspended inches from Eric's face. She ran toward him and pushed him out of the trajectory. Time resumed, and the rod bounced on the ground several yards behind him.

Westerfield narrowed his eyes. "How in the hell do you do that?"

He waved his hand with a snapping motion, and she went flying into Eric. Their bodies collided, sending them both to the ground. Eric gave her a fierce look. It said, *We're not going to make it.*

She gave him one back. *Yes, we are.*

The roar of the airplane engine filled the air. Except Westerfield wasn't in it. He was directing it, at them. Eric jumped to his feet, yanking her up with him. Westerfield was smiling, a satisfied smile that pissed her off. Eric, too, to judge by the snarl on his face.

"I'm going to distract him," she said. "Do as much damage as you can."

The plane was moving closer. She felt the suck of the air, the whining roar of the engine. She closed her eyes and projected herself behind Westerfield. Tapped him on the shoulder. He spun around, and Eric rushed him.

He threw Westerfield to the ground, his hands around his throat. The men struggled, and she raced toward them just as the plane moved up behind her. Run for the gun? No time. She had to distract Westerfield so he wouldn't do his wicked mind thing. Eric had a stranglehold on him, but Westerfield was moving enough to gasp for air and keep his strength.

She grabbed at his arms, digging her nails into his skin. The plane was behind them, the engine noise a hum in her brain now, the same sound as when she was projecting. Westerfield gasped, as though losing the battle. She didn't believe it, though.

She looked up. The plane was coming right at them. He was still controlling it. She felt her body lift, a crazy weightless sensation. Eric tilted backward. Westerfield pushed them toward the blur of the blades.

Can't win. No, can't give up!

He reared his arm back, as though to throw a ball at them. No, to give them a final, fatal push. Her feet left the ground. She felt the air sucking at her, pulling her in. Felt the vibration of the engine. Her body bumped Eric's. He grabbed her hand.

Stop. Time.

The engine stopped. Westerfield froze, his hand out toward them. She and Eric dropped to the ground. She blinked as he stared at the frozen blades.

"You're not frozen," she said.

"Move." Eric pulled her out from in front of the propeller. He faced Westerfield's still form and concentrated.

"Can't burn him, even now," he said, frustration grinding his voice to a fine point. "Get on the plane. I'll run him down like he tried to run us down."

The plane's engine came back to life as they climbed into the small cabin. Several silver canisters sat inside, with lines coming from them.

"Do you know how to fly?" she asked. "Or . . . drive?"

He'd jumped into the seat, and now took hold of the steering wheel. "I know enough to make me dangerous. A couple of years ago I had a friend who took me up in his plane a few times."

Westerfield scrambled out of the way as Eric aimed for him. "Can you freeze him again?"

She focused, but nothing happened. "I must be tapped out." She needed to learn how to hold the freeze longer.

"Where'd he go?" Eric's voice pitched higher as he strained to see where Westerfield had ducked. He turned in time to see him jump into the open doorway of the plane. But before Westerfield could do anything, Eric shot him. Westerfield fell backward into the plane's cargo area from the impact. Blood gushed from the bullet wound, but he was already holding his hand over it.

"Let's get out of here." Eric raced past him, grabbing her hand and jumping out of the plane and onto the tarmac with him.

The plane, now under no one's control, kept moving forward.

"Stay under it," he called out, tugging her beneath the moving body. "If he can't see us, he can't nail us."

"But the plane might," she said, eyeing the wheels. She'd learned to be quick on her feet long ago, though, and kept up with the movement.

"Stand behind me," he said, ducking in an attempt, it seemed, to stay in the plane's blind spot.

Westerfield was apparently more focused on taking off than finishing them off, because the plane turned, the engine whined louder, and then it started down the rutted and cracked runway. Eric stared, and a tree burst into flame near the end of the runway. Her heart started at the ferocity of the flames that licked into the sky, and potentially into the plane's path. It veered to the left, and Eric set another tree on fire, too. The wheel on the left went through it, but it didn't stop the plane's forward momentum. In seconds it was a speck in the sky.

He looked over at her. "You all right?"

She twisted her arm and grimaced at the scrape. "Funny how it hurts more when you look at it. I'm fine. You?"

"Pissed. How are we going to kill that son of a bitch? We'd better get out of here. He might be on the phone now with whoever he was talking to earlier, and I don't feel like another foray into the woods."

"What about the fire?"

"I'll call it in so they can stop it before it spreads."

"Well, at least you're a responsible arsonist."

He didn't look amused by her sort-of compliment. "I wasn't always. And yet, I hate when people throw their cigarette butts out the window of their car." He glanced back once more into the sky. The plane was out of sight, the sound of its engine fading in the distance. "I want to know what was on that plane, and why it was more important to him than wiping us."

She looked at the now empty sky, but her gaze went to the trees. A terrible weight settled into her chest. "Whatever he's up to, people are going to die."

CHAPTER 14

Out in the Wal-Mart parking lot, Eric opened the tube of antibiotic, and Fonda stretched out her scraped-up arm. He held her wrist and gently rubbed on the salve. Her wrist was so small, everything about her was small, but she wasn't delicate. She was strong, brave, and vulnerable. Even in danger, walking that thin plank around the water tank, she had the grace of a cat. Her dichotomies twisted him, but it wasn't unpleasant. Bothersome, yes, but not unpleasant.

She sucked in a breath but let out nothing more than that.

They'd done a mini clean-up in the restrooms. He had bought some mousse, and for the first time in days actually did something with his hair. Her hair looked soft, and the pink stripe caught the sunlight. He wondered if her nearly white-blond hair was natural.

There are ways to find out . . .

He remembered that she'd told Magnus it was. He now wondered if her pubic hair was that color, too. He pushed that thought out, because it took next to nothing to get him hard under normal circumstances, and being with Fonda was nowhere near normal. Besides, he didn't want her to think he was getting off treating her scrape.

She had bought a tank top and a pair of jeans, and obviously some makeup. Her eyes were smoky, her lips pink, and at the moment they were in a tight line.

He focused on her arm, the fine hairs against her skin that the sunlight made golden. And those scars. "The cuts that left these scars must have hurt." They bugged him, mostly because she wouldn't tell him about them.

"Yes, they did," she said, but didn't sound upset.

"How were they made?"

Her jaw tensed. "It's none of your business."

It was, somehow, though he couldn't figure out just how. He would find out, but he sensed now was not the time to push.

"Any other injuries?" he asked, surveying what he could see of her. His gaze zeroed in on a speck of blood at her earlobe. "Your earring's missing." He reached out to touch the soft skin, but her fingers were faster, inspecting her lobe.

"Whew. No rip."

He leaned closer to get a better look. "Just a scratch where it tore out."

She turned, finding him only an inch away, and turned her head to remove the other earring. "I tore my belly button ring once, out dancing, and that hurt like hell. Took three weeks to heal, and it was another month before I could put a ring in it."

She had a belly button ring. And tattoos in private places. He knew he would see them, all of them. The knowing settled hard and deep in his gut, and lower. Wanting her was no surprise. It was the other things he felt that tangled up his insides, because he'd never felt them before. Wanting to protect her, to make things right.

Calling her "little girl" wasn't his way of demeaning her, even though she obviously took it that way. It was an endearment that slipped out.

"I think I've got a scrape back here," she said, lifting her shirt to expose creamy pale skin at her waist marred by a road burn slashing at an angle.

"Yeah." He wished he were Petra, where he could wave his hand and take it away. He rubbed more salve on that, the best he could do. His fingers spread, touching the skin around the scrape. He didn't want to stop touching her.

"You had a scrape on your back, from Sayre," she said, turning toward him and moving out of his reach. She took the tube.

"It's okay," he said, even though it was damned nice of her to remember.

She pinned him with a look and twirled her finger. He turned around, lifting his shirt.

She didn't do anything for a second, and he thought it must be pretty bad. Infected, maybe. Then he felt her touch, one finger lightly rubbing across a tender place midway up his back. It was the first time they'd touched each other, he realized, other than the necessary, in-the-moment kind of touching when they were running for their lives.

She took her time, and he closed his eyes and savored the touch, even through the pain. How long since a woman had touched him? He heard her soft breathing, felt her fingers sliding against places where he wasn't scraped, as he'd done with her. When he was intimate with a woman, most of them focused on his penis, as though it was his only erogenous zone. But Fonda's touch on his back, the least e-zone he could think of, still rocked.

"You've got a bunch of little scrapes across your back," she said, her voice light and airy. She rubbed the salve on various spots, taking her time. Her other hand came to rest against his lower back, as though to brace him. He sank into her touch, her fingers rubbing slowly over the same areas, over and over, no pain, just the feel of her, warm, sensual, and before he could stop it, a low moan escaped his mouth.

She backed up with a jerk, and when he dropped his shirt and turned around, she was fumbling with the cap. She wasn't looking anywhere but at that cap. "That should help."

"Thanks. It felt good." No need to skirt the issue. "What was that eighties song, something about a fine line between pleasure and pain?"

"The Divinyls," she said, opening the passenger door for the truck and leaning in to put away the tube.

He got in the driver's seat. She was digging around in her duffel bag. She'd gotten as caught up in touching him as he had with her. Was she going to shoot him now?

"What are you looking for?" he asked.

"I thought I had another pair of earrings in here. I feel naked without them."

"You've got twenty others in your ear." He gestured to the row of tiny hoops on the upper edge of her ear.

"Not twenty. Ten." She gave him a smirk. "I like big ones that dangle."

"Ya do, huh?" He lifted an eyebrow at the provocative tone in his voice, and when she realized the double entendre, her cheeks pinkened.

She swiveled back to the duffel. Two pictures fell out when she pulled out a smaller bag, one of Jerryl, and another of her and Jerryl with their cheeks pressed together. She was grinning, he wasn't. He didn't get to see much more because she grabbed them and tossed them back into the bag.

His chest felt heavy at the sight of them. She was still in love with the guy, or at least the idea of loving him. Even though they had gotten past the anger, he couldn't imagine she would ever forgive him for killing her lover. Jerryl would always be the ghost between them. Not that there was a them, he reminded himself.

She said, "I know where we could go for tonight. I spent a month there after . . . the fire at the estate, when everything fell apart and I needed to escape for a while. Westerfield couldn't find me there, apparently. It was only when I returned to my apartment that he was waiting for me. My father's house."

His body tightened. "The man who didn't believe you when one of his buddies tried to assault you? The guy who didn't protect you?" Maybe the man who'd cut her.

"I don't need his protection anymore. I didn't go there to be comforted. I went to hibernate in one of the bedrooms."

"Is this in a bad part of the city?"

"He moved out of the worst area a couple of years ago. It's not the best section but it's not terrible. My stepmother isn't supposed to get out of jail until next week. She did time for drug possession. My dad, he's supposedly clean. I didn't see him using while I was there, but I stayed to myself, so I can't be sure. It'll give us a place to crash, and you look wiped."

He *felt* wiped, as though his energy was slowly draining down to his feet and out his toes. The wave hit him hard. More so since using his pyrokinesis. "I just need some sleep." But he wasn't sleeping, and the lack of it was taking a toll.

"I'll drive," Fonda said. "I know the way, and you can close your eyes. Before you object—which I see you're going to—there's nothing unmasculine about being in the passenger seat." She got out, walked around to the driver's side, and opened his door.

He wanted to argue, but honestly, he couldn't think of a good angle. He was tired enough that his reflexes could be compromised, and he didn't want to endanger her because of his pigheadedness. He'd done that enough times in his life.

He got out and climbed in on the other side. He did close his eyes, for a few minutes at a time, but never dozed. "What part of D.C. does your father live in? I don't want to be too far away from Annapolis."

"It's on the east side. But I want to go into D.C. first."

"Not to where you live."

"No, I want to go by where I worked before I left to work for Darkwell."

"They probably know your employment history."

"I haven't been back there, other than for short visits, since I started working for Darkwell. They won't be watching the place."

He hated sitting there doing nothing, and in general felt plain ornery. He checked in with the Rogues and gave them the latest. It gave him something to focus on instead of Fonda.

Lucas said, "You all right? You sound tense, and that's saying a lot when it comes to you."

He scrubbed his fingers through his hair. "I'm antsy, like I have little electrical shocks running through me." Which reminded him, and he'd much rather talk about someone else than himself anyway . . . "How are you feeling, bro?"

"I have more energy than I've had for a while. And no storms of images, even with all the stuff you've got going on. It's frustrating, because I can't warn you."

"Yeah, but you're not dying, either."

"Well, there's that. I can't get into anyone's dreams, even Sayre's."

"Hopefully he's on my case now. I'll take care of him."

"Like you don't have enough going on."

He glanced at Fonda, who looked his way. He didn't like that she was involved in the Sayre business. "I can handle it. How are things with you and Amy?"

"I have nothing to say on the subject."

She must be in the area, and by the hard tone in Lucas's voice, things weren't good. "Remember, she did it out of love."

"Eric Aruda is not giving me advice about love. Right? Now I know you're an imposter, trying to elicit information from me."

"I'm just saying . . . you didn't see the look on her face watching you bleed. She was terrified."

"You didn't stop her."

"Lucas, you were dying. That woman loves you like nothing else. If I had stopped her, and you died, she would have killed me. Cut her out of your life and you'll cut out part of yourself."

Where was this coming from? He glanced at Fonda, who was probably listening to every word.

"What's going on with you and Fonda Raine?" Lucas asked. " 'Cause if how you're talking is any indication—"

"Nothing. We're just trying to stay alive. I'll check in with you later."

He signed off, paying attention to their surroundings as she drove into the city. He liked to know where things were, like hiding places and alleyways. Paranoia worked for him these days.

The area wasn't bad, a mix of ethnic restaurants and multiuse brick buildings. Chinese food sounded good about then. They'd grabbed a sandwich, but he was ravenous again.

Fonda had a wistful expression as she looked around. "My apartment is down that street," she said, pointing across him. "It was so good to be back that one day. I thought . . . I had hoped that I could come back to my life after . . ." She glanced at him, a sheepish look on her face. " . . . well, after killing you. But I wasn't sure I could. I wasn't sure what I would be."

She pulled up alongside the curb in front of a grouping of buildings, one stacked right up next to another but each retaining its own style. A whimsical pink sign announced PASTIMES: VINTAGE CLOTHING. She took it in, along with a deep breath before getting out.

He scanned the area as he too got out. He wished he knew what the guy working with Westerfield looked like. "Know Your Enemy" was one of his favorite Green Day songs, and now it had even more meaning. "Tell me again why we're stopping here."

"I want to get some clothes that feel comfortable for me. And, well, just in case . . . things don't go well,

I'd like to see the store and my coworkers one more time." She'd been looking at the storefront, but now turned to him. "I told them the truth, that I was being tapped for a government program that I couldn't tell them about."

She pushed open the door before he could reach it, and a bell dinged. A redheaded woman in her fifties was unpacking a box. She looked up, and a warm smile broke out on her face. "Fonda!" She got to her feet and swept Fonda into her arms. "Are you back? I told you I'd keep a spot open for you, and I meant it."

The gratitude on Fonda's face softened the hard edges. Her smile, though, was tempered by the truth. "I'm afraid not, Marion. We don't have a lot of time, but I wanted to stop by and say hi. I've got a few more things to take care of jobwise. Hopefully soon."

Marion leaned back and took locks of Fonda's hair in her fingers. "What have you done to your hair? It looked so soft and pretty last time I saw you."

"I needed a change."

Marion nodded toward a large picture of a cute blonde in a pink dress, and Eric realized with a start that it was Fonda. "I liked you better when you looked like that."

Soft, without the dark smudgy makeup around her eyes, posing with her finger at her chin. Fonda before Darkwell and Jerryl and him. There were other blown-up pictures of her on the walls and columns, her blond hair tied back, lashes thick and dark. In one she wore a fringed dress, like something out of the sixties. In another, a two-piece short set with a crop top.

Some posters featured the woman who was walking up to the register with her gaze on him. "No wonder you're staying away. Who's this?"

Fonda's eyes widened when she realized she'd have to identify his role in her life. "Uh, this is Eric. He's a . . . coworker. Eric, this is Marion, the shop's owner, and Natalie, one of the employees."

Natalie, with black, straight hair that fell past her shoulders and eyes just as dark took his hand. "Pleasure to meet you." Those eyes took him in, head-to-toe, drawing out the words, "You're big." That didn't seem to bother her at all, not by the naughty smile on her face.

Fonda was watching, her eyes narrowed. "Not dating Chuck anymore, Nat?"

"Nope." She still hadn't looked at Fonda.

"You have a customer." Fonda nodded toward another young woman who was standing by one of the round racks holding a dress and watching them.

Damn, he hadn't been out among people in so long, he forgot the female attention he sometimes got. Normally he liked it, but he didn't care much now.

Marion looked at the posters with a smile. "I've had four customers who don't know you think those are pictures of Edie Sedgwick."

Fonda smiled. "I'll take that as a supreme compliment."

Marion drew Fonda's attention as she walked to a door behind the register. "I have some clothes for you, put them back in case you came by. They have your name written all over them."

"Oh, you shouldn't have," she said, but her smile returned as she focused on Marion, who was coming back with hangers of clothing. She hung them on a rack near the register.

Fonda's face glowed as she looked through the

outfits, the hangers clacking together. "Groovage. Thanks, Marion."

Marion looked at Eric. "Fonda went from a customer who spent more time here than at home, I think, to an employee, to manager. She knew how to sell, and the customers love her. Everybody misses her, so hurry up and finish that assignment of yours so she can come back to us."

"I miss it here," Fonda said, trying to hide her reaction to Marion's praise. As though she wasn't used to getting it. Well, she probably wasn't, and he knew why she spent more time here than at home. He doubted Marion did.

He felt that tightness in his chest again, picturing Fonda as a teenager, basically on her own. He couldn't wait to meet her father. His fingers flexed at the thought of it, and of what he wanted to do to the man.

Fonda zoomed over to a rack of earrings like a nail to a magnet. She was a kid again, enraptured by big plastic earrings, a huge smile on her face. He felt a tickle in his chest and coughed to dislodge it.

"I need some pajamas, too," Fonda said, setting three pairs of earrings on the counter.

The women wandered over to a rack in the back, and Natalie went with them, peppering Fonda with questions. He could hear her rapid whispers as he grabbed a couple of pairs of jeans from a rack in the men's section. "Hot damn, Fonda, you *work* with him? Is he a spy or something?"

"Or something," Fonda replied, glancing toward him. "Something else is more like it."

"Is he single?"

"I guess."

"You two . . . you're not . . ."

"*No.*"

"Good." And Natalie made a beeline for him, a predatory smile on her face. "Let's see what we have for you, maybe something from the eighties."

She showed him different shirts, then took his arm, as though they were going onto the dance floor, and led him to the dressing rooms, carrying three shirts for him to try on.

"I don't need to try—"

"Nonsense. Let's see how they look on you."

Fonda took one look at the two of them and disappeared into one of the dressing rooms, closing the door with a loud thump.

Natalie was touching him, her fingers squeezing his upper arm. Funny, it didn't have the same effect as when Fonda put the salve on his back. This woman was clearly interested, which should have awakened his hungry body. It didn't normally take much.

Like when Fonda came out of the dressing room in a form-fitting dark red bodysuit. She twirled around, looking at her reflection in the three-way mirror. "It's dreamy. I love it!"

"Me, too," he said before he could think better of it. Soft velvet clung to her breasts, over her flat stomach, and hugged her hips.

She met his heated gaze but quickly turned away. "Do you have any ankle boots?"

Natalie took Fonda's arm this time, yanking her toward the back where racks of shoes covered the rear wall. "You are so lying!" she whispered beneath her breath.

"What are you talking about?"

"You, him . . . Puh-leeze."

Marion walked up to him, so he couldn't keep lis-

tening while pretending not to. He gave her a smile.
"Ring everything up." He pulled out his wallet.

The woman regarded him with a smile, but not a
thank-you-for-purchasing-our-clothes one. "Fonda's
a special girl. I sort of see her as a daughter, but she
doesn't let people in, not really. I can see she likes you.
I may not get another chance to say this to you, and
I'm probably out of line, but so be it. I didn't get where
I am by holding back in life. She may look tough
on the outside, but be gentle with her. She's not that
tough on the inside. And she's got a big heart."

He handed her several bills. "No disrespect intended, but you're wrong, ma'am. She doesn't like
me, not like that." If he'd told her how they'd gotten
together . . . he nearly laughed at the thought. "But I'll
do my best to protect her."

She smiled, studying him. "I see that you will. I'm
going to hold you to that."

"To what?" Fonda said, coming up to the counter.

"Watching out for your safety." The woman was
smooth, he'd give her that.

She handed him back way too much change.
"Employee discount," she said before turning to
Fonda. "Come back soon, hon. Your job will be waiting. Oh, almost forgot. I have a bag of discards for
you." She went into the room again, coming back with
a big fat garbage bag.

Fonda opened it and pulled out several articles of
clothing. She seemed as excited about that as about
the clothing Marion had put aside for her. "Thank
you! I know exactly who to give them to." She hefted
the large bag over her shoulder, like Santa Claus.

"Discards?" he asked, taking it from her.

She turned to him, and her face was glowing, a

beautiful sight. Dimples creased her cheeks. "The clothes that don't sell. I give them to women who don't have nice clothes. It's funny, I hated wearing old clothing I'd bought at consignment shops before I started coming here. But now that's all I wear, though these are considered vintage."

Sounded like a label meant to up the price, but whatever.

"You didn't have to pay for everything," Fonda said as they walked out.

"No big deal. She hardly charged anything anyway." He walked over to the fast-food Asian restaurant three stores down. "Nice lady. She cares a lot about you."

"I doubled her store's sales."

Funny how she didn't acknowledge the caring part. "Let's eat. I'm starved."

"You just ate two big sandwiches. And three packages of Ho Hos."

But she went in with him and ordered a bowl of wonton soup. He devoured a General Tso's chicken. She kept hopping up, walking to the front window, then sitting down again for another spoonful.

"Natalie sure liked you," she said after standing again.

"Who?"

"Natalie. You know, the tall, attractive, dark-haired girl. Duh."

He pretended he couldn't offhand think of who she was talking about by giving her a blank look. Actually, he couldn't picture what she looked like. He could, however, picture Fonda's sour look when Natalie had escorted him to the dressing room.

"The one at the store," she said, throwing her hands

up in exasperation. "And you call yourself oversexed. She was practically throwing herself at you."

He tried to hide a smile. Was she jealous? "Oh, her. I just thought she was a good salesperson. I did buy all the shirts she picked out for me."

She dropped back into the plastic seat. "You did that because you were hot for her."

"I did that because I liked the shirts. Do you want me to like her? I could ask her out sometime—"

"No." The word came out too firmly, and she waved it away. "You can do whatever you want. *After* this is over with."

He gave her a toothy smile. "Gee, thanks."

She frowned at him, looking adorable and sexy, especially because her lips were pursed. "Just don't come in the store when you pick her up for a date. That would be awkward."

"What about after we're married? Won't the kids think it's strange that Daddy never goes to Mommy's place of employment?"

Her mouth dropped open.

"Well, you've got me dating her, so might as well take the next steps. Her parents love me, but her cat only tolerates my presence. We'll probably get a dog next spring." He gave her a guileless smile.

"You are exasperating."

Damn, she *was* jealous. Astonishing. So when she was probably expecting a smart-assed reply, he said, "And you're adorable." Before she could react to that, other than her stunned expression, he got up and dumped his empty plate into the garbage.

"Wait a minute." She went to the counter and ordered a plate of chicken kung pow to go.

"We can eat it here," he said.

She was big into avoidance, he noticed. He'd thrown her, and now she wouldn't meet his eyes. "It's not for me. It's for George."

His eyebrows jumped up. "Who's George?"

"A friend."

Now it was his turn to feel a twinge of jealousy. She paid for the order and took the plastic container the lady handed her. He grabbed the bag of discards. They walked out, and she headed down the block. He alternated his gaze on their surroundings and her small tight ass in that bodysuit. It had a diamond cutout in the back that matched the smaller one in the front at her neckline. The collar went high, with a rhinestone at the center, and even on her short frame, the outfit made her look tall and lean. What word had she used? Oh, yeah . . . groovage.

He remained just behind her, keeping up with her brisk pace. Finally she slowed at the end of the block and looked to the left. "Hi, George!" She disappeared from view for a second. He turned the corner and saw her handing the container to a black man who was sitting on the sidewalk, an old mail cart beside him probably holding his worldly belongings.

"You a blessin', Fonda, a God-given blessin'," he said, taking the container with a weathered hand. "Thank you."

"You're welcome. I'll see you later."

She walked past Eric and toward the truck. George opened the box as though she'd given him a treasure. She'd even remembered the spork, which confirmed that this wasn't the first time she'd done this.

"That was awfully nice of you," he said, coming up beside her.

"He never begs, never asks for anything. He's just happy to be alive."

Fonda got into the driver's side while he put the bag in the back of the truck. She took a deep, fortifying breath when he got in. "Now, on to my father's. Let me handle him. Last time, I told him I was recovering from a friend's death. I don't know what I'm going to tell him this time."

Like how she was going to explain him.

Neil walked out of Pastimes and called Malcolm. "They were here not twenty minutes ago. She doesn't work here anymore, but she and Aruda stopped by for a visit."

So close.

"Let me check." A few minutes later Malcolm said, "She's in that area east of D.C. again."

The one he couldn't find her in before. He'd been swamped by all of the emotions saturating the air: despair, anger, self-hatred. As much as he loved emotions, all of them, they interfered with his finding Fonda the first time.

"I'll try again," Neil said, disconnecting. Maybe he'd get lucky.

CHAPTER 15

Fonda felt a heaviness as they neared her father's. The neighborhood wasn't bad, not compared to where she'd grown up. It was more of a forlornness that oozed from the small houses with peeling paint and mold, the people sitting in plastic chairs on their front lawns.

Eric was checking it out, though she couldn't tell what he thought of the area. He looked at her. "We don't have to come here."

She pulled up to a small house, parking on the curb. After cutting the engine, she stared at the house. "No, it's okay."

"You looked completely different when we pulled up to Pastimes."

She turned to him. "How did I look?"

"Happy. You look far from those now."

"I was just thinking, this is the first time I'll see my father knowing that he isn't. I wonder if he ever suspected."

"My father did. There was always something missing, something different in the way he treated my sister and me."

She could see his pain, just a brief flash. She didn't want to see that, so she opened the door and stepped out.

"I've got the bags," he said, grabbing them out of the back.

She shored up her shoulders and faced the house. One night, where she might feel safe.

He came up beside her. "If you feel this way about being here, why did you come before?"

"I wanted to feel comfortably numb. Like that Pink Floyd song. That's how I lived my life for a long time."

"How bad was it?"

She glanced at him, and his expression was grave. "It could have been worse. But you know, I can't really blame my father. He was needy, lost, after my mother's suicide. I have vague memories of different women being in and out of our lives. I was ten when he met Connie. I think she kept the darker side of herself from him while they dated; at least I'd like to think he didn't marry her knowing she was an addict. Maybe her drug use became more than occasional after they married.

"She was nice to me then, but not affectionate. They partied a lot, and then it wasn't only on weekends but during the week. People hanging around and drinking and getting high. I got a bad feeling about them, so I hid in my room a lot. I remember coming out to ask my dad a question about my homework and caught him shooting up. It scared and disgusted me.

"Things got worse when I was about thirteen. I'd

wake up and find him and Connie and sometimes other people sprawled about the living room. I had a hard time waking him up in the mornings." She remembered the first time she'd thought he was dead. "Connie was spending money like crazy, buying clothes and shoes. I heard them fighting about it, but I still saw bags and bags. Dad lost his job. Then one day the police told us we had to leave our house. I thought it was the worst thing that had ever happened, but he didn't even seem to care."

She turned to him, and he was listening so intently his jaw was rigid. She continued. "The good thing that came out of that life was it helped me astral project. I was fifteen when I first 'left' my body. Dad and Connie were having a huge fight. I was locked in my room, lying on my bed wishing I was somewhere else. And then . . . I was. I was at Pastimes. I saw the women who worked there, but I stayed out of sight. It was so bizarre, I snapped out of it. The next time I went somewhere I'd never been before: Hollywood. That's when I knew it was real."

"I still don't understand why you'd want to come back here. I wouldn't go to my father, not if his house was the only safe place in the world."

"See, we are different." She forced a smile. She hadn't told him everything, but some part of her wanted him to know. "Connie won't be here, thank God. And it's only for a night."

She walked to the front door and rang the bell. Her dad had fixed the house up some since he'd been clean. He had a job. It was a start, but not one she was counting on sticking. He'd failed too many times.

To her surprise, Connie opened the door, her long, narrow face made even longer by thick, dirty-blond hair. She wrinkled her nose. "What are you doing back?" Of course she'd heard about Fonda's stay. She looked back into the house. "Bruce, the slut's back! And she's got a friend."

Eric took a step forward, leaning down into Connie's face even though he was one step lower than she. "Don't talk about her like that."

Fonda put her hand on his arm. "It's no big deal. That's just the way she is."

Anger flared in his eyes, and he kept that gaze on Connie. "It is a big deal. It's disrespectful, mean, and says a lot more about you than her." He raked her up and down with that fiery gaze. "Don't let me hear you call her that again, or anything like that."

Connie's eyes widened. She wasn't much bigger than Fonda, and was stick thin, and Eric towered over her. "I didn't mean it."

"Then don't say it," he ground out.

Her father, Bruce, walked up to the scene, looking confused. "What's going on?" He took Fonda in and then Eric. "Who are you?"

"You let this woman call your daughter ugly names?"

Bruce bristled, but a shadow of guilt crossed his face. "It's her way of joking around. She does that to everyone." He even managed a nervous laugh. "That's just Connie."

"Well, Connie needs to learn manners, and you need to stand up for your daughter."

Fonda's face flushed, but not in embarrassment. What Eric was saying, doing . . . in the place where she always felt so small and inconsequential, he was standing up for her.

Her father's expression told her he knew Eric was

right, but his ego clicked into place and his shame hardened. He looked at Fonda. "Who is this?"

"This is Eric. He's my boyfriend." She linked her arm around his, as she'd seen Natalie do earlier. "We're heading east, and I wanted him to meet you." She shifted her gaze to Connie, narrowing her eyes. "I didn't know you were out of jail."

"I got out a couple of days early," she said with a sneer.

Okay, it was awkward as hell, and Eric's bluster had thrown her off her course. "Eric, this is my father, Bruce Raine. And my stepmother, Connie."

She *hmphed* and stepped back. "I do not want them in my home."

Fonda was about to back down, to leave, but stopped herself. Eric had stood up for her. She could damn well stand up for herself. She looked at her father. "We need to stay the night."

Would he take Connie's side, as he had from the beginning? Normally he was too cowardly to take a side. He'd always ignored Connie's vicious barbs, and anything else he didn't want to deal with.

Her father looked at Eric and then at her. "All right."

She released a breath, feeling warmth flow through her.

"Bruce!" Connie whined. "Did you hear how her boyfriend talked to me?"

"It's just a night, Connie. Let it go."

"Some guy who's only authority is screwing your daughter bullies me, and that's all you have to say?"

Eric shook his head, his mouth in a snarl. "I'm not sleeping with her, you clueless b—" He took a deep breath, pulling back the word with every bit of his strength. Oh, how wonderful it would have been to hear him call her that!

He nailed her with a look. "It's about respecting people, especially your family. By blood or not, she is your family. Show some decency. And some self-respect."

Connie looked at Bruce, who shrugged. "Please, let's put this aside," he said. "Fonda, I told you if you needed to come back, you could." He turned to Connie. "Let's not burn the house down."

Fonda gave Eric a knowing smile at that turn of phrasing. She stepped inside, ignoring Connie but feeling her hatred as though it were a laser beam. She looked at her father and mouthed *Thank you*. His eyes were still clear. He wasn't using yet.

"Did you get my message?" he asked her. "I called after you left."

She nodded. "I've been kind of busy."

He flicked a glance to Eric and gave her a tentative smile. "Well, you look more alive than the last time I saw you."

She wanted to laugh at the irony of that but tempered it into a smile.

"Do you want something to eat? We've already had dinner, but I can throw something together."

He was trying. She'd give him that. "We've eaten, thank you." She'd planned that on purpose, not wanting to sit through a meal and answer awkward questions. "Mostly we're just beat. I'm going to get a shower." She swung a look at Eric as she led him down the short hall to the bedroom she'd slept in before and whispered, "Dare I leave you alone with them?"

His mouth quirked. "Probably."

She pulled out the pajamas she'd bought at the store, new panties, and the bottle of shampoo.

"I noticed your father didn't ask where I was sleeping. Considering I'm your boyfriend and all."

"It was easier to call you that than explain the situation. And I'm sure he assumes we'll be sleeping together, despite your claim."

"I'll sleep on the floor. It's not right to share a bed"—he glanced at the bed, which was only a double—"in your father's house. I'd sleep on the couch, except it's too far away from you. Sayre, Westerfield, we just don't know when they'll turn up next."

He kept surprising her, and she didn't like it. She wanted him to be what she'd been told he was. He'd stood up for her. Defended her. Now he was showing respect. Dammit, he'd made her like him a little.

"Thanks," she said, unable to say anything more because her throat felt tight. *Don't make a big deal out of it.* She went into the bathroom and took a quick shower.

The pajamas clung to her body, but they weren't tight or risqué. That's the last thing she needed, to give Connie ammunition. Then again, Connie had been calling her a whore before she was even kissed.

It hit her then, that those words were empty. As Eric had said, they reflected Connie, not her. They had nothing to do with her. Even though she'd never been promiscuous, she had felt, deep in her cells, that she was a whore. With a rush of relief, she released that old belief, one she didn't even know she'd held.

Here, with her father and Connie, she had always been the mouse. It was outside in the 'hood that she was tough. Now, for the first time, she felt strong here.

She walked out, finding the bedroom empty. Uh-oh. Voices drew her to the kitchen, where she heard Eric and her father talking. She slowed, curious about what they were saying.

Her father: "Connie would kill me if she heard me say this, but . . . I appreciate what you said. You're right. I never said what needed to be said."

"My father was the same way," Eric said. "I guess a man gets so lonely, he'll put up with anything just to have company. Even at the expense of his children."

She knew he spoke from his own pain, but she heard no bitterness in his voice. No judgment. Just the facts. His stepmother wanted to ship him and his sister away. It hit her then that they'd both grown up with men who weren't their biological fathers, stepmothers who resented them, and the legacy of a mother who'd died too young. They had so much in common.

"It says a lot about you . . . that you had the balls to say that to both of us," her father said. "My daughter, she deserves a lot more than she's ever gotten. I hope you're that man."

Her eyes prickled, a sure sign she was going to cry. *No, not here.*

Eric's voice: "Yes, she does. I'll take care of your daughter. She's safe with me."

Holy crap. She felt the first tear well up, slide down her cheek. *Dummy, he's only playing the role of your boyfriend.* She swiped it away but couldn't erase how those words made her feel.

"I need to know something." Eric's voice had an edge to it. "She's got scars from cuts on her arms and legs. Did you make those cuts? Did you or Connie hurt her?"

She opened her mouth to stop the conversation, but her father said, "Fonda did it. She cut herself."

She uprooted herself from her spot and walked into the kitchen, feeling heat sting her cheeks. *Her father knew.* "Excuse us for a minute." She grabbed Eric's arm and pulled him back to their bedroom.

As soon as the door closed, she turned and jabbed her finger at his chest, which only hurt her finger. "You don't get to ask personal questions about me! You are not my boyfriend. My scars are none of your business."

He leaned down into her face and in the same fierce whisper as hers said, "Yes, they are."

She blinked in surprise. "And what makes you think that?"

"Because when I saw them . . ." He took her wrist and pushed up the sleeve, running his fingers over those old, faint scars. His voice changed, going hoarse and low. "All I could think about was someone cutting you, over and over. That thought made me crazy. Since you wouldn't answer me, I had to ask someone else." His fingers stilled against her skin, and he pinned her with his icy blue gaze. "What the f— Why would you cut yourself?"

Everything was all tight inside her, and she yanked her arm out of his grasp. "You wouldn't understand."

He ran his hand through his hair, shaking his head. "I'm trying to understand."

"Why? You know someone else didn't do it, and wasn't that your big concern? What are you going to do, beat me up for it?"

He leaned closer, his nose almost touching hers. "My big concern was who cut you and why. I have the who. Now I want to know why."

"It's none of your business." She couldn't stand the thought of him looking at her as though she were a freak. She walked back to the kitchen, where her father was pouring a glass of soda.

She stared at the glass, wondering if there was liquor in it. Those were the rules when going clean: nothing addictive.

"It's just soda," he said, lifting it toward her so she could smell it.

She waved the glass away. "I trust you." She wasn't sure she did, but the words came out easily enough.

"I'm sorry I told your boyfriend about the cutting. I thought he might slam me through the wall thinking I'd done it. You should have seen the crazy light in his eyes."

"I've seen it." In the bedroom, when Eric talked about the scars.

"You never told me why you did it."

"It's personal, Dad." She glanced into the living room. "Where's Connie?"

"She went over to Sam and Macy's."

Bad influences, both of them. "Because of me. I'm sorry."

He leaned against the counter, looking at her. "No, I'm sorry. I'm sorry I let her talk to you that way. Not only this time, but all those times. Your boyfriend's right. I was a lousy father, more interested in my own comfort than yours. I got messed up for a long time, wallowing in my misery and ignoring what was important to me." He looked at her. "You, my daughter. But I'm clean, and I intend to stay that way. Before you got here, Connie and I were talking. I told her I want her to stay clean. She said she wanted that, too, but I could tell she wasn't committed. You got to want it bad, badder than you want the drug. She's not there yet. Now that she's out, I'm not letting her back until I know she's clean."

Her heart lifted. "She's moving out for good?"

He nodded, and she stepped forward to hug him before she could even think to stop herself. *Thank you, Eric.*

"You can stay longer if you want," he said. "Both of you."

"Thanks, but we have to go in the morning." She didn't know for sure that Westerfield couldn't find them here, and she didn't want to endanger him. He was her father, after all. Not by blood, maybe, but by heart. "I'll be back. I promise."

"Bring Eric. I like him and respect him."

"Uh, we'll see." By the time she could come back, it would be over, and so would she and Eric. Why that stabbed at her chest, she didn't know, didn't want to know. "Do you have any extra blankets? Eric's sleeping on the floor."

"You're a grown woman. He doesn't have to do that."

"I know." She caught herself smiling. "But he was telling the truth: we're not sleeping together."

Bruce went into his bedroom and returned with two folded blankets. "You have a good guy there. I can tell he cares a lot about you."

She felt a wash of prickles over her body, wanting to hear why he thought Eric cared but holding back. *Too desperate,* she told herself, and besides, Eric was just putting on an act. "Good night."

Her dad looked like he wanted to hug her but didn't know how. Her body strained to lean toward him, to give him the okay. She didn't want to get too close to him, not yet. One hug was good for now. She could come back and see where he was later.

In the bedroom, she heard the shower running in the bathroom. Thank God. It gave her a few minutes to gather her thoughts, to steel herself against Eric. He might have saved her father. The thought made her all gushy inside. If he walked into the room at that moment she might throw herself into his arms and bawl in gratitude.

I'll take care of your daughter. She's safe with me.

The impact of those words slammed into her chest. She fell back against the door and squeezed her eyes shut. This was crazy, the way she felt about him.

She remembered the pictures of Jerryl in her duffel bag. She'd put them there the night she went out to kill Eric. To give her strength, resolve. She looked at them now and felt a distance from the man, barely smiling because he didn't like his picture being taken. She even saw her distance from him in photos of the two of them, her mouth smiling, but not her eyes. She'd been clinging to an illusion about what they had. It had only been sex. She'd called it making love because she didn't like the word *sex.* It conjured up people screwing in the living room, mindlessly high. But she and Jerryl had not made love. No one had ever made love to her. She tore the pictures into strips as she walked to the small garbage can on the other side of the dresser.

She was watching the pieces flutter down when Eric walked into the bedroom, wearing a pair of cotton, drawstring pants. She eyed them, pretty sure he hadn't gotten them at the shop.

He tossed a toothbrush and tube of toothpaste in his bag. "I haven't slept in clothes in years," he said.

"I can't stand the feel of anything on my skin when I sleep. Last night all I had was jeans, and I couldn't sleep in those. Or try to sleep. But to be a decent sort of fellow, I bought these at Wal-Mart." He raised his arms out. "Happy now?"

Well, no. "Ecstatic." She forced a smile. "Thank you."

Even though he probably used the same soap and shampoo she did, he smelled good and fresh and yummy. His hair stuck up from being towel-dried, and there were three drops of water in the indent of his chest. She had the absurd impulse to lick them off and had to swallow it down. The bruise from his fight with Sayre, the bastard, bloomed purple on his stomach.

He walked over to the duffel bag and dug around for a brush. The fabric of his thin pants tightened across his ass. A sigh began to come out of her mouth, and she coughed to cover it.

"You don't have to sleep on the floor," she said.

He eyed her and then the small bed. "Oh yes I do."

She perched on the edge of the bed. "Why do you say it like that? Do I squirm and kick in my sleep?" Did he not want to be that close to her?

He pinned her with a heated look. "Remember what I said about the stretched rubber band?"

"But I'm not wearing a little nightgown."

"You could be wearing a muumuu."

He took the blanket and sheets and laid them on the floor, giving her a moment to think about his comment. He didn't trust himself around her. Or he was simply horny.

The stupid words came out before she could even think better of it: "I could call Natalie, hook you up."

She was bluffing, of course, and her body tightened at the thought of him taking her up on it.

He gave her a look that indicated she'd said the dumbest thing on earth. Beyond *duh*. "You don't get it, do you? I'm not hot for just any woman. Ever since you astral projected to me, you are all I can think about. So being around you every minute of the last two days, in that damned nightgown, or in the dress you got at Magnus's, that red jumpsuit, *hell*, talk about torture, or even in those pajamas where I can see just enough of your stomach to tease me with the glint of your belly button ring, to taunt my imagination about your tattoos in private places and imagine what the rest of you looks like, is driving me crazy. But from what I've seen, like in that towel, you're delectable, just enough curve, tone, proportioned perfectly, that sharing a bed mere inches from you last night was excruciating. I will sleep on the floor." He dropped down to where he'd placed the bedding on the floor.

She stood there, stunned, letting his words soak in, warming her right down to her core. And other places. Nobody had ever said something like that to her. She could say the same thing about his body, without the part about taunting her imagination, since she'd seen every inch of him. She could tell him that only made it worse, but held her tongue and got into bed.

In a few seconds he was up again. "I'm restless, edgy." He shook out his hands. "I need to do some exercise, work it out."

"There are some weights in the top drawer of the dresser." She'd worked out as best as she could while staying there before.

Eric opened the drawer and pulled out the five-pound weights. "Not heavy enough." He put them back and dropped down to the floor in push-up position. Except when he came up, he clapped his hands. It was impressive. His muscles bulged, his arms shook, and his face reddened, but he kept at it. He started groaning from the strain, and those groans sounded way too much like the sounds a man might make when he was on the verge of coming. Not that she'd ever heard a man make more than a grunt. Grunt and squirt, big romance.

Then she realized her father would think they were having dirty, sweaty sex. She jumped off the bed and opened the door. "Hope Eric's not too noisy *working out*," she said, aiming her voice toward the living room where a television was on.

Her father didn't reply.

"Why'd you say that?" Eric asked in a strained voice as he held his push-up inches above the floor.

She perched on the edge of the bed. "Because you sound like you're in the throes of ecstasy."

"Really?" He sank down, turned over, and started doing crunches. Now his abs were tensing, defining his six-pack. "Must be the pleasure/pain thing. 'Cause I'm feeling pain now."

A fine line between pleasure and pain. Heat curled between her legs and into her stomach. She wanted to straddle him, grind into his groin, kiss across that vast, gorgeous chest. From the beginning, she'd been physically drawn to him, even when she hated him. It was getting worse. Thank goodness she'd opened the door, thus damping her temptation.

Eric was pushing himself hard. His teeth were gritted, and those glorious sounds came out again. He made no attempt to muffle them. She wondered if he made those sounds when he came. She bet he let loose and wailed. She sighed.

He stopped. "Sorry, I'm keeping you awake, aren't I?"

"You have no idea." She crawled into bed, and he flopped back onto the blanket bed.

When she turned, he was watching her. "Who's Edie Sedgwick?"

She rolled onto her side, facing him. "Why do you ask?" she said, curious.

"In the store, Marion said there were customers who thought you were Edie Sedgwick."

"Oh . . . she was one of Andy Warhol's Factory Girls. Way before my time. When I was in my teens, a friend's dad told me I looked like Edie. I'd never heard of her, so I looked her up on the Internet. He was right. I devoured her story and her life, and I sort of became her for a while. Not the drugs. It was the sixties, and Edie had a huge problem with them. But I resonated with her life, the tragedy and fragility of her. I painted my eyes to look like hers. She had these big beautiful eyes, wore fake eyelashes. I wanted to be her; in a way, it was better than being myself."

She didn't know why she'd told him so much. She never did that with anyone else.

He stood and put his finger on the light switch, but his gaze was on her. "You're fine the way you are."

"Thanks." She rolled over as he killed the light. She didn't know if she could handle looking into those eyes any longer. The night-light she'd bought was still plugged in, casting a warm glow over the room.

She couldn't sleep. Eric kept shifting, restless. Every now and then he released a ragged sigh. The lights from the digital clock taunted her as the minutes ticked past. Her mind kept spinning. Being there. Sayre. Eric. Westerfield. Her father. Suddenly she had several men in her life. Most were a threat in one way or another.

After another forty minutes, she got up to use the bathroom in the hall. When she returned, closing the door behind her, she looked down at Eric. He had that same blank stare he'd had the first time she projected to him.

"Eric," she whispered. She knelt down in front of him, but he didn't respond. "Holy crap, you're burning up." She put her hand over his forehead and the heat nearly seared her.

His hand clamped around hers, and then she was lying flat on the blanket, Eric pressed down over her, his arm at her throat. He blinked, came awake and sat up. "Stop sneaking up on me like that. I could have killed you."

His voice sounded raspy. He helped her up. Her heart was pounding, the pulse beating in her throat.

He rubbed his face. "Sorry."

She forced a laugh. "For all you know, I might have been holding a gun again." She sat in front of him. "I was worried about you." She tried again, touching his forehead. It was damp. In fact, his whole body was soaked; sweat glistened in the dim light. "You're burning up."

He put his palm on his forehead, too. "I'll be right back." He stood and swayed, slapping his hand on the wall to balance himself.

"Are you all right?" she asked.

"It's just one of those waves of exhaustion I mentioned." His voice was slurred.

He walked out, and she heard water running.

When he returned a minute later, he was drying himself with a towel. He moved to the window, which faced out the front. She came up beside him. His expression was tense. More than tense; it was fearful.

"Lachlan said you had the same edge in your eyes that he had before he exploded."

He nodded. He probably also remembered the part about taking her with him.

"Your eyes are dilated."

He nodded again.

"Your mother accidentally set herself on fire. So she had pyrokinesis, too."

He finally turned to her. It was the first time she'd ever seen vulnerability on his face. It scared her.

"She lost her mind," he said.

Her hand went to her throat. "Could that happen to you?"

"I don't know." He saw her gesture, and his expression darkened further. He put his hand over hers, and the heat penetrated her skin. "I almost killed you just now. I thought you were . . . I don't even know who I thought you were."

"It's okay. I startled you." She laughed, though it came out hollow. "You couldn't even kill me when you had a good reason."

His hand went higher and he stroked her cheek with his thumb. His fingers trailed down the front of her throat to the hollow. "Be careful of me."

Don't I know it. But that's not what he meant. "What do you mean?"

"Lucas made me promise to kill him if he went crazy. He was scared of it happening like Lachlan said. Even then, he wasn't willing to take the antidote.

And we don't know if he's okay yet. It hasn't been long enough."

"What are you saying?"

"If you see anything that scares you about me . . . get the hell away. Don't be afraid to do whatever it takes to protect yourself."

Her chest tightened. "Are you telling me to kill you?"

"If you need to."

Now she was really scared.

He leaned down and kissed her forehead. "Get some sleep."

Yeah, right. She was supposed to tumble into slumberland after that?

Sayre poked into Fonda's consciousness first. She was a sexy, sassy little thing, at least as much as he'd seen of her. The fact that Eric had tried to get her to leave during their scuffle in the woods meant he cared about her. That was always a useful thing in the art of torturing people. And oh, he liked torturing people. Love was a funny thing, at least what he had seen of it.

So he drilled through the ether to find her. He hit a fuzzy barrier. She wasn't asleep, not even at two in the morning. Next he tried Eric, but that barrier was even bigger. He'd yet to slip into Eric's dreams. Odd.

He walked to the window of the cheap motel room he was renting. Eventually they would sleep. Then he would come in. He wanted Eric out of the picture. Then he would visit Fonda. He liked her, maybe even best of all. He wanted her in person. Then they would have fun.

CHAPTER 16

The ants under his skin, the restlessness, was getting worse. Eric tossed and turned, feeling hot and then cold as sweat broke out on him. He got up and walked to the window, checking for predators. Even at five in the morning he saw people outside, probably up to no good. He glanced at Fonda, lying on the bed. To crawl in with her, wrap his arms around her . . .

He wanted her, but in a way he'd never wanted a woman before. The wanting yawned like an enormous beast inside him, threatening to swallow them both. It was no good, not with their history, not with what they had going on. That didn't stop the wanting one bit.

Her body went rigid, fingers tensing into claws. He dropped down next to her. Sayre? She screamed, her eyes snapping open but not seeing him or the room.

"Put it out! Oh, my God, oh, my God!"

She was dreaming of the fire again. He pulled her into his arms and crushed her against his chest.

"*Nooooo!*" she screamed.

"Wake up, Fonda. It's only a dream."

He should have tapped her cheeks or gently shaken her. Instead he rained kisses on her face, whispering "Wake up" with each one.

Even in the dim light he saw the moment her eyes focused on reality. The terror remained, even as she looked at him.

She put her hands on either side of his face. "Eric."

He expected shock and anger at reliving what he'd put her through, not the relief he saw in her expression. She stayed in his arms, not pushing him away.

"It was just a dream," she said, reveling in that reality.

"The fire. I'm sorry."

She nodded, her jaw tensing again. "Fire." Her fingers tightened against his face. "You, Eric. You were on fire. You were burning up with fever, convulsing, and then a flame erupted"—she touched his chest—"right here. Within seconds you were engulfed. I dreamed you set yourself on fire. Like your mother." In a raw whisper, she said, "I couldn't put it out. I threw water on you, but the flames kept growing and growing. And you were screaming out my name, over and over."

The fear on her face, the worry, was for him. He smoothed back her hair, and that gulf inside him opened even wider. "It's okay. I'm not going to set myself on fire."

She stared into his eyes. "You don't know." Suddenly, she seemed to realize their position, how close they were, and scrambled off the bed, rubbing her hands over her face. "You don't know what could happen."

He also got up, standing behind her. Not too close, because he could barely fight the urge to pull her back against him. "If something happens to me, I want you to keep in touch with Magnus and the Rogues."

"I don't want to think about that."

"Right now the Rogues can't do much to help you, but when they get out, they will."

She turned to him. "Why would they help me? I worked for the man who was trying to kill them. I *helped* him." Her recrimination was clear.

He touched her cheek. "You didn't know. I do know my people, though, and they help their own."

"I'm not one of them. They're not my people."

"You are one of them. You're an Offspring. They'll help you."

He could see she wasn't convinced. He would talk to Lucas later.

She moved away from his touch. "I'm going for a walk. I don't want to go back to sleep and chance having that dream again."

"I'll go with you."

"I've walked alone in this neighborhood at night before. I've walked alone in worse places than this. You don't have to come."

"I know I don't 'have' to come." He hated the thought of her walking out there, tempting a dark fate. He sensed the kindred craving for recklessness. "But you're not walking alone now."

He felt her tension vibrate the air around them. "You . . . you . . ."

"I'm bossy, arrogant, a Neanderthal, whatever. Get over it."

"You so do not understand!" She turned and dug in her duffel bag for some clothes.

"Enlighten me." He pulled out jeans and one of the shirts he'd gotten at her shop.

"Forget it." She started to lift up her shirt. "Turn around."

He turned, dropping his pants and sliding on the jeans. As he bent to pick up his shirt, he glimpsed a flash of her ass, because she was wearing one of those thongs that barely covered anything. Above her right cheek was a tattoo, but he couldn't make out the details.

She glanced his way, both irritation and embarrassment coloring her expression. "Peeking!"

"You were, too."

"Was not. I sensed you looking." She pulled up her black leggings. "You have no honor."

He shrugged. "I'm a man. 'Nuff said."

She turned, pulling on a purple top that was long enough to be a miniskirt. It had long sleeves with ruffles at the end. She bent over and slid on black boots with rivets on them and thick heels.

With an annoyed glint in her eyes, she walked past him. She was being ornery. He followed her. He loved ornery.

They walked into the cool predawn morning. The sky was gray, barely thinking of waking. Fonda paused by the truck. "I'll leave the bag of discards on the girl's porch. I met her during one of my walks. She's married, got a baby, and she's barely twenty. The dad's around, at least, but they're struggling." She gestured to the area. "Obviously."

He reached out to take the bag from her, but she hefted it over her shoulder and walked on. Her hips swayed the way a cat might twitch its tail when it's aggravated. Even in those clunky boots, she moved with fluid grace.

They walked in silence. Usually, he would have

been antagonizing her. He craved conflict, the fight. But she'd been through a lot with the nightmare, so now he decided to leave her to her thoughts, try not to get caught up in her fear of him dying, ironic that it was.

Fonda stayed a foot ahead of him. He'd let her have that space but not an inch more. At the end of the block, she walked down a sidewalk and set the bag out of sight on a front porch. Even with all the crap going on in her life, she cared about others. He waited on the sidewalk, watching her as she came back toward him. He saw the wounded look in her big brown eyes, the tough facade, and the tenderness beneath it, all plain on her face. Her gaze was locked on his, her pace slowing, her mouth opening.

In that moment he knew why Lucas and Nicholas and Rand were willing to die for their women. Why Lucas had wanted him to kill him to protect Amy. Not out of loyalty or duty or even because they were a sort-of family. It went much deeper, cut into places he didn't even know were inside him, and what bled out took his breath away. He wanted Fonda in a way he had never wanted anyone, not only body, but soul and heart and everything that went with it.

As though she sensed the miasma going on inside him, scarier than anything he'd ever faced, she stopped a couple of feet away. Her eyes were wide and he saw her chest rising and falling.

"You have honor," she said, tucking her hair behind her ear in a quick, involuntary gesture.

Those words, and the apology in her voice, broke his tenuous thread of control He closed the gap between them, pulling her against him, tipping her chin up and kissing her. She was heaven, the taste of her, the feel of her tongue against his, her body moving closer to his. Her hands went around his back. His fingers braced her face, slid into her silky hair, wanting to feel her everywhere. A wave of dizziness swept over him, and he kissed her right through it. She made him dizzy, and she made him things he'd never been, like wanting to take away everything bad in her life, like . . . in love.

Yeah. In love.

Holy crap, as Fonda liked to say.

He'd been hit by a truck, blown away by a tornado. How had this happened? At the moment he didn't care. He slid his hand down her back, stopping himself from squeezing her ass because he had honor, standing there in the open for everyone to see. He rubbed the indent of her spine, that sweet spot where her back curved in. She sighed and pressed closer.

Her hands were on his back, holding onto him so hard he could feel the tips of her nails through his shirt.

"Eric . . ." She breathed his name, not a hint of *stop* anywhere in the word.

A catcall whistle from across the street broke him out of the spell. A guy pumped his fist, his white smile stark against his dark skin.

She stood there, her fingers lightly on her lips, a dazed look on her face. She let her hand drop. "Eric—"

He put his finger where hers had been. "Don't say anything." He didn't want to hear her tell him not to do that again, and he didn't think he could handle hearing her tell him to do it again. He was walking a fine edge.

She spoke anyway. "Are we going to forget this happened, like the thing in the closet?"

His mouth twisted in a smile. "Yeah, 'cause that

worked well." He looked across the street where the guy was watching them. "Let's walk." He took her hand and led her back to her father's house.

They reached the small front porch and she sat down on the steps. Streaks of pink lit the sky, giving her skin a warm glow. They sat in silence for a few minutes. That was okay with him. He didn't know what to say, what to think.

Fonda braced her hands on the edge of the step and looked at him. "The first time I cut myself, it was an accident. When the guy tried to rape me, there was a razor on the coffee table. I slashed his arm with it. He called me filthy names and tried to grab me, but I ran into my room and locked the door. Later, when I stopped shaking and I knew he'd left, I took the razor and cut my hair really short. I made a decision to get tough. To work out, be strong. And I accidentally cut myself. It bled and hurt but somehow . . . it felt good. It was weird, I knew it was weird, but I realized why I liked it. My mind and body—I had numbed them. I stuffed everything inside me. Feeling physical pain was a safe way to feel. A way I could control."

He knelt down in front of her, taking her hand, turning it so he could see the underside of her wrist. "You never tried to kill yourself?"

"No, it was never about that. Cutting was therapy, that's what I told myself. My teacher started asking about the cuts, so I cut in places no one could see. I knew on some level it wasn't healthy, but it felt good, and I started doing it more often. Then it hit me: cutting was a kind of drug, and the thought of doing any kind of drug was bad."

He pushed up her sleeve and ran his fingers along those faint scars. "You don't do it anymore?"

"Haven't for years. Sometimes, though, when I accidentally hurt myself, I sink into that feeling."

Again he was swamped by the desire to fix her past. If only he could travel back in time like Lachlan and Wallace could . . .

No, none of them could be fixed. They could only move on. Something else tugged at him, like a lost memory.

The front door opened and her father stepped out. "I thought you'd left." His relief at seeing them was plain on his gaunt face. "I'm making breakfast, bacon and eggs." He went back in the house.

Eric reached out, and she allowed him to pull her to her feet, which left them only a few inches apart. She was taller in those boots, only about eight inches shorter than him instead of a foot.

"Thank you for telling me," he said.

"I've never told anyone. When people ask—the few who have seen the scars—I tell them my parents raised Doberman pinschers and the puppies scratched me. Most people wouldn't understand." She tilted her head. "Do you? Or do you think I'm some kind of freak?"

She'd trusted him. She'd opened up to him. All he could do was kiss her, a soft kiss that took all of his restraint not to deepen. He pressed his forehead against hers, breathing her in. Finally he stepped back. She smiled, and those dimples punched him in the gut.

"We'd better go in," he said.

He watched the tentative connection between her and her father as they put the bacon and eggs on three plates. It gave him a pang of desire to know his real father. He'd peppered Amy with questions, but she didn't remember a lot about him.

He thought about Rick Aruda, too, the man who

had raised him knowing he wasn't his biological son. Rick had harbored resentment over the betrayal, no doubt, and that's what he'd sensed while growing up. Now he could see that Rick had done his best, given the circumstances. Once this was all over, he would pay the man a visit, make peace.

He watched Fonda. His chest tightened. Now that he'd let himself slip into that abyss, what was he going to do about it?

Nothing. Remember how getting involved is a bad idea when people are gunning for you. Keep your heads straight.

The news was on in the living room, and the reporters kept going back to a breaking story: a cult community in northern Maryland had committed mass homicide. Not coerced suicide, like the Jim Jones massacre. No, these people had apparently killed each other in a frenzy. The camera focused on a group of buildings surrounded by yellow crime-scene tape and swarming with people. A procession of stretchers were being carried, the forms on top covered in black tarps. A woman with long scraggly hair stood several yards away from the scene, her arms wrapped around her scrawny body.

The journalist stepped in front of the camera, her expression passive. "This group is called the Sun Veil, but little is known about them. They have never come under the scrutiny of authorities until now. This was a self-sustaining community, and people in the nearest town said they only came in once in a while and never talked to anyone other than necessary conversation." She turned to her right. "This woman, who chooses not to be identified, is the only survivor of the massacre. Can you tell us what happened?"

With a trembling hand, the woman anchored her

hair behind her ear. "We've been waiting for the Veil to come and take us to our home planet. We were getting the signs that they were coming. Yesterday morning we saw something in the sky. We don't get any air traffic out here, so we thought it was the mother ship finally coming to take us out of this sick world. The plane came low, spraying something, like one of those farm planes. We thought it was way off course and we went inside 'cause we didn't want to breathe any chemicals or pesticides—we send the bugs that eat our produce love, and they leave it alone. Then in minutes everyone started acting irritated. I felt it, too, anger, hatred, fear, like I was being bombarded by everything I've tried to keep out of my energy field since I moved here."

She put her hand to her chest, her voice going hoarse. "The Family started arguing at first, name calling, and then hitting each other, and before I knew it, they were stabbing and strangling . . ." Her voice broke. "Even the children. Even the children were hurting each other, and then the adults killed them. It was hell on earth."

"How did you survive this horrible massacre?" the journalist asked.

"I locked myself in a storage bin. When I came out, after it got quiet, everyone was dead." Her eyes were haunted.

A man came over and took the woman's arm. "Please, ma'am, come with me."

The journalist wasted no time. "Sir, do you have any idea what happened here? Have you found the plane?"

"We're working on all leads." He turned and led

the woman away, FBI emblazoned on the back of his jacket.

Fonda's face was white, and when a commercial came on, she broke away and looked at him. A plane that sprayed chemicals. She walked toward him, and without a word between them, they stepped outside.

She gripped his arms as soon as the door closed. "The plane!"

"I know, I know. It has to be the same one. He sprayed them with something."

"That's what he was talking about, not being able to enjoy killing people. Whatever he sprayed, it made them turn on each other. Even the children, Eric. *Children*."

He gritted his teeth over that. It was the worst part, the most heinous. "We have to stop him. Them."

His phone rang, and he pulled it out and looked at the display. "It's Amy." He answered.

"Eric, have you seen the news?" Her voice sounded rushed.

"The cult massacre?"

"You said the guy took a crop duster out, right?"

"It's got to be the same plane. He had canisters on-board."

"The woman who survived, she had a glow."

"An Offspring glow?"

"Not quite, but something like it. Whatever he sprayed on them, it's related to Blue Moon."

"He infected them with it." It sounded insane. "And it launched those people into a psychotic attack. Hold on a minute." He turned to Fonda. "Amy sees glows, like auras. Different colors mean different emotions. Offspring have a mixed glow, like static on a television. She said the survivor had a glow something like it. Which means Westerfield is more than just trying to wipe us to cover up the program. He's using Blue Moon like a weapon."

"He probably figured no one would question a cult going crazy. And think about it: that wrestler who went bonkers and killed his family. Last month, the guy with no history of violence shooting his coworkers. There have been several cases of random, senseless violence in the last few months in this area."

"She's right," Amy said, obviously having heard her. "The question is, why? They're risking Blue Moon being found in a tox scan."

Eric ran his fingers through his hair. "Another question is, who are these people? Not Offspring. Maybe someone in the original program. Westerfield is the right age for that."

The day was bright now, people moving about, leaving for work. He wished he were one of them, giving the wifey a kiss goodbye and heading off to the factory.

No, he didn't.

Fonda's face was tense. "This isn't just about us anymore," she said. "It's about innocent people getting killed and no one knowing why. Children are dying." She paced the porch. "If they found something unidentifiable in the tox scan they did on the wrestler, on any of those people, they didn't tell the media."

"Maybe it's not detectable," Eric said. "Our parents ingested who knows how much of that stuff. Enough to change our DNA and probably theirs, too. But a smaller dose may not show up. Amy," he said into the phone. "I know you don't like to do it, but you need to talk to Cyrus. Ask him if there was anyone else in the program we don't know about."

After a moment of silence she said, "Okay. I'll work on that now. Nicholas wants to talk to you."

"Hey. Amy said you mentioned a strange man outside the motel, that he gave you a really weird feeling."

"Yeah."

"Did he have a shaved head? Was he taller than you, with light violet-blue eyes? Did you get a strange feeling, like a current of electricity?"

Eric sorted through the barrage of questions. "Shaved head, yes. Taller than me, yes, but leaner. I couldn't see his eyes in the dark, but I did feel something like an electrical current when he looked at me." It clicked then. "That guy you told us about, the one who worked with Darkwell."

"Yeah. Sounds like Pope."

"Maybe he's the one Westerfield was talking to at the airfield."

"Except Pope didn't do anything to us when Olivia and I found the warehouse full of all that strange stuff. That's always baffled me. He could have easily nailed us. Obviously he knew we were there, because he materialized as though he were a ghost. But he didn't try to stop us or even question us."

"I don't like it," Eric said. "It's much better when people are cut and dried. They're either trying to kill us or not. Pope's a wild card, and that makes him dangerous. Put Lucas on for a second."

When Lucas came on the line, Eric asked, "What's the situation there?"

"Not good. The SWAT team is searching my house again. They obviously know we're here somewhere. I think they're on to us."

"I can be there in twenty minutes."

"You come here storming the place, they'll nab you and get us anyway."

He hated to admit that Lucas's fears were justified. The old Eric would have stormed in, guns blazing. "I'm not storming anything."

"We're prepared. They won't take us alive, that's for sure."

"Taking you dead is not a good alternative. We're going to find Westerfield and take him out. Hopefully his partner will be with him." He looked at Fonda, who no doubt was trying to make sense of the conversation. "If something happens to me, I'm sending Fonda your way. Once you're out of there."

"Fonda? Seriously? Don't tell me the hard-assed don't-get-involved Aruda has fallen for a woman, and a former enemy, no less."

"Just bring her in. She needs people like herself. I'll talk to you soon."

"I don't need people," Fonda said tersely.

"Yeah, you do. Let's fly. We've got a psycho bastard to find."

Neil drove all over the area. Dark emotions bombarded him, as though the residents were pelting him with slimy blobs. His phone rang. Malcolm. What did he want? They had already celebrated their victory. Almost everyone in the cult had succumbed to their own rage. If only he'd been there to witness it, to breathe it in. But he would. More and more people would be exposed to the Essence, creating that delicious chaos he loved so. He answered. "Yeah."

"I found exactly where they are, the simplistic way.

Fonda's father lives in the area." He rattled off an address.

Neil punched in the address in his GPS. "Two minutes away."

"Be careful."

"I'm always careful."

Malcolm's voice took on that deadly low tone Neil hated. "A man died four nights ago near Fonda's apartment. Right around the time you were there. His heart looked like a squashed tomato, according to the medical examiner. They're baffled."

"I don't have time for gossip. I've got people to dispatch."

"Neil, I will not allow you to destroy my life here."

"I'll check back when I've assessed the situation." He hung up, feeling a twitch in his cheek.

A minute later he pulled past the small house. No car in the driveway. No lights on. He called Malcolm and reported that.

"I had a thought while I was driving around," he went on. "They found me once. We don't know if Eric Aruda can project or view, but we know Fonda can. I'll bet she'll try again. I'm going to do what we did to Simeon."

"Yes, prepare for it. Go to the factory and remain there for a while."

Neil gritted his teeth. "That's what I was going to do." Damn him, giving orders. Maybe Malcolm did that in his role, but he did not like to take orders. Especially when they kept him from doing what he enjoyed most. He would soon have Fonda. And where Fonda went, Eric Aruda was sure to follow.

CHAPTER 17

Admit it. You think I'm weird because of the cutting." Fonda leaned against the passenger door, facing him.

He glanced at her and then back at the road ahead. "I don't think you're weird."

"You do, just a little. You won't hurt my feelings. I expect it, actually."

He looked at her, his head tilted. "When you told me why you did it, I finally understood something about myself. Why I was reckless. Why I jumped off roofs and picked fights with guys meaner than me, why I did a lot of the things I did. When I take risks, I feel alive."

She could only stare at him. That wasn't what she'd expected at all. He understood her, related to her oddness. She remembered her words to him . . . Was it only two days ago? *I don't want to like you, Eric Aruda. Don't make me.* Well, he had gone and made her like him. More than like him. Every day, he did something that touched her, breaking down her defenses. The way he'd kissed her, *ay carumba!* It would have been easier if it was a lustful moment, or like that shut-you-up kiss. No, he'd looked at her in a way that grabbed her heart like a soft glove taking hold, never to let go.

Oh, puh-lease, cut that out.

She fiddled with one of her earrings, faux gold chandeliers, tugging it down until she felt pain. Safe. Comfortable. Not scary like feeling something for Eric Aruda.

"I think that's the turnoff up there," he said, nodding ahead.

To the cemetery that they'd agreed was a good spot to find Westerfield again. A few minutes later they pulled into the small gravel parking lot. She found the same double headstone, husband and wife, Beatrice and Herbert; Beatrice still alive, while her husband was long gone. This time the thought of that tore her heart rather than plucking at it. She stretched out on the ground, her fingers grazing the cold granite.

He sat beside her. "In and out. You find his location, I'll go in and nail him. He must have sensed us last time. I still think taking him by surprise is the key. Then he can't block my abilities. Otherwise I have no idea how to take him out."

"Eric, are you up for this? You don't look well." He looked as pale and gray as the granite.

"I'm fine. But first I want to check out the Tomb. That's what we call our hideout. I need to assess the situation, see how many cops are there."

"Don't push yourself."

He dropped his head, giving her a look. "Are you mothering me?"

Wow, she was. "You look like you're going to drop.

If you do, there's no way I can drag your heavy self to the truck. I'll have to leave you here with the ghosts."

He smirked and then stretched out beside her. She did watch him, watched his body strain, the sweat pop out on his forehead and the veins engage in his neck. No, not watched; hovered. She didn't like the way he looked. He was worrying her, mother hen or not.

He opened his eyes, though only about halfway. "I saw a few guys watching the area. They definitely think my people are in the house somewhere." His voice sounded so soft she could hardly hear him. His eyes drifted shut again.

"Eric." She shook his shoulder but he didn't budge. His shirt was damp, his body hot. "Eric, wake up." She heard the fear in her voice.

He was pale, yet burning up. His face and neck were covered in a sheen of perspiration. His eyes fluttered beneath his closed lids but didn't open. His mouth moved as though he were trying to say something.

She leaned close, so close his heat enveloped her ear and cheek. "What? I can't hear you."

All she could hear was his exhalation of breath.

"If you're tricking me because of the ghosts remark, you win. I'm freaked. Wake up, so I can find Westerfield."

She hoped he was making her pay for the snide remark she'd made, since she couldn't admit she was worried about him.

He still didn't wake. She straddled him, her hands on his shoulders, and tried to shake him. "Eric, please. Don't do this. Don't leave me." The fear at that sucked her breath away. She'd made light of it, but she couldn't leave him here. "Eric!" Fear tore at her voice, stretching it taut as it echoed off the gravestones. She beat on his chest, her eyes stinging with heat. "Eric!"

Nothing. She leaned down to his heart, listening. Yes, still beating. But his mind was gone. Even his eyes weren't moving anymore. "Eric . . ." This time the word poured out in an agonized breath. "Don't leave me alone. I can't do this without you." She fell on him, sucking in deep breaths, rising and falling with his own breathing.

She sat up again. *Do something.* She dug into his pocket where he kept his cell phone and went down his list of contacts. Names she recognized, people she'd targeted, but she'd never spoken to any of them. He seemed close to Lucas. She dialed his number and waited for what seemed forever for him to answer.

"What's up?" he said.

Her words slammed together like a train wreck. "It's Fonda. Something's wrong with Eric. He was really tired, and his eyes started being dilated a few days ago, and last night he was burning up, and he just remote-viewed your Tomb and now he won't come back, and I don't know what to do!" She could hardly catch her breath.

"Dammit. Blue Moon is breaking him down."

"Magnus offered him the antidote, but Eric didn't want to lose his abilities."

"Give him a few minutes to come out. I had these storms that would wipe me out for fifteen minutes at a time. Maybe that's what he's going through, too. Then he can decide if he wants to take the antidote."

"He said you took it, right? And you're okay?"

She heard Lucas's bitter laugh. "It was given to

me," he clarified. "I don't know if I'm okay or not. It's only been a few days."

She was watching Eric the whole time. "It's worth it if it saves him, isn't it? Even if he loses his abilities?" Her voice caught. "I don't want him to die. If you care about him, if you love him, wouldn't you do whatever it takes to save him? The way he talks about you, all of you, I know he'd do anything to save you. That's how you people are. I know the things you've done for each other."

Lucas exhaled. "Yeah. That's what we do."

"You've risked your lives for each other. You risked getting caught to warn Amy because you loved her that much. Tell me, Lucas. In my position, with Eric dying before my eyes, what would you do?"

Silence for a moment. Then his quiet voice. "I'll give you Magnus's number."

She released a breath. Not exactly permission, but close enough. "I have it. Oh, and Eric said there are several men watching your place. I have to go."

Eric groaned and opened his eyes. They were even more dilated, the pupils as big as his irises. He tried to sit up, and she grabbed at his hands and pulled him the rest of the way.

He was back. Her heart soared.

"Get away from me," he said in a gravelly voice.

"What?" Was he possessed by Sayre? No, Sayre wouldn't be sending her away. He'd be attacking her.

"Get away from me." His voice was harsher now. "Take the truck and go."

"I was kidding about leaving you here."

He buried his face in his hands and shook his head. "Get the hell away from me. Now. I don't want to hurt you."

She thought of his mother setting herself on fire, the nightmare she'd had. He was spiraling down into a dark place.

She scooted closer and leaned next to his face. "Eric, get in the truck. I'll take you to Magnus. He'll give you the antidote."

"I'm not going in the truck with you." He shoved her away, got up and staggered a few feet before gripping one of the gravestones for support. "I don't want to be anywhere near you. Go to Magnus. He'll take care of you."

"Eric!"

He spun around again, wavering. "Do you want me to torch you? Remember how it felt, how horrible it was when it happened to Jerryl? I could do that to you. *Is that what you want?*" The snarl on his face matched his words. He was using her pain over Jerryl and her fear over what happened on purpose.

He pushed on, away from her. She went after him, and he spun around and gave her a look so acidic, so psychotic, she gasped. He continued walking toward the line of trees beyond the cemetery, his every step leaden.

She let him go, her body so full of fear, for and of him, she couldn't move for a second. "Fine! Go, you son of a bitch! Go off and die!"

He did, stepping into the woods, holding onto a pine tree trunk for balance and then moving forward again.

Her breath came in heaving gulps. For over two months she'd lived for the moment when he died. Now that could happen without her doing a thing.

Except everything was different. She couldn't find a speck of anger anywhere in her psyche toward him.

Especially since he was pushing her away for her own safety.

She had lived her whole life in self-preservation mode. Tangling with Eric was dangerous in more ways than one. She could die a most horrible death. She could watch yet another man she cared about die a horrible death.

You care about him. You care, and not because he's protecting you, not because he saved your ass more than once, and not because he's sexy as hell. And as much as that scares you, letting him die would be far worse than anything you can imagine, anything you've gone through.

She snapped out of it and fumbled with his phone, finding Magnus on the list.

"Magnus?" she whispered when a man answered.

"Yes. Who's this?"

"Fonda. I need your help. Eric's gone over the edge."

The world was spinning. All around Eric, trees swayed and spun in circles, and he had to keep holding onto them. He had waited too long.

He dropped to the ground, his legs giving out. Crap, if he set himself on fire here, he'd send up the whole forest. *Good move, Aruda.*

He already felt as though he were on fire. He managed to lift his head to make sure. No, not yet. He looked beyond, and though his vision was getting blurry, he saw that Fonda hadn't followed him in. Either she was smart, or he'd put her off. Either way, she was safe from him. He hated that he couldn't protect her anymore. With the Rogues trapped, they couldn't either. Magnus would. He had to believe that.

He remembered Lucas's fever after they'd rescued him, how Amy had watched over his every breath as she tried to keep him cool. Then he saw Fonda in his mind's eye, standing in the cemetery, fear in her eyes. Fear for him. Maybe she cared a little. That was the last thought he had before he succumbed to the darkness.

Lucas disconnected the phone and turned to the others, who were all waiting for news. He told them about Eric's situation. "Fonda's arranging to get him the antidote."

He saw Amy's surprised expression. "Is that why you offered to give her Magnus's number?"

He nodded, his gaze on her. "It's his only hope. She cares about him. She's scared and desperate and doesn't want him to die. She reminded me that sometimes we have to take risks to save the ones we love." He stepped closer to her, and everyone else in the room fell away in his consciousness. He saw only Amy's green eyes, filled with a different kind of desperation—and love. "She asked me if it was worth taking the chance. Even if he loses his abilities. I saw it from her side. Your side. If you were dying, I'd do anything to save you." He put his hand on her cheek, and she leaned into it. He saw all the pain she'd experienced because of his stubborn anger. "I'm sorry I put you through that. I'm sorry I punished you for it."

She leaned forward and kissed him, tears glistening at the corners of her eyes. He hadn't realized how much he'd missed seeing her smile.

He rubbed away her tears with his thumbs. "And I didn't lose my ability to get into people's dreams. I poked into yours last night for a second. Just to test it."

Her smile grew even wider. "Maybe you could come again tonight, and stay longer."

"How about we spend some time together in person instead?"

Fonda walked toward the line of trees where Eric had gone. She couldn't hear footsteps anymore. *Please don't have gone far.* As unbalanced as he'd been, she doubted he could physically make it very far. She quietly stepped into the woods. Her heart sank when she saw him on the ground. Her body strained to run to him, but she needed to stay near the cemetery when Magnus got there.

Eric's phone rang. Magnus! No, not the same number she called. She stepped away so Eric wouldn't hear her and answered.

"How's Eric?" a frantic female voice asked.

"Not good." Fonda's throat tightened on those words. "Who's this?"

"Petra, his sister."

Fonda pictured the tall, beautiful blonde from the pictures she'd seen. By the pain in her voice, she imagined Petra's face contorted in fear.

"Magnus is coming with the antidote."

"If I were there, I could heal him. Dammit, I've got to get out of here."

A woman in the background said, "No, you couldn't. Even if you were with him, you'd die trying."

Petra's words broke when she said, "Please don't let my baby brother die. I love him so much."

Her words and agony grabbed Fonda's heart as

painfully as Westerfield could. She hadn't even realized she'd walked closer to Eric. He was curled up on
his side, fingers in tight fists, eyes squeezed shut. His
breaths were shallow and rapid.

"I won't," she whispered.

The sound of tires on gravel snapped up her head.
"Magnus is here. I've got to go. I'll keep in touch."

She disconnected and broke out of the woods in a
run, her gaze going to both brothers getting out of a
newer truck. Magnus carried a small box.

She rushed over to meet him. "He's over there.
Come."

Lachlan followed at a short distance. "What's his
state of mind? I don't want him burning me up."

"He told me to stay away from him. He didn't want
me hurt. But now he's out of it."

Magnus lifted the box. "We'd better give this to
him while we can."

"I can do it if you want to stay at a safe distance,"
Fonda said. "I've never given an injection but I've seen
people do it."

"Let her do it," Lachlan said, remaining several
yards back. "If she wants to risk her life for him, fine.
We've lost enough because of these people."

Magnus turned to him, his expression hard. "We
lost our father because of our father. He was the one
who introduced this to innocent people, whether on
purpose or not. He kept ingesting it without knowing
what it really was. Blaming is not going to solve anything." He faced forward and kept walking. "I'll do
it. If he starts thrashing, you'll need muscle power to
hold him down."

That thought was startling.

Eric was still on his side. Magnus knelt down

beside him and took out the syringe. Those had only represented evil to her, or just plain pain when given in a doctor's office. Now it could be Eric's salvation.

Or not.

Would Eric be as bitter as Lucas or Lachlan seemed to be? Would he hate her for disobeying his orders to let him die alone? None of that mattered as much as the worry that this antidote might do him more harm than good. She put her hands on Eric's shoulder as Magnus injected the bluish fluid into his vein. Eric's heat made her palms sweat within seconds. He contorted, his eyes fluttering open, his body tensing. He grabbed her arm and squeezed hard, not realizing what he was doing. Magnus tried to pry his fingers off her but she shook her head. "It's okay."

The pain felt good but for a different reason: it drowned out the pain inside.

Eric took a sharp breath, like when Westerfield had him at the flea market.

"Is this normal?" she asked, never taking her eyes off Eric.

"There is no normal. Lachlan did his fair share of this, though, and then he slept for twenty-four hours. It was touch and go during that time. He would burn up, then be cold, then scream out as though someone was tearing out his soul. Then fall into something deeper than sleep. When he woke, he was fine."

"Except for my abilities being gone," Lachlan added.

She flicked a glance at him, though her gaze went back to Eric. "You guys are so worried about losing your freaking abilities, like they're part of your identity or manhood. Would you rather have died?"

"As a matter of fact, I would have," Lachlan said.

Eric's body went lax. She put her ear next to his chest and listened. *Please, be there.*

Yes, a heartbeat.

"Lachlan," Magnus said, "help me carry him to the truck."

Would Eric rather die than lose his abilities? She had to hope he had more to live for than that. His people. His sister, who loved him so much.

Not her, of course.

The men lifted Eric up with a groan of effort. She put her hands on his back to lend support. His shirt was soaked and his body still super heated. Heat meant alive, though.

They laid him in the back of their truck. Magnus, she presumed, had thoughtfully laid out a sleeping bag on the bed's surface. She climbed in next to Eric.

Magnus said, "Stay low. We don't want to attract any unnecessary attention."

Lachlan got into the truck they'd been using, and Magnus drove his truck. She stretched out beside Eric, her face at his neck, and breathed him in, earth, the musky scent of hot sweat. She slid her finger up to the pulse point under his jaw and counted his heartbeats.

CHAPTER 18

Fonda looked at the clock in the guest bedroom for the hundredth time. If this lasted twenty-four hours, there were twenty more agonizing ones to go. *If* this antidote worked the same as the others.

A big if.

She had let the Rogues know when they reached the compound but didn't tell them it was a different formula. No need to worry them yet. She'd take that on herself.

She sat by the bed and kept dabbing a cold washcloth over Eric's body. She had stripped off his clothes, telling herself he wasn't modest. Besides, he didn't like sleeping in clothing, and he was going to be sleeping for a long time. The sheet covered his pelvis area, but the rest of him was exposed to the cool air in the room. Amy had told her that's what she'd done when Lucas went through the same thing.

Eric hadn't moved, not so much as a flicker under his eyelids. Not a moan or an exhalation. He was as still as stone, except for the gentle rise and fall of his chest and for his pulse, which she kept checking.

The room was sparse, clean, done in light earth colors with a king-sized bed in the center and a dresser along one wall. A large window let in the sun and the bright greenery outside. She hardly looked at it.

Magnus appeared at the open doorway. "How's he doing?"

"No change. I don't know whether that's good or not." She hoped he would provide a clue. He must have watched Lachlan; he had endured this, too, though he probably didn't remember much.

He stepped inside and passed his hand a few inches above Eric's body. "Still burning up. Lachlan's temperature swung back and forth, so when Eric starts to shiver and get chill bumps, cover him and push up the thermostat. Like someone with a flu fever, you need to keep his body temperature as even as possible. He'll likely thrash around, so be careful as he'll have no idea what he's doing, and you could get hurt."

Lachlan hovered in the doorway.

In a hard voice, Fonda said, "He hasn't died yet." She didn't want Lachlan's negative energy impacting Eric's healing.

"I don't want him to die. I just want him to lose his abilities, is all." He smiled. "Just because he's such an arrogant son of a bitch."

"Get out."

He raised a thick eyebrow at her. "You're telling me what to do in my own home? And you the guest, an uninvited one at that?"

"Lachlan, please," Magnus said, not even looking at him. "They are invited, by me."

Fonda looked at Magnus. "The antidote you gave

to Eric. Why didn't your father use that one on you? What made him develop it further?"

Lachlan answered with a smug smile. "The mouse went into convulsions and died."

Her gaze flew back to Magnus. "Is that true? You gave *that* to Eric?"

Magnus shook his head. "Well, it is true that the mouse died, but we don't think it was the antidote that killed it, not as a whole. She—my father always called them by gender—had a reaction to an element in the antidote. Two other mice died, and my father went on to develop a different version that didn't use that exact compound. I don't know what he changed in it, but he felt the previous version wouldn't harm humans. Still, he didn't want to take a chance."

"But you did. You took a chance by giving it to Eric."

He met her furious glare with his neutral one. "You called me for help. That was the only help I could give you."

"I'm grateful—I am. I'm just afraid to lose him."

Magnus took a few steps back toward the door. "I've got a video of my father talking about Blue Moon, how he found it. If you want to watch it . . ."

She was shaking her head. "I don't want to leave Eric. Later. I'd like to watch it later."

"All right." He had a curious frown on his face. "When you were here only two nights ago, you made it very clear that you didn't think much of Eric. In fact, you seemed angry with him, said he'd killed your boyfriend. Now I see something very different in your eyes as you watch him. I see fear and grief and—"

"I forgave him," she said, not wanting to hear what

else Magnus thought he saw. A lot had changed since they were last here, and it was that scene in the closet that had started it.

He nodded, then turned toward Lachlan. "Forgiveness is a powerful thing. It transforms and transcends. You'd be well served to think on that." He turned back to her. "I'll leave you to it, then. Press the button on the intercom system if you need me."

A moment after he left, Eric's phone rang. It was plugged in to charge, and she walked over to the dresser to answer it.

"Fonda, it's Amy. How's Eric?"

"The same. When you gave Lucas the antidote, did he sweat and not move and then all of a sudden thrash around?"

"Yes, though he didn't stay asleep for twenty-four hours solid. He was groggy and fell back asleep a few times over the next day."

"He's mad at you for giving him the antidote, isn't he?"

"*Was* mad," Amy said. "Whatever you said to him earlier softened him. What did you say?"

"Just that I didn't want Eric to die, and wasn't it worth doing whatever I could to save him?"

"It is worth it. Eric's never been keen on the antidote either, but hopefully he'll understand and get over it. Then again, I am talking about the most stubborn man on earth." Silence for a moment. "You care about him, don't you?"

Fonda looked at him and felt something in her heart shift. "He saved my life. I owe him."

Amy chuckled. "Oh, so that's the reason." She didn't sound convinced, but before Fonda could say more to convince her, Amy said, "Talk to him. I told

Lucas how much I loved him, to please come back to me because I needed him. I don't know whether it helped or not, but I'd like to think it did."

"I will."

"Eric wanted me to ask my uncle about anyone else who was in the original program. Cyrus is dead, but I can talk to him when I'm brave enough. He said there were no others in the program besides the ones we know about. So whoever this Westerfield is, he's something entirely different."

"Great."

"Yeah, isn't it? Keep in touch. We're so tense around here, a sneeze could blow us apart. First those guys out there and now Eric. We need him—and you—to find out what's going on. Tell him that. And tell him we love him."

"I will."

Fonda disconnected and sat back down next to Eric. She dipped the cloth in the bowl of cool water and wiped it across his brow. "Eric, you'd better come back. In one piece. Mentally."

That last word struck fear into her. What if he came back but was not wholly himself?

"Magnus seems fine," she went on. "And it sounds like Lucas and Amy are okay, or at least a little better." She leaned closer to Eric's ear. "You'll be fine, too. Amy sends her love. And Petra. All of them." She laid her head down next to him as she sat in a chair beside the bed. "You are loved, Eric. And I . . . I need you. Don't make me do this alone." She stroked the line of his jaw, willing him to feel it. "I'm scared. There, I admitted it. I'm scared of these people who are hunting us, and of you dying, and I'm scared . . . of never talking to you again. Never kissing you again."

There was something about seeing a big strong man in a helpless position that reached beneath all her defenses, like smoke creeping under a door.

She started to run the washcloth over his head but stopped and put her hand on his forehead. He wasn't hot anymore. She pressed her finger against his pulse point. Still beating. Relief washed over her, even though she hadn't let herself think he was . . .

She dropped the cloth into the bucket and watched him. Just as Magnus had predicted, chill bumps rose on Eric's skin. Progress. Maybe. She turned the thermostat up to a higher setting, then returned and pulled up the blanket and tucked it over his shoulders, which left her face-to-face with him. Nose-to-nose. She kissed it. Even his nose was cool. His cheeks. His lips.

His mouth moved slightly beneath hers. Just a reflex, but it still sharpened her heartbeat. Maybe he could feel her. She kissed him again, over his face and then on each eye. Her earrings jangled as they brushed against his neck. She'd never kissed a man like this, and it felt odd. She'd never do it if he were awake. It was too . . . she couldn't even put a word to it, but if she had to find one, it would have been *uncomfortable*.

She smoothed back his hair. He took a deeper breath and turned on his side, in a fetal position. For warmth, she guessed. She slid beneath the blanket, wrapping her arms around him from behind. He wouldn't remember any of this. Even if on a deep level he felt her or heard her, he wouldn't consciously remember.

She tucked her chin over his shoulder, molding her body to his. The warmth in the room stole into her senses, drawing her eyes closed. All of her fear and worry had worn her out. Her fingers flexed against his bare chest, kneading him like a cat. Strange, she'd never done that before. Somehow it gave her comfort, maybe the same way it did for a cat. She didn't want to fall asleep, in case he needed her. But damn, she was so tired.

"Eric, come back," she whispered against his skin.

His body pressed into her with his every breath. She breathed when he did, in and out, in sync. She drifted into sleep, dreaming of the cold, of waking to find him dead, of being alone in a snow-covered plain. Then the sun came out from behind the clouds, filling her with warmth. The snow melted, and flowers bloomed across the field.

A figure in the distance walked into view, and she watched as he came closer. Eric! She ran toward him, through waist-high grass and flowers. He held out his arms, and she threw herself into them. Strong, big arms wrapped around her. His erection was hard against her thigh, and she pressed closer, wanting to feel all of his body.

Eric, Eric, Eric, you're here.

His hands slid up beneath her shirt, stroking her back. Finally, a good dream. It amazed her how the dream aroused her physically. Her whole body was alive with energy, flowing through her veins and down to places that throbbed with wanting. She became aware of her body, of the heat and electricity. *Aware. How can I be physically aware if I'm asleep?*

I'm not!

Her eyes flew open. Not a dream. Eric was holding her, sliding his hands over her body, and he was still totally, completely out of it. Well, not completely . . .

"Eric," she whispered, and he kissed her, bracing her face with his hands as he had earlier.

Or . . . Sayre? He'd said that if Sayre came in, his eyes would look blank. Eric's eyes were still closed, and his body was hot again. The gesture of his holding her face, that was something Eric did. So it was Eric, only Eric.

No one had told her about this possibility. Hot, cold, but not amorous.

The room was dark, which meant it was nighttime. She couldn't see the clock from her angle.

He felt so good, wrapping her in his arms, kissing her neck and the place beneath her ear. He let out a soft groan and slung his leg over her, pinning her within the bounds of his body. His hands slid down her back, all the way down beneath her pants, each hand nearly covering the whole cheek, and he squeezed. She let out a soft moan. *Touch me.* They slid back up, and one hand threaded up into her hair, anchoring there. The other wrapped around her waist. She was surrounded by his heat, his skin, his scent. Earth, fresh air, and Eric.

"Eric. Wake up."

How wrong was it to want him even if he was deep asleep? She wanted him. Her body was electric, hot and wet with it. She knew he wanted her when he was conscious. Deep in his unconsciousness, he still wanted her.

Eric, I'll give you whatever you want. Anything if it might bring you back.

He kissed her neck, across her collarbone, and then pulled up her shirt to kiss her breasts. She helped by pulling off the top and unhooking her bra. She dug her nails into his shoulders, so ready, so on the edge, that even his tongue swirling around her nipple was about to send her over.

She watched his face, waiting for some sign that he was coming out. His hands skimmed down her sides, her hips, under the waistband of her pants. She pushed them down, kicking them off with her feet. His fingers found her.

"Eric," she whispered.

Still no sign that he was waking up. She gasped as he traced her folds, slick and ready, then dipped his finger into her. Even in his mindless state it was as though he were preparing her for him. How far would this go? How far would she let it go?

He groaned and murmured her name. A sweet sound, because it meant he knew her. He hadn't lost his mind. She wrapped her legs around his waist, which pressed his hardened penis against her pubic area.

She put her hands on either side of his face. "Eric, we shouldn't do this . . . Unless it'll bring you back."

She did a quick mental calculation, sure she was past the time she could get pregnant. He'd said he always used condoms. Still . . .

Okay, she'd let him take it as far as he wanted, go along for the ride and hope it would bring him out. The feel of him grinding against her, oh hell, she wanted him inside her. She wrapped her fingers around his penis, rubbing the tip of him against her opening. With another groan, he pushed in. Slowly, at first, but she slid down on him. Pleasure far outweighed pain. He stretched her, just like he did in other ways. He filled her in a way she'd never felt before. The pleasure radiated out through her whole body, and she arched to press against him even more.

"Eric . . ."

She watched his eyes. What if he woke while they were doing this? What would he think?

He would flow right into it. She moved against him, and they quickly found their rhythm. There was something both edgy and safe about making love like this. His pubic bone pressed in the right place, and she felt the orgasm spill deliciously through her, over her. Her body tightened with it, and her fingers gripped his back.

They moved together for a long time, bringing on more of those waves of ecstasy. He kissed her as they made love, something different for her. The face-to-face position was usually the most uncomfortable for her psychologically. She liked closing herself in her world, focusing only on the physical sensations. Kissing made the act so much more intimate, but with Eric unaware, she could lose herself in it.

He came with a burst of power, as though exploding her insides. He gripped her hard against him, groaning the way he had when he was doing sit-ups, his breath coming heavy in her ear.

She held onto him, wrapped around him as though he were a buoy in a raging ocean. He felt so right, throbbing inside her, like no one else had, and those waves threatened to drown her.

He curled one hand gently around her neck and pressed his cheek against hers. In the faintest whisper, he said, "I love you, little girl."

Her eyes opened as the swell of those words took her dangerously high. She turned to see if he was awake. Eyes closed, a slight smile on his face. Dreaming, then. Had he actually said those words? She thought she'd heard *I love you* before when it had only been *That's nice* to her ugly sweater. She replayed Eric's faint words in her mind. She couldn't be sure, couldn't let herself believe that's how he felt.

His body slackened, feeling heavy where he lay on her.

"Eric."

No response. She'd lost him again. Her fingers tightened on his back. Still breathing.

You shouldn't have done this, shouldn't have let it happen.

Was it wrong? For him, for her? He probably wouldn't remember it, but she would. She would never forget the way he felt inside her, the way he made he feel. She whispered words back, words she'd be too afraid to ever tell him otherwise.

She needed to clean up. She relaxed her body, running her fingers through his soft hair. Not yet. She wasn't ready to move out of his arms. For now she was safe and happy, and so much more.

Eric felt as though he'd been in hell for days. Burning up, a vein of fire going from his arm all through his body. A brain synapses-induced play of lights like the Aurora Borealis. When he drifted away from that display, he sometimes heard voices, but he couldn't move or feel his body. Then he would drift into that strange place again.

At last he felt his body, and it was connected to something soft and warm. He felt a hand on his chest, the curve of a woman's body against his back. His mind filled in the image of that woman, with her white-blond hair and doe brown eyes, and before he knew it he was turning over and pulling her into his arms. A dream, or illusion, to taunt him with what he couldn't have. If this was hell, he'd take this bit of it, because even a taste was better than never having it.

His hands drank her in, the feel of her skin, the curve of her back and then lower, sliding beneath the waistband of her pants and cupping her small firm ass. His mouth tasted hers; he so was hungry, he wanted to eat her up. He curled his body around her as though he could absorb her. He threaded his fingers into her hair.

His body drank in the feel of her. An erotic dream, touching her, and then her touching him, and even in the dream he felt the jolt through his body. Then the exquisite feeling of pushing into her, feeling her tighten around him. Her calling out his name. He held onto her as tightly as he held onto the dream, not wanting to lose any of it. When he came, those undulating colors exploded in rays of light, like two stars crashing into each other.

I love you, little girl. The words crashed in his mind, too, as vivid as the colors.

The darkness crept in again. *No, not yet.* This was the hell part, taunt him and then haul him back to the nothingness.

"Eric."

Her pleading voice pulled him back, an inch, and then he slipped again. He opened his mouth to say something, or tried to, but he'd slid away from the controls on his body again.

He still felt her, their bodies intimately connected, the gossamer feel of her fingers on his face, her voice in his ear.

"Eric, please come back to me. I need you." The desperation in her voice tugged him back again. The sound of her breath against his ear, full of angst. "Not because you're strong. Not because we've got bad people after us. I need you because you're the only person who ever made me feel."

A dream? Had to be. Fonda would never say those things to him. He felt himself sliding down the slope into the darkness, mentally scrabbling like a man sliding down a cliff. Fonda in his arms, her words, he would take both with him to hell, and it wouldn't be quite so bad.

A knock woke her. Fonda opened her eyes and saw that once again sunlight filled the room. Her first thought was Eric, and she turned to him. He'd thrown off the sheets during the night and wasn't wrapped around her anymore, but his arm was across her stomach. It felt heavy, warm, and she didn't want to move yet.

Magnus stood at the doorway, his brown curls a mass. "Sorry to wake you, but you've been asleep since four o'clock yesterday. I left dinner, but you haven't touched it. You need to eat."

She glanced at the dresser where a tray sat, the bread curling up on the sandwich. Then what he said hit her. "I've been asleep since four . . . *yesterday*?"

He nodded. "You've had a hard few days. You obviously needed it."

She tried to look at the clock from her angle without moving Eric's arm. Eight-thirty.

Magnus approached the other side of the bed and placed his hand on Eric's forehead. "Still warm, but not hot. That's a good sign."

"He moved around last night." She wasn't about to tell him just how he'd moved. "That's good, too, right?"

He smiled, no doubt at her desperation for reassurance. "Yes. He should come out in the next couple of hours. Why don't you get something to eat? Yes, we have toast and tea. My father was a tea connoisseur."

The way he'd said that, as though he'd read her mind . . . "You can read minds, can't you?" He'd done that before, too, though she'd passed it off as a coincidence. But he *was* an Offspring, after all.

His mouth quirked in a smile. "Sorry, it's such a part of me, I don't think about it. Just words here and there. I heard 'tea' and 'toast.' "

"Do you get anything from Eric?" She wanted so badly for him to be thinking about something. Unless he was thinking about what they'd done last night; that could be embarrassing.

"It's indistinct. But I think he's thinking about you. I get the sense of you, anyway."

Eric's fingers twitched. She looked at his face, hoping for an awakening. Nothing.

"Get some nutrition into you. He's not coming around anytime real soon."

She started to slide out from beneath the sheet until she remembered she was naked. "I need a quick shower."

He nodded toward their duffel bags. "I brought those in from the truck."

She gave him a smile of appreciation.

"I'll leave toast, jelly, and tea in the kitchen. It's down the hall to the left."

She showered, checking on Eric before she even dried off. No change. His hand was in the place where she'd been not long ago, as though he'd reached for her. She was too scared, too overwrought, too . . . too involved. She'd only *thought* she loved Jerryl, and look at what a pitiful mess she'd become. She couldn't let that happen again. Jerryl had stood up for her at a bar; Eric had saved her life. That kind of thing made her weak in the knees, and worse, in the heart. That's what Eric did. He wouldn't let her die, no matter who she was. He was honorable.

Don't make more of it than it is, because that's what you do. He protects you, and you think you love him. Everything he'd done filled her with that need, with that scary feeling. What he made her feel was the scariest thing of all. Was it real or something contrived by that little girl inside her who yearned for someone to protect her?

She dug out the tie-dyed yellow jeans and a green tank top, put them on, and pushed herself to leave the room. Her stomach growled at the thought of toast now. The kitchen's walls were painted a taupe, with metallic red tiles going halfway up. The counters were dark stone, the light fixtures contemporary. Magnus had, to his word, left a loaf of whole-grain bread on the counter, a plate with a pat of butter and knife, and a tea set. She started the kettle and looked through the assortment of tea tins. Several exotic varieties tempted her, and she chose honey vanilla. She scooped the chunky blend into the tea diffuser.

While she waited for the tea to brew, she tuned into a strange clanging sound in the near distance. Alert for anything odd, she walked down the hall and looked out into an interior courtyard filled with flora and fauna. Across the way, she saw a studio with walls of glass and two men wearing Scottish garb, fencing. Their swords clashed, the sound bouncing off all the glass. She watched them for a minute, amazed at their grace and strength, which reminded her of Eric, which propelled her back to the kitchen.

Once she'd eaten her toast and brewed a second cup of tea, she returned to the bedroom. Eric was sitting up in bed, looking dazed. Her heart shot through the ceiling and she nearly dropped her teacup. Relief was quickly followed by guilt for not being there when he woke.

She tamped down her soaring excitement (Okay, she wanted to jump up and down), set down her cup and walked to the bed. "How are you feeling?"

He pulled his gaze from her and looked around the room. "Where am I?" His voice was hoarse. "This isn't hell, right?" His gaze settled on her, softening. "You wouldn't be in hell."

She perched on the bottom edge of the bed. Now she would have to tell him about the antidote. "You're at Wallace's compound."

He looked at her again, and she could see his muddled mind sorting through the pieces. "I didn't die?"

She shook her head.

"You got me here?"

"I called Magnus. He and Lachlan brought you here."

She saw the exact moment that he put it together. His face got pale and his icy blue eyes snapped to hers. "You gave me the antidote."

"I wasn't going to let you die."

"You could have gotten killed. I could have fried you. Or Magnus. That's why I told you to leave me alone."

"Yeah, well, I didn't, and everything turned out all right."

He looked at his hands. They were shaking a little, but then again, he hadn't eaten in more than a day.

"You're welcome," she said, with what was probably a forced smile, reminding him of the time she'd followed him when he'd gone to find Sayre.

"You disobeyed me, risked your life, and allowed some unstable substance to be put into my body. I don't know whether I want to thank you or throttle you."

She cat-walked across the bed to him. "If I were you, I'd kiss me and thank me. Be a lot less messy."

He was torn, and that was a good thing. Instead of doing either, he dropped back and covered his face with his hands. He'd gone almost as still as he had been through the night. "What the hell are the brothers doing?"

"Who?"

"Magnus and Lachlan. They're fighting with swords."

"Yeah, I saw them, though I was in too much of a hurry to get back to you to watch them." She blinked. "How did you—you can still remote-view."

His hands fell away, a ghost of a smile on his face. "Yeah. I didn't lose my abilities. Maybe I'd better test the pyrokinesis."

"No! Not here. Wouldn't be considered good guest-age."

"Guest-age?"

"You know, being a good guest." She inched closer, looking down on him. "So you don't hate me?"

He narrowed his eyes at her. "A little." He took her arm and pulled her closer. His hair was messier than she'd ever seen it, but that could be her fault. "Why? Why did you risk your life even after I'd ordered you to leave me alone? After everything I've done to you?"

Her throat tightened. The truth? The line from the movie *A Few Good Men* came to mind: *You can't handle the truth!* She couldn't handle the truth. So she improvised.

"We're working together. We're a team, and we need each other if we're going to kick this Westerfield's ass. And . . ." She glanced to the right of him. " . . . I couldn't help Jerryl. It's what haunted me the most, that I was right there and couldn't help him. I wasn't going to go through that with you."

He released her, and she swore he looked disappointed. "You have the soul of a soldier. You do what you have to do for your comrades."

"Isn't that why you saved *me*?"

He paused. "Yeah." He sat up again, scrubbing his hands through his hair, and then made a sniffing sound. "Damn, I need a shower."

"You were sweating buckets." She was almost afraid to ask. "Do you remember anything?"

He shook his head. "Lights, like the Aurora Borealis, in the darkest blackness I have ever seen. Thinking I was in hell because I was so hot. Feeling fire in my veins, probably after the injection." He looked at the bruise inside his elbow. His gaze lifted to her and his pupils dilated for an instant.

"What?"

"Nothing. I was probably delusional."

Did he remember their interlude? She turned away. "You'd better call your people. They've been tripping with worry." She got his phone and handed it to him. "They love you loads. You're lucky."

His hand closed around over hers, though his gaze was somewhere else. "Yeah. I am."

He talked to them for a few minutes and then got

out of bed. That's when he noticed he was naked. "You stripped me?" He looked shocked, giving her a raised eyebrow. "You bad girl."

"You were drenched." *Way to sound defensive.* Her face flushed with heat. *Oh, I did more than that.* She put her hands on her hips. "Besides, you don't care if I see you naked anyway. Like now, for instance."

He walked toward the bathroom, but swayed and grabbed onto the edge of the dresser for balance.

Fear spiked in her again as she rushed to his side. "Are you all right?"

"A little dizzy. I'm starved."

"Eat first, then shower."

"I'll be fine."

She rolled her eyes. "You are such a guy. I'm going in to the bathroom with you, then."

"If you insist."

A rush of relief and gratitude washed over her. He was the same Eric. She wanted to hug him but held back. "Go in. I'll be right here if you need me."

He gave her a curious look, as though he were figuring something out. Then he shook his head and started the shower. She sat on the lid of the toilet, her legs pulled up to her chest, cheek resting against her knees. The shower curtain was an opaque blue, revealing indistinct outlines of his body. She had to watch him, because he wouldn't call out if he felt dizzy. She'd have to try to catch his bonehead ass before he hit the tub.

You are so falling for that bonehead.

The truth she'd been trying to avoid now pulsed through her. She squeezed her eyes closed, trying to push it back.

You know the psychology, girlfriend. You did it with Jerryl, and so it's only logical that you'd do it with Eric.

Except I don't feel the same way about Eric that I did about Jerryl. Jerryl was lust, drama. He fed my anger. Eric calms me in some ways, and makes me crazier than ever in others. But he doesn't make me angry. He does make me feel safe.

The shower stopped and he pushed the curtain aside. Dammit, she had to stop seeing him naked. A woman could only take so much. She stood, threw a towel at him, and stalked out.

"Something I said?" he asked.

"No, something you are." She closed the door.

Sayre parked along the road, looking down the gravel drive. He'd finally gotten into Fonda's dreams enough to get her to clue him in as to where they were. When he had Fonda take a walk around, he recognized the place. Amy had stayed there once, and he'd given the information to Darkwell. For some reason, he couldn't get into Eric. Well, he could have plenty of fun with Fonda. Especially once he got rid of Eric.

It took some dicking around, but he'd finally found the road. It was out in the rural area south of Annapolis. He didn't know what this place was or who owned it, and the NO TRESPASSING signs made him wonder what the heck they were doing out here. He'd wait a bit. He had plenty of time.

CHAPTER 19

Eric could have eaten a horse, but he had to settle for a pound of bacon, ten eggs, and half a loaf of bread. Fonda wore an amused expression as she nibbled on a piece of bacon. He ought to be pissed at her, but he couldn't quite muster it. Mostly because he had some hazy memories of her, of things she'd said to him, of her tender toughness. The erotic thing could have been his imagination, but the other stuff . . . those memories made him feel something, which made him think they were real. Then she'd said she only saved him out of honor and responsibility.

Hell, if he knew.

Magnus sat at the table, too, leaning his chair back. "So what are your plans now?"

"We've still got to find a way to nail this guy."

"Amy said he wasn't part of the original program," Fonda said.

Eric mopped up the last of his egg yolk with the last of his bread and popped it into his mouth. "So how does he fit in?" He didn't wait for an answer, of course. He looked at Magnus. "We'll be out of here by noon."

"If you need my help, I'm here. Sounds like one way or another this guy will be hunting us all down."

Eric shook his head. "I appreciate that, but he and whoever he's working with might not know about you. No need to put you in danger." He looked at Fonda. "Wallace never told Darkwell about his sons. When their mother got pregnant, the program was deteriorating, and so were the subjects."

"Didn't seem like the right time to make the happy announcement," Magnus said. "By the time Lachlan was born, the subjects were dying, and my father suspected they weren't all because of mental illness. So he put my mother's last name on the birth certificates and left his name out altogether." He raised his thick eyebrow. "So on paper, we're bastards."

Eric recognized the hunger to fight in Magnus's eyes, remembered how they were sword fighting. "If we run into a situation where we need the extra manpower, we'll give you a shout." He didn't want to be responsible for another man's death. Besides, if Magnus died, he knew that Lachlan would have his head.

Fonda leaned her elbows on the table. "We've got to find out who Westerfield is affiliated with. He showed me an FBI badge, but that could be a fake. Is he really government? Most importantly, who's the guy on the other end of the phone? He might be the bigger threat, which means getting rid of Westerfield won't solve our problem. Let me find him, figure out where he is. Eric, you can remote-view him and gather more information." She looked at Magnus. "That's what we were doing when Eric took a nose-dive."

Eric pushed his plate away, his gaze on Magnus.

"Are there any dangers in astral projecting? With remote-viewing, I'm not really there. But her soul goes to where she projects."

"Other than the psychosis, I don't think so. Not that we ran into, anyway. But we never dealt with someone like us. Hitler, Martin Luther King, Jesus Christ—"

"You saw *Jesus*?" Eric asked.

"My father did. He was different after that, too. It was the most peaceful I'd ever seen him."

Fonda's face glowed. "I want to learn to do that. That would be incredible." The glow disappeared. "But first I've got to focus on the present. We're going to head out in a bit. I'm sure Lachlan will be glad to see us go."

Magnus shrugged. "You disappointed him, Eric."

"By not dying?"

"By not losing your abilities. Yours came back even faster than mine did. But really, he can't get much more bitter than he already is." He turned to Fonda. "Project from here. Let us know where this guy is, in case you and Eric never come back."

She gave him a forced smile. "That's optimistic."

He stood and tapped the table. "Got to be realistic with this business. Let me know what you find out."

Eric loaded his dishes into the dishwasher and followed Fonda down the hall to the room he'd spent the night in. He didn't realize that he put his hand on her lower back until he'd already done it. Fonda glanced back but didn't shrug away from him.

She climbed onto the bed and stretched out. Her lower body was encased in tie-dyed yellow jeans, and her green tank top tightened over the curves of her boobs. The pink stripe of hair caught the sunlight coming in, and her hair, parted on the side, brushed her cheek. She still wore those drippy gold earrings.

"What?" she asked when she noticed he'd stopped cold and was staring at her.

"You look . . ." He wasn't sure what to say. His brain was still in second gear. Something was bugging him, and seeing her like that jarred it again. "This is not the kind of question a guy likes to ask, but did something happen while I was out? Did we make love?"

Her body stiffened and her face flushed. So when she said "No," very definitely, he actually felt disappointed.

He sat on the bed. "Because I had this . . . well, I'm not sure it was a dream exactly—"

"Nothing happened."

He crawled up next to her. "I have these memories of you in my arms. Of touching you here." He put one hand on her stomach, his other hand around the back of her neck. "And here." He slid his hand to her waist, and then around to her back. "And here." He kissed her, taking her lips in his, just a taste.

Her eyes closed but her eyebrows were furrowed. Why was she fighting him? There was at the least an overpowering sexual chemistry between them. That, she couldn't deny, and yet she was. Her body moved into his touch, her mouth slackened, and he swept in with his tongue.

He held onto the words he'd heard her say, raw emotion saturating them: *Eric, please come back to me. I need you.* He'd come back, and now she was putting up the wall again.

She pushed back, a tangle of emotions on her face. "I can't."

He sat back, expelling a breath. "Because of Jerryl? You still think you love him, don't you?"

She looked genuinely surprised by his assumption. "Jerryl?"

"I saw the pictures in your bag."

"The pictures . . . oh, yeah, those. I threw them away at my father's house."

"You threw them away?"

She nodded, tracing infinity circles on the sheet. "You were right; I never loved him."

"You're mad that I popped that bubble?"

She stretched out on her side, her gaze on her finger as she continued to trace circles. "At first, yes. You made me see things about myself, things I didn't want to see. Even worse, it was you putting that mirror in front of my face." She exhaled a soft breath and looked at him. "But I'm glad you did."

He lay on his side, arm propped up by his hand, facing her. Hearing those words sent a surge of relief through him. It mattered, and given the way he felt, it mattered a lot to him that she'd come to her senses where Jerryl was concerned. He reached out and skimmed his hand along her side and the curve of her hip. He said something he didn't think he would ever say. "Do you forgive me for putting you through that? For killing him?" That mattered, too, and he would do anything to hear her say the words.

He didn't have to pay any price. Her eyes were clear and filled with compassion. "Yes, I've forgiven you."

He cupped her cheek. "Thank you." The words came out in almost a whisper. She did things to him, broke down his hard shell, made him into someone he'd never been before. She still had her shell, though, and he knew in that moment he would do whatever it took to break through it. He grazed her mouth with his thumb, brushing slowly back and forth. "Do you feel safe with me?"

She nodded.

He shook his head. "Some part of you doesn't. I see it now, and whenever I touch you. I won't ever hurt you. Do you know that?"

She nodded again, and he saw the shell in her eyes, the shell and the yearning.

"I want you," he said. "You know that, too, don't you?"

She hesitated, shifting her gaze away. Uncomfortable territory. Yeah, well, this was unfamiliar terrain to him, too. He'd always gone into new situations without fear, guns blazing, not taking the time to think things through. He was done doing that. She was too important to risk, to scare away. Walking a fine line, however, was as foreign as what he was feeling for her.

She cleared her throat. "You know I have this thing, this weakness for someone protecting me. I based everything I thought I felt for Jerryl on that. Now I feel . . . something for you, and even though it's different, I'm afraid it's because of that. You've saved me—"

"I thought we weren't keeping score."

"We're not. I'm not. You've done more than just save my life, like making me see the truth . . . you've done more than anyone else in my life has. You didn't let me stay blind and comfortably numb. I don't trust what I feel."

"What do you feel?"

She searched his eyes, a flicker of panic in hers. "Eric, don't make me—"

"Like you?" He smiled, easing the moment.

She smiled, too, and looked at the ceiling. "You made me like you. Oh, yeah, you definitely made me like you."

A soft knock on the door preceded its opening. Magnus stepped in. "Did you find him?"

"We haven't started yet," Eric said.

Fonda jumped at the chance to move out of a conversation that had her teetering on the edge of either running from the room screaming or throwing herself into Eric's arms. Of all the risks she'd taken, admitting what he'd come to mean to her was the biggest, and not one she was ready to take. Yes, she was scared that those feelings were based on what he'd done for her. Even scarier was the sense of just how deep they went.

She rolled onto her back. Much safer to focus on the psychic creep than those arctic eyes she'd once thought masked Eric's feelings. So not true.

She pictured Westerfield's face, his taunting voice when he talked about smelling her fear. She went through the familiar process, and then she was in a room, like a lab of some kind. She stood behind a man sitting at a desk on the far side. Westerfield. Seemed odd to find him doing something mundane like paperwork. She stepped farther out of his view.

Tacks were stuck in a random pattern on a map of the D.C./Maryland area on the wall. No indication of where this place was, though. Eric needed a location before he could remote-view. Interesting that he could talk while he did so. She tried to describe what she saw but was completely disconnected to her physical self.

She walked around a tall shelving unit filled with notebooks, intending to go through the wall.

Westerfield stood there, looking right at her. Her heart jumped. *Get out!*

"Got you," he said.

She saw a blinding flash of light, felt something close in around her. *Can't see anything. Get back, now!* She felt an odd tightening sensation, as though a cloud had surrounded her and now squeezed from all sides. She'd never felt pain in her etheric form before, but now she did. The humming was more like a searing buzz, vibrating through her being.

She couldn't get back. *No!*

The buzz lessened in its intensity and the cloud thinned. Okay, she was going back. It was just different this time. Different . . .

The cloud dissipated. Eric's face was warped. No, not Eric. Westerfield! He was smiling at her, that much she could see, but the image was stretched and shiny. Glass. She spun around and saw glass all around her. Fear gripped her, pounding as fast as her heartbeat. She was trapped in a glass jar. Judging by the size of his face, she was small. He'd grabbed her soul! And shrunk her.

Eric wouldn't be able to find her. How long could Westerfield keep her? What would happen to her body? Was there a way to get back to it? To Eric? She tried, focusing on that gorgeous face and his expression when she'd said she forgave him, as though she'd given him a precious gift.

Nothing. Whatever this was, it blocked her from leaving.

Everything tilted when Westerfield picked up the jar. He shook it, sending her crashing against the sides. His mouth was moving but she couldn't hear what he was saying, only a murmur. What she could see was how pleased he was. Could he smell her emotions here? She steeled herself, cramming down her fear and anger. One feeling got through, though: grief at not being able to contact Eric. At the thought of not seeing him again.

That's what got to her most of all.

Eric watched her body tighten, her breath come in an airless gasp. She hadn't done that last time. He looked at Magnus, whose eyebrows furrowed. What happened next worried him even more. Her body wilted. He could feel the absence of her, like an emptiness that sucked the air out of the room.

He grabbed her hand and felt her pulse. Light and thready. "Fonda!" He shook her and kept screaming her name. No response. He gave Magnus a desperate look. "How do I get her back?"

"What you're doing is how my father said to do it. That's how we got Lachlan back." He sat on the other side of her and slapped her cheeks.

Eric kept hold of her hand, squeezing it hard, leaning down next to her ear. "Fonda, get back here, now! Come back to me!"

Not a twitch, not a sign that she was in there.

Magnus looked concerned. "I'm getting Lachlan. He knows more about astral projection than I do."

He ran out of the room, his footsteps heavy down the hall. Minutes later two sets pounded back toward Eric.

Eric didn't care if Lachlan was an angry asshole. He'd been one once, too. He met the man's dark eyes. "Help us. How do we get her back?"

Lachlan looked at Fonda. "How long has she been gone?"

Eric looked at the clock. "Five minutes. She's already been gone for *five minutes*." Too long. The words beat through his head: *Too damned long*.

Lachlan perched on the edge of the bed beside her. "Dad told me there was a chance something could go wrong. What happened to me was different. I was partially connected to my body, acting out what my soul was experiencing." He picked up her hand and let it drop. "That's not what's happening to her, obviously."

"She's not here at all." Eric heard the strain in his voice.

Lachlan shook his head. He also felt her pulse at her wrist. "She's barely here physically."

"What did Wallace say could go wrong?"

Lachlan was studying Fonda's face. "He intuitively felt there were dangers, aside from the psychosis. Once, he'd gone to a place he couldn't describe. It was like nothing he'd ever seen before, a world like ours but not quite. Something pulled at his soul, like a magnet. He had a struggle getting back. When he did, he was shaken, something my father was rarely. He felt that if that thing had grabbed him, he wouldn't have come back."

Eric's mouth moved and words came out, but he had no idea where they were coming from. "We have to find her Essence, her soul, and bring her body to it. If we don't within an hour, she'll die."

Both men looked at him, and Eric knew his expression was probably as surprised as theirs. It wasn't like Jerryl's voice in his head, not an order. It was not something he'd ever experienced before.

"How do you know that?" Lachlan asked.

"I don't know, but I know it's true. How do I find

where she is? I can't remote-view without having some idea where she went." The answer came to him from his own mind this time. "I took Amy with me once, when I remote-viewed Lucas, by connecting our souls. He was being held prisoner, and she needed to see him." He straddled Fonda's body, putting his hands on her face, leaning low over her. "I'm going to go to her the same way."

He closed his eyes, merging his energy with hers. The void he felt scared him, almost enough to bring him back to the surface, but he focused only on filling her with his energy, becoming one with her in a way he could never do physically.

He left his body, flying through the ether, following a faint trail that looked like the stream of clouds a jet leaves in the sky. Her trail, and it was fading fast. He clung to the last particles that led him into a thick white cloud. He dove into it, scrabbling for those last crumbs of her. One more. He reached for it, tumbling, breaking through the cloud.

In a room. Westerfield at a desk, on the phone. He strained to hear. Sounds were always muffled or warbled.

"I've got her Essence. It worked just as it did for Simeon. I'll watch her fade away, as I did with him . . . yes, I'll let you know when she's gone. Then we'll find the other one."

Her Essence, the word his mind had conjured up. Or someone else's mind. Eric frantically searched for her. His heart plunged when he saw the jar at Westerfield's elbow, a small version of her ghostly presence in the glass cylinder with a metal rim on the top and bottom. The bands bore hieroglyphic symbols engraved in the metal. One of them was the Eye that he had tattooed on his arm. How had Westerfield captured her? Could he get her out?

Eric wanted to try to communicate with her, but Westerfield would either capture him or send him hurtling back to his body. More important was figuring out her location. He floated higher, above a remote building in the woods like Wallace's compound. He found the nearest street sign, and then another. That was enough. He pulled out.

"He's got her," he said, fear and exhaustion permeating his voice. "He's got her Essence in some kind of glass container. She's going to die if I don't get her back to her body."

"I'll go with you," Magnus said.

Before Lachlan could protest, as he was about to do, Eric said, "I'm not exposing you." Like Fonda had exposed herself to Sayre.

"Look, mate—"

"I can handle this. If I need help, I'll call you. What I do need is a computer connected to the Internet. I saw a couple of street signs."

"Give me the names, and I'll print out a map for you," Magnus said. "Rest for a few minutes. You'll need all the strength you can get."

CHAPTER 20

Eric had thirty minutes left to reunite Fonda's soul to her body. He drove, his gaze going to her limp body on the passenger seat. She looked so small, like a child asleep. Had she gone through what he was now suffering: worrying, scared to frigging death? If what he heard her say was any indication, yes. Except he had a time element to deal with.

This place was closer to D.C., and out in the woods off several rural roads. He kept looking at her, at the clock, the map, her . . . he was hardly looking at the damned road.

Westerfield would be there. The question was, would he be expecting him? *Count on it.* He paused at a stop sign and looked at the satellite map. He'd recognize the building, chair-shaped from above, when he saw it.

He pulled down a gravel road marked with more ominous NO TRESPASSING signs than the Wallace compound. He parked a few hundred feet in. From the map, the building appeared to be a quarter mile from the road. He walked around to the passenger side and opened the door.

"We're here, baby. Hang on."

He brushed her hair from her face, then gently picked her up. She weighed next to nothing but wasn't as vulnerable as she looked. That gave him hope.

Several minutes down the road he heard a noise, like a door closing. He searched the woods. He hadn't spotted the building yet and saw no one moving in the distance. Only heard the breeze rustling through the leaves and his footsteps.

How close did her body need to be? He'd gotten the answer to the time limit, so he cleared his thoughts and heard *Fifteen feet*. Sort of his voice, but not his knowledge. He looked around again. That was creepy as hell, having someone putting thoughts in his head. Maybe it was Cheveyo, the mysterious Offspring who helped them but had never talked to anyone but Zoe and Petra. He seemed to know a lot about this stuff. Or maybe it was his imagination. Still, it made sense that she needed to be near her physical body. The hard part would be getting hold of the jar.

The building came into view, blending well with the trees. He paused, remote-viewed, and saw Westerfield still sitting at the desk. Damn. As he neared the building, he looked for cameras. Nothing he could see, but who knew what the guy had in place, both physically and psychically? He knew he had to be ready, and he sure as hell didn't want Fonda in his arms if the dude came out.

"You killed her," a voice said from behind him, wrapped in a southern accent. "Now why'd you go and do that? I was looking forward to having some fun with her once you were out of the picture."

Eric's heart slammed as he turned to see Sayre standing only a few yards away.

"Shut the hell up," Eric whispered.

"Is this your hideout? The famous place Darkwell couldn't find?"

"You don't know what you're into here. The guy in there is more of a badass than Darkwell ever was. Than you are."

Sayre laughed. "Nobody's more of a badass than me. You saw what I did to Nicholas, didn't you?"

Eric wanted to kill him, to just torch him right then. But no way could he take the chance of setting a fire with Fonda here. He set her down next to the building and stalked toward Sayre, his hands twitching to go around his throat and shut him up.

"Well, well, I've got company," another male voice said.

There went his element of surprise. Eric hoped Westerfield hadn't seen Fonda's body.

"Who the hell are you?" Sayre asked, not looking the least bit perturbed.

"Shouldn't I be asking you that, since you are, after all, on my private property?" Westerfield smiled. "You're one of them, the one who's wanted by the police."

"Nah, that's my twin brother. I'm the good guy."

Eric stepped very slowly toward Westerfield as the two men talked. Maybe he could get inside—

Westerfield turned and held out his hand, squeezing his fist at Eric. Pain exploded in his head. He dropped to his knees, fighting all the way.

"Hey, that's a cool ability you got there," he heard Sayre say.

Then Sayre's scream of agony. Through blurred vision, Eric saw Sayre crumple to the ground, too, clutching his head.

Can't die. Got to break that jar, release her.

Everything went dark.

He opened his eyes, with no idea how much time had passed. Still not dead. His eyes snapped fully open and he tried to get to his feet. Except he couldn't move. He was staring at the ceiling, lying flat on his back. He couldn't move his limbs and felt cuffs strain against his ankles and wrists. His fingers wrapped around the edges of a metal table.

"Good. I didn't use too much force." Westerfield stood beside him, looking down. "It's a fine line between incapacitating and slaughtering." He breathed in, his nostrils flaring. "Only a little fear. That will change."

Eric's gaze went to the jar, still on the desk: inside, Fonda's ethereal form was shrunk as small as a Barbie doll. Her hands were on the glass and she was facing him, but he couldn't see the details of her face. She was more transparent than before. Fading. *Got to get her out of there.* He searched and found a clock on the wall. Less than fifteen minutes to save her.

"Ah, not fear for yourself," Westerfield amended. "For her. How sweet. But how did you know to bring her body here?"

That struck even more fear into him. He knew. Eric frantically looked for her body but couldn't see it. "What do you want with us? Let her go. She's no threat to you."

"You are all threats, just by your existence. And for me, you are a curiosity."

A groan pulled his and Westerfield's attention to the floor. Eric lifted his head and saw Sayre slumped there, cuffed to a metal loop in the wall. Sayre pulled against the cuff. "What the f—" He narrowed his eyes at Westerfield. "Now, that wasn't very nice. I mean, it was okay doing it to that son of a bitch, but you and me, we ain't got no beef."

"You didn't come here together to save Fonda Raine?" Westerfield said to him.

"Save her?" Sayre pointed to Eric. "He killed her. I followed him here and saw him carrying her body."

"Interesting." Westerfield's smile grew. "Yes, this could be very interesting indeed. How will two adversaries react?"

"What the hell are you talking 'bout?" Sayre said.

Eric was taking in the room, all the while testing his own cuffs. They were solid. The clock ticked louder and louder with each passing minute. He had to break that jar and release her. At least then she'd have a chance of surviving. And he had to do it soon.

He saw newspaper clippings tacked to a huge bulletin board. All he could read were the headlines: 'QUIET' MAN GOES ON RAMPAGE, SHOOTS FOUR CO-WORKERS; 'FAMILY MAN' MURDERS WIFE, TWO SONS, THEN SELF; PEACEFUL CULT MEMBERS TURN ON ONE ANOTHER, BRUTAL BLOOD FEST.

Westerfield was infecting people with something that made them turn on other people, even their loved ones. Now he was going to use it on them—that's what he'd meant about the adversaries remark.

"What was in those canisters on the plane?" Eric asked. "Was it Blue Moon?"

Westerfield scoffed. "That's what the botanist called it. Somehow that man got hold of it and then was insane enough to ingest it. Now you carry it in your bodies. We can mask it when we spray it on people so no tox scan will pick it up. But it's in your DNA. Can't be masked there."

"What is it?"

"You have the Essence of someone's life in you."

"Extraterrestrial life."

Westerfield only smiled. "Is that what you've deduced? Martians, maybe? Green beings with huge eyes?" He made circles around his eyes with his fingers, then laughed. "Well, it won't matter much longer."

Sayre said, "Are you saying we've got some alien stuff in us? Is that what you are, some freaking alien who can look like us? What did you do to us out there? It felt like a brain freeze. Shit, it was a mind probe thing, wasn't it?"

Westerfield turned toward him, his voice deadly low. "You talk too much."

"I want answers, dammit. You squeeze my head without touching me, cuff me, and you ain't even told me why. Now you're saying you're some kind of alien freakazoid who—"

Westerfield flung his hand toward Sayre, whose head jerked with a *crack*. His eyes widened in pain and he tried to say something and grimaced in even more pain. He put his free hand on his jaw like he was holding it in place.

Lesson one: don't talk too much. Eric already knew he had to play it cool if he was going to have a chance of saving Fonda.

Westerfield picked up something that looked like a

steel fire extinguisher. He knelt down and unlocked Sayre's cuff. "I trust you'll cooperate now. I do love making people's brains and guts explode in grand and spectacular ways, but I have something even more fun in mind."

Sayre couldn't talk, but he went along toward a room Eric could only see if he lifted his head. There was a large window to the left of the steel door where Westerfield led Sayre. As they moved away, he tried desperately to break free, but couldn't budge the cuffs. Then he heard the door slam and the lock click shut, followed by a spraying sound.

Westerfield came into view a moment later. "I was hoping to do some experimentation."

Eric remembered how he'd been whining that he couldn't witness or directly participate in the killing of people. All those innocent people.

Westerfield took a deep breath. Eric tried to quell his fear and anger, but Westerfield's smile indicated he'd picked up something. His eyes rolled in pleasure. "Rage. Confusion. Bloodlust." He nodded in the direction he'd taken Sayre, toward the window on the other side of the room. "He's not nearly as controlled as you."

Westerfield walked over to a video camera on a tripod and turned a switch at the wall. Sayre's grunting noises belched out of a speaker above the window.

"He'll be ready in a few minutes."

Which Eric realized meant he had ten more minutes to break out Fonda's soul.

Westerfield regarded him. "Don't you want to know what I'm going to do? You don't seem scared, or much of anything."

Answering was a lose-lose proposition. Whatever

was going to happen, he wanted to get it started. He had to get off this table.

A loud thump caught both their attention. Sayre was throwing himself at the window, trying to break through. Westerfield moved the table, obviously on wheels, so Eric could watch the show. Was this his intent, to make both of them go crazy and beat themselves to death?

Sayre had a wild look in his eyes, which was even spookier because the man looked so much like Lucas. Foam spittle dribbled from the corners his mouth and smeared on the glass. He pounded on the window, even smashing his forehead into it.

"I'd say it's working splendidly. The glass won't break." Westerfield shot Eric a grin. "In case you were worried."

Watching Sayre was unnerving; watching the clock ticking away was terrifying.

Westerfield's arms were loosely crossed in front of him as he watched, a satisfied look on his face. He turned from the window to him. "Have you ever been to a dogfight? They mistreat the dogs, get them riled up so their rage builds, and as soon as they see the other dog, they attack. Let's see how a noncrazed man will do against a crazed one. And no fair using your pyro skills. I'll be blocking them, as usual. Don't want you to burn the place down, after all."

Eric felt a dull thumping in his chest. His blood slowed to a crawl of dread. It reminded him of when Darkwell had thrown Nicholas into Sayre's room to let him kill him. Even not crazed, Sayre had beat the hell out of him. This, though, Westerfield was doing for friggin' entertainment. Under normal circumstances Eric would have been happy to nail Sayre's ass to the floor, and he knew he could have easily done it. But with Sayre psychotic . . . he wasn't sure.

"Let's get on with it then," he said, tightening his jaw.

Westerfield chuckled. "I'd heard you were blood-thirsty."

Funny thing, he'd probably heard that from Fonda.

Another minute ticked by, each second an agony. Westerfield checked the camera that was aimed at the window, peering at the small screen. Eric tilted up his chin, trying to catch a glimpse of Fonda. She was barely visible.

"*Now* I smell some real fear coming from you." Westerfield pulled out a ring of keys. "We can do this the civil way, you cooperating, and maybe you'll have a chance to win."

As though the guy would let him live.

"Or, if you try to escape, you'll be struck down and face him already in a state of pain, a distinct disadvantage. You don't impress me as someone who would want to go in disadvantaged."

Two minutes left!

Westerfield unlocked the cuffs. Eric got to his feet, pretending to shake his numbed limbs, but then sprinted toward the jar. She was only a mist now. Pain seared his stomach but he pushed on. His knees went out from under him. He started to fall. Reached out. *Almost there. Break it. Have to break the glass.* He fell. His hands knocked the jar to the side. It tilted. He fought his body's instinct to curl up with the pain. The jar fell. Westerfield's footsteps pounded behind him.

The jar hit the floor. Rolled. Didn't break. Pain. Westerfield behind him. Eric reached up—*pain . . . must do it*—and smashed his hand down on the glass.

It broke, cutting the side of his palm. The mist evaporated.

Westerfield stood above him, hands on his hips. "You think that's going to save her?"

Eric had a heart-stopping thought. Where was her body? In the room with Sayre? He got up and ran to the room, pain rocketing through his insides. Sayre threw himself at the glass in front of him, his hands like claws. Nothing human remained in his eyes, not that there was much in there to begin with. Eric searched behind him but didn't see Fonda. Westerfield put his hand on the doorknob. "I'll disable him temporarily so you can go in clean."

Sayre crumpled, the door opened, and Eric felt a hand push him inside. He had no choice, not when the guy could and would crush his insides. Sayre jumped to his feet, eyes blazing with the bloodlust Westerfield had just mentioned. The door closed.

CHAPTER 21

Fonda felt herself fading by degrees. Every time Westerfield had looked at her, his face warped in the curve of the glass, it gave her the creeps. She faced the opposite direction, where papers were spread out on the desk. Because she needed something to think about, she focused on those papers and pictures. She saw the word *Amish* several times and a red circle on a map. The pictures she could see, slightly distorted though they were, looked like surveillance photos of Amish people. One was of a woman and two young children.

They'd infected that Sun Veil cult. Were they looking for other groups to infect? But why? An Amish community, peaceful, not waiting for some UFO to take them away.

She was trapped there, unable to help. In fact, dying. She didn't know how long she had, but it wouldn't be long. Losing that connection to her body felt like a huge void that grew larger and larger.

Westerfield suddenly stood and walked away. She

pushed against the glass wall, trying to knock the jar off the desk. If she could break it, maybe she could escape. Her soul had no power to touch or move things in this jar, though. And she was so weak.

Movement in the room caught her eye. He was dragging a body inside. *Eric! No!* She squinted, trying to see more of the man. No, not big enough. Wait. She recognized the close-shaved head: Sayre. She could hardly feel relief when Westerfield left, because he returned dragging another man in. Her heart dropped, even though she didn't *have* a heart in a literal sense. *Eric.* How had he found her? Was he dead? She couldn't see any blood, but she knew what Westerfield could do.

The longest minutes of her life crept by as she watched him secure both men. Finally Eric woke, and Westerfield talked to both men, though she couldn't hear what anyone said. They walked out of her sight as she strained to see what was going on. Suddenly, a man came running toward her, stumbling, and then she saw Eric's face for a second before his hand knocked the jar down. She fell to the floor, spinning dizzily, and then his hand smashed down on the glass and she was sucked away.

She woke with a gasp . . . in her body. Pins and needles everywhere, but at least she could feel again. She ran her hands over herself, thank God, back. What about Eric? She looked around. *Huh?* She was in a bathroom. She ran to the door. The knob turned but the door wouldn't budge.

She pushed, and then it abruptly opened. Westerfield stood in front of her, his hand on the knob. "Ah. Just in time to watch your boyfriend die."

She heard a thump nearby and jerked her gaze to a window: Eric and Sayre going at it, and the sound of flesh pounding against flesh coming out of a speaker.

"It's a death match," he said.

He explained about the Essence and how it had made Sayre psychotic. Sayre, not Eric, thank God. Westerfield's words, though, were lost as she watched the horror inside that room. Sayre, foaming at the mouth, his jaw at a strange angle, throwing himself at Eric, who deflected him, knocking him to the floor. Eric kicked at his face, and Sayre's eyes bugged in pain.

She couldn't breathe. Eric looked up and saw her, his face blanching. The distraction gave Sayre a chance to ram his knee into Eric's stomach. She felt it, too, gripping her stomach.

I'm so sorry, Eric. You came for me and now this.

Eric doubled over, and when she thought he might be done, rammed his head into Sayre's, sending him backward. Eric had claw marks down his arms, and Sayre scrambled up with those claws ready to slash again. Her hand went to her mouth as she watched, unable to pull her gaze away.

"Stop them," she said. "This is mad."

But she knew that Westerfield would never stop a show he was enjoying so much. She thought about freezing time, but Eric would be frozen, too, and she couldn't get him out in any case.

I love you, I love you, I love you. The words kept rolling through her mind. She wanted to scream them out but didn't want to distract him again.

Eric slammed Sayre against the wall and started punching him in the face. Blood spurted everywhere. Sayre kicked Eric in the groin, and she watched his face tighten and body curl inward. He didn't stop pounding. Sayre tried to kick again, but Eric stepped sideways. Sayre lost his balance and slipped to the floor. He could hardly move to get up.

Eric didn't stop pounding on him, his breath heaving as he dropped to his knees and delivered one last blow. He bowed over, head hanging down, catching his breath. After a few seconds he checked Sayre's pulse and then dropped his arm. He pushed to his feet and faced the window. She gasped at his face, bruised and bloodied.

Eric looked at Westerfield. "Your little experiment is done. Let her go and I'll cooperate in whatever way you want." His gaze shifted to her.

He was offering himself to save her! She felt the impact of that like a boulder to the chest. She shook her head, but Westerfield was smiling that amused grin again.

He pressed a button on the speaker. "Very impressive, Aruda. *Very* impressive. Not only your physical strength, but your sacrificial desire to save your girl. I find that kind of behavior so interesting but very rare. I'll bet cooperating doesn't come easy for you, especially when you know death will be at the end. Sayre had an even stronger reaction to the Essence than normal people, so I suspect it's because of the Essence that's already in you. Let's see what more does to you."

He pressed a button on a silver canister attached to the wall. A mist filled the room Eric was in.

"No!" She lunged for Westerfield, and he grabbed her wrists.

"Don't make me hurt you. It would spoil all the fun."

That last word sank into her like talons.

He kept a hold on her wrists but was looking at Eric. "Death match two: throw your girlfriend in with you, see what happens when it's someone you love. I'll wait until the mist settles so she'll be perfectly sane as you maul her. It's so much more enjoyable that way. Then I'll finally experience some emotion. Hers, not yours, of course. You'll have none as you tear her apart, because you'll be mad."

Eric looked at her, a fierce expression on his face. "I'll never hurt her." He'd said that to her before, but hadn't counted on being infected by madness. No, she couldn't stand the thought of him mindlessly killing her. By the agony in his eyes, neither could he.

"Do you think that loving cult thought they'd harm any living thing?" Westerfield turned to her. "He's exhausted and already injured. You'll have a small advantage there, though I'm not so sure how long it will last. You saw Sayre. He started the fight with a broken jaw."

Westerfield opened the door and shoved her in. Eric rushed forward but Westerfield slammed the door before he could reach it. Eric pulled her into his arms and kissed her hard.

She put her arms around him and pulled back to look at him, her hand touching one of the few places on his face that wasn't bruised or bloody. "I'm sorry, Eric. I'm sorry I caused this to happen to you. To us."

"I came here because I wanted to, not because I had to. And you didn't cause this."

She lifted his hand, wincing at the cut on the side of his palm. "You are my hero. No matter what happens—" The words choked in her throat. She met his gaze. "We made love when you were out. You weren't dreaming that. And it was beautiful and wonderful, and I felt not-quite-right about it, but I hoped it would bring you back, and—"

He kissed her, bracing her face, moving close to her. "Keep kissing me. Don't stop."

An order, as though that would stop the madness. She complied, because kissing him seemed a lot better than standing around waiting.

Several minutes passed. "It's working," she whispered.

"How much could you hear from the speaker out there?" he whispered back.

"It wasn't very clear."

"I don't think it's the kissing. I bet it's the antidote."

The antidote! Holy crap, she hadn't even thought about that. The antidote stopped the psychosis.

"How well can you act?" he asked again, nuzzling her neck.

"Good enough. What's on your mind?"

"I pretend to go crazy and strangle you. Then I collapse in grief. He opens the door."

"I freeze time."

"Uh-huh. Then I torch the place. I can't get to him directly, but maybe it'll work indirectly."

"I'm game." Her heart beat the strains of sweet, splendid hope.

"Do what you have to do to make it look authentic: scratch, kick, whatever. Pretend I've bitten your neck."

She screamed, holding her neck. "No, Eric! It's me, Fonda. You came here to save me, remember! Which means you care about me. You. Care. About. Me." He did. "Eric, look at me."

He did, his mouth twisting as though he were fighting a demon inside him. If she didn't know better, she would have wondered if the Essence was working. His hands slipped from her face to her throat.

"*No.*" The word came out strangled as she squeezed it out of her mouth.

His eyes went blank. He pushed her down to the floor. She fought him, kicking at his legs, and found herself in a familiar position—pinned beneath his body. His arms trembled with the strength he was supposedly using to strangle her. She scratched at his clothes, gasping, pushing all the blood up to her face. Her eyes bulged out. She shuddered and went limp.

He growled and screamed and laid her on the floor, pacing, hitting the walls, or at least that's what it sounded like. He made so many strange noises that she had to fight to keep from looking up to see what he was doing. Playing out the craziness, she guessed, and then he would come to his senses. He knelt beside her, checking her pulse, letting her hand drop to the floor as he had with Sayre.

"No. *Noooo!*" He dropped his head on her stomach and released the agonized cries of a wounded animal.

She heard the door lock click and then open. Waited a heartbeat until she heard Westerfield say, "Eric, you—"

She opened her eyes. Westerfield was frozen in front of the door, mouth ajar. She leapt to her feet while Eric ran to Westerfield and pushed him, sending him to the floor. "Lock him in."

"Good idea."

They rushed out and locked the door. "Get out of his sight as soon as you can."

As they ran to the door, they heard the lock click. Westerfield had unlocked it with his ability.

A fire erupted at the desk, and another at the door as they passed through the opening. They ran, and she held her side as a stitch cramped. Eric's fingers were curled around hers.

Sunlight slanted through the trees, lighting their way. They reached the truck and Eric swiveled around to look behind them. So did she. He came from behind one of the tree trunks, his footsteps heavy. Without a word they both jumped in and Eric tore away. She looked back, terrified Westerfield would send the truck rolling. Smoke already billowed into the sky.

"I can't see him. I don't know whether that's a good thing or not."

He pulled her against him, driving with one hand. "Are you all right?"

She nodded, afraid if she opened her mouth too much would come tumbling out. How scared she'd been of losing him, how incredible and shocking that he'd tried to bargain with his life, and mostly that he'd come for her in the first place.

Finally she asked, "How about you? You're a mess."

"I'm fine. Bruised, scratched. As long as he didn't have rabies. Son of a bitch bit me." He lifted his arm and looked at a bite mark above his wrist.

She touched the outer edge of the mark. "How did Sayre end up there? That was totally trippy, seeing him."

He filled her in on everything. The part about the voice that told Eric her body needed to be close to her soul was the eeriest.

"But it was right," Eric said. "If I hadn't known that, I might have done everything for nothing, because I wouldn't have risked taking your body there.

And you would have still . . ." He squeezed her closer instead of saying the word. After a few minutes he said, "Call Magnus and let him know we're all right."

She did, giving him a brief rundown of events.

"Are you coming back here?" Magnus asked on the speaker phone.

"No, we're staying away," Eric answered. "No need to draw them there. But I have a job for you: make up a batch of antidotes. It saved my ass. And it might save the rest of my people's assess, too." He was looking at her.

He signed off, and she settled next to him, reveling in the feel of being in her skin again. Of being with Eric. As soon as she got comfortable, she sat up. "Westerfield's targeting an Amish village. I heard him talking to someone named Malcolm, right after he captured me. His name is Neil, not the same first name as on the identification he showed me, so Westerfield probably isn't his last name. Anyway, he said something about the Essence being ready for tomorrow. I saw pictures of people, *kids*, and a tack on a map in southern Maryland. They're going to kill more children. We have to stop them."

"They'll probably use the same plane, same hangar. So we head out tonight, disable the plane, and wait for him to show up. And we do our damnedest to put this guy out."

"We have to. He's hurt enough people. Enough children. Seeing those pictures . . ."

He pulled her against him and rubbed her arm. She looked up and saw a severe look on his face. "We'll stop him."

* * *

Neil called Malcolm from a safe distance, watching smoke billow up into the sky. "I've run into a difficulty."

"Would that be why I hear sirens in the background?" he asked, his voice terse.

"I had three of them, one a surprise Offspring named Sayre, Lucas Vanderwyck's twin." He filled Malcolm in on the experiment, and how Eric Aruda hadn't succumbed to the Essence. "I thought the Essence would affect them differently, because they already had it in them. What their parents got was a purer form, which didn't have the immediate effect of insanity. Sayre went within minutes, but Eric had enough wherewithal to pretend he'd succumbed. He and the girl escaped, and he set the building on fire. I've masked it so the firefighters will only see an open field."

"Did you get the Essence out?"

"Yes. When I couldn't catch up to the two, I ran back and retrieved it. We're still set for our next experiment, except Fonda's soul was there when I spoke to you about it. The pictures, map, everything. I'm not sure how much she could hear or see."

"It's time to shift our focus. I wasn't fond of infecting the village so soon after the cult."

"It would have looked like the cult's massacre set someone off in the village. It happens, one spree shooter hits the news and then there's another." The more chaos they created, the more he craved. It was like a drug.

"We'll put it off for another week," Malcolm said. "If Aruda and Raine know about the plan, they'll probably try to stop you. Or kill you. Either way, they'll be at the hangar. This time, take care of them any way you have to. Explode their bodies like you enjoy so much, as long as no one is around. But get rid of them now." He heard Malcolm's teeth grinding together.

"That was what I was going to suggest. Any luck finding the others?"

"Yes, finally. Every spare minute I have, I've been working on the shield that's present at the gallery location." That's how they knew the Offspring were there. No need to protect the gallery otherwise. "It's beginning to weaken. I've got a press conference to attend this afternoon, and then I'll be able to spend more time on it. I'll see what's there, and more importantly, who's there. The blueprints for the gallery were delivered here this morning, but some moron has misplaced or misdirected them. The pieces are coming together. I'll breathe a lot easier knowing this situation has been taken care of."

"Me, too."

Neil disconnected. He had to admit, though, these Offspring were a challenge. He'd been so very disappointed when Eric hadn't torn into Fonda. What a delight that would have been to watch. There were other ways to destroy them, though. The thought of exploding them, something he hadn't done in many, many years, sent a thrill through him. Messy, but well worth the clean-up.

CHAPTER 22

Eric and Fonda found another small motel just off the main road, but this one looked quaint, each unit painted a different color, with a small porch and two chairs. "Stay here," he said. "I'll get us checked in."

She put her hand on his shoulder. "I'd better go. You look like you were stomped by a herd of elephants."

He looked down at himself, clothing torn, bloodied. "Good point."

She checked in and got the room at the end. He grabbed both bags and they went inside. The owner obviously took pride in his establishment, as the room was clean and painted bright yellow, with a queen-sized bed covered in a quilt.

Fonda locked the door and threw herself at Eric, and everything she'd been holding in for the last hour gushed out. "You tried to bargain for my life with yours. You were going to throw your life away, suffer unimaginable torture, to get him to release me."

He rubbed her back. "It was worth a shot. But it didn't w—"

"Eric, look what you did!" She ran her fingers through her hair and leaned back to look at him. "My God, who does that? I mean, I know you'll risk your life to save mine, but you *offered* your life to . . . to . . ." Her voice was trembling, her eyes filling with tears.

He wiped them away. "Hey, hey, it's okay."

She buried her face against him, her fingers twisting in his shirt and not gripping him because she didn't want to hurt him. She couldn't get her head around it. Always, those words would pound through her head, her heart.

He kissed the top of her head. What he did to her, whether it was throwing himself on the fire for her or something tender like that gesture.

"You're just in shock, from everything," he said. He tilted her face up to his. "Come on, let's get a shower." He took her hand and led her to the bathroom.

She nodded. Let *us*? He let go of her to lean in and start the shower, and she stripped out of her clothes. He turned to find her standing there naked, and the fire in his eyes flared.

"Together," she said, her heart thumping pleasantly in her chest.

He nodded, a smile coloring his expression. "Together."

She stepped closer to him and unbuttoned the ruined shirt, flinging it toward the waste can. He relaxed his arms and let her unbutton his jeans and push them down his legs. He stepped out of them and kicked them aside. Bruises, scratches, and dried blood marred his beautiful body. All to save her. She took his cut hand and kissed along the edge of it. A ragged breath came out of her, and he tilted her chin up so she was looking into his eyes.

"Don't blame yourself," he said. "Coming for you was my choice. And it wasn't a hard one. I'll be fine."

She nodded, but those words didn't soften the impact of what he'd done. She took his hand and led him into the shower. It barely fit them both.

She opened the soap and grabbed a washcloth from the towel bar. After lathering up, she washed him, being gentle over the damaged areas, smiling as his fingers tensed when she concentrated on other, more interesting areas. She trailed her fingers after the cloth, wanting to feel his skin, the sprinkling of hairs on his body, the curves and dips of his muscles. She leaned close, kissing his chest as the water ran down over her face. She'd almost lost him, lost the chance to touch him again.

He took the cloth, rinsed and lathered it, and washed her. He took her in, every inch, cleaning her as a man might wax his most precious car. She was instantly back in bed with him the night before, his hands on her body, fingers sliding between her folds as he gently cleaned without the cloth.

"So these are the infamous tattoos," he said with a grin, running his finger over the black kitten on her left hip, sweet, with huge doe eyes. The one on her right hip had narrowed eyes, claws glistening at the razor tips.

"The two sides of me." She turned to show him the one above her right butt cheek: a fairy with black wings and a pissed-off *I'm going to get you* expression on her beautiful face.

His hands slid over her bottom, taking his time stroking up and down. "I sense a theme here."

She laughed, but her smile faded. "Like you said about the flames having that allure, but not anymore. I used to love being angry. It's not an easy way to be."

He shook his head, looking as though he totally understood. "It becomes comfortable."

"Not anymore."

"Seems pointless, really."

Then he stepped back and lifted her foot onto his bent leg, washing her thigh, knee, calf, and even between her toes.

The pressure was building inside her as he lovingly tended to her other leg, and then he poured shampoo on her head and massaged it through her scalp. She closed her eyes and sank into the sensation, letting out an *"Mmmmm."*

"Tell me no one's ever washed your hair before," he said.

She looked at him, and he wasn't teasing. "Except my hairdresser, no one's ever washed my hair like this. My hairdresser's cute, but he's never been naked."

He smiled then, tilted her head back and let the water rinse out the soap. Once she'd squeegeed the water from her hair with her fingers, she stepped onto the edge of the tub and poured shampoo from the bottle into her hands.

"How about you?" She didn't want to hear how some other woman had done this to him before. *So why'd you ask, dummy?*

"Nope, never taken a shower with a woman."

She understood the smile he'd had on his face. "Any sore spots on your head?"

"I don't think so."

She gently scraped her fingernails across his scalp, eliciting that same sound from him. He had thick

hair, the color of a field of wheat, and it felt silky beneath her fingers as the water rinsed out the soap.
He turned and wrapped his arms around her, turning her back into the stream of water, letting her body
slide down his until they were face-to-face, and then
he kissed her crazy.

When she could barely breathe, he stepped out of
the stream.

"You said we made love last night," he said.

Her cheeks fired hot. "Oh . . . that. I thought you
were going to die. It doesn't count."

He raised an eyebrow.

"Okay, it wasn't a dream. We made love. I was
lying next to you because you were so cold, and you
wrapped your body around mine, and then you
kissed me and touched me, and I thought maybe I
could reach you, that I could get you to come back."
Her mouth quirked. "You did come, but you didn't
come back. Am I the most terrible person in the world
for taking advantage of you?"

His expression was serious. "Awful."

"You're mad? Disgusted?"

"Both. Very." Then the corner of his mouth twitched.
Twitched again. Then the laugh exploded. He tilted his
head back, his whole body shaking, his arms tightening around her to keep her from sliding down.

"What's so funny?"

Finally, he composed himself and looked at her.
"The best sex in my life, and you're worried that you
took advantage of me? No, baby, you can attack me
any time, awake or not."

He kissed her again, sweeping his tongue into her
mouth. He'd called her "baby." What did that mean?
Should she tell him that he'd said he loved her? Just

the thought of opening that subject made that huge, scary shadow move closer. No, not yet.

"We . . . we didn't use anything," she felt compelled to say. "I won't get pregnant, and I don't have anything, but if you want to use a condom—"

He kept kissing her. "I'm clean."

She slid down a little farther, feeling the tip of his penis pressing against her opening. He held on tight, and she maneuvered onto him, feeling that rush once again as he filled her. He sucked in a breath, his head rocked back, eyes closed.

"I can't believe this didn't bring me back," he said in a hoarse voice. "But I promise you, I enjoyed every second of it." He looked at her as she moved against him, clinging to his shoulders because looking at him while he was inside her felt too . . . something. She wove her fingers into his hair, kissing his neck, loving the feel of her breasts brushing against him.

He moaned, his fingers tightening on her back. She was caught up in their movements, in the build of pressure that swirled through her body. Her breath came in quick gasps, and his moans got louder, echoing off the tiles, making that pressure build even more. He was enjoying it, and he wasn't shy about letting her—and the rest of the motel—know. That was why she'd requested the end unit.

She'd never made noise before, but gasping, yelping sounds came out of her mouth as her orgasm built, built, and then burst out. She arched, trying to catch her breath, feeling dizzy with it all. He jerked, and she felt him throbbing inside her as his body spasmed again and again. He, too, was having trouble catching his breath.

He leaned back to look at her, a flushed smile on his face.

"It's much nicer when you're awake," she said with a wicked grin.

"Let's continue this in a better place."

"Continue?"

He gave her a pointed look. "Uh, we're not done."

But they'd made love. He'd gotten off. It was always over after that.

He set her on her feet, and she stood beneath the spray of water for a minute. She cut the water, and they stepped out of the shower and dried off. He swept her back into his arms and walked into the room.

"Carrying you like this is also nicer when you're awake," he said.

He threw off the quilt, laid her down on the bed and kissed her. He was looking at her, his eyes filled with awe as his hands skimmed over her wet skin.

"Yes, this is so much better when I'm awake," he said between kisses. "That was torture, feeling you, and yet not feeling you." He looked at her. "You are absolutely beautiful."

"So are you."

He glanced down. "I'm a wreck."

"A beautiful wreck."

He chuckled and kissed her mouth, then that place beneath her ear, murmuring, "This is my favorite place—well, my favorite nonerotic place—on a woman's body."

Chills washed over her as he kissed and licked down the side of her neck, trailing down to lavish attention on her breasts and then down her stomach. When he nuzzled her pubic hair, the growing discomfort shot her to a sitting position.

"What are you doing?"

He gave her one of those *Duh* looks. "What does it look like I'm doing?"

"Why? I mean, we've already . . . you know, and you don't have to do that."

"I know I don't 'have' to do it. I want to. Sex isn't just about the penetration. I mean, yeah, that's a great part of it, but it's also about pleasuring each other, on and on, for hours on end until we're so exhausted and sated we can't move."

His words tantalized her and scared her because she wanted what he was talking about. She pulled her legs up, and he set his chin on his hands, studying her.

She said, "It's about sex, the act, and then it's over."

He reached out and clamped a hand on her leg. "Maybe for some guys. Not for me. Not with you." He tugged on her leg as though to pull her back down.

She held strong. "No, it's okay. I like it that way." *With you.* What did that mean?

"You like wham, bam, thank you, ma'am? Or sir, rather?"

"I'm comfortable with that."

"Doing other things isn't comfortable?" His fingers trailed up her inner thigh, a devilish gleam in his eyes. "Like this?" His hand went higher. "Or this?"

She shifted away from him. "What's wrong with the sex part? Isn't that the best part, the most important part?"

His gleam dulled, his mouth twisting in a frown. "Is that how you feel?"

She nodded.

"You don't like oral sex?"

She shook her head so hard it made her dizzy. The thought of opening herself, even to Eric . . . no way.

"Have you ever had it done to you?"

"I've given it. It's okay, I don't mind. But receiving it . . ." She shook her head.

He sat up and tilted his head at her, and she felt like a specimen. She'd been there before, of course, though Jerryl had only offered to do it once. After she demurred, he dropped it. She hoped Eric would, too.

Dumb thought.

"You've never had someone go down on you?" he asked again, incredulous.

She shook her head again, this time careful not to be too exuberant. "It's just not my thing." She didn't want him to think she was some kind of prude, so she got to her knees and pushed him back, climbing on top of him. Men were incredibly easy to distract when it came to their penises, so she knew the subject would soon be dropped.

He was still as hard as he'd been before. She kissed and nipped at the places that weren't bruised, loving the brush of her lips against his skin. His breath came faster, deeper, as she moved over his body, licking at his nipples while her hands roamed across his pelvis. When she took him into her mouth, she knew she'd succeeded.

And she found it was more than okay. With Eric, she actually liked it, liked making him groan and arch and flex his toes. When he jerked in orgasm, it was dry since he'd already come.

He grabbed her by the shoulders and threw her down to the bed, pinning her at her waist and kissing her thighs.

She wiggled and squirmed, and finally he stopped. "It's more than that you don't like it. You said you were uncomfortable, which is different than it not being 'your thing.' Uncomfortable is inside stuff. Why? You trust me, don't you? I mean, if you can't trust me by now—"

"I trust you like I've never trusted anyone."

Those words made him smile. "Good. Then . . . why?"

She scooted back against the white metal headboard and crossed her arms over her chest. "I don't want to talk about this anymore." She felt like a gawky teenager, and she didn't like it one bit.

He braced himself in front of her. "Uh-uh. After everything we've been through, good and bad, you don't get away with telling me that."

She liked the anger that flared inside her. "You think because we had sex that you own me?"

"First off, I've had sex with women before, and I've never felt like I owned them. I feel like I *possess* you and you *possess* me, and though I don't know exactly what it means, it's a totally different feeling. Second, help me to figure out why you're acting the way women always accuse men of acting after sex."

The word "possess" and the way he said it, emphasized it, with his eyes sparking . . . good Lord, he'd deflated her anger completely.

He said, "Whoever you were with in the past treated sex as just a way to get off. Am I right?"

She shrugged, then nodded. Jerryl couldn't get out of bed fast enough, his mind already back on work, on hunting. When she complained once, he said sex fired him up. So much for the afterglow.

Eric got to his hands and knees, hovering in her face. "Forget that. For me, sex is an experience, mind, body, and soul. I am in the moment, and the only thing on my mind is the woman I'm with, pleasuring her, and making it last as long as possible. Not just the sex part, but everything. I want to enjoy her body, every inch of it, I want to watch her react to everything I do to her. I don't want it to end."

She dug her fingernails into her palms. Pain. Comfort. Familiar.

"It's just that my father used to have sex right there in the living room with Connie," she said. "Other people did, too. I used to think sex was dirty, sleazy, because it was something you did anywhere. There was nothing sacred about it."

"No, I don't think that's it. The guy who almost raped you, did he hurt you?"

She shook her head hard again. "I hurt him. I slashed him with a razor blade."

"You hang a lot of weight on being protected. You thought you loved a guy because he stood up for you at a bar. Fonda, help me understand."

She curled her hands around the sheets. "Why do you want to understand me? Why is that so important to you?" First the reason she'd cut herself, and now this.

He released a long breath, his eyebrows furrowed. "Damned if I know. Probably because you're the most fascinating, vexing, frustrating dichotomy of a woman I've ever known. Definitely because you mean something to me."

She heard those whispered words echoing in her head: *I love you.* Even though she wasn't positive he'd said them, they pressed against her heart. She wanted to hear them, and she was scared to death to hear them. Hell, *she* didn't even understand herself.

He said, "When I mentioned the guy who tried to rape you, your body stiffened, your face tensed, and it was like you stopped breathing. Tell me what happened that night."

"I don't want to relive it. Why would you make me do that?"

He leaned even closer and his voice got soft. "Because I think you need to."

She took a deep breath, looking to the side. "He was a good friend of my father's. He brought over drugs, helped him out at times, got him a job once. He'd always been nice to me, though. Brought me little gifts, asked me how school was. He paid attention to me, listened, and made me feel . . . comfortable. Special."

"That's what predators do. They target kids who need attention and love, and seduce them."

She could see that now. When Eric waited for her to continue, she pushed on. "One time he came over and I was alone. I didn't even think about it when he walked in and said he'd wait. I was sitting on the couch doing homework. He sat next to me and turned on the television."

She was back in that dingy apartment, the fabric on the couch so worn she could see the foam beneath it. Smell of stale cigarettes. Coffee table scarred, always a mirror and a razor blade and a few granules of powder left on the surface. She usually blew them away.

"He put his hand around my shoulder and told me I looked sad. Just a simple touch, safe, comforting. I melted against him. Nobody had touched me in so long, not a hug or kiss good-night. All I remember next is him trying to pull down my shorts, me kicking and screaming . . ."

Eric's fingers wrapped around her arm, squeezing gently. "Something happened between those two things."

"No. Nothing happened."

A memory nudged at her. Like a cockroach, it peered out from a dark crack and scurried back.

"Nothing." She shook her head, slowly, and then stopped when the memory peered out again. She looked past Eric, deep in her mind. "He touched my breast. Just a graze, and I thought he'd done it on accident. Then he kissed me. He said I was so beautiful, and he'd wanted me for so long, and for a few seconds . . ." Her mouth slackened. "I ignored the rest because he wanted me. He pushed me back on the sofa and said he wanted to make me feel good, like I'd never felt before. I hardly ever felt good, and so I let him . . ."

Her eyes widened as that last frame of the buried memory snapped into place. "He pulled down my pants and put his mouth down there. And it did feel good." Her eyes watered at the shame, and her hands curled into the sheets again. "I let him do it, though I didn't come. Then he pushed his pants down and said it was his turn, and I knew it was all wrong, that I'd done wrong, and he was mad and that's when he tried to rape me."

Eric pulled her into his arms and she clung to him, the waves of shame rolling over her.

"You were only a kid then. You were a kid hungry for affection, and he was a predator who lured you in."

Her voice squeaked when she said, "But I let him. And it felt good. It was my fault."

"You didn't know any better. Sick bastard used your need. Don't let him steal anything more from you." He stroked her back. "You were innocent, baby. Just an innocent. Let it out. It's okay."

That's when she realized she was crying, softly, but he must have felt her body heaving, the tears dripping onto his back.

Those horrible memories had been living inside her all these years, like a cancer, tainting her life. The shame turned to violation, to grief, and then to release, and through it all he held her. No one had ever held her like this other than as a prelude to sex. He held her tight, whispering, "Let it out, little girl, just let it out."

After several minutes she felt as though she were impinging on him, putting him through too much. It was too weird, this comforting.

She backed up and wiped her face. "I want you to do it."

"Do . . . ?"

She gestured to the vee between her legs.

"Now?"

"Yes. If you're up for it."

"Let's get one thing straight: I'm always up for it. But you're not ready."

"Yes, I am." She lay down and spread her legs. "Please." A challenge for herself, to move past it.

He kissed down the tender insides of her thighs, easing her in, moving his mouth over her stomach and then closer. She recognized the feeling now, the fear of being touched there and the shame of enjoying it. So she could get over it, right? Because she felt aroused, oh yes.

He stopped and came to a sitting position.

She sat up, too. "What's wrong?"

He wasn't in the mood anymore. Well, of course,

she couldn't blame him. Or maybe he was turned off now that he knew the truth.

"You're clenching your thigh with your hand so hard, you're leaving marks."

She saw the red crescents on her pale skin. "Pain. It comforts me, and makes feeling safe." She put her forehead in her palm. "I'm so screwed up."

He pulled her hand away, tipping her chin up so she had no choice but to face him. "You're not screwed up. You've just got issues. We've all got issues. I've got an idea, and I must be crazy to even suggest it, but here it is. You still trust me?"

"With my life."

He took a breath at that, and she saw something in his eyes soften. "I'm proposing a test for both of us. We touch each other everywhere but the erotic places. No sex. Not until you're ready to see that it's not just sex and not until you're begging me to go down on you. When I do, you're going to spread your legs wide and move against my mouth desperate and hungry, because I'm making you feel so good you're losing your mind. And you won't be impaling yourself."

She laughed at that last bit, but the rest? "Well, you're pretty darned sure of yourself."

He raised one eyebrow. "I'm good." Not cocky, but definitely sure of himself. She felt a stirring down there despite her misgivings. He touched her cheek. "If I can do this test—and it'll be excruciating—then you can do it."

She took a deep breath. "Okay. When do we start?"

"Later today." He pulled her down to the bed and into his arms. "Now we sleep. It's going to be a long night."

She was facing him, and she reached out and

touched his face the way he did hers sometimes. "Why are you putting us through this? You could write me off as damaged goods, leave it at that."

"You don't get it, do you? No, you don't. Because you're worth it, Fonda. Because you're worth fighting psychotic creeps and having an aching hard-on so I can break through that wall you hide behind. You're worth all of that and more."

She closed her eyes, because they were tearing up. His words filled her with hope and pain and everything that came with love. She knew, absolutely for sure, that she did not love him because he'd saved her. She loved him because he was Eric Aruda.

With her fingers still grazing his face, she let her body relax. She listened to his breathing as it became deep and steady. He'd almost died twice in the last twenty-four hours. She synchronized her breathing with his and felt as though she were rising and falling on the ocean.

If she took all the times of her life that she was brave, walking the mean streets, dealing with Westerfield, and put them together, she wasn't sure she had enough courage to tell Eric how she felt. Or risk her heart. But she was willing to take the first step.

CHAPTER 23

Eric's phone rang, a space-age chirp, and he shot straight out of sleep. Sleep. He'd actually dropped off into glorious sleep with dreams and everything. The afternoon sun slanted through a crack between the drapes. He grabbed the phone off the dresser, where he'd plugged it in to charge.

"Yeah," he whispered, hoping not to disturb Fonda. Which didn't matter, he saw. She was sitting up, her eyes wide.

"It's Amy. Are you near a television?"

"I can be. Hold on." He clicked the remote and sat on the edge of the bed. "What am I looking for?"

Fonda scooted up next to him, leaning close to hear. He put the call on speaker phone.

"Any major channel, the President is talking about the economy."

He flipped through a few channels and found one with the President standing at the podium. "What am I looking for? I'm assuming you don't have a sudden interest in what's going on in the real world."

"I wish. No, look at the man on the President's left, in the back. Vice President Bishop, right?"

A good-looking man barely in his fifties stood erect, his hands loosely crossed in front of him.

"Yeah."

"Eric, he's got the Offspring glow."

"Like the woman at the cult?"

"No. His is more powerful. Even more than ours."

He stared at Bishop, the golden boy of politics, poised to run for President in the next election, when the President's second term would end.

"Bishop's too old to be an Offspring," he said. "Like our buddy Westerfield."

Fonda looked at Eric, touching his arm. "What's Bishop's first name?"

"Mike? No, wait a minute. Malcolm."

Her face went a shade paler. "No way. No freaking way."

"What?" he asked.

"Have Amy look him up on the Internet, find out everything she can about him. Like if he has a brother named Neil."

"I heard her," Amy said. "I'll call you right back."

He stared at Bishop, trying to see a family resemblance. "They could be related."

The President fielded questions from the press, and finally the phone rang again. "You're right," Amy said. "He has a brother named Neil. They were orphans, parents died in a car wreck when they were young, you probably know the heart-tugging story. You want to fill me in?"

"Are you ready for this? The people after us? The friggin' Vice President of the United States. And his brother."

"No shit. Wait, Lucas just handed me something else he printed off from the Internet . . . Back in the mid-eighties, around the time that Darkwell was starting his program, Malcolm was a colonel in the Army. I'll bet he was somehow involved in BLUE EYES, one of the two dangerous people Cyrus warned me about. He and Neil must have been ingesting Blue Moon, too."

Fonda leaned against Eric's arm. "No wonder they want us out of here. Malcolm Bishop can't take a chance of anyone finding out what he was involved in."

They sat in silence, digesting all that for a moment.

Finally, Eric said to Amy, "On a brighter subject, tell Lucas he doesn't have to worry about Sayre anymore." He filled her in on recent events.

"Do you want to tell him yourself?"

"No, you do it. It might help, good news coming from you."

"It's okay between us. Thanks to what Fonda said to Lucas."

That baffled him. "What'd she say?"

"When she was desperately trying to help you, weighing whether to give you the antidote . . . Lucas saw what I went through. He sensed how much she cared about you, and the agony of making that decision. She helped him to understand."

He smiled at Fonda, and she gave him a sweet smile. He focused on the call again. "What's going on there?"

"We're still waiting, but the guys are getting antsy. They're talking about going up and taking out the officers. I don't think it's a good idea. Thank goodness we've got supplies, but pretty soon we'll have to break into all of that preserved food. Who knows what that'll taste like?"

"Hang in there. Now we know who's after us. Getting to the veep will be impossible. But we know where Neil's going to be tomorrow. I plan to get rid of that son of a bitch once and for all."

"Please be careful, both of you."

He signed off. Fonda was watching the closing of the press conference, a somber look on her face. "How are we supposed to win against someone that powerful?"

"The good thing is that he's got to be careful. He can't come after us himself, not unless he brings his Secret Service people along. I don't think they'd cover for him killing two people without provocation."

"We don't know what his abilities are."

"No. But if he were more powerful than Neil, we'd be dead." He touched her chin. "Let's get something to eat, go over our plan. Then we'll come back and do some touching."

He took her hand and pulled her to her feet. He must be crazy, he thought. Crazy in love. Yeah, because as much as he craved sex, he wanted much more from her. He wanted all of her. He knew she wasn't ready to hear any of that yet, though, and he didn't want to scare her away. They would take it slow, and it would kill him, but in the end it would be worth it.

Petra started to crack her knuckles and then stopped, even though Eric wasn't there to get on her case about it. She missed him, and she missed being outside and feeling safe. Knowing who their enemy was didn't help, not one tiny bit.

Everyone sat in the large living area talking about the implications, but it all became a buzz in her head.

Four days of being trapped down there was getting to them. Some were talking explosives, but the others didn't want to give away their position.

"I'm going to lie down," she said, heading to her room. She'd gotten very little sleep lately.

She drifted into sleep quickly, dreaming of Lucas, and the men they'd seen on their security monitors, explosions, and . . . Cheveyo.

He stood in a void, his dark brown hair brushing the shoulders of his leather jacket, his blue-gray eyes intense as they took her in. He held out his hand to her, and she felt herself floating toward him.

"Cheveyo."

He had protected them by putting a psychic shield over their shelter, and he'd saved her life.

He pulled her close and ran his fingers along her hairline. "Yaponcha."

"The Hopi wind god."

He smiled. "You remembered."

They'd come up with a code word so she would know it was him and not an imposter. "I remember everything about you, the way you kissed me, and especially the way you keep telling me you can't be with me." Despite the special connection he said they had, which just about drove her crazy.

His expression grew dark, and he kept his hands on her face like he didn't want to let go of her because he was going to lose her forever. She could be imagining it, of course. She did tend toward the dramatic.

"Like Lucas, I get flashes of images from the future, though not painful. I usually see maybe a day ahead. I saw a man shooting you, but before I could warn you, you'd already gone to the shelter. So it changed the future. I saw the men watching this place and put the shield back up. Someone has been trying to break down my shield. Someone very powerful."

"It's the Vice President and his brother." She told him everything they'd learned, surprised he didn't already know. He seemed to know a lot more than they did. "They're not Offspring. We figure they ingested Blue Moon like Wallace did."

He shook his head. "They *are* Blue Moon."

"I don't understand."

"Right now that's not important." His expression darkened. "I saw another vision. It doesn't make any sense to me, but my visions have never been wrong. I see you all dead."

Dread washed over her like black oil. "How?"

"I don't know, but you're all in the shelter."

"They're going to get in! We have to go on the offensive."

He shook his head, running his fingers through his hair. "I've gone through scenarios where I tell you to evacuate, and it's no better. You're gunned down as you come out. I've made a plan to go there and take out the men, but they take me out, and you all still die."

She fell against him, clutching him. "What do we do?"

He put his hands over hers, pressing them against his chest. "I don't see how it happens, only the aftermath." His beautiful face was rigid, taut with anger and frustration. "The door is still closed. I don't understand it, but it's as though a ghost gets in and shoots you all. I don't see anyone else, only all of you dead. It doesn't make sense."

"I'm scared. Where am I? Where do I die?"

"You're hiding in the range, behind the buckets you use as targets. Whoever the bastard is, he finds you. Find a better place to hide." He pulled her close, his hands on her face, and kissed her. Even in the wake of those terrible words, the feel of his mouth on hers filled her. The fierceness of his kiss filled her with hope—and fear. A last kiss. A kiss goodbye.

His hands were still on her face. "I'm not giving up. I'll find a way to help you."

She heard the conviction in his voice, saw it in the agony on his face. As she started to say something, he evaporated. She sat up, startled by his sudden disappearance. He'd never left like that before. They'd been cut off. Had the enemy broken through the shield? She jumped off the bed and tore into the living room to tell the others.

Fonda took her time getting out of the truck. It was just touching. Why was she so nervous?

"We don't have a lot of time before we leave," she said as they walked to their room.

"That's because you dawdled through dinner."

"I didn't dawdle. I was enjoying it."

He raised one eyebrow, which told her he didn't believe her. "Strip naked and get your ass on that bed, pronto."

She grinned. "Yes, master."

"I like that. You can keep calling me that."

She narrowed her eyes. "I'll call you other things, too, like hard-ass and—"

He gave her a quick kiss, to shut her up, no doubt. "Stop stalling and get naked." He watched her strip, his eyes hungry. "I must be friggin' crazy."

"We don't have to do this."

He wasn't going to relent, despite the erection she could see straining his jeans.

She sat in the center of the bed. "What about you?"

He pulled off his shirt and shoes, but remained in his jeans. "I'm not that strong. Besides, this is about you." She started to get up, but he pressed her back down with one finger on her shoulder. "You. And we're going to do this until you're ready for more, because when we make love, you will let me in everywhere." His eyes glowed like aquamarines. "Close your eyes."

She rolled them first, just to make a point.

He touched her arm. "Focus all your attention on my touch, but only on my touch. Any thought or emotion, let it go."

After a moment she raised her eyebrows in surprise. "That's weird."

"What?"

"I can feel your touch, but I also feel a pulsing energy."

"Good. That's what I want you to focus on wherever I touch you. I want you to feel the energy as much as the physical touch. Lay down."

She stretched out on her back, watching him. He walked across the bed toward her on his hands and knees, a predatory gleam in his eyes. His gaze swept over her. "This is incredibly hard."

"And so are you."

"Exactly why my pants are staying on. Keep your eyes closed."

He leaned over her, planting kisses on her forehead, down her temple, at the corner of her eye. He took his time, each kiss lasting several seconds. She reached out to touch him, but he stilled her hand. "You." One word; an order, that. She let out a huff of breath and dropped her hand.

He kissed very deliberately at the edge of her mouth but not her lips. She started to turn to kiss him but he held her face. "Uh-uh."

"Eric—"

"Shh."

"This is painful."

"You like pain."

"Not like this. It's . . ."

"Uncomfortable. Good. Focus on my touch."

He lingered a long time at that place below her ear, then moved over her shoulders, down her arms. The inside crook of her elbow was a surprisingly erotic place. And her wrist, where her energy pulsed even more, and then the palm of her hand. He flicked his tongue between her fingers, overtly erotic. It was hard to focus on her energy when he was doing that. It reminded her of his tongue in other places. *Energy.* Wow, it was changing to a deep, throbbing pulse.

He kissed down the back of her arm, even her armpit, which made her giggle, and down her side, which was almost as ticklish. Thankfully, he didn't linger there. He moved to the other side and went through the same procedure. She realized she'd lost the need to touch him or try to get out of it. She gave in to it, concentrating on the feel of his mouth or his hands moving over her.

Not foreplay. Just a man worshipping a woman's body, her essence. Her. The sheer tenderness of it brought tears to her eyes, and that someone as big and tough and sexy as Eric could do this for her . . . she had to fight the urge to wipe her eyes.

He ran his fingers across her stomach, planting kisses on her hip bones, where her tattoos were, and belly button, flipping her ring back and forth, before moving down her leg. He bent her leg and ran his finger in that space behind her knees. She was so entranced by the feeling, she didn't notice right away that she was exposed to him. She trusted that he wouldn't go there until she was ready. He moved down her calf, both stroking and kissing his way around her ankle, and then her foot.

Oh, those kisses were so exquisite that, yes, they *were* painful. The Metric song played through her mind again. *Help, I'm alive.* Heart beating like a hammer, pulse like a runaway train. It *was* hard to be soft, tough to be tender.

He moved along the inside of her thighs, but before he got too close for comfort, he moved to her other leg. Her energy was pulsing everywhere, oh yes, there, too. When he'd lavished affection all the way down to her toes and back up again, he said, "Roll over."

She took the opportunity to swipe her eyes as she rolled. She couldn't take much more of this. He brushed her hair aside and nuzzled her neck and every inch of her back, stroking the base of her spine with his tongue, only lightly touching the curve of her bottom, and then moving down her leg. He flicked his tongue over the back of her knee in a way that must be like what he would do down there. Slow, soft, gentle. *Whoa.* She could feel it there, too, as though the energy had a directly line from one place to the other.

When he got to her other knee, she held her breath, wondering if it would feel the same. It did. Warmth spread over her. She hadn't realized she'd spread her legs. Energy was swirling in her lower stomach, over her entire pubic area. When he moved up the back of her leg, she imagined him dipping between her legs this time . . . and the panic didn't come. She was throbbing, and just the thought of it stepped up her breathing. He left one last kiss at the base of her spine.

She rolled over, curling her hands behind his neck and pulling his face to hers. "That was the most beautiful thing I have ever experienced."

He looked as caught up in the moment as she felt. "Want me to do it again?"

"I want you to go down on me. More than anything in the world, I want that. With you. Right now."

He took her in, and he must have seen her sincerity because he kissed her, thoroughly, deeply, and then made his way down a curved path to her coarse hairs, which he nuzzled. Even that made her breath hitch, and when he went lower and touched the tip of her with his tongue, she nearly went over. He didn't rush in, taking his ever-loving time, bringing her to the edge and then backing off, until finally he let her go.

She let out a long low moan, feeling free to do that because, hey, *he* was loud. He kept moving his tongue over her, making her body contort with the most intense feelings she'd ever had, and then she went again.

"No more," she panted. "I can't take any more."

"You didn't even give me a chance to do my thing."

"Oh, you did your thing, Eric. You definitely did your thing."

When he pulled himself up to face her, she pushed him back on the bed and undressed him, then climbed on top of him. She liked this kind of impaling herself better. She moved in rhythm, and he braced her hips with his hands. Their gazes locked to each other's as they moved. He moaned and groaned, and she let out a few of her own as her climax built and then exploded.

He still moved, the veins in his neck and arms prominent, and several long minutes later he finally came with a most delicious groan. The man enjoyed making love, no doubt about it. She couldn't call it sex anymore, not with Eric. He hadn't called it that either.

He rolled her to the side, sliding his hands into her hair, a sweet, satisfied smile on his face. "You were incredible." He gave her a quick kiss, looking at her as though he might never let her go.

"We were incredible." The panic fluttered in her stomach. She put her hand on his cheek. "Don't make me love you, Eric."

"What am I doing that's making you say that? Because I saved you?"

"You risked your life and almost died, and I can't tell you how much that means to me. But no, that's not why I said that. I know it's not. You saved my soul, Eric. My *soul*. What you said to me in the closet at Magnus's, that you wouldn't let me walk alone in my father's neighborhood, pressing me to face my darkest shadows so I could slay them . . . I can because you're beside me. It's the way you touch my face when you kiss me, the way you loved on every inch of my body without any expectations of getting pleasure back. That's what makes me want to run away screaming."

His thumb scraped across her cheek. "What are you afraid of?"

"I'm afraid of feeling something that's so foreign, so overwhelming. I'm afraid of loving you and then you letting me down when you realize I'm not what you want. Every man I've ever loved, or thought I loved, let me down."

His gaze riveted hers. "I won't ever let you down."

"How can you say that? You don't know what's going to happen between us. You might get tired of me or—"

He pulled her close and kissed her. "I love you. That's all I know right now. It's enough."

I love you. Unmistakably clear this time. He wasn't dreaming, and neither was she. The words pushed and pulled and tangled up inside her, but she couldn't let herself believe them. "You said you'd never loved a woman before. How do you know?"

"I feel it down to my bones." He bracketed her face, moving his close to hers. "Remember how you let go and let me go down on you? How that felt?" She nodded. "I want you to do that with your heart."

She wanted to do that, too, but her fears were stronger. "If I let go, I'll be needy. I'll cling to you and I'll want to hold onto you all the time and try to get you to say 'I love you' over and over so I'll believe it, and I'll be a pitiful mess. I didn't realize it at the time but that's how I was with Jerryl. I don't ever want to be that way again."

"You acted that way because deep down you knew he didn't love you, and you didn't love him either. But what if you had a man who let you hold onto him whenever you want, who's always there to cling to, who says he loves you over and over without you having to try? You wouldn't be needy because you wouldn't need anything. You'll have it. Here." He pressed his fingers over her heart.

She took a deep shuddering breath. His phone made a strange ringing sound.

"I set the alarm, in case we lost track of time. We have to go." He gave her a pointed look. "We will continue this conversation."

He got up and started dressing. There was a lot going on between now and when they would be able to do that. She just hoped they survived it.

CHAPTER 24

Oddly enough, Eric pushing her to face the horrors of her near rape gave Fonda strength to face what was ahead. That didn't stop the fear that pulsed through her, though, or the way her nerves burned. She looked at him, driving the truck, and her heart ached at the thought of going through another battle where he could get hurt. Or worse.

Don't think about worse.

He was already so bruised and beat up. She loved him. So much her heart throbbed with it, that those words wanted to bound out of her mouth and fill the cab. Now wasn't the right time, just like telling him they'd made love when they were locked in that room wasn't exactly the greatest timing. *Duh.* Emotions were distracting; that's what he'd said. He was right, because she was thinking about hers instead of what was ahead.

"Are we going to try the surprise tactic again?" she asked.

"That hasn't exactly been working for us. I've been thinking about this. My friend Steve—the one who took me up in his plane—told me about this guy he knew who was inspecting the new paint job on his plane. He accidentally turned the propeller and started the engine. The prop sliced him up so bad, there was blood all the way up to the ceiling of the hangar. Neil can heal himself, right? A bullet wound, a cut, that kind of thing. But what if he were hacked into a thousand pieces?"

She grimaced at the mental picture. Oh, the gruesomeness. Neil deserved that, and more.

Eric's face glowed with his idea. "In that condition, he wouldn't be able to stop my abilities, and if he *does* begin to regenerate, I can torch him before he's whole. It's our only chance."

"Then we do it."

"If their plan is to spray the village today, I doubt he'll be at the hangar tonight. That gives us plenty of time to get in and into position. I want you in the plane. Remember where he got the key from the last time? We'll figure out how to start the plane, get ready. I don't want him to know you're there. I'll engage him, get him near the prop, you start it, and I push him in."

"I don't like the engaging part or the being near the prop part. Not with what Neil can do."

"It's the only way."

His face froze. He slammed on the brakes and swerved onto the shoulder of the road. "No, not again." He looked over at her. "I'm hearing a man's voice in my head."

"It can't be Jerryl."

"Wait." He closed his eyes, his expression tensed. "Not Jerryl."

She relaxed a smidge. But who?

He opened his eyes a minute later. "Cheveyo. He can communicate psychically. He's done it with Nicholas and my sister, but never with me."

"What did he want?"

"He had a warning. He can see into the future, and he told me not to go to the Tomb, that we'll die. He saw me and a woman—you—dead." His mouth trembled. "He said he can't get through to Petra anymore. Something's happened to the shield he put over them."

"Is this guy reliable? Trustworthy?"

"I don't trust people as a rule, especially ones I haven't met. But he put a shield over the Tomb to keep Darkwell from finding us. He saved Petra's life when Jerryl tried to kill her, so I'd say he's on our side. He knew Zoe was in trouble and saved her, too. I have to guess his visions are pretty accurate."

Eric grabbed his phone and tried to call Amy, then Lucas, and down the list of Rogues. His face got paler with each unsuccessful call. "The calls all go right to voice mail." He left a message on the last one pleading with them to call him. She scooted next to him and wrapped her arms around his neck. He was scared, and he wasn't scared of much.

He looked past her. "I've got to get over there."

"He said we'd die."

"I didn't say anything about you going."

"Oh, no, you don't. He didn't say that your friends were going to die, did he?"

Eric shook his head.

"Then we stick to our plan. We have an opportunity to get to Neil because we know where he'll be. We can't help anyone if we die. If we can kill Neil, we can break our enemies down. Think of the children, all those innocent, peaceful people he's going to infect. We take out Neil, then go to the Tomb, all right?"

He looked at her. "All right."

"Do you think it was Cheveyo who was in your head before, telling you how close my body had to be to my soul?"

"No. He didn't know who you were. He only described you." He shuddered, and she knew he was imagining whatever he'd said. And wondering who else had been in his head.

They continued on until they reached the road near the airfield's closed entrance. Eric parked a short distance past it. He turned to her, cupping her cheek with his hand. "Don't do anything to put yourself in danger. I don't want to lose you."

"Ditto," she said, her heart tight.

He kissed her long and hard, as though drawing strength for the hours ahead. She drew that strength back.

"Let's go."

Amy came out of the computer room after having checked the video surveillance. "I don't see the officers outside anymore."

The others looked hopeful, but Petra didn't see it that way. Not because she was a pessimistic, overly dramatic person . . . okay, she was, but it was Cheveyo's warning, and the fact that he'd suddenly disappeared, that squashed any hope.

Lucas said, "Let's get out of here. I say we split up, some of us take the entrance into the gallery and some go outside through the shed. We meet in the garage and get the hell out of here. Head to the docks tonight if we get split up."

Amy dashed down the hall. "I've got to put Orn'ry in a safe place and leave him with plenty of food and water."

"I'll help," Lucas said. A minute later they were carrying the bird cage, with the obnoxious cockatoo inside, into the room behind the kitchen.

"It's too dangerous to go out there," Petra said, panic clawing up her throat. "What if they're just hiding?"

"We can't stay here anymore. If what Cheveyo saw comes true, this is where we die. So we get out there and take our chances."

She nodded. "Okay. I'm going with you and Amy."

Amy joined them a few seconds later. They all grabbed their cell phones and went in two different directions. Petra followed Lucas and Amy into their bedroom, where the gallery entrance came in. He grabbed at the handle and pulled. It wouldn't budge. The door was solid metal, to keep out desperate and infected citizens who might have found out about the shelter when the big bomb went off.

"It won't open." He jerked and tugged.

"Let's go with the others, then," Amy said.

They started toward the door and stopped when they saw the rest of the group coming their way. "The door is jammed," Nicholas said.

Petra put her hand to her throat. "They've trapped us down here! They're going to come in and kill us!"

Lucas's expression grew grim. "Not without a fight. They don't know what we have down here. Everyone grabs a gun and watches the entrances. As soon as the door opens, start shooting. Make sure it's not Eric, first, though."

They remained in their groups and got into positions, facing the doors to wait. For death. For destruction. For the end.

Malcolm Bishop had pulled the officers out of the area the night before. He could only tie up resources for so long without any proof that there was a threat to the President lurking around the premises. Besides, he didn't want any witnesses or questions when he took care of things.

It wasn't easy to get away from those sworn to protect him. He'd told his Secret Service agents he had personal business to attend to in downtown Annapolis, an early morning meeting with an attorney. The advanced team was already in place. Two agents were posted outside the conference room, where he was now alone, ostensibly going over documents in private. More agents were posted by the motorcade at the curb.

He set an illusion in place so the agents, or anyone else, wouldn't see him exit the room and go out the back door. He walked two buildings over to where the art gallery—now closed—was located. He walked along the back, to the small porch, and laid out the blueprints on a small table. Everything was in place. Doors sealed. Psychic shield disrupted and his own shield put in place. One more thing to do and then it would be finished, no one wiser.

The hangar looked deserted, closed up tight. Eric and Fonda walked around it, finding a couple of windows on the side that looked into a small office.

"No sign of him," she said, peering in.

Eric took off his shirt, wrapped it around his hand, and smashed the glass. He broke out the shards.

"Climb in and open the whole window from the inside."

Yeah, no way was he fitting into that small space. She supposed he could have broken out the middle pane, too, but that would look more obvious.

He hoisted her up, and she climbed through and stepped onto the desk below the window. With a dusty magazine that was dated three years earlier, she swept the glass off the desk. She twisted the clasp and slid the window up, then helped him climb in.

"If he comes in here, he'll know something's up," she said. "But it doesn't look like he uses this office much."

Eric walked out the door and closed it, looking in through the hazy pane of glass in the door and opened it again. "You can see a slight difference between the clearness of the opening and the grimy glass, but through this window it's not as obvious. We'll be okay if he just glances over. Not so much if he takes a close look."

He walked to the tool chest and took the key out of the third drawer. The side door on the plane was open. There were blocks in front of the wheels.

She looked at the propeller as they passed it, at the edges that looked so sharp. "I don't like this plan."

"Don't look when it happens; you'll never get the image out of your head."

"That's not what I'm worried about. If he throws you at the running prop, even if I freeze time, I'll be in the plane and you'll be out there. I doubt I'll have enough time to run down and push you to the floor."

"I'll be ready for him."

They both climbed in. The canisters weren't in place. Nothing looked ready.

"What if he changed the plan?"

"We give him through the morning, then decide what to do if he doesn't show." He turned to her, his expression stern. "If something happens to me, I don't want you feeling guilty because you couldn't stop it. Okay? And I want you out of here. He can't hurt you if he can't see you. Stay out of his sight."

She put her hand on his arm. "I don't want to think about that." It was like those moments when he was burning up all over again, the thought of losing him. "Don't leave me, Eric," she said, just as she had then. "I don't want to lose you."

He touched her cheek. "You won't."

He couldn't be sure of that. They were empty words of reassurance. And they didn't make her feel one iota better.

"Come here, let me show you what to do, if I can re-member it." He sat in the pilot's seat. "First you have to push this mixture knob, this red one, all the way forward, to Rich, so the gas gets to the engine." He put the key in a switch marked Mags. "Turn the key past Left and Right to Both. Push hard to get past the spring to Start. It'll start and snap back to Both. Try it."

She went through the steps, and the engine started.

"Pull the red lever back to cut the engine."

She did it, and the engine went quiet.

He sat down on the floor of the cargo area and pulled her onto his lap. "It's been a few years, but I was curious about how things worked when Steve took me up. I was all jazzed about getting my pilot's license, maybe even becoming an instructor. Then Steve got transferred to California, and I never fol-lowed through on it. You're lucky you have something you love to do. I haven't figured that out yet."

She leaned into him. "What have you been doing up till now? Besides arm wrestling for money," she added with a smile.

"A lot of nothing. I was a bouncer, a repo dude, jobs that used muscle." He looked around the plane. "Being inside the cabin again makes me want to go back to my earlier goal."

She turned to look at him. "I can tell it's something you have a passion for. That's what life is all about, you know. Finding your passion. Living it." She liked talking about the future. Believing they had one.

He leaned back, taking her with him, keeping her in his arms. She rested her head on his chest and dozed. She dreamed of planes, of Eric as a captain of a charter plane service, of a normal life . . . together.

The sound of metal against metal woke them. They sprang to a sitting position. Fonda crept to the cockpit, and Eric slipped to the floor and hid around the back of some cabinets.

The hangar door opened, but from the sound of it, only partially. Then it closed again. It was eight in the morning. Neil's voice echoed against the metal walls. "I know you're in here. I can smell your apprehension, your fear for each other's safety." He made sniffing sounds and then let out a satisfied sigh.

Fonda peered from the bottom edge of the window. She could barely see him. She reached for the red lever and then clenched the key with her fingers.

Eric stepped out, putting himself way too close to Neil. There was no place for him to get out of sight if Neil started his crushing thing.

Eric crossed his arms over his chest. "We finish this, here and now."

Neil let out a dramatic breath of relief. "Finally."

"Take me on like a man. No abilities. Don't hide behind your powers."

Neil chuckled. "You are trying to appeal to my ego? My sense of fairness. Or manliness? That might work if I were a man."

Eric took another step closer to Neil. "What are you?"

"Far more powerful than you. I'm sure you would have already incinerated me if you could. What you did to my building was irritating, and I will enjoy crushing you just for that. You know you can't defeat me, and yet you keep trying. It's amusing, admirable even, but as you said, it's time to finish it."

Eric's gaze flicked twice to the left, her signal. She started the engine and Eric pushed Neil back. He wasn't expecting that, and his arms windmilled as he lost his balance and fell backward. The propeller was instantly a blur.

Neil's hand went up. The propeller stopped. His face was ashen, though eerily passive. "Now, that wasn't fair at all."

No, no, no.

She pulled the red lever back in case the propeller started again. Neil twisted to the right, reaching out as though to grab something and fling it toward Eric. A pipe flew through the air. She froze time and launched out of the plane's cabin. How many seconds did she have? At any moment time would resume, and that pipe would slam into Eric's beautiful face. Fear squeezed her chest. Just one more second, that's all she needed. She leapt, fingers reaching for the pipe. *Hold, another few seconds.* She grabbed it out of the air, throwing it to the floor where it clanged on the concrete.

Time resumed as soon as she reached the plane. Neil blinked, looking at the pipe.

"No, little girl, you don't get to use that trick on me again." He held out his hand toward her, and she ducked out of sight. Nothing happened.

Little girl, like Eric called her. Bastard had no right to call her that.

The plane jerked, as though a giant had hit it. It didn't tip over, but she fell against the side door. Before she could right herself, Neil threw Eric against the corrugated metal wall, his hand shaking as he pinned Eric there. Eric's face was in a painful grimace as he twisted to get free.

"Want down?"

Eric dropped to the floor, landing on top of the tool chest and toppling them both to the floor. Tools hit the floor and scattered. He pushed away the chest and staggered to his feet.

Neil looked toward the ceiling of the hangar and moved his fingers in a clawlike action. The metal tore at the top, like a cut, making a screeching noise. He left it sticking out. Then he pointed at Eric, and like a psychotic orchestra director, waved his hand to send Eric flying toward the jagged edge.

She froze time. Eric kept flying toward it. Neil had disabled her ability, too. *Noooo!*

Eric put out his hands as he reached the sharp edge, grabbing onto the opening as his body hit the wall. His hands bled as he held on and pushed away from the sharp edge, physical force against psychic force. She heard his grunts of strain.

Stop!

Neil pulled Eric back, and he lost his grip. Her heart stopped beating, she stopped breathing. Eric's body slammed toward the edge. He put his hand out, and the metal tore through it. He let out a scream of agony as blood streamed down the metal. He tried to fight the force by using his good hand. It wasn't enough.

Neil turned Eric sideways, pinning him against the wall just below the edge. The top of the metal peeled farther, curling around him. He rolled, the metal peeling back with the screeching sound, curling around and around him. Only his head and lower legs were visible. It stopped, leaving him suspended halfway up the wall. Trapped. A slice of morning sky showed in the strip of opening above him.

Eric tried to wriggle out but he was pinned tight.

Neil walked closer, looking up at him. "You have a bond with the girl, and I know how it pains you to see her hurt. So you shall watch her die, and I will breathe in your agony, draw it into my cells. I can't manufacture those feelings myself, you see. I need to experience them through you humans, and you give me such a variety. It seems you thrive on them, too, though mostly the negative ones. Where I am from, the humans self-destructed." He inhaled deeply and then turned toward the plane. "Watch me explode her. It'll make such a mess in the plane, but I have time to clean it up before my next mission."

The Amish village. The children, the innocent.

Neil smiled. "Before you both go, you should know that your friends are, at this moment, being infected with the Essence. My brother is at the ventilation pipe, ready to send it down into the air system. I want you to think about how they'll turn on each other, become animals, like Sayre, mindlessly killing anyone in sight. You can see it clearly, can't you? Yes, I feel it."

Eric's fury reddened his face and he tried even

harder to break free. She started the plane again and pushed the black knob forward like she'd seen Eric do before. It didn't move. Blocks! She'd seen blocks next to the tires. Dammit!

Neil walked closer to her, their eyes locking. His were blank, empty of anything that resembled being human. He wasn't human, that's what he'd implied.

Pain rocketed through her body. She tried to push him out but he was too strong. She curled up, unable to move out of his view. White lights burst behind her closed eyes. *Have to stop this. Stop him.*

Pain. I can't take . . . much . . . more.

Wait. An idea.

She had one last chance. She projected out of her dying body, through the propeller, to stand behind Neil. He walked closer to the plane. One step. Then another. Gathering what strength she had, she pushed him. His energy was dense, heavy. He fell forward, his head turning back to her, eyes stark. In an instant the air from the propeller sucked him in.

She flew back to her body. The plane shook. She rolled to the floor. The unearthly sound of flesh and blood splattering everywhere rocked her senses. The engine gasped and choked, and then ground to a halt. Silence descended like death. She dared to look out the window. Blood and matter covered the windshield. On the outside, not the inside, as he'd intended. Not hers, but his.

Eric!

She scrambled out, sliding on the blood all over the concrete floor, fighting to keep her balance as she ran to him.

"You were fantastic, baby," Eric said in a strained voice. "You all right?"

She was breathless. "Yes. You? Are you . . . okay?"

"I can't take deep breaths, but I could be worse. I have no idea how I'm going to get down."

A low male voice said, "I can help."

They both looked toward the front of the hangar. A man stood there, extraordinarily tall, shaved head and eerie, light violet eyes. He wore a black trench coat, and his shoes scraped on the floor as he walked toward them.

Eric said, "Fonda, get out of here."

She didn't take her eyes off the man. "I'm not leaving you."

"She's perfectly safe," the man said, coming to a stop beside her. He acknowledged her with a nod, his expression blank, neutral. "Nice job."

"You're Pope," Eric said.

The wild card who'd worked with Darkwell. She'd never seen him during her time there.

He hadn't hurt Nicholas and Olivia. That's what she latched onto. "You said you could help."

He raised his hands toward Eric. Her heart tightened. His arms shook with the strain, as Neil's had. Eric started to roll upward, the strip of metal unfurling, warped and wavy beneath him. Once Eric was free, Pope slowly lowered his arms, and Eric floated down in sync with his movement. The second his feet touched the floor, he ran to Fonda, putting himself between her and Pope, one hand twining around hers and pulling her against him.

He held his other hand, cut and bleeding, out to his side. His face was pale from the pain, and she could hear how it stole his breath away. "Who are you?"

"It seems you already know. We don't have time to chat. Your friends are in trouble."

The Essence! "And why does that matter to you?"

"I'm your ally. And you do matter to me, very much. All of you."

Eric's body stiffened. "If you're our ally, why didn't you step in when that son of a bitch was wrapping me up like a lid on an anchovy tin?"

He smiled. "Because I knew you would succeed here. You won't succeed in saving your friends without my help."

Eric said, "Neil told us his brother is infecting my people with the Essence."

"Yes, that is his plan."

"Lucas won't be affected. He's had the antidote."

"No, he'll be killed by the others. They're sitting there waiting, all armed and ready to kill. Very easy to turn their guns on each other."

"But you worked with Darkwell," Eric said.

"I let Darkwell think I was working with him. What I was doing was protecting you. I cleaned the messes that might have exposed you. By the laws of where I come from, I cannot interfere, but I have broken those laws in small ways."

"Like letting me know that Fonda's body had to be close to her soul."

"Yes." Pope walked several yards away, stopping in front of a smattering of glowing jellylike substance roughly the color of his eyes. Eric stepped to the side to see what he was doing, taking her with him.

"This is Neil Bishop's Essence. His life force." Pope turned to them. "This is what Richard Wallace found that day he followed the supposed meteorite. This is what was in your parents, what's in you." He turned toward the blob again, reaching his hand toward it.

His fingers splayed, vibrated. "I can't leave this here. He's not dead until his life force is gone."

The blob glowed, first white, and then red, and then smoke rose from it. It turned black, drying into a crusty black pile of coal, and then burned down to a black spot on the concrete.

Eric walked toward the door, which was still closed. How had Pope gotten in? "We have to go to Magnus's place and get the antidotes before we go to the shelter. It's the only way to save them."

"It'll be far too late by the time you drive there. But I can get you there in seconds."

They both stopped, turning to look at him. "Seconds?" she asked.

"How do you think I got here?"

Or to the warehouse when he found Nicholas and Olivia. He'd appeared like a ghost, they said.

"I can teletransport. If you hold onto me, you go, too."

Eric looked at her, worried.

"Let's do it," she said. "We have nothing to lose."

Eric's mouth tightened. "I don't like it."

"I can't do anything to help them," Pope said. "If I use my power to kill in combat, I will be executed. You'll have to face Malcolm. And the only way you can reach them in time is to go with me."

"Okay." Eric turned to her. "You take the truck back."

"Oh, no, you don't. I'm going, too."

He released a quick, frustrated breath. "To Magnus's. Then you stay there."

Yeah, right. He needed her. And she needed to help him save his people. She tried to ignore the fatigue that stole through her, the aftereffect of using her abilities. *No time to be tired now.*

Pope said, "Quickly, I must tell you what you'll be facing when you reach the bomb shelter. Malcolm has a shield over it, so we cannot transport into the shelter itself. We will arrive exactly where Malcolm is, and hopefully we can stop him before he infects your friends. He can't squeeze your insides or move things, but he can make you see things that aren't there. He will use that to weaken you. You will have to kill him before you can get into the shelter. It's the only way to destroy the shield." He pointed to Eric's ruined hand. "You're going to need both your hands." They watched, she in astonishment, as Eric's hand healed, and then every bruise, scratch, and cut disappeared, too.

They walked toward Pope, who held out his arms. "Put your hands on me. You'll feel a whoosh through your body, and everything will go dark for a second."

The moment they touched him, that's exactly what happened.

CHAPTER 25

Eric could see it was exactly as Pope had described. Luckily, he grabbed Fonda's hand just before they went into the darkness and could still feel her. Thank God he could leave her with Magnus for safekeeping. They appeared in the inner courtyard of the compound, where a fountain in a black pond bubbled. The koi in the pond ducked with several splashes. He felt his body, solid, and he sought out Fonda. She smiled, relief on her face.

Pope looked around.

Eric, his grip still on Fonda, ran toward the front part of the house where a light was on. He banged on the door, and Magnus and Lachlan appeared.

Magnus opened the door, surprise on his expression. "What the hell—"

"I need the antidotes. Hurry, we don't have time to explain."

Magnus ran past him to the lab, though he was looking back at Pope.

Lachlan nodded toward Pope. "Who is that? Don't tell me I have another surprise sibling."

"He's someone who's helping us," Eric said. Magnus returned, and Eric grabbed the box from his hand. "Thanks. I'll explain everything later, including what you're about to see. I'm leaving Fonda here. Keep her safe."

He ran back to Pope, Fonda right behind him. "You're *not* leaving me."

"Yes, I am. You don't need to risk your life for people you don't even know." He kissed her and looked at Pope. "Let's roll."

Just before the whoosh and darkness, he saw Fonda grab onto Pope's arm. Dammit, he was going to kill her.

They materialized behind Lucas's gallery. He recognized the man standing on the porch from his appearances on television: Malcolm Bishop. He eyed the three of them, his brown eyes narrowing on Pope. Eric took advantage of his focus and set the box of syringes out of sight.

"Pope," Malcolm said. "I knew you had to be involved in this. But surely you did not kill my brother. That would be against the rules, and you've always adhered to the rules." His smile had a taunt in it, as did his voice. The two men had a history together, obviously.

Eric said, "I killed him." He didn't want the man to shift his focus to Fonda.

"And so shall you die as well." He turned to Pope again. "You destroyed his Essence, didn't you?"

"It couldn't be discovered. You know the rules. And I always follow them, as you pointed out."

"No, you don't. You brought them here. You are not our Liaison. You cannot interfere in any way. You've overstepped your bounds."

"As have you. I don't believe infecting people was part of your mission here."

What mission? What laws? No time to ask.

"You've tried to start trouble for us before," Malcolm said, "but no one believed you. And they won't now, if you were to try again. Besides, I have diplomatic immunity. I've accomplished too much during my stay here, and you, Pope, have accomplished so little. You haven't even been able to find out what happened to Simeon."

"I know you killed him. You stole his Essence, didn't you? He was on to you, and you put him in the receptacle."

"He was a pest, as you are." Malcolm heaved a sigh. "I can see this is going to get messier than I thought." He waved his hand, and a shimmering veil surrounded them. "A little privacy."

The illusion Pope had mentioned.

Malcolm turned to Eric. "Now, on to you. No, you can't use your powers on me. I can feel the heat right about . . . here." He gestured to about a foot away from him.

Eric lunged for him. A flash of white-pink light seared him and sent him to the ground. His vision blurred for a second, but he could see Malcolm wringing out his hand. "I'm a bit rusty at that," Malcolm said. "Don't get to use the bolt much. Too flashy." He shot a look at Pope. "Too bad you can't use your deadly powers. They'll know, and you'll have to explain yourself. You know what they'll do, and you don't want them to know about these people." He flashed the bolt at Eric again.

Eric rolled to the side, ready for it this time. Malcolm shot out his hand and aimed at Fonda. The bolt went right through her, leaving a gaping hole in her stomach. Eric heaved, like that hole was in him. She looked down at herself, her face ashen, and crumpled to the ground.

"No!" Eric screamed.

It's not real, Pope said. *Remember, illusion*. This time Pope's voice in his head was distinct.

His gaze was on Fonda. It looked real. So real. Agony froze her face. She reached for him, her hand trembling. "Eric . . . help me."

He wants you distracted. Weakened. Focus on Malcolm.

She was screaming in pain, calling his name over and over. His body strained to run to her. He had to trust Pope. Even if Pope hadn't warned him about the bolts. He went for Malcolm again, body slammed him to the ground. He rammed his knee into Malcolm's stomach, shoving the breath out of him. He had to put this guy down. No more.

Malcolm reached out and grabbed his arm. The electric shock sent him flying backward, rocketing through his veins and organs. He jerked and twitched. Whatever the hell Malcolm was doing, he was getting stronger.

Fonda rushed him. Fonda—without a hole in her stomach. If electrical aftershocks weren't firing inside his guts, he'd have been overwhelmed with relief. She launched herself at Malcolm and he flung her away. She screamed as the jolt went through her. He aimed his hand at her, everything went dark for a second, and then she was several feet away. The bolt struck the empty ground.

She'd frozen time.

"You won't do that again," Malcolm said. "You won't be alive to do that again." White-pink sparks flew from his fingertips, vibrated along the outer edges of his hands. He was definitely getting stronger.

Fonda was looking at Eric, her eyes wide. "You're alive. I thought he'd killed you. I saw you dead."

"Fonda, get out of here!"

He didn't know why he even bothered, except out of instinct. She never listened.

She rolled out of the way of another bolt that seared the grass and left a black crater in the ground. The blades of grass sizzled, the pungent smell stinging his nostrils. He saw the fatigue on her face, along with the tracks of tears she'd cried thinking he was dead. Her movements were getting slower. Malcolm was playing with her, wearing her out. Eric leapt to his feet and went for him again.

Before he could reach him, however, a white hot glow surrounded Malcolm, washing him out. It wasn't anything Malcolm was doing, not by the shocked look on his face. He screamed as the light flashed brighter and then exploded in a shower of sparks. The heat blew Eric back. He landed hard on the ground. On the porch where Malcolm had been standing, he saw a charred section of wood.

Eric turned to see Pope standing with his arm out, a resolved, grim look on his face. "You weren't going to win."

He had broken some rule. A big one.

Eric ran over to Fonda, who was struggling to get to her feet. He helped her up, and she wrapped her arms around his waist and sagged against him.

"Stay here and rest," he said. "I'm going down."

The canister lying on the porch not far from the charred spot caught his eye. The lid was off. He ran over to the ventilation pipe. The screen had been removed. Dread hit him like a wave. The canister was empty.

"He's already fumigated them!"

Pope was standing next to them, his expression even more grim.

Eric grabbed the box of syringes. "I'm going to stop them from killing each other." He looked at Pope. "Take me down."

Fonda put her hand on Pope's arm. "I'll freeze time so you can administer the antidotes."

"You don't have the strength to do that," Eric said. "You're about to drop as it is."

"I'm not letting your people die."

He felt the whoosh, and they materialized in the living area of the shelter. If he could have imagined a nightmare, this was it. Nicholas had a gun aimed at Lucas, who looked shocked and sane.

"Nicholas, you don't even like to shoot the bad guys. What the hell is wrong with you? Put the damned gun down!"

Eric heard a struggle in the back bedroom. Rand pulled the trigger of his gun and nearly shot Zoe, who dropped to the floor and aimed her gun at him. Rand's crazed eyes shifted to Fonda, Eric, and Pope, and he swung the barrel toward them and pulled the trigger again.

The moment froze, the bullet suspended only inches in front of Eric's face. Fonda was still holding onto both Pope and Eric. "We don't have much time," she said, grabbing several syringes out of the box. "I'll go down the hall. You take care of these guys."

Pope took one out and turned to Rand, the immediate threat. Eric injected Zoe and then ran to

Nicholas. He didn't need to inject Lucas, so he ran down the hall.

Fonda called out, "Watch the bullet. Time will resume any second."

Eric went into Lucas's room, where Amy, Petra, and Olivia were in the middle of a physical fight. Fonda's face looked strained as she tried to inject Amy. "I'm trying to hold on, but I don't think I can do it anymore."

He took two syringes from her. "I'll take care of them."

Amy came to life just as he slid the needle into her arm. She screamed and slugged him. She had the same crazy look as he'd seen on Sayre.

"Get that away from me!" Petra screamed, fighting off Fonda, who was holding the syringe.

Eric threw her to the bed and leaned down low over her. "It's your little brother, Eric. Listen to me. I'm going to give you a shot, and you'll feel better. Understand?"

She blinked. Fonda moved up beside him while he had Petra pinned and injected her.

"Nice move," he said.

Olivia ran screaming from the room. Eric and Fonda went after her, only to find Lucas holding a gun to Pope. Nicholas and Rand looked dazed. Nicholas held up one of the empty syringes. "What the hell did you inject into us?"

Eric held Lucas's tense gaze. "Don't shoot him."

Lucas's eyes narrowed. "You brought him here. Are you nuts?"

Eric laughed at the irony, which was lost on Lucas, of course. He held up a hand as a signal to wait and joined Fonda, who had pinned down Olivia on the couch.

She was trying the same tactic he'd used on Petra. "Olivia, do remember me?" Fonda said. "You helped me once, after the fire. Now let me help you."

Her eyes were moving back and forth. "No!"

Fonda injected her. Eric turned around and found Nicholas and Rand pointing their guns at him now, though their eyes were clear. Lucas still had his gun on Pope, who looked oddly unperturbed. Petra and Amy had come out of the hallway, rubbing the spots where they'd been injected, looking lost and confused.

Eric took them all in. "You're okay now. Everything's okay."

Lucas tightened his finger on the gun aimed at Pope. "Everything's 'okay'? You brought the enemy here. You, the one who was the most paranoid about that. I saw you just . . . materialize right there with him."

Petra gave him a betrayed look. "Eric, how could you? They've turned you. First you join up with her, and now *him*?"

"This guy just saved all of your asses. And our asses *while* we were trying to save your asses. Remember, I'm the one who shoots first and asks questions later."

The three men lowered their guns, but their suspicion didn't lessen.

"'Splain, Lucy," Petra said, using a phrase he'd used on her before.

"Yeah, 'splain." Lucas leaned against the wall as though all the energy had drained out of him. "Because one minute we're down here, trapped with the doors jammed but otherwise normal, and the next, everybody starts freaking out and trying to kill each other."

Petra said, "I felt this horrible anger, like a bolt inside me, and all I wanted was to kill someone—anyone. I don't remember anything after that."

"Sit down." Eric gestured to the long dining table, tugging Fonda down into the chair beside him. "We've got a lot to fill you in on. First, everyone, this is Fonda. Nicholas, Olivia, you already know her, but you don't know her at all. Just like you, she had no idea she was working for the wrong side. So whatever feelings you might have about her being the enemy, drop them now."

Eric told them what had happened that day, but he still had a lot of questions of his own. "Neil said he couldn't manufacture emotions, so he got off on ours. He said he needed to experience emotions through us humans. Which means he isn't human, and also means part of us isn't human. We already figured out that part is alien."

Pope actually smiled at that. "No, not alien. This dimension hasn't quite nailed it down yet, though some of your top quantum physics scientists are getting closer. There are many dimensions besides the one you live in. We—meaning Neil, Malcolm, and I—come from one of those dimensions. It's a world not completely different from this one in some ways. In other ways, it's very different."

All the Rogues sat in silence and listened to the truth they had been wanting to know for so long. Eric squeezed Fonda's hand and pressed it against his mouth. Petra, across the table, watched with widened eyes but quickly shifted her attention back to Pope.

Nicholas said, "Parallel dimensions. So this world

exists right alongside ours without us even knowing about it?"

"Precisely. Ours and many others. In our dimension, a different organism became the dominant species and humans became extinct."

"Neil said they self-destructed," Eric recalled.

"In a matter of speaking. A bacterium, what you call a biological weapon, was developed by one country to kill off its enemies. It only affected the brains of humans, not animals or plants. That was why they embraced this particular weapon. It didn't condemn the natural world, the innocent creatures, like a nuclear weapon does. It was unleashed on the intended enemy, and the destruction was complete.

"But no one could have predicted how virulent the bacterium was. Or how well it would travel on air and ocean currents. It contaminated the water supplies, drifted into the air of one country after another. It took twenty years, but it eventually killed every human being." He smiled. "But we were underground, and we were not human."

"What are you?" Fonda asked.

"We are called 'Callorian.' From the beginning of our race, we lived underground but monitored what was happening on the surface, what we called Surfacia. When the last of the planet's humans died, we came up to see what was left. And we liked being on the surface, feeling the sun, the colors, the variety of animals and plants and bugs . . . everything the humans had taken for granted.

"So we took over all those abandoned places and built a new world. But a carefully constructed one. Each country is managed by what you would call a president or king; we simply call them leaders. Each leader is answerable to the Collaborate in all things, like your United Nations, but with power.

"Having watched humans succumb to their emotions, they were forbidden in our society and eventually grew dormant. There is no anger or fear or egos. We have no wars or feuds. We don't age as quickly as humans because of this. We use our sixth senses as a regular part of our lives, unlike here where it is considered an anomaly or something to be feared. We protect our planet. Aggressive, manic, or overly sexual behavior is extinguished. And if one breaks the law, he or she is executed by the Collaborate."

"How do they know if the person is guilty?"

"They are mind-scanned, which is usually fatal in itself. Very few people break the laws."

"And you might have to answer to these people?" Fonda asked, her attention fully on him. "Because you saved us?"

He nodded, a slow, grim nod. "There was no other way. You fought well, but Malcolm would have killed you and Eric. And the others"—he looked around to include them all—"would have died, too."

"You might be executed?" Eric said. "Or mind-scanned?"

"I will face the consequences, whatever they might be."

Eric said, "You told me that we matter to you. Obviously we do. Why?"

Pope's mouth quirked in that odd way again, though no emotion hit his eyes. Of course, he *had* no emotions. "In a way, I'm your brother."

He gave them a moment to digest that, and Eric swore he was enjoying it in his deadpan way. "Because the ozone layer has been compromised by the humans, cracks have been forming in the wall between our dimensions. Sometimes a Callorian accidentally slips through. The meteorite Wallace thought he saw was actually one of our aircraft, and it crashed. The pilot died on impact, the aircraft shattering.

"My brother, Allistair, was assigned to collect the pilot's Essence and the pieces of the aircraft. He missed one small piece of Essence . . . the piece Wallace found. When he ingested it, it became part of him, then part of the subjects in the first program, and now part of you. That pilot was our father.

"As a Liaison, my role is to interface with and monitor those from Surfacia who study your world by taking a human guise and living here. While on a mission here, I sensed my father's Essence, which was very odd since he was deceased. I tracked it to Wallace. That's how I learned about the first program. I couldn't tell the Collaborate because that would mean my brother failed in his duty to retrieve all of our father's Essence, which would incur a stiff penalty and loss of honor."

Eric saw the faintest flicker of emotion when Pope talked about his brother. Maybe emotions hadn't been completely bred out of them. "Would they kill him?"

That flicker again, though Pope's voice remained neutral. "Possibly, if they knew his mistake exposed our dimension to yours. And since I knew about it and did not report it, I now have committed an act of treason."

Eric leaned back in his chair. This was way better than being a friggin' alien. "So where do Malcolm and Neil fit into all this?"

"They are two of our people who live here.

Obviously, Malcolm has done an exemplary job, which is why no one believed me when I tried to report that they were up to no good. Not to mention they are the sons of one of the leaders. I suspected they'd killed their last Liaison, Simeon, who disappeared. I believe it is a form of his Essence they used to infect people. They were seduced by the emotions here and began to crave chaos, something lacking in our dimension."

Eric asked the question that probably nobody wanted to think about. "What happens if this Collaborate finds out about us?"

"They will destroy you. You have the potential to expose our DNA, and thus, our dimension. We don't want humans to find the portals. Occasionally they do, and they are immediately destroyed. That is why your people sometimes disappear without a trace."

Rand leaned forward. "So UFOs, weird phenomena, that's you guys?"

"Or those from other dimensions." He looked at Nicholas. "All those parts you saw at the warehouse, those were from rogue or errant planes. I store them in a building I can make disappear at will."

"You let us find it," Nicholas said.

"I wanted to see what you would do, just as when I hired you to find that piece of aircraft with the symbol on it." He nodded toward the Eye on Eric's arm. "I see you've adopted it."

Zoe said, "That's why I dreamed it. Because it's in my DNA. But what does it mean?"

"It is a symbol for highly elite pilots and spies. My father was one of those. He was training in an experimental aircraft when he lost control and came through a crack."

Eric nodded, relieved that the Eye wasn't for the

Collaborate itself. "That's cool." He grinned, looking at his tattoo. "The highly elite."

Petra rolled her eyes. "Oh, brother."

Pope stood. "I'm being summoned back. They have obviously sensed that I used my power to kill."

Fonda stood, too, facing him. "Can't you just stay here?"

"If I stay, I become a Scarlett, an outlaw, the very thing I am sometimes tasked with hunting down. I would dishonor my family and disrupt a long history of high-ranking service to our leader. But I will not reveal your existence. Unless I am mind-scanned."

Eric stood, too, feeling strange looking so far up to the man. "How many of us are there? There were only so many people in the program."

"My sister," Nicholas said.

"Jerryl had a sister, too," Fonda said.

"Cheveyo," Petra said, her eyes getting gooey and dewy. "Maybe he'll come around now."

Pope said, "More Offspring than you think. One of the participants donated sperm to a bank for infertile couples." His eyes sparkled at that, or maybe it was the words that came next as he looked at Amy. "By the way, you're pregnant. Eat well and take care of yourself. Oh, one more thing: Eric, Zoe, Lucas, the phony charges against you have mysteriously disappeared from your police computers. You're free to go back to your lives, all of you."

There was a flash of light, and he was gone.

"That's wild," Rand said, scrubbing his fingers through his spiky hair.

Petra stalked over and shoved at Eric's chest. "You fell in love! You, of all people. That is so totally unfair." She stomped off.

Eric looked at Fonda and shrugged. "She's just jealous because she can't be with the guy she's in love with."

A moment later Petra ran back toward him and threw her arms around him. "I love you. I was so worried about you!"

He hugged her back. "I love you, too. Cheveyo will come around one of these days."

She leaned back, hope on her face. "You think so?"

Not really, but heck, what did he know? "Sure, why not?"

Amy hugged him, too, and introduced herself to Fonda. Then they were all thanking her for saving Eric's life, and before long Fonda's defensive demeanor melted. When cónversation shifted to Amy being pregnant, to their lives now, Eric took Fonda's hand and turned to the group. "We're heading out. I don't think I ever want to see this place again."

There was a murmur of agreement.

He leaned close to her ear. "Give me one more minute." He looked at Lucas. "Bro." He nodded toward the storage room behind the kitchen.

"You've forgiven Amy?" he asked when they were alone.

"Yeah."

"Fonda tried to kill me. That's how we met, and please keep that to yourself. But because she lured me out that night, I didn't get trapped here. So in a way, she saved all of us by trying to kill me, as crazy-assed as that sounds. Because Amy gave you the antidote, you didn't go insane and join them. It might have gone a lot worse if you had. So go beyond forgiving her. Get down on your knees and thank her. You know I'm no expert at love—"

Lucas's laugh was more like a bark. "You're a total newbie. So you're not angry that Fonda gave you the antidote?"

Eric shook his head. "My woman did what she had to do to save me. I don't know if it was out of love then, but she cared enough to risk her safety to get me to Magnus's. She doesn't know it yet, but she's going to be putting up with me for a long, long time. I'm sorry I gave you such a hard time about getting involved. I can see that when you meet the right one, logic goes out the window."

Lucas held out his hand, and Eric clasped it in a shake. "Welcome to the crazy world of love. Best place to be."

Eric knew everything would be all right. He could go now. He went back, grabbed Fonda's hand, and pulled her into his room. "Remember this place?"

Her cheeks colored. "I feel awful about that."

He swung her into his arms. "You saved not only my life, but all of our lives, because you tried to kill me."

"Huh?"

"I'll 'splain later. I want to pack up my stuff. I'll come back for the paintings, or maybe, since I now have my own sensual, alluring woman, I won't need them anymore." He tightened his hold on her. "I do have my own sensual, alluring woman, right?"

She stepped out of his arms and turned toward the door, and he got a sinking feeling in his stomach. But she didn't walk out. She closed the door, turned, and threw herself against him, burying her face against his chest.

"I love you, I love you, I love you," she said on a breath, over and over again, like a burst dam. Her fingers tangled in his hair, and her emotions saturated her voice.

Hearing those words filled every hole in his soul, every need, every want. He held her close, stroking her back. "Hey, hey, hey, are you all right?"

He bracketed her face and pulled back to look at her. Tears shined on her cheeks and dotted her eyelashes.

"I've been fighting everything I've felt for you for so long, first because I was supposed to hate you, then because I was afraid that what I felt was the protection thing, then because I was afraid . . ." She wiped at her tears, shaking her head. "I didn't risk my life to take you to Magnus's because of a fear of feeling *guilty*. I saved you because, even then, I loved you. I didn't want to admit it, even to myself, but I know it now.

"What you did to me, touching me so tenderly it almost hurt, what you said before we left the motel, God, Eric, you killed me, just killed me right there. But we had to go, and all I could think about was telling you I loved you, but it was such a bad time to do that. When I saw Malcolm shoot one of those bolts right through you, and I thought you were dead . . ." She squeezed her eyes shut, more tears streaming out.

He rubbed them with his thumbs and then kissed them away.

She smiled. "See, this is the kind of thing that made me love you. You're sexy as hell, fantastic in bed, strong, gorgeous, but none of that mattered. Do you have any idea how incredible you are?"

He laughed, leaning close to kiss her mouth. "No, but keep telling me."

"Take me home, Eric. To our home. I want you in my bed for the rest of my life."

He widened his eyes. "You mean like a sex slave?" He pretended to mull it over, his finger on his chin. "Mm, I like that idea."

She nudged him, and he grabbed her hand and kissed her knuckles. She walked over to the painting of the female angel, a man kneeling before her. "Let's keep this one. It'll look great in our living room." She turned back to him. "Let's go home."

Home. He liked the sound of that. No, he loved the sound of it. He pulled her into his arms. "I already am, baby."

ACKNOWLEDGMENTS

A big fat thank you to everyone who helped me get things right:

Steve Kantor for answering plane questions, like how to murder someone via prop! Good thing you know I'm a writer. And a shout out to Anne Marie, too!

Antonio "Tony" Sanchez, MSM, CLET, Captain, Biscayne Park Police Department . . . you da best!

To critique bud Marty Ambrose.

To Terri Garey for vintage clothing help, and for writing fun ghost books.

To Eric and Fonda, for being such fabulous and fun characters to write. You made writing my story so easy.

To my editor, Tessa Woodward, and my agent, Joe Veltre, for your guidance, support, and enthusiasm.

To my support team at Avon, including but not limited to Pamela Spengler-Jaffee, Shawn Nicholls, Megan Traynor, and Wendy Ho.

Here's a sneak peek at
Book Five
in the Offspring series!

Petra Aruda leaned back and surveyed the woman in front of her with a critical eye. "You are so going to knock 'em dead."

Sharla's eyes lit up, which was saying something now that they were properly lined and shadowed, just a hint of mascara. Perfect for a job interview.

Sharla took in her reflection and let out a whistle. "You sure know your stuff. Were you a model or something?"

Petra was jotting down makeup tips. "Or something." Not that she was embarrassed about having been a Hooter's waitress. It was why she'd become one that bothered her. She handed the paper to Sharla. "Good luck. You can do it."

"Thank you for doing this." She gestured to the outfit Petra had chosen, a professional suit and skirt from the store at the Women's Center for Independence.

"I enjoy it." Actually, she loved it.

She smiled as Sharla gave her a quick hug and zipped off, looking at her reflection for as long as she could.

Gwen Stefani's "Hollaback Girl" trilled from Petra's purse, a big plum bag she'd bought yesterday to go with her witchy boots. She pulled out her pink phone and stared at the number: no one she knew. She almost tossed it back into the bag but something stopped her. If it were a telemarketer, she'd just hang up.

She answered, and a man's low, smooth voice said, "Petra?"

Her breath hitched for a second before she realized it wasn't *him*. "Yes?"

"It's Pope."

Pope. It took a moment to register. She'd only met him once, but the man had gone against the rules to save her and the lives of those she cared most about. They hadn't heard from him in three months, since he went home to his dimension to face the consequences.

"You're back? And all right?" she asked.

"I'm back," he said, not answering the second question. "Eric gave me your number. I need to meet with you as soon as possible."

Her heart plunged, sucking away her breath. *No, not again. No more running for her life, getting shot at.* "There's not . . . we're not . . ." She couldn't even utter the words *in danger again.*

"You're all fine. I'll explain more when I see you. Can we have lunch?"

"Sure. Do you know where Sally Sue's is?" She gave him the general location.

"I'll find it. See you in a few minutes."

Her throat was tight as she looked for the shift supervisor. The Women's Center helped those who were out of work and needed a makeover, job skills, and more importantly, self-confidence. Petra volunteered her time and skills as often as her classes allowed.

"I've got a family issue," she told the woman in the office. "I'll try to get back before my afternoon class."

What could Pope want to talk with *her* about? The question weighed heavily in her chest as she got into her bright yellow VW Bug and drove to Sally Sue's in downtown Annapolis. If he needed help, he could ask any of the other Rogues, like the ones who had balls, literally or figuratively. She wanted to forget about those six weeks of Hell with a capital H. Being hunted by the government, having someone mind-control her into trying to kill herself, running around with guns . . . H-E-L-L. All caps. The last time she thought it was finally over, they'd had to go back to the Tomb and hide again.

Yes, everything about those six weeks, she reminded the little voice that whispered, *Are you sure you want to forget about him, too?*

She was in full fidget mode by the time she walked into the noisy seafood restaurant that overlooked the docks in downtown Annapolis. Pope was sitting at a table near the window, and her gaze was drawn to him as though he'd mentally flagged her down. Well, he probably had. She sat down across from him and forced a smile. Her brother, Eric, had pretty much squashed her habit of cracking her knuckles, but she'd picked up a new one: braiding her hair.

His light violet eyes held not a trace of anything to give her a hint about the reason behind his cryptic summons.

"You came back," she said. "Does that mean things went well over there?"

Please, please let things have gone well.

People glanced over at them, though it was Pope who commanded their attention. At six-foot-five, with a shaved head and dramatic, defined features, he was striking. He seemed to either ignore or not notice the attention he garnered.

Pope shook his head, and only spoke when the waitress came over to take their order. He ordered nothing but ice tea; she ordered a latte, glad when the waitress departed so she could hear more.

"I stood before the Collaborate and had to explain why I used my powers in a deadly way," Pope began. "They can track us while we're in this dimension, at least when we use our major powers. They didn't believe that their agents had turned bad. They mind-scanned me and saw deception. They locked me away, neutralized my deadly abilities, intending to do a SCANE on me. Something like your lobotomy, only they extract your memories, your knowledge. That the subjects usually don't survive it is a nice side benefit for them."

She inhaled a deep breath at the thought of it, and of his facing the panel of leaders who resembled a powerful United Nations. "How did you escape?"

"It took several weeks, as my counsel tried to appeal, dragging out the process much like your own legal system here. When their appeal failed, I escaped. Now I am a Scarlett."

Only then did she see a flicker of emotion, perhaps disappointment or shame.

"An outlaw." Like those he had been tasked to hunt during his tenure with the Collaborate.

Her hand automatically went to her chest. "You saved our lives but put your own in danger. I'm sorry."

"I can live with that. Or . . . not." He actually smiled, that grin that looked so out of place on him. "But the Extractor they've sent to hunt me down is very dangerous. He is what you call 'evil' here. I have known him for many years. He came here on independent business before he joined the C."

"You want our help to get rid of this guy? Because we will. You helped us, after all." *Oh, boy. Here comes that scary feeling again.* Three months of being normal was addicting. She wasn't sure she could give that up.

"Just one of you."

Her eyes widened. "Me? B-But I'm not all that great at this killing stuff, and I don't have any deadly powers, just healing and hearing, and I've got this habit of—"

"Rambling?"

"Yeah, and freaking out." Already her fingers automatically worked the long strands her hair.

The waitress brought their drinks. Petra looked at her. "Nothing else for me." The thought of eating turned her stomach.

The waitress looked at Pope, who waved away any order he might have as well.

When she left, he said, "You did well, Petra. You overcame a lot." He gave her that smile again. "But it is not your help I require. Cheveyo is the one I seek."

His name thrummed in her veins, which was quite annoying. "Cheveyo? Why him?"

"The rest of you have been through enough."

A hysterical laugh bubbled out of her. "You got that right." She must be schizo, because she actually felt let down that he wasn't asking for her help. "So you're telling me this because . . ."

"I've heard you have a connection to him."

She rolled her eyes. "You talked to Eric."

"He said you two had a . . ." He waved his hands, but he was having trouble saying the words. Had he ever been with someone romantically? Had he been in love with someone and felt the ache of their loss? Probably not.

Finally he said, "Something about you being gooey and dewy whenever you saw him. Can you explain the meaning?"

"Never mind." She rolled her eyes. "Argh. Eric, who gave everybody a hard time about falling in love while we were in danger and then fell the hardest." That still stung, that her boneheaded little brother found love, that everyone she knew was all cozied up in their lives—except her.

Pope was watching her with curiosity. "I sense anger from you."

"You can sense my feelings?"

"Since our feelings have been bred out of us over recent generations, they are that much more apparent in humans. Like a loud sound in a quiet marsh."

She forced a smile. "It's not anger, only frustration." She waved it away. "Anyhoo, I saw the man twice. Yeah, maybe I was a little gooey and dewy—hate that expression—but that's only because he's mysterious and sexy, and he looks so much like Lucas, who I had a crush on for years. Not to mention that Cheveyo saved my life, and we kissed." The memory still gripped her, just as it did every time she thought about the damned kiss, which was hardly ever. "I haven't heard boo from him since he said goodbye when he thought we were all going to die." Yeah, she was rambling again. "I mean, three months have passed, life is back to normal, and still, not even a lousy call." Okay, it hurt. She thought she'd shored herself better. "He's never told me why we can't be together, other than it being dangerous for all of us. Whatever that means. I'm not gooey and dewy anymore." She latched onto her braid again. "I'm so over him."

Except for when she dreamed about him every now and then. Not the kind of dream where he actually came to her, just ordinary dreams where he touched her, and she woke up all hot and bothered.

Pope tilted his head, a puzzled expression on his face. "What am I feeling now from you?"

She was *not* going to explain sexual frustration to him. "Just annoyed, or I was annoyed when I wanted to see him, but I don't want to see him anymore."

"I'm not sure if that is a good thing or not."

"It's a good thing. I don't kick my couch anymore or punch pillows." She gave him a forced smile because she'd said too much. "I have a date tonight. A date with someone who hopefully hasn't killed anyone or been hunted by the government or has any kind of psychic ability."

"A date." He nodded. "So you have no troublesome feelings for Cheveyo?"

"None at all. Just a lingering frustration, and only because I never found out why he couldn't contact me. It's like, you know, when you date someone once or twice and never hear from him again. You just wonder why." She smiled. "Have you ever been on a date?"

"No. That's never been part of my assignment here. Not my desire, as I see the chaos it creates in humans."

She snorted. "Probably a good idea. You want to

know about Cheveyo? I really can't tell you all that much."

"I need you to contact him. Your untroubled feelings for him will make that easier, right?"

"I don't understand why you need me. Can't you, like, teletransport to wherever or whoever? Or did you lose that ability?"

"My transport skills are still weak. Even when they were fully operational, I could not go to him. He's different."

Yes, he was. "He can turn into a panther. Did you know that? He did it in front of me once. It was freaky, sexy, cool, even if I am afraid of large animals with sharp teeth." Pope's mouth twitched slightly, making her replay the words she'd just said. "Anyhoo, he seems more advanced than any of us."

"Indeed. Since he trusts you, I want you to bring him to me."

Her chest tightened at the thought of contacting him. She hadn't even tried, out of pure pride. If he couldn't be bothered to contact her, why should she be the one to go begging him to come see her?

She shuddered. Cheveyo, damn him, wasn't easy to forget, but she was sure trying. Taking a college program on esthetics, accepting a date with a guy who couldn't do amazing, crazy things with his mind. She could pretend she was totally normal and that she loved her life the way it was.

No, not pretend that last part. She did love her life now.

So why was the prospect of seeing or even talking to Cheveyo pumping up her heartbeat?

"I'll try, but he absolutely refused to even come down to the shelter and talk to Lucas, even though he's his half brother. What do you want me to tell him?"

"It might be better not to tell him about me until you get him to our meeting place. I've tried to find him over the years, and I think he suspects I'm an enemy." His mouth twitched again. "Use what you call here feminine wileys, if you must."

Now her mouth twitched. "Wiles, you mean. Yeah, well, I don't really have any of those." People seemed to think that just because she was pretty, that she was (a) easy, (b) had tons of dates, or (c) was a man stealer. "If you think this will be easy because we have some psychic connection to each other, that doesn't seem to mean anything to him. Or me," she added. *Anymore.*

Pope merely gave her a Mona Lisa smile. "I think you'll be able to bring him to me."

Pope had confidence in her. Cheveyo had once told her she was stronger than she thought, and he'd been right.

"I'll try. That's all I can promise. Are you going to tell me why you're having me summon him?"

His smile faded. "Do you want to be involved?"

"No."

"Wise answer. Bring us together, and your part will be done."

He left a twenty on the table, and they stood. His violet-blue eyes scanned the restaurant. "You walk out first. In case the assassin has found me, I don't want him to know we're linked in any way." In a low voice he said, "You will need to be even more careful when we meet next."

She blinked as an image flashed in her mind.

"That is where we'll meet," he said. "Speak not of it, not to Cheveyo, either. Just bring him to the location."

She nodded, knowing where it was. "This is starting to sound scary again." Scary, yes, but her heart was thrumming with adrenaline. Good God, she couldn't actually miss the danger, could she? That would be sick. *Sick*.

"I'm doing everything I can to protect you. All of you. But I need Cheveyo's help."

She nodded. "I'll make sure you get it."

Yurek watched a blond woman walk out of the restaurant. She headed to the right, unraveling her long straight hair from its braid. Pope emerged a few seconds later, watching the woman for a moment. She looked back, and in that glance he saw a connection between them. Yurek was close enough to pick up on the woman's emotions: an odd mix of excitement and trepidation. But he also picked up something from Pope. Was it . . . caring that came from him? Yes, he cared about the girl. Interesting. They weren't supposed to have those feelings, and yet . . .

He also picked up something else from the girl. The Geo Wave, an almost electric sense whenever one of their kind met up with another. It shouldn't be coming from the girl.

Intrigued, he followed her, making sure he wasn't picking up Pope's Wave. She was beautiful in Earth terms, like the women he saw in advertisements here: tall, full mouth, long legs in black, tight pants. Her bag matched her shoes and earrings.

Anyone who came from their dimension was warned not to get physically involved with the humans here. Mixing their blood, a bad idea.

People streamed past them, many tourists who were paying more attention to what was in the shop windows than where they were going. Some looked at him, at the handsome visage he had chosen for his costume here.

The woman stopped at an intersecting road, and he nearly bumped into her. She turned and looked at him, and he apologized. She gave him a quick, forgiving smile and turned forward again.

Yes, a beautiful woman . . . who was part Callorian, his species. Then the pieces clicked together. Pope had been coming to the Earth dimension for many years on various assignments. He was a valued dignitary, before he went Scarlett. He had obviously had an assignation with a human, and this lovely creature was the result. It explained why Pope cared about her.

The crowd surged forward again, and he continued to follow her. He smiled. Now that he worked for the Collaborate, his duties included eradicating anything troublesome on this dimension. This woman was troublesome. It would trouble Pope if his daughter was killed, and that would further weaken him. Yurek liked the idea of bringing down the last vestiges of the once powerful Pope.

Next month, don't miss these exciting new love stories only from Avon Books

Hunger Untamed by Pamela Palmer
For a thousand years, Kougar, a Feral Warrior, believed his lover, Ariana, Queen of the Ilinas, to be dead. So when Kougar discovers Ariana's betrayal, he must overcome his rage in order to save them from approaching evil. But the biggest danger of all could be the love they once shared.

What I Did For a Duke by Julie Anne Long
Reeling with rage after Ian Eversea crosses him, Alexander Moncrieffe, the Duke of Falconbridge, decides to avenge the wrong-doing by seducing Eversea's sister, Genevieve. Will his plan be sweet revenge or will lust have something else in store?

One Night Is Never Enough by Anne Mallory
In order to quench his thirst for Charlotte Chatsworth, the object of his infatuation, Roman Merrick engages the girl's father in a wager for one night with his daughter. Though Charlotte is devastated by the bet, the result of their tryst will leave them both gambling for their hearts.

Seducing the Governess by Margo Maguire
Hoping for a fresh start from her cold and sheltered upbringing, Mercy Franklin takes a governess position in a far-off manor. But when a passionate kiss with her employer, Nash Farris, melts both of their hearts, they are torn between what's right...and what feels even better.

At Avon Books, we know your passion for romance—once you finish one of our novels, you find yourself wanting more.

May we tempt you with . . .